MURDER, MYSTERY AND INTRIGUE—
Fight crime and put away the bad guys with 15 of fiction's most notable sleuths

In "No One Likes to Be Played for a Sucker," Michael Collins's hero Dan Fortune realizes that it can be a mistake to be too smart when trying to pick a locked-room murder.

Investigate a suicide with the determined Matthew Scudder in Lawrence Block's urban tale, "Out the Window."

Asked by a husband to locate his missing wife, Kinsey Millhone stumbles upon an intricate plot of secrets, embezzlement, and death in "Long Gone" by Sue Grafton.

"The Strawberry Teardrop" by Max Allan Collins finds Nate Heller searching for a serial killer and solving another historical question.

A deadly game of Japanese Go has Sara Paretsky's V. I. Warshawski piecing together "The Takamoku *Joseki*."

FIRST CASES

First Appearances of Classic Private Eyes

EDITED BY

Robert J. Randisi

A SIGNET BOOK

SIGNET
Published by the Penguin Group
Penguin Books USA Inc., 375 Hudson Street,
New York, New York 10014, U.S.A.
Penguin Books Ltd, 27 Wrights Lane,
London W8 5TZ, England
Penguin Books Australia Ltd, Ringwood,
Victoria, Australia
Penguin Books Canada Ltd, 10 Alcorn Avenue,
Toronto, Ontario, Canada M4V 3B2
Penguin Books (N.Z.) Ltd, 182–190 Wairau Road,
Auckland 10, New Zealand

Penguin Books Ltd, Registered Offices:
Harmondsworth, Middlesex, England

Published by Signet, an imprint of Dutton Signet,
a division of Penguin Books USA Inc. Previously appeared in a Dutton edition.

First Signet Printing, February, 1997
10 9 8 7 6 5 4 3 2 1

 REGISTERED TRADEMARK—MARCA REGISTRADA

Printed in the United States of America

PUBLISHER'S NOTE
These are works of fiction. Names, characters, places, and incidents either are the product of the authors' imagination or are used fictitiously, and any resemblance to actual persons, living or dead, events, or locales is entirely coincidental.

BOOKS ARE AVAILABLE AT QUANTITY DISCOUNTS WHEN USED TO PROMOTE PRODUCTS OR SERVICES. FOR INFORMATION PLEASE WRITE TO PREMIUM MARKETING DIVISION, PENGUIN BOOKS USA INC., 375 HUDSON STREET, NEW YORK, NEW YORK 10014.

CONTENTS

Introduction 7

No One Likes to Be Played For a Sucker
  by Michael Collins 8

It's a Lousy World
  by Bill Pronzini 24

File #1: The Mayfield Case
  by Joe Gores 43

Out the Window
  by Lawrence Block 60

Where Is Harry Beal?
  by John Lutz 94

Merrill-Go-Round
  by Marcia Muller 109

The Steinway Collection
  by Robert J. Randisi 119

Robbers' Roost
  by Loren D. Estleman 134

The Takamoku *Joseki*
  by Sara Paretsky 147

Long Gone
by Sue Grafton 158

C Is for Cookie
by Rob Kantner 175

The Strawberry Teardrop
by Max Allan Collins 191

Till Tuesday
by Jeremiah Healy 208

Lucky Penny
by Linda Barnes 222

Mary, Mary, Shut the Door
by Benjamin M. Schutz 243

INTRODUCTION

A recent review of my Miles Jacoby novel *Stand Up* called it the third book in a series, when actually it is the sixth. That started me wondering how many readers of series don't know how many books there are, or when the character first appeared.

This book features the first short story appearances of fifteen of the most famous and enduring series private detectives. In the case of some of them—like Linda Barnes's Carlotta Carlyle and Joe Gores's DKA series—it was also their very first appearance ever. For others—such as Lawrence Block's Matt Scudder and Jeremiah Healy's John Francis Cuddy—the characters first appeared in novels.

It's interesting to go back and read an early story about a series character you've been following for years. In some cases—such as my own Miles Jacoby—the character you meet in this story is very different from the character as he or she appears in later stories and in novels.

So what I have done in this collection is given readers—new as well as regular—a chance to meet these characters as they appeared in their earliest short stories. I've also indicated where and when the detective first appeared.

This is actually *First Cases I*. I am presently working on a second book which will collect the earliest short story appearances of series characters other than private detectives.

You see, I believe in equal time.

Good reading!

Robert J. Randisi
St. Louis, Mo.
February 1995

NO ONE LIKES TO BE PLAYED FOR A SUCKER
Michael Collins

FIRST APPEARANCE: *Act of Fear*, 1967

In terms of service and volume the Dan Fortune series ranks just ahead of Bill Pronzini's Nameless series as the longest running contemporary PI series. With nearly twenty books about the one-armed detective, Michael Collins (real name: Dennis Lynds) continues to produce Fortune novels that chronicle the detective's ever-evolving career and life. From New York to Santa Barbara Mr. Collins continues to use the PI form to produce what he has called "sociodramas." The very first Fortune novel, *Act of Fear* (Dodd, Mead), won the MWA Edgar Award for best first novel of 1967. "No One Likes to Be Played for a Sucker" first appeared in *Ellery Queen's Mystery Magazine* in 1969.

Although Dennis Lynds has created other series detectives under other pseudonyms, Michael Collins and Dan Fortune remain his most enduring team.

It can be a mistake to be too smart. Deviousness takes real practice, judgment of human nature as fine as a hair, and something else—call it ice. The ice a person has inside.

Old Tercio Osso came to me with his suspicions on a Thursday morning. That alone showed his uneasiness. Old Tercio hadn't been out of his Carmine Street office in the morning for twenty years—not even for a relative's funeral.

"Business don't come and find you," Tercio pronounced regularly.

Osso & Vitanza, Jewelry, Religious Supplies, and Real Estate, and if you wanted to do business with Tercio, or pay your rent, you went to his office in the morning. In the afternoon Tercio presided in his corner at the Mazzini Political Club—a little cards, a little boccie out back.

Lean old Cology Vitanza, Tercio's partner of thirty years, reversed the procedure, and at night they both held down the office—thieves struck at night on Carmine Street, and there was safety in numbers.

It was Cology Vitanza that old Tercio came to me about.

"We got troubles, Mr. Fortune. I think Cology he makes plans."

The old man sat like a solemn frog on my one extra chair. He wore his usual ancient black suit, white shirt, and black tie with its shiny knot so small it looked as if it had been tied under pressure. The shabbiness of my one-room office did not bother Tercio. On Carmine Street, no matter how much cash a businessman has in various banks, he knows the value of a shabby front: it gives the poor confidence that a man is like them.

"What kind of plans?"

Tercio shrugged. "Business it's not good. We make some big mistakes. The stock market, buildings not worth so much as we pay, inventory that don't sell."

"I didn't know you made mistakes, Mr. Osso."

"So?" Tercio said. "Maybe I'm old. Vitanza he's old. We lose the touch, the neighborhood it's change. The new people they don't buy what we got. Maybe we been playin' too much boccie, sit around tellin' too many stories from the old days."

"All right," I said. "What plans do you figure Vitanza is making?"

Tercio folded his plump hands in his broad lap. "For six year Cology he got no wife. He got ten kids what got lotsa kids of their own. We both gettin' old. We got insurance, big. We talk about what we do next year and after and we don't think the same, so? Then I see Cology talking to people."

"What kind of insurance have you got?"

"On the inventory, on both of us, for the partners."

I sat back in the gray light from my one window that opens on the air shaft. "You're saying you think Vitanza is making plans to collect on the insurance?"

"I see him talk to Sid Nelson yesterday. Three days ago he drinks coffee alone with Don Primo."

Don Primo Veronese was a lawyer, a member of the Mazzini Club, and, by strong rumor, a fence for small hoods. Sid Nelson was a hood, not small but not big—sort of in between. A thief, a killer, and a careful operator.

"You and Vitanza talk to a lot of people."

"Sure, I talk to Don Primo myself," Tercio agreed. "I don't talk to no Sid Nelson. I don't say we should make a special inventory. I don't take big money from the bank, put in envelope, carry in my pocket. I don't go to mass five times in one week."

"What do you want me to do, Mr. Osso?"

A slow shrug. "In winter the wolf comes to the streets of the city. The old lion he got to learn new tricks or starve. Maybe I'm crazy, okay. Only you watch Cology. You be a detective."

"That's my work," I said. "All right, a hundred in advance."

"A horse works on hay," Tercio said, and counted out two nice crisp fifties. "You tell me nine o'clock every night."

After old Tercio had gone, I rubbed at the stump of my missing arm, then phoned Lieutenant Marx at the precinct. I told him Tercio's story.

"What do you want me to do?" Marx said.

"I don't know," I said. "Tell me that Tercio Osso is a smart old man."

"Tercio is a smart old man," Marx said. "All I can do is stand by, Dan. At least until you get something that can be called reasonable suspicion."

"I know," I said.

"You can check out most of it," Marx pointed out.

That's what I did. I checked out old Osso's story.

It checked. Other people had seen Cology Vitanza talking to Don Primo Veronese, and, especially, to Sid Nelson. The firm of Osso & Vitanza was in trouble—cash tied up, notes overdue, interest not paid, a few bad deals the other Carmine Street financiers were grinning about, and the jewelry stock not moving at all.

Vitanza had been going to mass almost every day. He had withdrawn five thousand dollars in cash. (A teller I knew, and ten bucks, got me that information.) I had to take Tercio Osso's word about the special inventory of the unmoving stock, but I was sure it would turn out to be true.

I began tailing Cology Vitanza. It wasn't a hard tail. The tall old man was easy to follow and a man of routine. He never took me out of the ten-square-block area of Little Italy. I reported to Osso every night at nine o'clock by telephone.

On Friday I spotted Vitanza talking again to Sid Nelson. The hoodlum seemed interested in what Vitanza had to say.

I ate a lot of spaghetti and drank a lot of wine for two days. I saw one bad movie, and visited the homes of twenty old men. That is, Vitanza visited and I lurked outside in the cold, getting more bored every minute. I wore out my knees kneeling at the back of a dim church.

But I was there in the Capri Tavern at six o'clock Saturday night when Vitanza stopped to talk to a seedy-looking character in a rear booth. A white envelope passed from Vitanza to the seedy type. I waited until the new man downed his glass of wine and ambled out. Then I switched to tailing him.

I followed the seedy man through Little Italy and across to the East Side. He looked around a lot, and did all kinds of twists and turns, as if he figured he might be followed. That made it hard work, but I kept up with him. He finally headed for the Bowery.

A block south of Houston he suddenly ducked into a wino joint. I sprinted and went in, but he was out the back way and gone. I went around through the alleys and streets of the Bowery for another hour trying to pick up his trail, but I had no luck.

I went back to Carmine Street to find Cology Vitanza. He wasn't at the Mazzini Club, and neither was Osso. I tried their other haunts and didn't find them. The lights were on behind the curtained windows of the shop and office on Carmine Street, but I couldn't go in without tipping my hand, so I took up a stakeout.

Nothing happened for half an hour. Then some people tried to get into the store, but the front door was locked.

That wasn't right for a Saturday night. It was almost nine o'clock by then. I made my call to Osso from a booth where I could watch the front door of the store. There was no answer, so I called Lieutenant Marx.

"I don't like how it sounds," Marx said. "Too bad you lost that Bowery character. I've done some checking on their insurance. They've got fifty thousand dollars on the inventory, twenty-five thousand dollars life on each payable to the other, and fifty thousand dollars surviving-partner insurance with option to buy out the heirs."

"A nice haul," I said. "What do we do?"

"Sid Nelson hasn't moved. I put a man on him for you."

"The commissioner wouldn't like that."

"The commissioner won't know," Marx said, and then was silent a few seconds. "We've got no cause to bust in yet."

"And if nothing's wrong we tip off Vitanza."

"But they shouldn't be locked up on Saturday night," Marx said. "The patrolman on the beat ought to be suspicious."

"I guess he ought to," I said.

"I'll be right over," Marx said.

Marx arrived with two of his squad inside three minutes. He'd picked up the beat patrolman on the way. I joined them at the door to the store. We couldn't see anything through the curtains.

"Pound the door and give a call," Marx instructed the beat patrolman.

The patrolman pounded and called out. Nothing happened. Marx chewed his lip and looked at me. Then, as if from far off, we heard a voice. It was from somewhere inside the store, and it was calling for help.

"I guess we go in," Marx said.

He kicked in the glass of the door and reached inside for the lock.

At first we saw nothing wrong in the jewelry store. Then Marx pointed to the showcases where the expensive jewelry was kept. They were unlocked and empty.

In the office in the back a rear window was open. A man lay on the floor in a pool of not-quite-dry blood. A .38-

caliber automatic was on the floor about five feet from the body, toward the right wall of the office. There was a solid door in the right wall, and behind it someone was knocking and calling, "What's happen out there? Hey, who's out there?"

Marx and I looked at each other as one of his men bent over the body on the floor. It was not Tercio Osso, it was Cology Vitanza. Marx's second man swung the door of the safe open. It had been closed but not locked. It was empty.

Marx went to the solid door. "Who's in there?"

"Osso! He knock me out, lock me in. What's happen?"

Marx studied the door. There was no key in the lock. I went and searched the dead man. I shook my head at Marx—no key. One of Marx's men pointed to the floor.

"There."

The key was on the floor not far from the gun. I picked it up. It was one of those common old house keys, rough and rusted, and there would be no prints. Marx took the key and opened the door.

Tercio Osso blinked at us. "Mr. Fortune, Lieutenant. Where's Cology, he—"

Osso stepped out into the office and saw his dead partner. He just stood and stared. Nothing happened to his face. I watched him. If anything had shown on his face I would have been surprised. Everyone knew he was a tough old man.

"So," he said, nodding, "he kill Cology. It figure. The crazy old man. Crazy."

"You want to tell us what happened?" Marx said.

"Sure, sure," the old man said. He walked to his desk and sat down heavily. I saw a trickle of blood over his left ear. He looked at Vitanza's body. "He come in maybe hour, two hours ago. What time is it?"

"Nine-twenty," Marx said.

"That long?" Osso said. "So two hours since. Seven-thirty, maybe. One guy. He comes in the front. I go out to see. He got a mask and a gun. He push me back to office, me and Cology. He makes us go lock the front door, clean out the cases and then the safe. He work fast. He shove me in storeroom, knock me out."

The old man touched his head, winced. "I wake up, I

don't know what time. I listen. Nothing, no noise. I listen long time, I don't want him to come back for me. Nothing happen. I hear phone ring. So I start yelling. Then I hear you bust in."

Osso looked around. "He got it all, huh? Out the window. Only he don't keep the deal, no. Cology is crazy man. A guy like that don't keep no deals."

There was a long silence in the office. Sirens were growing in the cold night air outside as the police began to arrive at Marx's summons. Marx was chewing his lip and looking at me. I looked at Osso.

"You're telling us you figure Vitanza hired a guy to rob the store for the insurance, and then the guy killed him? Why?"

Osso shrugged. "Who know? Maybe the guy don't want to split with Cology. Maybe the guy figures the jewels is worth more than a cut of the insurance. They fight, Cology's dead. How do I know, I'm locked inside the storeroom."

The assistant medical examiner arrived, the fingerprint team, and two men from Safe and Loft. I went into the storeroom. It was small and windowless. There was no other door. The walls were white and clean, and the room was piled with lumber, cans, tools, and assorted junk. I found a small stain of blood on the floor near the door. The walls seemed solid.

When I went back out, Marx's men had finished marking the locations of the body, the gun, and the key. The ME stood up and motioned to his men to bring their basket.

"Shot twice in the back," the ME said. "Two hours ago, maybe more, maybe a little less. Rigor is just starting. He's a skinny old man. Died pretty quick, I'd say. The slugs are still in him—thirty-eight caliber looks about right."

"The gun's been fired twice," one of Marx's men said, "not long ago."

"Prints all over the place, all kinds," the fingerprint man said. "It won't be easy to lift them clean."

Marx growled. "Prints won't help. What about you Safe and Loft guys?"

A Safe and Loft man said, "Rear window opened from inside. Some marks on the sill could have been a man climbing out. The yard is all concrete, no traces, but we found this."

The Safe and Loft man held up a child's rubber Halloween mask. Marx looked at it sourly.

"They all use that trick now. The movies and TV tell them how to do everything," Marx said, and came over to me. He lit a cigarette. "Well, Dan?"

"Everything fits," I said. "Just about what I was supposed to figure that Vitanza was planning—except for his killing."

"Neat," Marx said.

"Too neat," I said. "Let's talk to Osso."

While his men and the experts went on working, Marx took Osso into the storeroom. I went with them. The old man watched us with cold, black eyes.

"This is just what you expected when you went to Fortune," Marx said to the old man.

"I got a hunch," Osso said.

"What does Cology figure on getting out of it, Tercio?" I said. "The insurance on the stock, no more. Maybe he figures on keeping most of the jewels, too, okay. But figure what you get out of it. You get the whole works—stock insurance, life insurance on Cology, partnership insurance, option to buy it all."

"So?" Osso said, watched me.

"So if Cology was going to set up a risky deal like this it ought to be you who's dead, not him. The thief should have killed you and knocked Cology out. Then there's a big pie to split with Cology."

"You think I set this up?"

I nodded. "It smells, Tercio. We're supposed to figure that Vitanza hired a punk to fake a holdup, but not kill you when there was more riding on you than on the stock? Then the hired hood kills Cology for some reason and leaves his gun here on the floor? Leaves his mask out in the yard to prove he was here? Leaves the key on the floor so we know you were locked in?"

Osso shrugged. "You figure I set it up, take me down and book me. I call my lawyer. You find the guy I hire. You do that. I tell the truth. I hire no one, you won't find no one. I'm inside the storeroom, so how I kill Cology?"

Marx said, "It's too neat, Osso. You practically told Fortune how it was going to happen."

"So book me. I get my lawyer. You find the man I hire." And the old man smiled. "Or maybe you figure I kill from inside locked room?"

Marx snapped, "Take the old man down, book him on suspicion. Go over the place with a vacuum cleaner. Send anything you find to Technical Services."

They took Osso. Marx followed and I left with him.

The police had gone, except for a patrolman posted at the broken door in front, when I jimmied the back window and went in. I dropped into the dark office and flicked on my flashlight. I focused the beam on the marks that showed where the gun, the key, and the body had been.

I heard the steps too late. The lights went on, and I turned from pure reflex. I never carry a gun, and if I'd had a gun I couldn't have pulled it with my flash still in my lone hand. I was glad I didn't have a gun. I might have shot by reflex, and it was Lieutenant Marx in the doorway. That's the trouble with a gun, you tend to depend on it if you have one.

I said, "You, too, Lieutenant?"

"What's your idea?" Marx said.

"The old man's too confident," I said. "He damn near begged you to book him on suspicion of having hired a man to fake the robbery and kill Vitanza."

"Yeah," Marx said, "he did. You think he didn't hire anyone?"

I nodded. I didn't like it, but unless Cology Vitanza had set it up after all, which I didn't believe, there had to be another answer. Marx didn't like it either.

"You know what that gives us," Marx said.

"I know," I said, "but Tercio's too smart to hire a killing and have a monkey on his back the rest of his life. No, he'd do it himself."

"You got more than a hunch, Dan?"

"The gun," I said. "It's the flaw in the setup. It sticks out. A thief who kills takes his gun away with him. Osso would know that."

"So?"

"So the gun being in the office has to be the clue to the answer," I said. "It was here because Osso couldn't do anything else with it. The jewels are gone, the mask was out in the yard, the front door was locked on the inside out in the shop. If Osso had had a choice he'd have taken the gun away and the key too. He didn't. Why?"

Marx rubbed his jaw. "So if he did it, it reads like this: He took the ice and stashed it. He planted the mask and left the rear window open. He killed Vitanza, and then he got into that storeroom and somehow locked himself in with the key outside and a long way from the door."

"Yes and no," I said. "If he killed Vitanza *before* he got into that room, he could have disposed of the gun to make it look more like an outside killer. He didn't. So he must have killed Vitanza from *inside* the locked storeroom."

"And then got the gun and key out?"

"That's it," I said.

Marx nodded. "Let's find it."

We went to work. The locked room is an exercise in illusion—a magician's trick. Otherwise it's impossible, and the impossible can't be done, period. Since it *had* been done, it must be a trick, a matter of distracting attention, and once you know what you're really looking for, the answer is never hard.

When we had dismissed the distraction—the hired robber and killer theory—the rest was just a matter of logic. I sighted along the line from the body to the seemingly solid wall. The line pointed directly to a light fixture set in the wall. Sighting the other way, the line led to Vitanza's desk and telephone.

"Vitanza came in," I said. "Osso was already inside the locked room. Vitanza went to his desk. He probably always did that, and Osso could count on it. Or maybe he saw that the jewels were gone and went to his desk to telephone the police. Osso probably knew he would be sure to do that, too. They'd been partners thirty years."

"And Osso had to shoot him in the back," Marx said. "The desk faces the other way."

"Let's look at that light fixture," I said.

It was one of those small modern wall lamps with a wide circular metal base. It had been attached to the wall recently and was not painted over. The wall behind it sounded hollow, but we could not move the lamp.

"It doesn't come off, Dan," Marx said.

"Not from this side," I said.

We went into the storeroom. I measured off from the door to exactly where the light fixture was attached on the other side of the wall. We studied the wall. The whole wall had been recently painted. The cans of quick-drying paint were among the litter in the storeroom. On the floor there were a few crumbs of dried plaster.

"Quick-drying plaster," I said to Marx.

Marx found a hammer and chisel in the storeroom. There were flecks of plaster on the chisel. He opened a hole directly behind the light fixture. It opened easily. The back of the light fixture was clearly visible about two inches in, between vertical two-by-fours. The fixture had a metal eye on the back. It was held in place by a metal bar that passed through the eye and was angled to catch the two-by-fours.

"That's it," I said. "Simple and clever."

Marx had two hands. He reached in with his left, turned the metal bar, and held the fixture. He pushed the fixture out and to the left and aimed his pistol through the hole with his right hand. He had a clear shot at the desk five feet away—in direct line with where the body of Cology Vitanza had fallen.

I said, "He had this hole open on this side. He heard Vitanza come in and head for the desk. He pushed out the fixture. It didn't matter if Vitanza heard or not—Osso was ready, didn't care if he hit Vitanza front or back. He shot Vitanza, tossed the gun and key through the hole, pulled the fixture back and re-fastened it, plastered up the hole, and painted the wall. He knew no one would break in until after I called at nine o'clock. He hid here and waited."

I shook my head in admiration for the old man. "If we believe that Vitanza had set it up, fine, we'd be looking for a nonexistent thief and killer. If we think Osso hired a man, fine, too. We're still looking for a nonexistent thief and killer, and in a few weeks Osso cleans up this storeroom, and the new plaster sets so it can't be told from the old plaster. Maybe he fixes the light fixture so it's permanent in the wall. All the evidence is gone, and he's in the clear."

"Only now the lab boys should be able to prove some of the plaster is newer," Marx said, "the fixture moves out, and the evidence is in this room. We've got the old bastard."

Marx called in Captain Gazzo of Homicide. Gazzo took it to Chief of Detectives McGuire, who got a judge to order the office and storeroom sealed. The DA would want the jury to see the office and storeroom just as they were when Vitanza was killed.

I gave my statement, Marx made his report, and Gazzo faced the old man with it. Osso was a tough old bird.

"I want my lawyer," Osso said.

He got his lawyer, they booked the old man, and I went home to bed. I felt good. I don't get many locked rooms to play with, so I was pleased with myself.

Until morning.

"It's not the gun," Captain Gazzo said.

I was in Gazzo's office. So was Marx. Gazzo held the .38 automatic that had been on the office floor—the gun that had been the tip-off, the weak link, the key to it all.

"This gun didn't kill Vitanza," Gazzo said. "Ballistics just reported. Vitanza was killed with a thirty-eight, yes, but not this one."

I said nothing. Neither did Marx.

"A locked room," Gazzo said sarcastically. "Great work, boys. Clever, very clever."

I said it at the start: it can be a mistake to be too smart. A locked-room murder is an illusionist's trick, a matter of the misdirection of attention. And the one who had been too smart was me.

"All he threw out was the key," I said. "That was all he had to throw out all along. The rest was to distract us."

There had never been any reason why Osso had to kill from inside the storeroom, only that he lock himself in from the inside and get the key out. The whole locked room had been a trick to distract us. A gun on the floor by a dead man. The right caliber gun fired recently and the right number of times. Who would dream it was the wrong gun?

"The key now," Gazzo said. "First he's brought in on

suspicion of having hired a man to fake a robbery and kill his partner. Next he's booked for having killed his partner from inside a locked room with a trick scheme. Now he killed his partner outside the room, switched guns, locked himself in, and tossed the key out. What next?"

"He killed Vitanza," Marx said. "I'm sure he did."

"I'm sure too," Gazzo agreed, "but what jury will believe us now with the speech his lawyer'll make about dumb cops and police persecution? You guys like fairy tales? How do you like the one about the boy who cried wolf? The DA is bawling on his desk thinking about facing a jury against Osso now."

"We'll find out what he did," Marx said. "We'll find the right gun and the jewels."

"Sure we will," Gazzo said. "Some day."

"And I bet it won't do us any good," I said.

It didn't. Three days after the killing the superintendent of a cheap rooming house on the Lower East Side reported that a tenant hadn't come out of his room for three days. The police broke in and found the man dead. It was the seedy character I had followed and lost.

He had been shot in the shoulder. The bullet was still in the wound. But that was not what had killed him. He had died from drinking whiskey with lye in it. The bottle was in the room. The police found some of the missing jewels in the room, but not all. They also found a .38-caliber automatic that had been fired twice.

"It's the gun that killed Vitanza," Ballistics reported.

"Only the bum's prints on the gun," Fingerprinting said.

"It's certain he died four or five hours *after* Vitanza died," the ME said. "The bad whiskey killed him. He might have been unconscious most of the time, but after three days we'll never prove it. He lost blood from that shoulder wound."

Ballistics then added the final touch. "The bullet in the bum's shoulder came from the gun you found on the floor of Osso and Vitanza's office. The gun was registered to Cology Vitanza himself."

With my statement and report on what I had observed Cology Vitanza do, on the actions Osso had reported and I had checked out, the evidence logically added up to only one story: the seedy character had been hired by Cology Vitanza to rob the jewelry store. For some reason there had been a fight while Osso was unconscious in the locked room. (Osso stated he had plastered the hole in the storeroom the day before. With the evidence against the bum his story was better than Marx's and mine.)

Vitanza had wounded the bum, and the bum had killed Vitanza. Then the wounded bum had run for his room with the loot, but hid some of it on the way. In his room, weak from his wound, he had drunk the bad whiskey, passed out, and died. It was just the way a wounded bum would die.

I had a different story. The day after they dropped all charges against Tercio Osso I went to his office. He didn't try to evade me.

"I owe you a couple days and expenses," Osso said.

"You hired me in the first place just to make me and Marx suspicious," I said. "You figured I'd talk to the police and you knew we'd suspect a trick. You wanted us to accuse you right away of hiring someone to kill Vitanza."

Osso said nothing.

"You arranged all those suspicious acts of Vitanza's. It wouldn't have been hard. You were partners, old friends, and he'd do anything you asked him to do if you said it was business. You asked him to talk to Sid Nelson about something innocent, to take out five thousand dollars in cash for you, to meet the bum with a note, even to go to a lot of masses."

The old man was like a fat black frog in the chair.

"You played us like trout. It was too easy and not smart for you to have hired a killer. We were sure to look for more. That's when you handed us the locked room and the gun on the floor."

Osso smiled.

"That gun would have made any cop wonder, and you expected us to figure out the locked-room trick. You wanted us to charge you with it, and you wanted time. You needed at least a few hours to be sure the bum was dead, and the locked room would keep us nice and busy for at least a few hours."

The old man began to light a thin black cigar.

"You killed Vitanza while I was tailing the bum. You

took the jewels, locked up, went out the back window. You went to the bum's room and filled him with the bad whiskey, then shot him with Vitanza's gun. A wound that would bleed but not kill.

"Then you planted the gun that had killed Vitanza in the bum's room with some of the jewels. You knew no one would look for the bum for days. You went back to the office and laid out Vitanza. You put the gun that had shot the bum on the office floor. You locked yourself in the storeroom from the inside and tossed out the key through the light fixture hole in the wall.

"Then you sat back and led me and Marx into being too smart for our own good. You got the time you needed. You kept us away from the bum until it was too late. You've got what you were after, and you're safe." I stopped and looked at the old man. "One thing I want to know, Osso. Why did you pick me?"

Old Tercio Osso blew smoke and looked solemn. He shrugged. He took the black stogie from his mouth and studied it. Then he laughed aloud.

"You got one arm," Osso said, grinned at me. "You're easy to spot. I got to know where you are all the time to make it work, see? I got to make it easy for that bum to spot you and lead you a chase before he loses you. And I got to make it easy for the man watching you all the time."

"You had a man watching me?"

"Sure, what else? Good man, a relative, never talk." Osso studied his cigar some more. "You got good friends on the cops, and you're a real smart man, see? I mean, I know you figure out that locked room."

And Osso laughed again. He was very pleased with his shenanigans. I said nothing, just stared at him. He studied me.

"I got to do it, see?" Osso said at last. "I'm in trouble. Vitanza he don't agree with me no more. He was gonna ruin me if I don't stop him. So I stop him. And I fix it so you smart guys outsmart yourselves."

I stood up. "That's okay, Osso. You see, you made the same mistake Marx and I made."

"So?" he said, his black eyes narrowing.

"That's right. You forgot other people can be as smart

as you. You fixed it good so that no one can prove in court what you did. But you made it too good. Everyone knows you did it. You made it too complicated, Osso. You're the only one who could have worked it all. What I figured out, and just told you, I also told Vitanza's ten kids, and the members of the Mazzini Club. They're smart, too."

"I kill you too!" Osso croaked.

"You couldn't get away with it twice, not with everyone knowing what you did. You're too smart to try. Bad odds, and you always play the odds."

I left him chewing his lip, his shrewd mind working fast. Who knows, he's a smart man, and maybe he'll still get away with it. But I doubt it. As I said, other men are smart, too, and Vitanza's kids and the Mazzini Club boys believed the story I had figured out.

I read the newspapers carefully now. I'm waiting for a small item about an old man named Tercio Osso being hit by a truck, or found in the river drowned by accident, or maybe the victim of an unfortunate food poisoning in a restaurant that just happens to be run by a member of the Mazzini Club.

Nothing fancy or complicated this time, just a simple, everyday accident. Of course, everyone will know what really happened, but no one will ever prove it. Whoever gets Tercio Osso won't even have to be particularly careful. A reasonably believable accident will do the trick.

After all, we're all human and have a sense of justice, and no one likes to be played for a sucker.

IT'S A LOUSY WORLD
Bill Pronzini

FIRST APPEARANCE: *This Story*, 1968

I wonder if Bill Pronzini had any inkling when this story was first published in *Alfred Hitchcock's Mystery Magazine* in 1968 that the Nameless Detective series would last as long as it has. Two Shamus Awards—one for best PI novel (*Hoodwink* [St. Martin's Press, 1981]) and one for best PI short story ("Cat's Paw")—over twenty novels, and twenty-seven years later, and Nameless is one of the longest running—and best— PI series in the genre. Mr. Pronzini has also served as the very first president of the PWA, and has earned the PWA Life Achievement Award. The first Nameless novel, *The Snatch* (Random House), appeared in 1971.

Odd that it should have all started with a story called "It's a Lousy World," isn't it?

Colly Babcock was shot to death on the night of September 9, in an alley between Twenty-ninth and Valley streets in the Glen Park District of San Francisco. Two police officers, cruising, spotted him coming out the rear door of Budget Liquors there, carrying a metal box. Colly ran when he saw them. The officers gave chase, calling out for him to halt, but he just kept running; one of the cops fired a warning shot, and when Colly didn't heed it the officer pulled up and fired again. He was aiming low, trying for the legs, but in the half-light of the alley it was a blind shot. The bullet hit Colly in the small of the back and killed him instantly.

I read about it the following morning over coffee and undercooked eggs in a cafeteria on Taylor Street, a block and a half from my office. The story was on an inside page, concise and dispassionate; they teach that kind of objective writing in the journalism classes. Just the cold facts. A man dies, but he's nothing more than a statistic, a name in black type, a faceless nonentity to be considered and then forgotten along with your breakfast coffee.

Unless you knew him.

Unless he was your friend.

Very carefully I folded the newspaper and put it into my coat pocket. Then I stood from the table, went out to the street. The wind was up, blowing in off the Bay; rubble swirled and eddied in the Tenderloin gutters. The air smelled of salt and dark rain and human pollution.

I walked into the face of the wind, toward my office.

"How's the job, Colly?"

"Oh, fine, just fine."

"No problems?"

"No, none at all."

"Stick with it, Colly."

"Sure. I'm a new man."

"Straight all the way?"

"Straight all the way."

Inside the lobby of my building, I found an Out of Order sign taped to the closed elevator doors. Yeah, that figured. I went around to the stairs, up to the second floor, and along the hallway to my office.

The door was unlocked, standing open a few inches. I tensed when I saw it like that, and reached out with the tips of my fingers and pushed it all the way open. But there was no trouble. The woman sitting in the chair in front of my desk had never been trouble for anyone.

Colly Babcock's widow.

I moved inside, shut the door, and crossed toward her. "Hello, Lucille."

Her hands were clasped tightly in the lap of a plain black dress. She said, "The man down the hall, the CPA—he let me in. He said you wouldn't mind."

"I don't mind."

"You heard, I guess? About Colly?"

"Yes." I said. "What can I say, Lucille?"

"You were his friend. You helped him."

"Maybe I didn't help him enough."

"He didn't do it," Lucille said. "He didn't steal that money. He didn't do all those robberies like they're saying."

"Lucille . . ."

"Colly and I were married thirty-one years," she said. "Don't you think I would have known?"

I did not say anything.

"I always knew," she said.

I sat down, looking at her. She was a big woman, handsome—a strong woman. There was strength in the line of her mouth, and in her eyes, round and gray, tinged with red now from the crying. She had stuck by Colly through two prison terms and twenty-odd years of running, and hiding, and looking over her shoulder. Yes, I thought, she would always have known.

But I said, "The papers said Colly was coming out the back door of the liquor store carrying a metal box. The police found a hundred and six dollars in the box, and the door jimmied open."

"I know what the papers said, and I know what the police are saying. But they're wrong. *Wrong.*"

"He was there, Lucille."

"I know that," she said. "Colly liked to walk in the evenings. A long walk and then a drink when he came home; it helped him to relax. That was how he came to be there."

I shifted position on my chair, not speaking.

Lucille said, "Colly was always nervous when he was doing burglaries. That was one of the ways I could tell. He'd get irritable, and he couldn't sleep."

"He wasn't like that lately?"

"You saw him a few weeks ago," she said. "Did he look that way to you?"

"No," I said, "he didn't."

"We were happy," Lucille said. "No more running. And no more waiting. We were truly happy."

My mouth felt dry. "What about his job?"

"They gave Colly a raise last week. A fifteen-dollar raise. We went to dinner to celebrate, down on the Wharf."

"You were getting along all right on what he made?" I said. "Nothing came up?"

"Nothing. We even had a little bank account started."

She bit her lower lip. "We were going to Hawaii next year, or the year after. Colly always wanted to go to Hawaii."

I looked at my hands. They seemed big and awkward resting on the desktop; I took them away and put them in my lap. "These Glen Park robberies started a month and a half ago," I said. "The police estimate the total amount taken at close to five thousand dollars. You could get to Hawaii pretty well on that kind of money."

"Colly didn't do those robberies," she said.

What could I say? God knew, and Lucille knew, that Colly had never been a saint; but this time she was convinced he'd been innocent. Nothing, it seemed, was going to change that in her eyes.

I got a cigarette from my pocket and made a thing of lighting it. The smoke added more dryness to my mouth. Without looking at her, I said, "What do you want me to do, Lucille?"

"I want you to prove Colly didn't do what they're saying he did."

"I'd like nothing better, you know that. But how can I do it? The evidence—"

"Damn the evidence!" Her wide mouth trembled with the sudden emotion. "Colly was innocent, I tell you! I won't have him buried with this last mark against his name. I won't have it."

"Lucille, listen to me . . ."

"I won't listen," she said. "Colly was your friend. You stood up for him with the parole board. You helped him find his job. You talked to him, gave him guidance. He was a different man, a new man, and you helped make him that way. Will you sit here and tell me you believe he threw it all away for five thousand dollars?"

I didn't say anything; I still could not meet her eyes. I stared down at the burning cigarette in my fingers, watching the smoke rise, curling, a gray spiral in the cold air of the office.

"Or don't you care whether he was innocent or not?" she said.

"I care, Lucille."

"Then help me. Find out the truth."

"All right," I said. Her anger and grief, and her absolute

certainty that Colly had been innocent, had finally got through to me; I could not have turned her down now if there had been ten times the evidence there was. "All right, Lucille, I'll see what I can do."

It was drizzling when I got to the Hall of Justice. Some of the chill had gone out of the air, but the wind was stronger now. The clouds overhead looked black and swollen, ready to burst.

I parked my car on Bryant Street, went past the sycamores on the narrow front lawn, up the concrete steps and inside. The plainclothes detective division, General Works, was on the fourth floor; I took the elevator. Eberhardt had been promoted to lieutenant not too long ago and had his own private office now, but I caught myself glancing over toward his old desk. Force of habit; it had been a while since I'd visited him at the Hall.

He was in and willing to see me. When I entered his office he was shuffling through some reports and scowling. He was my age, pushing fifty, and he seemed to have been fashioned of an odd contrast of sharp angles and smooth, blunt planes: square forehead, sharp nose and chin, thick and blocky upper body, long legs and angular hands. Today he was wearing a brown suit that hadn't been pressed in a month; his tie was crooked; there was a collar button missing from his shirt. And he had a fat, purplish bruise over his left eye.

"All right," he said, "make it quick."

"What happened to your eye?"

"I bumped into a doorknob."

"Sure you did."

"Yeah," he said. "You come here to pass the time of day, or was there something?"

"I'd like a favor, Eb."

"Sure. And I'd like three weeks' vacation."

"I want to look at an officer's felony report."

"Are you nuts? Get the hell out of here."

The words didn't mean anything. He was always gruff and grumbly while he was working; and we'd been friends for more years than either of us cared to remember, ever since we went through the police academy together after World War II and then joined the force here in the city.

I said, "There was a shooting last night. Two squad-car cops killed a man running away from the scene of a burglary in Glen Park."

"So?"

"The victim was a friend of mine."

He gave me a look. "Since when do you have burglars for friends?"

"His name was Colly Babcock," I said. "He did two stretches in San Quentin, both for burglary; I helped send him up the first time. I also helped get him out on parole the second time and into a decent job."

"Uh-huh. I remember the name. I also heard about the shooting last night. Too bad this pal of yours turned bad again, but then a lot of them do—as if you didn't know."

I was silent.

"I get it," Eberhardt said. "You don't think so. That's why you're here."

"Colly's wife doesn't think so. I guess maybe I don't, either."

"I can't let you look at any reports. And even if I could, it's not my department. Robbery'll be handling it. Internal Affairs, too."

"You could pull some strings."

"I could," he said, "but I won't. I'm up to my ass in work. I just don't have the time."

I got to my feet. "Well, thanks anyway, Eb." I went to the door, put my hand on the knob, but before I turned it he made a noise behind me. I turned.

"If things go all right," he said, scowling at me, "I'll be off duty in a couple of hours. If I happen to get down by Robbery on the way out, maybe I'll stop in. Maybe."

"I'd appreciate it if you would."

"Give me a call later on. At home."

"Thanks, Eb."

"Yeah," he said. "So what are you standing there for? Get the hell out of here and let me work."

I found Tommy Belknap in a bar called Luigi's, out in the Mission District.

He was drinking whiskey at the long bar, leaning his head on his arms and staring at the wall. Two men in work clothes were drinking beer and eating sandwiches from lunch pails at the other end, and in the middle an old lady in a black shawl sipped red wine from a glass held with arthritic fingers. I sat on a stool next to Tommy and said hello.

He turned his head slowly, his eyes moving upward. His face was an anemic white, and his bald head shone with beaded perspiration. He had trouble focusing his eyes; he swiped at them with the back of one veined hand. He was pretty drunk. And I was pretty sure I knew why.

"Hey," he said when he recognized me, "have a drink, will you?"

"Not just now."

He got his glass to his lips with shaky fingers, managed to drink without spilling any of the whiskey. "Colly's dead," he said.

"Yeah. I know."

"They killed him last night," Tommy said. "They shot him in the back."

"Take it easy, Tommy."

"He was my friend."

"He was my friend, too."

"Colly was a nice guy. Lousy goddamn cops had no right to shoot him like that."

"He was robbing a liquor store," I said.

"Hell he was!" Tommy said. He swiveled on the stool and pushed a finger at my chest. "Colly was straight, you hear that? Just like me. Ever since we both got out of Q."

"You sure about that, Tommy?"

"Damn right I am."

"Then who did do those burglaries in Glen Park?"

"How should I know?"

"Come on, you get around. You know people, you hear things. There must be something on the earie."

"Nothing," he said. "Don't know."

"Kids?" I said. "Street punks?"

"Don't *know*."

"But it wasn't Colly? You'd know if it was Colly?"

"Colly was straight," Tommy said. "And now he's dead."

He put his head down on his arms again. The bartender came over; he was a fat man with a reddish handlebar mustache. "You can't sleep in here, Tommy," he said. "You ain't even supposed to *be* in here while you're on parole."

"Colly's dead," Tommy said, and there were tears in his eyes.

"Let him alone," I said to the bartender.

"I can't have him sleeping in here."

I took out my wallet and put a five-dollar bill on the bar. "Give him another drink," I said, "and then let him sleep it off in the back room. The rest of the money is for you."

The bartender looked at me, looked at the finif, looked at Tommy. "All right," he said. "What the hell."

I went out into the rain.

D. E. O'Mira and Company, Wholesale Plumbing Supplies, was a big two-storied building that took up three-quarters of a block on Berry Street, out near China Basin. I parked in front and went inside. In the center of a good-sized office was a switchboard walled in glass, with a card taped to the front that said Information. A dark-haired girl wearing a set of headphones was sitting inside, and when I asked her if Mr. Templeton was in she said he was at a meeting uptown and wouldn't be back all day. Mr. Templeton was the office manager, the man I had spoken to about giving Colly Babcock a job when he was paroled from San Quentin.

Colly had worked in the warehouse, and his immediate supervisor was a man I had never met named Harlin. I went through a set of swing doors opposite the main entrance, down a narrow, dark passage screened on both sides. On my left when I emerged into the warehouse was a long service counter; behind it were display shelves, and behind them long rows of bins that stretched the length and width of the building. Straight ahead, through an open doorway, I could see the loading dock and a yard cluttered with soil pipe and other supplies. On my right was a windowed office with two desks, neither occupied; an old man in a pair of baggy brown slacks, a brown vest, and a battered slouch hat stood before a side counter under the windows.

The old man didn't look up when I came into the office.

A foul-smelling cigar danced in his thin mouth as he shuffled papers. I cleared my throat and said, "Excuse me."

He looked at me then, grudgingly. "What is it?"

"Are you Mr. Harlin?"

"That's right."

I told him who I was and what I did. I was about to ask him about Colly when a couple of guys came into the office and one of them plunked himself down at the nearest desk. I said to Harlin, "Could we talk someplace private?"

"Why? What're you here about?"

"Colly Babcock," I said.

He made a grunting sound, scribbled on one of his papers with a pencil stub, and then led me out onto the dock. We walked along there, past a warehouseman loading crated cast-iron sinks from a pallet into a pickup truck, and up to the wide, double-door entrance to an adjoining warehouse.

The old man stopped and turned to me. "We can talk here."

"Fine. You were Colly's supervisor, is that right?"

"I was."

"Tell me how you felt about him."

"You won't hear anything bad, if that's what you're looking for."

"That's not what I'm looking for."

He considered that for a moment, then shrugged and said, "Colly was a good worker. Did what you told him, no fuss. Quiet sort, kept to himself mostly."

"You knew about his prison record?"

"I knew. All of us here did. Nothing was ever said to Colly about it, though. I saw to that."

"Did he seem happy with the job?"

"Happy enough," Harlin said. "Never complained, if that's what you mean."

"No friction with any of the other men?"

"No. He got along fine with everybody."

A horn sounded from inside the adjoining warehouse and a yellow forklift carrying a pallet of lavatories came out. We stepped out of the way as the thing clanked and belched past.

I asked Harlin, "When you heard about what happened to Colly last night—what was your reaction?"

"Didn't believe it," he answered. "Still don't. None of us do."

I nodded. "Did Colly have any particular friend here? Somebody he ate lunch with regularly—like that?"

"Kept to himself for the most part, like I said. But he stopped with Sam Biehler for a beer a time or two after work; Sam mentioned it."

"I'd like to talk to Biehler, if it's all right."

"Is with me," the old man said. He paused, chewing on his cigar. "Listen, there any chance Colly didn't do what the papers say he did?"

"There might be. That's what I'm trying to find out."

"Anything I can do," he said, "you let me know."

"I'll do that."

We went back inside and I spoke to Sam Biehler, a tall, slender guy with a mane of silver hair that gave him, despite his work clothes, a rather distinguished appearance.

"I don't mind telling you," he said, "I don't believe a damned word of it. I'd have had to be there to see it with my own eyes before I'd believe it, and maybe not even then."

"I understand you and Colly stopped for a beer occasionally?"

"Once a week maybe, after work. Not in a bar; Colly couldn't go to a bar because of his parole. At my place. Then afterward I'd give him a ride home."

"What did you talk about?"

"The job, mostly," Biehler said. "What the company could do to improve things out here in the warehouse. I guess you know the way fellows talk."

"Uh-huh. Anything else?"

"About Colly's past, that what you're getting at?"

"Yes."

"Just once," Biehler said. "Colly told me a few things. But I never pressed him on it. I don't like to pry."

"What was it he told you?"

"That he was never going back to prison. That he was through with the kind of life he'd led before." Biehler's eyes sparked, as if challenging me. "And you know something? I been on this earth for fifty-nine years and I've known a lot of men in that time. You get so you can tell."

"Tell what, Mr. Biehler?"

"Colly wasn't lying," he said.

I spent an hour at the main branch of the library in Civic Center, reading through back issues of the *Chronicle* and the *Examiner*. The Glen Park robberies had begun a month and a half ago, and I had paid only passing attention to them at the time.

When I had acquainted myself with the details I went back to my office and checked in with my answering service. No calls. Then I called Lucille Babcock.

"The police were here earlier," she said. "They had a search warrant."

"Did they find anything?"

"There was nothing to find."

"What did they say?"

"They asked a lot of questions. They wanted to know about bank accounts and safe-deposit boxes."

"Did you cooperate with them?"

"Of course."

"Good," I said. I told her what I had been doing all day, what the people I'd talked with had said.

"You see?" she said. "Nobody who knew Colly can believe he was guilty."

"Nobody but the police."

"Damn the police," she said.

I sat holding the phone. There were things I wanted to say, but they all seemed trite and meaningless. Pretty soon I told her I would be in touch, leaving it at that, and put the receiver back in its cradle.

It was almost five o'clock. I locked up the office, drove home to my flat in Pacific Heights, drank a beer and ate a pastrami sandwich, and then lit a cigarette and dialed Eberhardt's home number. It was his gruff voice that answered.

"Did you stop by Robbery before you left the Hall?" I asked.

"Yeah. I don't know why."

"We're friends, that's why."

"That doesn't stop you from being a pain in the ass sometimes."

"Can I come over, Eb?"

"You can if you get here before eight o'clock," he said. "I'm going to bed then, and Dana has orders to bar all the doors and windows and take the telephone off the hook. I plan to get a good night's sleep for a change."

"I'll be there in twenty minutes," I said.

Eberhardt lived in Noe Valley, up at the back end near Twin Peaks. The house was big and painted white, a two-storied frame job with a trimmed lawn and lots of flowers in front. If you knew Eberhardt, the house was sort of symbolic; it typified everything the honest, hardworking cop was dedicated to protecting. I had a hunch he knew it, too; and if he did, he got a certain amount of satisfaction from the knowledge. That was the way he was.

I parked in his sloping driveway and went up and rang the bell. His wife, Dana, a slender and very attractive brunet with a lot of patience, let me in, asked how I was, and showed me into the kitchen, closing the door behind her as she left.

Eberhardt was sitting at the table having a pipe and a cup of coffee. The bruise over his eye had been smeared with some kind of pinkish ointment; it made him look a little silly, but I knew better than to tell him so.

"Have a seat," he said, and I had one. "You want some coffee?"

"Thanks."

He got me a cup, then indicated a manila envelope lying on the table. Without saying anything, sucking at his pipe, he made an elaborate effort to ignore me as I picked up the envelope and opened it.

Inside was the report made by the two patrolmen, Avinisi and Carstairs, who had shot and killed Colly Babcock in the act of robbing the Budget Liquor Store. I read it over carefully—and my eye caught on one part, a couple of sentences, under "Effects." When I was through I put the report back in the envelope and returned it to the table.

Eberhardt looked at me then. "Well?"

"One item," I said, "that wasn't in the papers."

"What's that?"

"They found a pint of Kessler's in a paper bag in Colly's coat pocket."

He shrugged. "It was a liquor store, wasn't it? Maybe he slipped it into his pocket on the way out."

"And put it into a paper bag first?"

"People do funny things," he said.

"Yeah," I said. I drank some of the coffee and then got on my feet. "I'll let you get to bed, Eb. Thanks again."

He grunted. "You owe me a favor. Just remember that."

"I won't forget."

"You and the elephants," he said.

It was still raining the next morning—another dismal day. I drove to Chenery Street and wedged my car into a downhill parking slot a half block from the three-room apartment Lucille and Colly Babcock had called home for the past year. I hurried through the rain, feeling the chill of it on my face, and mounted sagging wooden steps to the door.

Lucille answered immediately. She wore the same black dress she'd had on yesterday, and the same controlled mask of grief; it would be a long time before that grief faded and she was able to get on with her life. Maybe never, unless somebody proved her right about Colly's innocence.

I sat in the old, stuffed leather chair by the window: Colly's chair. Lucille said, "Can I get you something?"

I shook my head. "What about you? Have you eaten anything today? Or yesterday?"

"No" she answered.

"You have to eat, Lucille."

"Maybe later. Don't worry, I'm not suicidal. I won't starve myself to death."

I managed a small smile. "All right," I said.

"Why are you here?" she asked. "Do you have any news?"

"No, not yet." I had an idea, but it was only that, and too early. I did not want to instill any false hopes. "I just wanted to ask you a few more questions."

"Oh. What questions?"

"You mentioned yesterday that Colly liked to take walks in the evening. Was he in the habit of walking to any particular place, or in any particular direction?"

"No," Lucille said. "He just liked to walk. He was gone for a couple of hours sometimes."

"He never told you where he'd been?"

"Just here and there in the neighborhood."

Here and there in the neighborhood, I thought. The alley where Colly had been shot was eleven blocks from this apartment. He could have walked in a straight line, or he could have gone roundabout in any direction.

I asked, "Colly liked to have a nightcap when he came back from these walks, didn't he?"

"He did, yes."

"He kept liquor here, then?"

"One bottle of bourbon. That's all."

I rotated my hat in my hands. "I wonder if I could have a small drink, Lucille. I know it's early, but . . ."

She nodded and got up and went to a squat cabinet near the kitchen door. She bent, slid the panel open in front, looked inside. Then she straightened. "I'm sorry," she said. "We . . . I seem to be out."

I stood. "It's okay. I should be going anyway."

"Where will you go now?"

"To see some people." I paused. "Would you happen to have a photograph of Colly? A snapshot, something like that?"

"I think so. Why do you want it?"

"I might need to show it around," I said. "Here in the neighborhood."

She seemed satisfied with that. "I'll see if I can find one for you."

I waited while she went into the bedroom. A couple of minutes later she returned with a black-and-white snap of Colly, head and shoulders, that had been taken in a park somewhere. He was smiling, one eyebrow raised in mock raffishness.

I put the snap into my pocket and thanked Lucille and told her I would be in touch again pretty soon. Then I went to the door and let myself out.

The skies seemed to have parted like the Red Sea. Drops of rain as big as hail pellets lashed the sidewalk. Thunder rumbled in the distance, edging closer. I pulled the collar of my overcoat tight around my neck and made a run for my car.

It was after four o'clock when I came inside a place called Tay's Liquors on Whitney Street and stood dripping water on the floor. There was a heater on a shelf just inside the door, and I allowed myself the luxury of its warmth for a few seconds. Then I crossed to the counter.

A young guy wearing a white shirt and a Hitler mustache got up from a stool near the cash register and walked over to me. He smiled, letting me see crooked teeth that weren't very clean. "Wet enough for you?" he said.

No, I thought, I want it to get a lot wetter so I can drown. Dumb question, dumb answer. But all I said was, "Maybe you can help me."

"Sure," he said. "Name your poison."

He was brimming with originality. I took the snapshot of Colly Babcock from my pocket, extended it across the counter, and asked, "Did you see this man two nights ago, sometime around eleven o'clock?" It was the same thing I had done and the same question I had asked at least twenty times already. I had been driving and walking the streets of Glen Park for four hours now, and I had been to four liquor stores, five corner groceries, two large chain markets, a delicatessen, and half a dozen bars that sold off-sale liquor. So far I had come up with nothing except possibly a head cold.

The young guy gave me a slanted look. "Cop?" he asked, but his voice was still cheerful.

I showed him the photostat of my investigator's license. He shrugged, then studied the photograph. "Yeah," he said finally, "I did see this fellow a couple of nights ago. Nice old duck. We talked a little about the Forty-niners."

I stopped feeling cold and I stopped feeling frustrated. I said, "About what time did he come in?"

"Let's see. Eleven-thirty or so, I think."

Fifteen minutes before Colly had been shot in an alley three and a half blocks away. "Do you remember what he bought?"

"Bourbon—a pint. Medium price."

"Kessler's?"

"Yeah, I think it was."

"Okay, good. What's your name?"

"My name? Hey, wait a minute, I don't want to get involved in anything. . . ."

"Don't worry, it's not what you're thinking."

It took a little more convincing, but he gave me his name finally and I wrote it down in my notebook. And thanked him and hurried out of there.

I had something more than an idea now.

Eberhardt said, "I ought to knock you flat on your ass."

He had just come out of his bedroom, eyes foggy with sleep, hair standing straight up, wearing a wine-colored bathrobe. Dana stood beside him looking fretful.

"I'm sorry I woke you up, Eb," I said. "But I didn't think you'd be in bed this early. It's only six o'clock."

He said something I didn't hear, but that Dana heard. She cracked him on the arm to show her disapproval, then turned and left us alone.

Eberhardt went over and sat on the couch and glared at me. "I've had about six hours' sleep in the past forty-eight," he said. "I got called out last night after you left, I didn't get home until three A.M., I was up at seven, I worked all goddamn day and knocked off early so I could get some *sleep,* and what happens? I'm in bed ten minutes and you show up."

"Eb, it's important."

"What is?"

"Colly Babcock."

"Ah, Christ, you don't give up, do you?"

"Sometimes I do, but not this time. Not now." I told him what I had learned from the guy at Tay's Liquors.

"So Babcock bought a bottle there," Eberhardt said. "So what?"

"If he was planning to burglarize a liquor store, do you think he'd have bothered to *buy* a bottle fifteen minutes before?"

"Hell, the job might have been spur-of-the-moment."

"Colly didn't work that way. When he was pulling them, they were all carefully planned well in advance. Always."

"He was getting old," Eberhardt said. "People change."

"You didn't know Colly. Besides, there are a few other things."

"Such as?"

"The burglaries themselves. They were all done the same way—back door jimmied, marks on the jamb and lock made with a hand bar or something." I paused. "They didn't find any tool like that on Colly. Or inside the store either."

"Maybe he got rid of it."

"When did he have time? They caught him coming out the door."

Eberhardt scowled. I had his interest now. "Go ahead," he said.

"The pattern of the burglaries, like I was saying, is doors jimmied, drawers rifled, papers and things strewn about. No fingerprints, but it smacks of amateurism. Or somebody trying to make it look like amateurism."

"And Babcock was a professional."

"He could have done the book," I said. "He used lock picks and glass cutters to get into a place, never anything like a hand bar. He didn't ransack; he always knew exactly what he was after. He never deviated from that, Eb. Not once."

Eberhardt got to his feet and paced around for a time. Then he stopped in front of me and said, "So what do you think, then?"

"You figure it."

"Yeah," he said slowly, "I can figure it, all right. But I don't like it. I don't like it at all."

"And Colly?" I said. "You think he liked it?"

Eberhardt turned abruptly, went to the telephone. He spoke to someone at the Hall of Justice, then someone else. When he hung up, he was already shrugging out of his bathrobe.

He gave me a grim look. "I hope you're wrong, you know that."

"I hope I'm not," I said.

I was sitting in my flat, reading one of the pulps from my collection of several thousand issues, when the telephone rang just before eleven o'clock. It was Eberhardt, and the first thing he said was, "You weren't wrong."

I didn't say anything, waiting.

"Avinisi and Carstairs," he said bitterly. "Each of them on the force a little more than two years. The old story: bills, long hours, not enough pay—and greed. They cooked up the idea one night while they were cruising Glen Park, and it worked just fine until two nights ago. Who'd figure the cops for it?"

"You have any trouble with them?"

"No. I wish they'd given me some so I could have slapped them with a resisting-arrest charge, too."

"How did it happen with Colly?"

"It was the other way around," he said. "Babcock was cutting through the alley when he saw them coming out the rear door. He turned to run and they panicked and Avinisi shot him in the back. When they went to check, Carstairs found a note from Babcock's parole officer in one of his pockets, identifying him as an ex-con. That's when they decided to frame him."

"Look, Eb, I—"

"Forget it," he said. "I know what you're going to say."

"You can't help it if a couple of cops turn out that way. . . ."

"I said forget it, all right?" And the line went dead.

I listened to the empty buzzing for a couple of seconds. It's a lousy world, I thought. But sometimes, at least, there is justice.

Then I called Lucille Babcock and told her why her husband had died.

They had a nice funeral for Colly.

The services were held in a small nondenominational church on Monterey Boulevard. There were a lot of flowers, carnations mostly; Lucille said they had been Colly's favorites. Quite a few people came. Tommy Belknap was there, and Sam Biehler and old man Harlin and the rest of them from D. E. O'Mira. Eberhardt, too, which might have seemed surprising unless you knew him. I also saw faces I didn't recognize; the whole thing had gotten a big play in the media.

Afterward, there was the funeral procession to the cemetery in Colma, where we listened to the minister's final words and watched them put Colly into the ground. When it was done I offered to drive Lucille home, but she said no, there were some arrangements she wanted to make with the caretaker for upkeep of the plot; one of her neighbors would stay with her and see to it she got home all right. Then she held my hand and kissed me on the cheek and told me again how grateful she was.

I went to where my car was parked. Eberhardt was waiting; he had ridden down with me.

"I don't like funerals," he said.

"No," I said.

We got into the car. "So what are you planning to do when we get back to the city?" Eberhardt asked.

"I hadn't thought about it."

"Come over to my place. Dana's gone off to visit her sister, and I've got a refrigerator full of beer."

"All right."

"Maybe we'll get drunk," he said.

I nodded. "Maybe we will at that."

FILE #1:
THE MAYFIELD CASE
Joe Gores

FIRST APPEARANCE: *This Story, 1968*

It was at the urging of famed critic Anthony Boucher that Joe Gores first donned the cap of storyteller while he was still a working PI. This story was the result, published in 1968 by *Ellery Queen's Mystery Magazine*. It led to many more DKA stories, as well as four novels, the most recent being *32 Cadillacs* (Mysterious Press, 1993). The first novel in the series, *Dead Skip,* was published in 1972. This, then, is the actual first appearance of Dan Kearny and company.

Tuesday May 23: 8:15 A.M.

Larry Ballard was halfway to the Daniel Kearny Associates office before he remembered to switch on his radio. After a whine and a blast of static, O'Bannon's voice came on loudly in midtransmission.

". . . Bay Bridge yet, Oakland Three?"

"Coming up to the toll plaza now. The subject is three cars ahead of me. I'll need a front tail once he's off the bridge, over."

"Stand by. KDM Three sixty-six Control calling any San Francisco unit."

Ballard unclipped his mike and pressed the red Transmit button. "This is SF Six. My location is Oak and Buchanan, moving east, over."

"Oakland Three is tailing a red Comet convertible across Bay Bridge, license Charlie, X ray, Kenneth, eight-eight-one. The legal owner, California Citizens Bank on Polk Street, wants *car only*—contract outlawed."

Oakland Three cut in: "Wait by the Ninth and Bryant off-ramp, SF Six."

"Control standing by," said O'Bannon. "KDM Three sixty-six clear."

O'Bannon set down the hand mike on Giselle Marc's desk, leaving it flipped to Monitor. He was a wiry red-haired man about forty, with twinkling blue eyes, freckles, and a hard-bitten drinker's face.

"Who's SF Six? The new kid?"

"Right. Larry Ballard. With us a month yesterday." Giselle was a tall lean blond who had started with DKA as a part-time file girl while in college; after graduation two years before, she had taken over the Cal-Cit Bank desk. "He's a green pea but he's eager and maybe—just maybe—he can think. Kathy's putting him on his own this week."

O'Bannon grunted. "The Great White Father around?"

"Down in his cubbyhole—in a vile mood."

O'Bannon grimaced and laid his expense-account item-ization on her desk with great reverence. Giselle regarded it without enthusiasm.

"Why don't you do your own dirty work, O'B?" she demanded.

Same day: 10:00 A.M.

Ballard was lanky, well-knit, in his early twenties, with blue eyes already hardened by his month with DKA. He was stopped, by Dan Kearny himself, at the top of the narrow stairs leading to the second floor of the old Victorian building that housed the company offices.

"That Comet in the barn?"

"Yes, sir," said Ballard.

"Terrif. Any static?" Kearny was compact and powerful, with a square pugnacious face, massive jaw, and cold gray eyes which invariably regarded the world through a wisp of cigarette smoke.

"I front-tailed him from the freeway. When he parked on Howard Street, Oakland Three and I just wired up the Comet and drove it away."

Kearny clapped Ballard's shoulder and went on. Ballard entered the front office, which overlooked Golden Gate

Avenue through unwashed bay windows. Three assignments were in his basket on the desk of Jane Goldson, the phone receptionist with the Liverpool accent: through her were channeled all assignments, memos, and field reports.

Carrying the case sheets, Ballard descended to the garage under the building. Along the right wall were banks of lockers for personal property; along the left, small partitioned offices used by the seven San Francisco field men. He paused to review his new cases before leaving.

The most puzzling one involved a new Continental, financed through Cal-Cit Bank, which had been purchased by a Jocelyn Mayfield, age twenty-three. She and her roommate, Victoria Goodrich, lived at 31 Edith Alley and were case workers for San Francisco Social Services. What startled Ballard was the size of the delinquent payments—$198.67 each—and the contract balance of over $7,000. On a welfare worker's salary? Even though her parents lived in the exclusive St. Francis Woods area, they were not co-signers on the contract.

From his small soundproofed office at the rear of the garage Dan Kearny watched Ballard leave. Kearny had been in the game for over half of his forty-three years, and still hadn't figured out the qualities which made a good investigator; only time would tell if Ballard had them. Kearny jabbed an intercom button with a blunt finger.

"Giselle? Send O'Bannon down here, will you?"

He lit a Lucky, leaned back to blow smoke at the ceiling. O'B had come with him six years before, when Kearny had resigned from Walter's Auto Detectives to start DKA with one car and this old Victorian building which had been a bawdy house in the nineties; and reviewing O'B's expense accounts still furnished Kearny with his chief catharsis.

He smeared out the cigarette; through the one-way glass he could see O'Bannon approaching the office, whistling, his hands in pockets, his blue eyes innocent of guile. When he came in, Kearny shook out a cigarette for himself and offered the pack. "How's Bella O'B?"

"She asks when you're bringing the kids for cioppino again."

Kearny indicated the littered desk. "I'm two weeks behind in my billing. Oh . . . this *expense* account, O'B." Without warning his fist smashed down in sudden fury. *"Damn it, if you think ..."*

O'Bannon remained strangely tranquil during the storm. When Kearny finally ran down, the redheaded man cleared his throat and spoke.

"Giants leading three-two, bottom of the third. Marichal—"

"What do you mean?" Kearny looked stunned. "What the—"

O'Bannon fished a tiny transistor radio from his pocket, then apologetically removed miniature speakers from both his ears. Kearny gaped.

"You mean—while I—you were *listening to the ball game*?"

O'Bannon nodded dolorously. Speechless with rage, Kearny jerked out the expense-account checkbook; but then his shoulders began shaking with silent laughter.

Same day: 9:30 P.M.

Larry Ballard parked on upper Grant; above him, on Telegraph Hill, loomed the concrete cone of Coit Tower, like a giant artillery piece about to be fired. Edith Alley ran half a block downhill toward Stockton; Jocelyn Mayfield and her roommate, Victoria Goodrich, had the lower apartment in a two-story frame building.

The girl who answered the bell wore jeans and sweatshirt over a chunky figure; her short hair was tinted almost white. Wide cheekbones gave her a Slavic look.

"Is Jocelyn here?" Ballard asked.

"Are you a friend of hers?" Her voice was harshly attractive.

Ballard took a flier. "I was in one of her sociology classes."

"At Stanford?" She stepped back. "Sorry if I sounded antisocial. Sometimes male clients get ideas, y'know?"

He followed her into the apartment. "You must be Vikki—Josie has mentioned you. You don't act like a social worker."

" 'Say something to me in psychology'? Actually, I was a waitress down in North Beach before I started with Social Services."

There were cheap shades at the windows of the rather barren living room, a grass mat on the floor, a wicker chair and a couch, and an ugly black coffee table. The walls were a depressing brown. It was not a room in keeping with monthly automobile payments of two hundred dollars.

"We're going to repaint eventually," Vikki said. "I guess." Ballard nodded. "Has Josie mentioned selling the Continental?"

"The Continental?" She frowned. "That belongs to Hank—*we* both use my Triumph. I don't think he wants to sell it; he just got it."

"Hank, huh? Say, what's his name and address? I can—"

Just then a key grated in the front door. Damn! Two minutes more would have done it. Now the subject was in the room, talking breathlessly. "Did Hank call? He wasn't at his apartment, and—"

"Here's an old friend of yours," Vikki cut in brightly.

Ballard was staring. Jocelyn Mayfield was the loveliest girl he had ever seen, her fawnlike beauty accented by shimmering jet hair. Her mouth was small but full-lipped, her brows slightly heavy for a girl, her brown liquid eyes full-lashed. She had one of those supple patrician figures maintained by tennis on chilly mornings.

"Old friend?" Her voice was low. "But I don't even know him!"

That tore it. Ballard blurted, "I'm—uh—representing California Citizens Bank. We've been employed to investigate your six-hundred-dollar delinquency on the 1967 Continental. We—"

"You dirty—" The rest of Vikki's remark was not that of a welfare worker. "I bet you practice lying to yourself in front of a mirror. I bet—"

"Vikki, hush." Jocelyn was blushing, deeply embarrassed. Vikki stopped and her eyes popped open wide.

"You mean you *did* make the down payment on that car? It's registered in *your* name? You fool! He couldn't make a monthly payment on a free lunch, and you—" She stopped, turned on Ballard. "Okay, buster. Out."

"Vikki, please." Then Jocelyn said to Ballard, "I thought—I had no idea the payments—by Friday I can have all the money."

"I said *out,* buster," Vikki snapped. "You heard her—you'll get your pound of flesh. And that's *all* you'll get—unless I tear Josie's dress and run out into that alley yelling rape."

Ballard retreated; he had no experience in handling a Vikki Goodrich. And there was something about Jocelyn Mayfield—private stock, O'Bannon would have called her. She'd been so obviously let down by this Hank character; and she *had* promised to pay by Friday.

Monday May 29: 3:30 P.M.

Jane Goldson winked and pointed toward the office manager's half-closed door. "She's in a proper pet, she is, Larry."

He went in. Kathy Onoda waved him to a chair without removing the phone from her ear. She was an angular girl in her late twenties, with classical Japanese features. Speaking into the phone her voice was hesitant, nearly unintelligible with sibilants.

"I jus' rittre Joponee girr in your country verry littre time." She winked at Ballard. "So sorry, too, preese. I roose job I . . . ah . . . ah so. Sank you verry much. Buddha shower bressings."

She hung up and exclaimed jubilantly, "Why do those stupid S.O.Bs always fall for that phony Buddha-head accent?" All trace of it had disappeared. "You, hotshot, you sleeping with this Mayfield chick? One report, dated last Tuesday, car in hands of a third party, three payments down—and you take a promise. Which isn't kept."

"Well, you see, Kathy, I thought—"

"You want me to come along and hold your hand?" Her black eyes glittered and her lips thinned with scorn. "Go to Welfare and hint that she's sleeping around; tell her mother that our investigation is going to hit the society pages; get a line on this Hank no-goodnik." She jabbed a finger at him. "Go gettem bears!"

Ballard fled, slightly dazed as always after a session with Kathy. Driving toward Twin Peaks, he wondered why Jocelyn had broken her promise. Just another deadbeat? He hated to believe that, apart from the Mayfield case he was doing a good job. He still carried a light case load, but he knew that eventually he would be responsible for as many as seventy-five files simultaneously, with reports due every three days on each of them except skips, holds, and contingents.

The Mayfield home was on Darien Way in St. Francis Woods; it was a huge pseudo-Colonial with square columns and a closely trimmed lawn like a gigantic golf green. Inside the double garage was a new Mercedes. A maid with iron gray hair took his card, returned with Jocelyn's mother— an erect, pleasant-faced woman in her fifties.

"I'm afraid I'm not familiar with Daniel Kearny Associates."

"We represent California Citizens Bank," said Ballard. "We've been engaged to investigate certain aspects of your daughter's finances."

"Jocelyn's finances?" Her eyes were lighter than her daughter's, with none of their melting quality. "Whatever in the world for?"

"She's six hundred dollars delinquent on a 1967 Continental."

"Indeed?" Her voice was frigid. "Perhaps you had better come in."

The living room had a red brick fireplace and was made strangely tranquil by the measured ticking of an old-fashioned grandfather's clock. There was a grand piano and a magnificent oriental rug.

"Now. Why would my daughter supposedly do such a thing?"

"She bought it for a"—his voice gave the word emphasis—"man."

She stiffened. "You cannot be intimating that my daughter's personal life is anything but exemplary! When Mr. Mayfield hears this ... this infamous gossip, he ... he is most important in local financial circles."

"So is California Citizens Bank."

"Oh!" She stood up abruptly. "I suggest you leave this house."

Driving back, Ballard knew he had made the right move to bring parental pressure on Jocelyn Mayfield, but the knowledge gave him scant pleasure. There had been a framed picture of her on the piano; somehow his own thoughts, coupled with the picture, had made his memory of their brief meeting sharper, almost poignant.

Same day: 5:15 P.M.

Dan Kearny lit a Lucky. "I think you know why I had you come back in, Ballard. The Mayfield case. Are you *proud* of that file?"

"No sir." He tried to meet Kearny's gaze. "But I think she broke her promise to pay because this deadbeat talked her into it."

"You took a *week* to find that out?" Kearny demanded. "Giselle found out that the subject walked off her job at Welfare last Friday night—took an indefinite leave without bothering to leave any forwarding address."

Kearny paused to form a smoke ring. He could blast this kid right out of the tank, but he didn't want to do that. "I started in this game in high school, Ballard, during the depression. Night-hawking cars for Old Man Walters down in L.A. at five bucks per repo—cover your own expenses, investigate on your own time. Some of those Okies would have made you weep, but I couldn't *afford* to feel sorry for them. This Mayfield dame's in a mess. Is that *our* fault? Or the *bank's*?"

"No, sir. But there are special circumstances—"

"Circumstances be *damned!* We're hired to investigate people who have defaulted, defrauded, or embezzled—money or goods—to find them if they've skipped out, and to return the property to the legal owner. Mayfield's contract is *three months* delinquent and *you* spin your wheels for a whole week. Right now the bank is looking at a seven-thousand-dollar loss." He ground out his cigarette and stood up. "Let's take a ride."

Later, ringing the bell at 31 Edith Alley, Ballard warned, "This Victoria Goodrich is tough. I know she won't tell us anything."

Vikki opened the door and glared at him. "*You* again?"

Kearny moved past Ballard so smoothly that the girl had to step back to avoid being walked on, and they were inside. "My name is Turk," he said. "I'm with the legal department of the bank."

She had recovered. "You should be *ashamed,* hiring this

person to stir up trouble for Josie with her folks. Okay, so she's two lousy payments behind. I'll make one of them now, and next week she can—"

"*Three* payments. And since the vehicle is in the hands of a third party, the contract is void." He shot a single encompassing look around the living room, then brought his cold gray eyes back to her face. "We know Miss Mayfield has moved out. Where is she living now?"

"I don't know." She met his gaze stubbornly.

Kearny nodded. "Fraudulent contract; flight to avoid prosecution. We'll get a grand-theft warrant for her seven-thousand-dollar embezzle—"

"Good God!" Vikki's face crumbled with dismay. "Really, I don't know Hank's addr—I mean I don't know where she's gone. I—" Under his unwinking stare, tears suddenly came into her voice. "His wife's on welfare; he's no damn good. Once when he'd been drinking he—he put his hands on me. I guess she's with him, but I don't know where."

"Then what's Hank's last name?"

She sank down on the couch with her face in her hands and merely shook her head. Ignoring her, Kearny turned to Ballard. "Sweet kid, this Mayfield. She *steals* the woman's husband, then a car, then—"

"No!" Vikki was sobbing openly. "It isn't like that! They were separated—"

Kearny's voice lashed out. *"What's his last name?"*

"I won't—"

"Hank *what*?"

"You've no right to—"

"—to throw your trashy roommate in jail? We can and we *will*."

She raised a tear-ravaged face. "If you find the car will Josie stay out of prison?"

"I can't make promises of immunity on behalf of the bank."

"His name is Stuber. Harold Stuber." She wailed suddenly to Ballard. "Make him stop! I've told everything I know—everything."

Kearny grunted. "You've been most helpful," he said,

then strode out. Ballard took a hesitant step toward the hunched, sobbing girl, hesitated, and then ran after Kearny.

"Why did you do that to her?" he raged. "Now she's crying—"

"And we've got the information we came after," Kearny said.

"But you said to her—"

"But, *hell.*" He called Control on the radio. When Giselle answered, he said, "Mayfield unit reportedly in the hands of a Harold Stuber—S-t-u-b-e-r. Checked him through the Polk Directory." He lit a cigarette and puffed placidly at it, the mike lying in his lap.

"The only listing under Harold Stuber shows a residence at 1597 Eighteenth Street; employment, bartender; wife, Edith."

"Thanks, Giselle. SF Six clear."

"KDM Three sixty-six Control clear."

Driving out to Eighteenth Street, Ballard was glad it had been Vikki, not Jocelyn Mayfield, who had been put through the meat grinder. Vikki wasn't soft, yet Kearny had reduced her to tears in just a few vicious minutes.

The address on Eighteenth Street was a dirty, weathered stucco building above the heavy industrial area fringing Potrero Hill. It was a neighborhood losing its identity in its battle against the wrecker's ball. Inside the apartment house, the first-floor hall wore an ancient threadbare carpet with a design like spilled animal intestines.

"Some of this rubbed off on your true love," remarked Kearny.

Ballard gritted his teeth. Their knock was answered by a man two inches over six feet, wide as the doorway. His rolled-up sleeves showed hairy, muscle-knotted arms; his eyes were red-rimmed and he carried a glass of whiskey. He looked as predictable as a runaway truck.

Kearny was unimpressed. "Harold Stuber?"

"He don't live here no more." The door began to close.

"How about Edith Stuber?"

The hand on the door hesitated. "Who's askin'?"

"Welfare." When Kearny went forward the huge man wavered, lost his inner battle, and stepped back. The apartment smelled of chili and unwashed diapers; somewhere in one of the rooms a baby was screaming.

"Edie," yelled the big man, "coupla guys from Welfare."

She was a boldly handsome woman in her thirties, with dark hair and flashing black eyes. Under a black sweater and black slacks her body was full-breasted, wide-hipped, heavily sensual.

"Welfare?" Her voice became a whine. "D'ya have my check?"

"Your *check*?" Kearny's eyes flicked to the big man with simulated contempt. He whirled to Ballard. "Johnson, note that the recipient is living common-law with a Caucasian male, height six-two, weight two-twenty, estimated age thirty-nine. Recipient should—"

"Hey!" yelled the woman, turning furiously on the big man, "if I lose my welfare check—"

Kearny cut in brusquely, "We're only interested in your legal spouse, Mrs. Stuber."

Her yells stopped like a knife slash. "You come about Hank? He ain't lived here in five months. When he abandoned me an' the kid—"

"But the bureau knows he gets in touch with you."

"You could call it that." She gave a coarse laugh. "Last Wednesday he come over in a big Continental, woke us— woke *me* up an' made a row 'bout Mr. Kleist here slee— bein' my acquaintance. Then the p'lice come an' Hank, he slugged one of 'em. So they took him off."

Kearny said sharply, "What about the Continental?"

"It set here to the weekend, then it was gone."

"What's your husband's current residence address?"

She waved a vague arm. "He never said." Her eyes widened. "He give me a phone number, but I never did call it; knew it wouldn't do no good." Behind her the baby began crying; the big man went away. Her eyes were round with the effort of remembering. "Yeah. Eight six zero, four six four five."

Back in the agency car, Kearny lit a cigarette. "If it's any consolation, there's the reason for her broken promise. He gets busted Wednesday night, gets word to Mayfield Thursday, on Friday she quits her job. Saturday she sees him at the county jail, finds out where he left the car, drops it into dead storage somewhere near his apartment, and holes up there to wait until he gets out. Find her, you find the car."

"Can't we trace the phone number this one gave us?"

Kearny gestured impatiently. "That'll just be some gin mill."

The next day the Mayfield folder went into the Skip tub and a request went to the client for a copy of the subject's credit application. Skip tracing began on the case. The phone number proved to be that of a tough Valencia Street bar. DKA's Peninsula agent found that Stuber had drawn a thirty-to-ninety-day rap in the county jail, the heavy sentence resulting from a prior arrest on the same charge. Stuber said he still lived at Eighteenth Street and denied knowing the subject. A stakeout of the jail's parking lot during visiting hours was negative.

Police contacts reported that the Continental had not been impounded, nor was it picking up parking tags anywhere in San Francisco. Stuber had no current utilities service, no phone listing. The time involved in checking dead-storage garages would have been excessive. By phone Giselle covered Welfare, neighbors around the Edith Alley and Eighteenth Street addresses, the subject's former contacts at Stanford, Bartender's Local Number 41, all the references on the credit application. Ballard supplemented with field contact of postmen, gas station attendants, newsboys, and small store owners.

None of it did any good.

Thursday June 9: 7:15 P.M.

Ballard was typing reports at home when his phone rang. He had worked thirteen cases that day, including two skips besides Mayfield; it took him a few moments to realize that it was her voice.

"What have I done to make you hate me so?" she asked.

"I'm all for you personally, Josie, but I've got a job to do. Anyway, if I let up it just would mean that someone else would keep looking."

"I love him." She said it without emotion—a fact by which she lived. "I love him and he said he would leave me if I let them take his car while he's—away. I couldn't stand that. It's the first thing of beauty he's ever possessed, and he can't give it up."

Ballard was swept by a sudden wave of sympathy, almost of desire for her; he could picture her, wearing something soft, probably cashmere, her face serious, her mouth a pink bud. How could Stuber have such a woman bestowed on him, yet keep thinking of a damned automobile? How could he make Jocelyn see Stuber as he really was?

"Josie, the bank objects so strongly to Stuber that they've declared the contract void; as long as he had possession, they'd hold the account in jeopardy. Surrender it. Get him something you can afford."

"I couldn't do that," she said gravely, and hung up.

Ballard got a beer from the refrigerator and sat down at the kitchen table to drink it. After only one meeting and a single phone conversation, was he falling for Jocelyn Mayfield? He felt a deep physical attraction, sure; but it wasn't unsatisfied desire which was oppressing him now. It was the knowledge that he was going to keep looking for the car, that there was no way to close the case without Jocelyn being badly hurt emotionally.

Friday, June 17: 10:15 A.M.

"If I see her mother once more, she'll call the cops," Ballard objected. "Stuber gets out June twenty-ninth. We could tail him—"

"The bank's deadline is next *Tuesday*—the twenty-first," said Kearny. "Then their dealer recourse expires and they have to *eat* their loss—whatever it is: Find the girl, Ballard, and get the car."

The intercom buzzed and Jane Goldson said, "Larry's got a funny sort of call on fifteen oh four, Mr. Kearny. She sounds drunk or something."

Kearny gestured and stayed on as Ballard picked up. The voice, which Ballard recognized as Jocelyn's, was overflowing with hysteria.

"I can't stand it anymore and I want you to know you're to blame!" she cried. "My parentsh hate me—can't see Hank on weekends 'cause I know you'll be waiting, like vultures—sho—I did it." She gave a sleepy giggle. "I killed myself."

"You're a lively sounding corpse," said Kearny in a syrupy voice.

"I know who you are!" Surprisingly, she giggled again. "You made Vikki cry. Poor Vikki'll be all sad. I took all the pillsh."

Kearny, who appeared to have been doodling on a sheet of scratch paper, held up a crudely printed note: Have Kathy trace call. Ballard switched off, jabbed Kathy's intercom button. Please God, he thought, let her be all right. What had brought her to this extremity?

"I'll trace it," rapped Kathy. "Keep that connection open."

He punched back into 1504. ". . . Ballard's shoul when I die . . . lose car, lose Hank, sho . . ." Her singsong trailed off with a tired sigh; there was a sudden heavy jar. After a moment a light tapping began, as if the receiver were swinging at the end of the cord and striking a table leg. They stared at one another across the empty line.

The intercom buzzed, making Ballard jump. Kathy said, "Four sixty-nine Eddy Street, apartment two oh six, listed under Harold Stein—that'll be Stuber. The phone company'll get an ambulance and oxygen over there. Good hunting."

Ballard was already out of his chair. "It's a place on Eddy Street—we've got to get to her!"

As they rocketed up Franklin for the turn into Eddy Street, Ballard said, "We shouldn't have hounded her that way. Do you think she'll be all right?"

"Depends on how many of what she took. That address—between Jones and Leavenworth in the Tenderloin—crummy neighborhood. The nearest dead-storage garage is around the corner on Jones Street. We can—hey! What the hell are you doing?"

Ballard had slammed the car to a stop in front of a rundown apartment building. "I've got to get to her!" he cried. He was halfway out the car door when Kearny's thick fingers closed around Ballard's tie and yanked him bodily back inside.

"You're a repo man, Ballard," he growled. "That might not mean much to you but it does to me, a hell of a lot. *First* we get the car." Ballard, suddenly desperate, drew back a threatening fist. Kearny's slaty eyes didn't flicker; he said, "Don't let my gray hairs make a coward of you, sonny."

Ballard slumped back on the seat. He nodded. "Okay. Drive on, damn you."

As they turned into Jones Street, a boxy white Public Health ambulance wheeled into Eddy and smoked to a stop on the wrong side of the street. At the garage half a block down, Kearny went in while Ballard waited in the car. Why had he almost slugged Kearny? For that matter, why had he backed down?

Kearny stuck his head in the window. "It's easy when you know where to look." He laid a hand on Ballard's arm. "On your way up there call Giselle and have her send me a Hold Harmless letter."

Ballard circled the block and parked behind the ambulance. On the second floor he saw three tenants gaping by the open door of apartment 206. A uniformed cop put a hand on Ballard's chest.

"I was on the phone with her when she . . . fainted."

"Okay. The sergeant'll wanna talk with you anyway."

She was on the floor by the phone stand, her head back and her mouth open. Her skin was very pale; the beautifully luminous eyes were shut. A tracheal tube was down her throat so that she could breathe. The skirt had ridden high up one sprawled thigh, and Ballard pulled it down.

"Is she—will she—?"

The intern was barely older than Ballard, but his hair already was thinning. "We'll give her oxygen in the ambulance." He opened his hand to display a bottle. "Unless she had something in here besides what's on the label, she should be okay."

Ballard glanced around the tiny two-roomer. There was a rumpled wall bed with a careless pile of paperbacks on the floor beside it; he could picture her cooped up there day after day, while her depression deepened. Above the flaked-silver radiator was a large brown water stain from the apartment upstairs; it was a room where dreams would die without a whimper.

Ballard backed off; instead of talking to the detective in charge he would call her folks so that their own doctor could be at the hospital to prevent it being listed as an attempted suicide.

That afternoon DKA closed the file on the Mayfield case. She was released from the hospital a few days later and returned to 31 Edith Alley. Without really knowing why, Ballard went over there one Tuesday evening to see her; she refused to come out of the bedroom, and he ended up in the living room, drinking tea with Vikki Goodrich.

"She's grateful for what you did, Larry. But, as far as anything further . . ." She paused delicately. "Hank Stuber will be out tomorrow." She paused again, her face suddenly troubled. "She's going to surprise him and pick him up in my Triumph; he doesn't know about the Continental. After that I guess she'll be . . . well, sort of busy."

Leaving the apartment, Ballard told himself that ended it: Yet he sat behind the wheel of his car for a long time without turning the ignition key. Damn it, that *didn't* end it! Too much raw emotion had been bared. . . .

Thursday June 30: 8:15 A.M.

Each short journalistic phrase in the *Chronicle,* read over his forgotten restaurant eggs, deepened his sense of loss, his realization that something bright in his life had been permanently darkened.

Police officers, answering a call late last night to 31 Edith Alley, were greeted by Miss Victoria Goodrich, 24, a case worker with San Francisco Social Services. The hysterical Miss Goodrich said that her roommate, Jocelyn Mayfield, 23, and Harold P. Stuber, 38, had entered the apartment at eight P.M. Stuber had been drinking, she said; by ten P.M. he had become so abusive that he struck Miss Mayfield. According to Miss Goodrich he then departed, and Miss Mayfield locked herself in the bathroom.

At eleven P.M. Miss Goodrich called for police assistance. They broke down the locked door to find Miss Mayfield on the tile floor in a pool of blood. Both wrists had been slashed with a razor blade. The girl was D.O.A. at San Francisco General Hospital. Stuber, an unemployed bartender who was released only yesterday after-

noon from the county jail, is being sought on an assault
charge.

Ballard thought, I've never even seen the son of a—I
could pass him on the street and not even know it. He felt
a sudden revulsion, almost a nausea, at his own role in
the destruction of Jocelyn Mayfield. Half an hour later he
slammed the *Chronicle* down on Kearny's desk.

"Stuber said he'd leave her if we took the Continental
while he was in jail. He left her, all right."

Kearny looked at him blandly. "I've already seen it."

"If we hadn't taken the car—"

"—she would have killed herself next month or next year
over some other deadbeat. She was an emotional loser,
Ballard, a picker of wrong men." He paused, then continued dryly, "It's the end of the month, Ballard. I'd like to
review your case file."

Ballard dropped his briefcase on the littered desk. "You
know what you can do with your case file, Kearny? You
can take it and—"

Kearny listened without heat, then reached for his cigarettes. He lit one and sneered, through the new smoke,
"What will you do now, Ballard—go home and cry into
your pillow? She's going to be dead for a long long time."

Ballard stared at him, speechless, as if at a new species
of animal—the square pugnacious face, the hard eyes which
had seen too much, the heavy cleft chin, the nose slightly
askew from some old argument which had gone beyond
words. A long slow shudder ran through the younger man's
frame. Work—that was Kearny's answer to everything.
Work, while Jocelyn Mayfield lay with a morgue tag on her
toe. Work, while scar tissue began its slow accretion over
the wound.

All right, then—work. Very slowly he drew his assignments from the briefcase. "Let's get at it then," he said in
a choked voice.

Dan Kearny nodded to himself. A girl had died; a man
had had his first bitter taste of reality. And in the process
DKA bought themselves an investigator. Maybe, with a few
more rough edges knocked off, a damned good investigator.

OUT THE WINDOW
Lawrence Block

FIRST APPEARANCE: *In the Midst of Death*, 1976

The first Matthew Scudder novel, *In the Midst of Death*, appeared in 1976 as a Dell paperback original. It was quickly followed by *The Sins of the Father* (Dell, 1976) and *Time to Murder and Create* (Dell, 1977). It was, however, with the appearance of the novel *A Stab in the Dark* (Arbor House, 1981), the first to appear in hardcover, that the series began to gain the stature it deserved. Since then Scudder has garnered his creator two best PI novel Shamus Awards, two best PI short story Shamus Awards, a best novel Edgar Award, and a best short story Edgar Award. As of this writing, the latest Scudder novel, *A Long Line of Dead Men*, had been nominated for an Edgar Award for best mystery novel of 1994.

"Out the Window" first appeared in *Alfred Hitchcock's Mystery Magazine* in 1977.

There was nothing special about her last day. She seemed a little jittery, preoccupied with something or with nothing at all. But this was nothing new for Paula.

She was never much of a waitress in the three months she spent at Armstrong's. She'd forget some orders and mix up others, and when you wanted the check or another round of drinks you could go crazy trying to attract her attention. There were days when she walked through her shift like a ghost through walls, and it was as though she had perfected some arcane technique of astral projection, sending her mind out for a walk while her long lean body went on serving food and drinks and wiping down empty tables.

She did make an effort, though. She damn well tried. She

could always manage a smile. Sometimes it was the brave smile of the walking wounded and other times it was a tight-jawed, brittle grin with a couple tabs of amphetamine behind it, but you take what you can to get through the days and any smile is better than none at all. She knew most of Armstrong's regulars by name and her greeting always made you feel as though you'd come home. When that's all the home you have, you tend to appreciate that sort of thing.

And if the career wasn't perfect for her, well, it certainly hadn't been what she'd had in mind when she came to New York in the first place. You no more set out to be a waitress in a Ninth Avenue gin mill than you intentionally become an excop coasting through the months on bourbon and coffee. We have that sort of greatness thrust upon us. When you're as young as Paula Wittlauer you hang in there, knowing things are going to get better. When you're my age you just hope they don't get too much worse.

She worked the early shift, noon to eight, Tuesday through Saturday. Trina came on at six so there were two girls on the floor during the dinner rush. At eight Paula would go wherever she went and Trina would keep on bringing cups of coffee and glasses of bourbon for another six hours or so.

Paula's last day was a Thursday in late September. The heat of the summer was starting to break up. There was a cooling rain that morning and the sun never did show its face. I wandered in around four in the afternoon with a copy of the *Post* and read through it while I had my first drink of the day. At eight o'clock I was talking with a couple of nurses from Roosevelt Hospital who wanted to grouse about a resident surgeon with a messiah complex. I was making sympathetic noises when Paula swept past our table and told me to have a good evening.

I said, "You too, kid." Did I look up? Did we smile at each other? Hell, I don't remember.

"See you tomorrow, Matt."

"Right," I said. "God willing."

But he evidently wasn't. Around three Justin closed up and I went around the block to my hotel. It didn't take

long for the coffee and bourbon to cancel each other out.
I got into bed and slept.

My hotel is on Fifty-seventh Street between Eighth and
Ninth. It's on the uptown side of the block and my window
is on the street side looking south. I can see the World
Trade Center at the tip of Manhattan from my window.

I can also see Paula's building. It's on the other side of
Fifty-seventh Street a hundred yards or so to the east, a
towering high-rise that, had it been directly across from me,
would have blocked my view of the trade center.

She lived on the seventeenth floor. Sometime after four
she went out a high window. She swung out past the sidewalk and landed in the street a few feet from the curb,
touching down between a couple of parked cars.

In high school physics they teach you that falling bodies
accelerate at a speed of thirty-two feet per second. So she
would have fallen thirty-two feet in the first second, another
sixty-four feet the next second, then ninety-six feet in the
third. Since she fell something like two hundred feet, I
don't suppose she could have spent more than four seconds
in the actual act of falling.

It must have seemed a lot longer than that.

I got up around ten, ten-thirty. When I stopped at the desk
for my mail Vinnie told me they'd had a jumper across the
street during the night. "A dame," he said, which is a word
you don't hear much anymore. "She went out without a
stitch on. You could catch your death that way."

I looked at him.

"Landed in the street, just missed somebody's Caddy.
How'd you like to find something like that for a hood orna-
ment? I wonder if your insurance would cover that. What
do you call it, act of God?" He came out from behind the
desk and walked with me to the door. "Over there," he
said, pointing. "The florist's van there is covering the spot
where she flopped. Nothing to see anyway. They scooped
her up with a spatula and a sponge and then they hosed
it all down. By the time I came on duty there wasn't a
trace left."

"Who was she?"

"Who knows?"

I had things to do that morning, and as I did them I thought from time to time of the jumper. They're not that rare and they usually do the deed in the hours before dawn. They say it's always darkest then.

Sometime in the early afternoon I was passing Armstrong's and stopped in for a short one. I stood at the bar and looked around to say hello to Paula but she wasn't there. A doughy redhead named Rita was taking her shift.

Dean was behind the bar. I asked him where Paula was. "She skipping school today?"

"You didn't hear?"

"Jimmy fired her?"

He shook his head, and before I could venture any further guesses he told me.

I drank my drink. I had an appointment to see somebody about something, but suddenly it ceased to seem important. I put a dime in the phone and canceled my appointment and came back and had another drink. My hand was trembling slightly when I picked up the glass. It was a little steadier when I set it down.

I crossed Ninth Avenue and sat in St. Paul's for a while. Ten, twenty minutes. Something like that. I lit a candle for Paula and a few other candles for a few other corpses, and I sat there and thought about life and death and high windows. Around the time I left the police force I discovered that churches were very good places for thinking about that sort of thing.

After a while I walked over to her building and stood on the pavement in front of it. The florist's truck had moved on and I examined the street where she'd landed. There was, as Vinnie had assured me, no trace of what had happened. I tilted my head back and looked up, wondering what window she might have fallen from, and then I looked down at the pavement and then up again, and a sudden rush of vertigo made my head spin. In the course of all this I managed to attract the attention of the building's doorman and he came out to the curb anxious to talk about the former tenant. He was a black man about my age and he looked as proud of his uniform as the guy in the Marine

Corps recruiting poster. It was a good-looking uniform, shades of brown, epaulets, gleaming brass buttons.

"Terrible thing," he said. "A young girl like that with her whole life ahead of her."

"Did you know her well?"

He shook his head. "She would give me a smile, always say hello, always call me by name. Always in a hurry, rushing in, rushing out again. You wouldn't think she had a care in the world. But you never know."

"You never do."

"She lived on the seventeenth floor. I wouldn't live that high above the ground if you gave me the place rent-free."

"Heights bother you?"

I don't know if he heard the question. "I live up one flight of stairs. That's just fine for me. No elevator and no, no high window." His brow clouded and he looked on the verge of saying something else, but then someone started to enter his building's lobby and he moved to intercept him. I looked up again, trying to count windows to the seventeenth floor, but the vertigo returned and I gave it up.

"Are you Matthew Scudder?"

I looked up. The girl who'd asked the question was very young, with long straight brown hair and enormous light brown eyes. Her face was open and defenseless and her lower lip was quivering. I said I was Matthew Scudder and pointed at the chair opposite mine. She remained on her feet.

"I'm Ruth Wittlauer," she said.

The name didn't register until she said, "Paula's sister." Then I nodded and studied her face for signs of a family resemblance. If they were there I couldn't find them. It was ten in the evening and Paula Wittlauer had been dead for eighteen hours and her sister was standing expectantly before me, her face a curious blend of determination and uncertainty.

I said, "I'm sorry. Won't you sit down? And will you have something to drink?"

"I don't drink."

"Coffee?"

"I've been drinking coffee all day. I'm shaky from all the damn coffee. Do I *have* to order something?"

She was on the edge, all right. I said, "No, of course not. You don't have to order anything." And I caught Trina's eye and warned her off and she nodded shortly and let us alone. I sipped my own coffee and watched Ruth Wittlauer over the brim of the cup.

"You knew my sister, Mr. Scudder."

"In a superficial way, as a customer knows a waitress."

"The police say she killed herself."

"And you don't think so?"

"I know she didn't."

I watched her eyes while she spoke and I was willing to believe she meant what she said. She didn't believe that Paula went out the window of her own accord, not for a moment. Of course, that didn't mean she was right.

"What do you think happened?"

"She was murdered." She made the statement quite matter-of-factly. "I know she was murdered. I think I know who did it."

"Who?"

"Cary McCloud."

"I don't know him."

"But it may have been somebody else," she went on. She lit a cigarette, smoked for a few moments in silence. "I'm pretty sure it was Cary," she said.

"Why?"

"They were living together." She frowned, as if in recognition of the fact that cohabitation was small evidence of murder. "He could do it," she said carefully. "That's why I think he did. I don't think just anyone could commit murder. In the heat of the moment, sure, I guess people fly off the handle, but to do it deliberately and throw someone out of a, out of a, to just deliberately throw someone out of a—"

I put my hand on top of hers. She had long small-boned hands and her skin was cool and dry to the touch. I thought she was going to cry or break or something but she didn't. It was just not going to be possible for her to say the word *window* and she would stall every time she came to it.

"What do the police say?"

"Suicide. They say she killed herself." She drew on the cigarette. "But they don't know her, they never knew her. If Paula wanted to kill herself she would have taken pills. She liked pills."

"I figured she took ups."

"Ups, tranquilizers, ludes, barbiturates. And she liked grass and she liked to drink." She lowered her eyes. My hand was still on top of hers and she looked at our two hands and I removed mine. "I don't do any of those things. I drink coffee, that's my one vice, and I don't even do that much because it makes me jittery. It's the coffee that's making me nervous tonight. Not . . . all of this."

"Okay."

"She was twenty-four. I'm twenty. Baby sister, square baby sister, except that was always how she *wanted* me to be. She did all these things and at the same time she told me not to do them, that it was a bad scene. I think she kept me straight. I really do. Not so much because of what she was saying as that I looked at the way she was living and what it was doing to her and I didn't want that for myself. I thought it was crazy, what she was doing to herself, but at the same time I guess I worshipped her, she was always my heroine. I loved her, God, I really did, I'm just starting to realize how much, and she's dead and he killed her, I *know* he killed her, I just know it."

After a while I asked her what she wanted me to do.

"You're a detective."

"Not in an official sense. I used to be a cop."

"Could you . . . find out what happened?"

"I don't know."

"I tried talking to the police. It was like talking to the wall. I can't just turn around and do nothing. Do you understand me?"

"I think so. Suppose I look into it and it still looks like suicide?"

"She didn't kill herself."

"Well, suppose I wind up thinking that she did."

She thought it over. "I still wouldn't have to believe it."

"No," I agreed. "We get to choose what we believe."

"I have some money." She put her purse on the table.

"I'm the straight sister, I have an office job, I save money. I have five hundred dollars with me."

"That's too much to carry in this neighborhood."

"Is it enough to hire you?"

I didn't want to take her money. She had five hundred dollars and a dead sister, and parting with one wouldn't bring the other back to life. I'd have worked for nothing but that wouldn't have been good because neither of us would have taken it seriously enough.

And I have rent to pay and two sons to support, and Armstrong's charges for the coffee and the bourbon. I took four fifty-dollar bills from her and told her I'd do my best to earn them.

After Paula Wittlauer hit the pavement, a black-and-white from the Eighteenth Precinct caught the squeal and took charge of the case. One of the cops in the car was a guy named Guzik. I hadn't known him when I was on the force but we'd met since then. I didn't like him and I don't think he cared for me either, but he was reasonably honest and had struck me as competent. I got him on the phone the next morning and offered to buy him a lunch.

We met at an Italian place on Fifty-sixth Street. He had veal and peppers and a couple glasses of red wine. I wasn't hungry but I made myself eat a small steak.

Between bites of veal he said, "The kid sister, huh? I talked to her, you know. She's so clean and so pretty it could break your heart if you let it. And of course she don't want to believe sis did the Dutch act. I asked is she Catholic because then there's the religious angle but that wasn't it. Anyway your average priest'll stretch a point. They're the best lawyers going, the hell, two thousand years of practice, they oughta be good. I took that attitude myself. I said, 'Look, there's all these pills. Let's say your sister had herself some pills and drank a little wine and smoked a little pot and then she went to the window for some fresh air. So she got a little dizzy and maybe she blacked out and most likely she never knew what was happening.' Because there's no question of insurance, Matt, so if she wants to think it's an accident I'm not gonna shout suicide in her ear. But that's what it says in the file."

"You close it out?"

"Sure. No question."

"She thinks murder."

He nodded. "Tell me something I don't know. She says this McCloud killed sis. McCloud's the boyfriend. Thing is he was at an after-hours club at Fifty-third and Twelfth about the time sis was going skydiving."

"You confirm that?"

He shrugged. "It ain't airtight. He was in and out of the place, he coulda doubled back and all, but there was the whole business with the door."

"What business?"

"She didn't tell you? Paula Wittlauer's apartment was locked and the chain bolt was on. The super unlocked the door for us but we had to send him back to the basement for a bolt cutter so's we could get through the chain bolt. You can only fasten the chain bolt from inside and you can only open the door a few inches with it on, so either Wittlauer launched her own self out the window or she was shoved out by Plastic Man, and then he went and slithered out the door without unhooking the chain bolt."

"Or the killer never left the apartment."

"Huh?"

"Did you search the apartment after the super came back and cut the chain for you?"

"We looked around, of course. There was an open window, there was a pile of clothes next to it. You know she went out naked, don't you?"

"Uh-huh."

"There was no burly killer crouching in the shrubbery, if that's what you're getting at."

"You checked the place carefully?"

"We did our job."

"Uh-huh. Look under the bed?"

"It was a platform bed. No crawl space under it."

"Closets?"

He drank some wine, put the glass down hard, glared at me. "What the hell are you getting at? You got reason to believe there was somebody in the apartment when we went in there?"

"Just exploring the possibilities."

"Jesus. You honestly think somebody's gonna be stupid enough to stay in the apartment after shoving her out of it? She musta been on the street ten minutes before we hit the building. If somebody did kill her, which never happened, but if they did they coulda been halfway to Texas by the time we hit the door, and don't that make more sense than jumping in the closet and hiding behind the coats?"

"Unless the killer didn't want to pass the doorman."

"So he's still got the whole building to hide in. Just the one man on the front door is the only security the building's got, anyway, and what does he amount to? And suppose he hides in the apartment and we happen to spot him. Then where is he? With his neck in the noose, that's where he is."

"Except you didn't spot him."

"Because he wasn't there, and when I start seeing little men who aren't there is when I put in my papers and quit the department."

There was an unvoiced challenge in his words. I had quit the department, but not because I'd seen little men. One night some years ago I broke up a bar holdup and went into the street after the pair who'd killed the bartender. One of my shots went wide and a little girl died, and after that I didn't see little men or hear voices, not exactly, but I did leave my wife and kids and quit the force and start drinking on a more serious level. But maybe it all would have happened just that way even if I'd never killed Estrellita Rivera. People go through changes and life does the damnedest things to us all.

"It was just a thought," I said. "The sister thinks it's murder so I was looking for a way for her to be right."

"Forget it."

"I suppose. I wonder why she did it."

"Do they even need a reason? I went in the bathroom and she had a medicine cabinet like a drugstore. Ups, downs, sideways. Maybe she was so stoned she thought she could fly. That would explain her being naked. You don't fly with your clothes on. Everybody knows that."

I nodded. "They find drugs in her system?"

"Drugs in her . . . oh, Jesus, Matt. She came down seventeen flights and she came down fast."

"Under four seconds."

"Huh?"

"Nothing," I said. I didn't bother telling him about high school physics and falling bodies. "No autopsy?"

"Of course not. You've seen jumpers. You were in the department a lot of years, you know what a person looks like after a drop like that. You want to be technical, there coulda been a bullet in her and nobody was gonna go and look for it. Cause of death was falling from a great height. That's what it says and that's what it was, and don't ask me was she stoned or was she pregnant or any of those questions because who the hell knows and who the hell cares, right?"

"How'd you even know it was her?"

"We got a positive ID from the sister."

I shook my head. "I mean how did you know what apartment to go to? She was naked so she didn't have any identification on her. Did the doorman recognize her?"

"You kidding? He wouldn't go close enough to look. He was alongside the building throwing up a few pints of cheap wine. He couldn't have identified his own ass."

"Then how'd you know who she was?"

"The window." I looked at him. "Hers was the only window that was open more than a couple of inches, Matt. Plus her lights were on. That made it easy."

"I didn't think of that."

"Yeah, well, I was there, and we just looked up and there was an open window and a light behind it, and that was the first place we went to. You'da thought of it if you were there."

"I suppose."

He finished his wine, burped delicately against the back of his hand. "It's suicide," he said. "You can tell the sister as much."

"I will. Okay if I look at the apartment?"

"Wittlauer's apartment? We didn't seal it, if that's what you mean. You oughta be able to con the super out of a key."

"Ruth Wittlauer gave me a key."

"Then there you go. There's no department seal on the door. You want to look around?"

"So I can tell the sister I was there."

"Yeah. Maybe you'll come across a suicide note. That's what I was looking for, a note. You turn up something like that and it clears up doubts for the friends and relatives. If it was up to me I'd get a law passed. No suicide without a note."

"Be hard to enforce."

"Simple," he said. "If you don't leave a note you gotta come back and be alive again." He laughed. "That'd start 'em scribbling away. Count on it."

The doorman was the same man I'd talked to the day before. It never occurred to him to ask me my business. I rode up in the elevator and walked along the corridor to 17G. The key Ruth Wittlauer had given me opened the door. There was just the one lock. That's the way it usually is in high-rises. A doorman, however slipshod he may be, endows tenants with a sense of security. The residents of unserviced walk-ups affix three or four extra locks to their doors and still cower behind them.

The apartment had an unfinished air about it, and I sensed that Paula had lived there for a few months without ever making the place her own. There were no rugs on the wood parquet floor. The walls were decorated with a few unframed posters held up by scraps of red Mystik tape. The apartment was an L-shaped studio with a platform bed occupying the foot of the L. There were newspapers and magazines scattered around the place but no books. I noticed copies of *Variety* and *Rolling Stone* and *People* and the *Village Voice*.

The television set was a tiny Sony perched on top of a chest of drawers. There was no stereo, but there were a few dozen records, mostly classical with a sprinkling of folk music, Pete Seeger and Joan Baez and Dave Van Ronk. There was a dust-free rectangle on top of the dresser next to the Sony.

I looked through the drawers and closets. A lot of Paula's clothes. I recognized some of the outfits, or thought I did.

Someone had closed the window. There were two windows that opened, one in the sleeping alcove, the other in the living room section, but a row of undisturbed potted plants in front of the bedroom window made it evident she'd gone out of the other one. I wondered why anyone had bothered to close it. In case of rain, I supposed. That was only sensible. But I suspect the gesture must have been less calculated than that, a reflexive act akin to tugging a sheet over the face of a corpse.

I went into the bathroom. A killer could have hidden in the stall shower. If there'd been a killer.

Why was I still thinking in terms of a killer?

I checked the medicine cabinet. There were little tubes and vials of cosmetics, though only a handful compared with the array on one of the bedside tables. Here were containers of aspirin and other headache remedies, a tube of antibiotic ointment, several prescriptions and nonprescription hay fever preparations, a cardboard packet of Band-Aids, a roll of adhesive tape, a box of gauze pads. Some Q-Tips, a hairbrush, a couple of combs. A toothbrush in the holder.

There were no footprints on the floor of the stall shower. Of course he could have been barefoot. Or he could have run water and washed away the traces of his presence before he left.

I went over and examined the windowsill. I hadn't asked Guzik if they'd dusted for prints and I was reasonably certain no one had bothered. I wouldn't have taken the trouble in their position. I couldn't learn anything looking at the sill. I opened the window a foot or so and stuck my head out, but when I looked down the vertigo was extremely unpleasant and I drew my head back inside at once. I left the window open, though. The room could stand a change of air.

There were four folding chairs in the room, two of them closed and leaning against a wall, one near the bed, the fourth alongside the window. They were royal blue and made of high-impact plastic. The one by the window had her clothes piled on it. I went through the stack. She'd placed them deliberately on the chair but hadn't bothered folding them.

You never know what suicides will do. One man will put

on a tuxedo before blowing his brains out. Another one
will take off everything. Naked I came into the world and
naked will I go out of it, something like that.

A skirt. Beneath it a pair of panty hose. Then a blouse,
and under it a bra with two small, lightly padded cups. I put
the clothing back as I had found it, feeling like a violator of
the dead.

The bed was unmade. I sat on the edge of it and looked
across the room at a poster of Mick Jagger. I don't know
how long I sat there. Ten minutes, maybe.

On the way out I looked at the chain bolt. I hadn't even
noticed it when I came in. The chain had been neatly severed. Half of it was still in the slot on the door while the
other half hung from its mounting on the jamb. I closed
the door and fitted the two halves together, then released
them and let them dangle. Then I touched their ends together again. I unhooked the end of the chain from the
slot and went to the bathroom for the roll of adhesive tape.
I brought the tape back with me, tore off a piece and used
it to fasten the chain back together again. Then I let myself
out of the apartment and tried to engage the chain bolt
from outside, but the tape slipped whenever I put any pressure on it.

I went inside again and studied the chain bolt. I decided
I was behaving erratically, that Paula Wittlauer had gone
out the window of her own accord. I looked at the windowsill again. The light dusting of soot didn't tell me anything
one way or the other. New York's air is filthy and the
accumulation of soot could have been deposited in a couple
of hours, even with the window shut. It didn't mean
anything.

I looked at the heap of clothes on the chair, and I looked
again at the chain bolt, and I rode the elevator to the basement and found either the superintendent or one of his
assistants. I asked to borrow a screwdriver. He gave me a
long screwdriver with an amber plastic grip. He didn't ask
me who I was or what I wanted it for.

I returned to Paula Wittlauer's apartment and removed
the chain bolt from its moorings on the door and jamb. I
left the building and walked around the corner to a hardware store on Ninth Avenue. They had a good selection of

chain bolts but I wanted one identical to the one I'd removed and I had to walk down Ninth Avenue as far as Fiftieth Street and check four stores before I found what I was looking for.

Back in Paula's apartment I mounted the new chain bolt, using the holes in which the original had been mounted. I tightened the screws with the super's screwdriver and stood out in the corridor and played with the chain. My hands are large and not terribly skillful, but even so I was able to lock and unlock the chain bolt from outside the apartment.

I don't know who put it up, Paula or a previous tenant or someone on the building staff, but that chain bolt had been as much protection as the sanitized wrapper on a motel toilet seat. As evidence that Paula'd been alone when she went out the window, well, it wasn't worth a thing.

I replaced the original chain bolt, put the new one in my pocket, returned to the elevator, and gave back the screwdriver. The man I returned it to seemed surprised to get it back.

It took me a couple of hours to find Cary McCloud. I'd learned that he tended bar evenings at a club in the West Village called the Spider's Web. I got down there around five. The guy behind the bar had knobby wrists and an underslung jaw and he wasn't Cary McCloud. "He don't come on till eight," he told me "and he's off tonight anyway." I asked where I could find McCloud. "Sometimes he's here afternoons but he ain't been in today. As far as where you could look for him, that I couldn't tell you."

A lot of people couldn't tell me but eventually I ran across someone who could. You can quit the police force but you can't stop looking and sounding like a cop, and while that's a hindrance in some situations it's a help in others. Ultimately I found a man in a bar down the block from the Spider's Web who'd learned it was best to cooperate with the police if it didn't cost you anything. He gave me an address on Barrow Street and told me which bell to ring.

I went to the building but I rang several other bells until somebody buzzed me through the downstairs door. I didn't want Cary to know he had company coming. I climbed two flights of stairs to the apartment he was supposed to be occupying. The bell downstairs hadn't had his name on it. It hadn't had any name at all.

Loud rock music was coming through his door. I stood in front of it for a minute, then hammered on it loud enough to make myself heard over the electric guitars. After a moment the music dropped in volume. I pounded on the door again and a male voice asked who I was.

I said, "Police. Open up." That's a misdemeanor but I didn't expect to get in trouble for it.

"What's it about?"

"Open up, McCloud."

"Oh, Jesus," he said. He sounded tired, aggravated. "How did you find me, anyway? Give me a minute, huh? I want to put some clothes on."

Sometimes that's what they say while they're putting a clip into an automatic. Then they pump a handful of shots through the door and into you if you're still standing behind it. But his voice didn't have that kind of edge to it and I couldn't summon up enough anxiety to get out of the way. Instead I put my ear against the door and heard whispering within. I couldn't make out what they were whispering about or get any sense of the person who was with him. The music was down in volume but there was still enough of it to cover their conversation.

The door opened. He was tall and thin, with hollow cheeks and prominent eyebrows and a worn, wasted look to him. He must have been in his early thirties and he didn't really look much older than that but you sensed that in another ten years he'd look twenty years older. If he lived that long. He wore patched jeans and a T-shirt with the Spider's Web silk-screened on it. Beneath the legend there was a sketch of a web. A macho spider stood at one end of it, grinning, extending two of his eight arms to welcome a hesitant girlish fly.

He noticed me noticing the shirt and managed a grin. "Place where I work," he said.

"I know."

"So come into my parlor. It ain't much but it's home."

I followed him inside, drew the door shut after me. The room was about fifteen feet square and held nothing you could call furniture. There was a mattress on the floor in one corner and a couple of cardboard cartons alongside it. The music was coming from a stereo, turntable and tuner and two speakers all in a row along the far wall. There was a closed door over on the right. I figured it led to the bathroom, and that there was a woman on the other side of it.

"I guess this is about Paula," he said. I nodded. "I been over this with you guys," he said. "I was nowhere near there when it happened. The last I saw her was five, six hours before she killed herself. I was working at the Web and she came down and sat at the bar. I gave her a couple of drinks and she split."

"And you went on working."

"Until I closed up. I kicked everybody out a little after three and it was close to four by the time I had the place swept up and the garbage on the street and the window gates locked. Then I came over here and picked up Sunny and we went up to the place on Fifty-third."

"And you got there when?"

"Hell, I don't know. I wear a watch but I don't look at it every damn minute. I suppose it took five minutes to walk here and then Sunny and I hopped right in a cab and we were at Patsy's in ten minutes at the outside, that's the after-hours place, I told you people all of this, I really wish you would talk to each other and leave me the hell alone."

"Why doesn't Sunny come out and tell me about it?" I nodded at the bathroom door. "Maybe she can remember the time a little more clearly."

"Sunny? She stepped out a little while ago."

"She's not in the bathroom?"

"Nope. Nobody's in the bathroom."

"Mind if I see for myself?"

"Not if you can show me a warrant."

We looked at each other. I told him I figured I could take his word for it. He said he could always be trusted to tell the truth. I said I sensed as much about him.

He said, "What's the hassle, huh? I know you guys got forms to fill out, but why not give me a break? She killed herself and I wasn't anywhere near her when it happened."

He could have been. The times were vague, and whoever

Sunny turned out to be, the odds were good that she'd have no more time sense than a koala bear. There were any number of ways he could have found a few minutes to go up to Fifty-seventh Street and heave Paula out a window, but it didn't add up that way and he just didn't feel like a killer to me. I knew what Ruth meant and I agreed with her that he was capable of murder but I don't think he'd been capable of this particular murder.

I said, "When did you go back to the apartment?"

"Who said I did?"

"You picked up your clothes, Cary."

"That was yesterday afternoon. The hell, I needed my clothes and stuff."

"How long were you living there?"

He hedged. "I wasn't exactly living there."

"Where were you exactly living?"

"I wasn't exactly living anywhere. I kept most of my stuff at Paula's place and I stayed with her most of the time but it wasn't as serious as actual living together. We were both too loose for anything like that. Anyway, the thing with Paula, it was pretty much winding itself down. She was a little too crazy for me." He smiled with his mouth. "They have to be a little crazy," he said, "but when they're too crazy it gets to be too much of a hassle."

Oh, he could have killed her. He could kill anyone if he had to, if someone was making too much of a hassle. But if he were to kill cleverly, faking the suicide in such an artful fashion, fastening the chain bolt on his way out, he'd pick a time when he had a solid alibi. He was not the sort to be so precise and so slipshod all at the same time.

"So you went and picked up your stuff."

"Right."

"Including the stereo and records."

"The stereo was mine. The records, I left the folk music and the classical shit because that belonged to Paula. I just took my records."

"And the stereo."

"Right."

"You got a bill of sale for it, I suppose."

"Who keeps that crap?"

"What if I said Paula kept the bill of sale? What if I said it was in with her papers and canceled checks?"

"You're fishing."

"You sure of that?"

"Nope. But if you did say that, I suppose I'd say the stereo was a gift from her to me. You're not really gonna charge me with stealing a stereo, are you?"

"Why should I? Robbing the dead's a sacred tradition. You took the drugs, too, didn't you? Her medicine cabinet used to look like a drugstore but there was nothing stronger than Excedrin when I took a look. That's why Sunny's in the bathroom. If I hit the door all the pretty little pills go down the toilet."

"I guess you can think that if you want."

"And I can come back with a warrant if I want."

"That's the idea."

"I ought to rap on the door just to do you out of the drugs but it doesn't seem worth the trouble. That's Paula Wittlauer's stereo. I suppose it's worth a couple hundred dollars. And you're not her heir. Unplug that thing and wrap it up, McCloud. I'm taking it with me."

"The hell you are."

"The hell I'm not."

"You want to take anything but your own ass out of here, you come back with a warrant. Then we'll talk about it."

"I don't need a warrant."

"You can't—"

"I don't need a warrant because I'm not a cop. I'm a detective, McCloud, I'm private, and I'm working for Ruth Wittlauer, and that's who's getting the stereo. I don't know if she wants it or not, but that's her problem. She doesn't want Paula's pills so you can pop them yourself or give them to your girlfriend. You can shove 'em up your ass for all I care. But I'm walking out of here with that stereo and I'll walk through you if I have to, and don't think I wouldn't enjoy it."

"You're not even a cop."

"Right."

"You got no authority at all." He spoke in tones of wonder. "You said you were a cop."

"You can always sue me."

"You can't take that stereo. You can't even be in this room."

"That's right." I was itching for him. I could feel my blood in my veins. "I'm bigger than you," I said, "and I'm a whole lot harder, and I'd get a certain amount of satisfaction in beating the crap out of you. I don't like you. It bothers me that you didn't kill her because somebody did and it would be a pleasure to hang it on you. But you didn't do it. Unplug the stereo and pack it up so I can carry it or I'm going to take you apart."

I meant it and he realized as much. He thought about taking a shot at me and he decided it wasn't worth it. Maybe it wasn't all that much of a stereo. While he was unhooking it I dumped a carton of his clothes on the floor and we packed the stereo in it. On my way out the door he said he could always go to the cops and tell them what I'd done.

"I don't think you want to do that," I said.

"You said somebody killed her."

"That's right."

"You just making noise?"

"No."

"You're serious?" I nodded. "She didn't kill herself? I thought it was open and shut, from what the cops said. It's interesting. In a way, I guess you could say it's a load off my mind."

"How do you figure that?"

He shrugged. "I thought, you know, maybe she was upset it wasn't working out between us. At the Web the vibes were on the heavy side, if you follow me. Our thing was falling apart and I was seeing Sunny and she was seeing other guys and I thought maybe that was what did it for her. I suppose I blamed myself, like."

"I can see it was eating away at you."

"I just said it was on my mind."

I didn't say anything.

"Man," he said, "*nothing* eats away at me. You let things get to you that way and it's death."

I shouldered the carton and headed on down the stairs.

*　　　*　　　*

Ruth Wittlauer had supplied me with an Irving Place address and a GRamercy 5 telephone number. I called the number and didn't get an answer, so I walked over to Hudson and caught a northbound cab. There were no messages for me at the hotel desk. I put Paula's stereo in my room, tried Ruth's number again, then walked over to the Eighteenth Precinct. Guzik had gone off duty but the deskman told me to try a restaurant around the corner, and I found him there drinking draft Heinekens with another cop named Birnbaum. I sat at their table and ordered bourbon for myself and another round for the two of them.

I said, "I have a favor to ask. I'd like you to seal Paula Wittlauer's apartment."

"We closed that out," Guzik reminded me.

"I know, and the boyfriend closed out the dead girl's stereo." I told him how I'd reclaimed the unit from Cary McCloud. "I'm working for Ruth, Paula's sister. The least I can do is make sure she gets what's coming to her. She's not up to cleaning out the apartment now and it's rented through the first of October. McCloud's got a key and God knows how many other people have keys. If you slap a seal on the door it'd keep the grave robbers away."

"I guess we can do that. Tomorrow all right?"

"Tonight would be better."

"What's there to steal? You got the stereo out of there and I didn't see anything else around that was worth much."

"Things have a sentimental value."

He eyed me, frowned. "I'll make a phone call," he said. He went to the booth in the back and I jawed with Birnbaum until he came back and told me it was all taken care of.

I said, "Another thing I was wondering. You must have had a photographer on the scene. Somebody to take pictures of the body and all that."

"Sure. That's routine."

"Did he go up to the apartment while he was at it? Take a roll of interior shots?"

"Yeah. Why?"

"I thought maybe I could have a look at them."

"What for?"

"You never know. The reason I knew it was Paula's stereo in McCloud's apartment was I could see the pattern in the dust on top of the dresser where it had been. If you've got interior pictures maybe I'll see something else that's not there anymore and I can lean on McCloud a little and recover it for my client."

"And that's why you'd like to see the pictures."

"Right."

He gave me a look. "That door was bolted from the inside, Matt. With a chain bolt."

"I know."

"And there was no one in the apartment when we went in there."

"I know that, too."

"You're still barking up the murder tree, aren't you? Jesus, the case is closed and the reason it's closed is the ditsy broad killed herself. What are you making waves for?"

"I'm not. I just wanted to see the pictures."

"To see if somebody stole her diaphragm or something."

"Something like that." I drank what remained of my drink. "You need a new hat anyway, Guzik. The weather's turning and a fellow like you needs a hat for fall."

"If I had the price of a hat, maybe I'd go out and get one."

"You got it," I said.

He nodded and we told Birnbaum we wouldn't be long. I walked with Guzik around the corner to the Eighteenth. On the way I palmed him two tens and a five, twenty-five dollars, the price of a hat in police parlance. He made the bills disappear.

I waited at his desk while he pulled the Paula Wittlauer file. There were about a dozen black-and-white prints, eight-by-tens, high-contrast glossies. Perhaps half of them showed Paula's corpse from various angles. I had no interest in these but I made myself look at them as a sort of reinforcement, so I wouldn't forget what I was doing on the case.

The other pictures were interior shots of the L-shaped apartment. I noted the wide-open window, the dresser with the stereo sitting on it, the chair with her clothing piled

haphazardly upon it. I separated the interior pictures from
the ones showing the corpse and told Guzik I wanted to
keep them for the time being. He didn't mind.

He cocked his head and looked at me. "You got something, Matt?"

"Nothing worth talking about."

"If you ever do, I'll want to hear about it."

"Sure."

"You like the life you're leading? Working private, scuf-
fling around?"

"It seems to suit me."

He thought it over, nodded. Then he started for the stairs
and I followed after him.

Later that evening I managed to reach Ruth Wittlauer. I
bundled the stereo into a cab and took it to her place. She
lived in a well-kept brownstone a block and a half from
Gramercy Park. Her apartment was inexpensively furnished
but the pieces looked to have been chosen with care. The
place was clean and neat. Her clock radio was turned to
an FM station that was playing chamber music. She had
coffee made and I accepted a cup and sipped it while I told
her about recovering the stereo from Cary McCloud.

"I wasn't sure whether you could use it," I said, "but I
couldn't see any reason why he should keep it. You can
always sell it."

"No, I'll keep it. I just have a twenty-dollar record player
that I bought on Fourteenth Street. Paula's stereo cost a
couple of hundred dollars." She managed a smile. "So
you've already more than earned what I gave you. Did he
kill her?"

"No."

"You're sure of that?"

I nodded. "He'd kill if he had a reason but I don't think
he did. And if he did kill her he'd never have taken the
stereo or the drugs, and he wouldn't have acted the way
he did. There was never a moment when I had the feeling
that he'd killed her. And you have to follow your instincts
in this kind of situation. Once they point things out to you,
then you can usually find the facts to go with them."

"And you're sure my sister killed herself?"

"No. I'm pretty sure someone gave her a hand."

Her eyes widened.

I said, "It's mostly intuition. But there are a few facts to support it." I told her about the chain bolt, how it had proved to the police that Paula'd killed herself, how my experiment had shown it could have been fastened from the corridor. Ruth got very excited at this but I explained that it didn't prove anything in and of itself, only that suicide remained a theoretical possibility.

Then I showed her the pictures I'd obtained from Guzik. I selected one shot which showed the chair with Paula's clothing without showing too much of the window. I didn't want to make Ruth look at the window.

"The chair," I said, pointing to it. "I noticed this when I was in your sister's apartment. I wanted to see a photograph taken at the time to make sure things hadn't been rearranged by the cops or McCloud or somebody else. But that clothing's exactly the way it was when I saw it."

"I don't understand."

"The supposition is that Paula got undressed, put her clothes on the chair, then went to the window and jumped." Her lip was trembling but she was holding herself together and I went right on talking. "Or she'd taken her clothes off earlier and maybe she took a shower or a nap and then came back and jumped. But look at the chair. She didn't fold her clothes neatly, she didn't put them away. And she didn't just drop them on the floor, either. I'm no authority on the way women get undressed but I don't think many people would do it that way."

Ruth nodded. Her face was thoughtful.

"That wouldn't mean very much by itself. If she were upset or stoned or confused she might have thrown things on the chair as she took them off. But that's not what happened. The order of the clothing is all wrong. The bra's underneath the blouse, the panty hose are underneath the skirt. She took her bra off after she took her blouse off, obviously, so it should have wound up on top of the blouse, not under it."

"Of course."

I held up a hand. "It's nothing like proof, Ruth. There are any number of other explanations. Maybe she knocked the stuff onto the floor and then picked it up and the order of the garments got switched around. Maybe one of the cops went through the clothing before the photographer came around with his camera. I don't really have anything terribly strong to go on."

"But you think she was murdered."

"Yes, I guess I do."

"That's what I thought all along. Of course I had a reason to think so."

"Maybe I've got one, too. I don't know."

"What are you going to do now?"

"I think I'll poke around a little. I don't know much about Paula's life. I'll have to learn more if I'm going to find out who killed her. But it's up to you to decide whether you want me to stay with it."

"Of course I do. Why wouldn't I?"

"Because it probably won't lead anywhere. Suppose she was upset after her conversation with McCloud and she picked up a stranger and took him home with her and he killed her. If that's the case we'll never know who he was."

"You're going to stay with it, aren't you?"

"I suppose I want to."

"It'll be complicated, though. It'll take you some time. I suppose you'll want more money." Her gaze was very direct. "I gave you two hundred dollars. I have three hundred more that I can afford to pay. I don't mind paying it, Mr. Scudder. I already got ... I got my money's worth for the first two hundred, didn't I? The stereo. When the three hundred runs out, well, you can tell me if you think it's worth staying with the case. I couldn't afford more cash right away, but I could arrange to pay you later on or something like that."

I shook my head. "It won't come to more than that," I said. "No matter how much time I spend on it. And you keep the three hundred for the time being, all right? I'll take it from you later on. If I need it, and if I've earned it."

"That doesn't seem right."

"It seems right to me," I said. "And don't make the mistake of thinking I'm being charitable."

"But your time's valuable."

I shook my head. "Not to me it isn't."

*   *   *

I spent the next five days picking the scabs off Paula Wittlauer's life. It kept turning out to be a waste of time but
the time's always gone before you realize you've wasted it.
And I'd been telling the truth when I said my time wasn't
valuable. I had nothing better to do, and my peeks into the
corners of Paula's world kept me busy.

Her life involved more than a saloon on Ninth Avenue
and an apartment on Fifty-seventh Street, more than serving drinks and sharing a bed with Cary McCloud. She did
other things. She went one evening a week to group ther-
apy on West Seventy-ninth Street. She took voice lessons
every Tuesday morning on Amsterdam Avenue. She had
an ex-boyfriend she saw once in a while. She hung out in
a couple of bars in the neighborhood and a couple of others
in the Village. She did this, she did that, she went here,
she went there, and I kept busy dragging myself around
town and talking to all sorts of people, and I managed to
learn quite a bit about the person she'd been and the life
she'd led without learning anything at all about the person
who'd put her on the pavement.

At the same time, I tried to track her movements on the
final night of her life. She'd evidently gone more or less
directly to the Spider's Web after finishing her shift at Armstrong's. Maybe she'd stopped at her apartment for a
shower and a change of clothes, but without further ado
she'd headed downtown. Somewhere around ten she left
the Web, and I traced her from there to a couple of other
Village bars. She hadn't stayed at either of them long, taking a quick drink or two and moving on. She'd left alone
as far as anyone seemed to remember. This didn't prove
a thing because she could have stopped elsewhere before
continuing uptown, or she could have picked someone up
on the street, which I'd learned was something she'd done
more than once in her young life. She could have found
her killer loitering on a street corner or she could have
phoned him and arranged to meet him at her apartment.

Her apartment. The doormen changed off at midnight,
but it was impossible to determine whether she'd returned
before or after the changing of the guard. She'd lived there,
she was a regular tenant, and when she entered or left the

building it was not a noteworthy occasion. It was something she did every night, so when she came home for the final time the man at the door had no reason to know it was the final time and thus no reason to take mental notes.

Had she come in alone or with a companion? No one could say, which did suggest that she'd come in alone. If she'd been with someone her entrance would have been a shade more memorable. But this also proved nothing, because I stood on the other side of Fifty-seventh Street one night and watched the doorway of her building, and the doorman didn't take the pride in his position that the afternoon doorman had shown. He was away from the door almost as often as he was on it. She could have walked in flanked by six Turkish sailors and there was a chance no one would have seen her.

The doorman who'd been on duty when she went out the window was a rheumy-eyed Irishman with liver-spotted hands. He hadn't actually seen her land. He'd been in the lobby, keeping himself out of the wind, and then he came rushing out when he heard the impact of the body on the street.

He couldn't get over the sound she made.

"All of a sudden there was this noise," he said. "Just out of the blue there was this noise and it must be it's my imagination but I swear I felt it in my feet. I swear she shook the earth. I had no idea what it was, and then I came rushing out, and Jesus God, there she was."

"Didn't you hear a scream?"

"Street was empty just then. This side, anyway. Nobody around to scream."

"Didn't *she* scream on the way down?"

"Did somebody say she screamed? I never heard it."

Do people scream as they fall? They generally do in films and on television. During my days on the force I saw several of them after they jumped, and by the time I got to them there were no screams echoing in the air. And a few times I'd been on hand while they talked someone in off a ledge, but in each instance the talking was successful and I didn't have to watch a falling body accelerate according to the immutable laws of physics.

Could you get much of a scream out in four seconds?

I stood in the street where she'd fallen and I looked up toward her window. I counted off four seconds in my mind. A voice shrieked in my brain. It was Thursday night, actually Friday morning, one o'clock. Time I got myself around the corner to Armstrong's, because in another couple of hours Justin would be closing for the night and I'd want to be drunk enough to sleep.

And an hour or so after that she'd be one week dead.

I'd worked myself into a reasonably bleak mood by the time I got to Armstrong's. I skipped the coffee and crawled straight into the bourbon bottle, and before long it began to do what it was supposed to do. It blurred the corners of the mind so I couldn't see the bad dark things that lurked there.

When Trina finished for the night she joined me and I bought her a couple of drinks. I don't remember what we talked about. Some but by no means all of our conversation touched upon Paula Wittlauer. Trina hadn't known Paula terribly well—their contact had been largely limited to the two hours a day when their shifts overlapped—but she knew a little about the sort of life Paula had been leading. There'd been a year or two when her own life had not been terribly different from Paula's. Now she had things more or less under control, and maybe there would have come a time when Paula would have taken charge of her life, but that was something we'd never know now.

I suppose it was close to three when I walked Trina home. Our conversation had turned thoughtful and reflective. On the street she said it was a lousy night for being alone. I thought of high windows and evil shapes in dark corners and took her hand in mine.

She lives on Fifty-sixth between Ninth and Tenth. While we waited for the light to change at Fifty-seventh Street I looked over at Paula's building. We were far enough away to look at the high floors. Only a couple of windows were lighted.

That was when I got it.

I've never understood how people think of things, how little perceptions trigger greater insights. Thoughts just seem to come to me. I had it now, and something clicked within me and a source of tension unwound itself.

I said something to that effect to Trina.

"You know who killed her?"

"Not exactly," I said. "But I know how to find out. And it can wait until tomorrow."

The light changed and we crossed the street.

She was still sleeping when I left. I got out of bed and dressed in silence, then let myself out of her apartment. I had some coffee and a toasted English muffin at the Red Flame. Then I went across the street to Paula's building. I started on the tenth floor and worked my way up, checking the three or four possible apartments on each floor. A lot of people weren't home. I worked my way clear to the top floor, the twenty-fourth, and by the time I was done I had three possibles listed in my notebook and a list of over a dozen apartments I'd have to check that evening.

At eight-thirty that night I rang the bell of Apartment 21G. It was directly in line with Paula's apartment and four flights above it. The man who answered the bell wore a pair of Lee corduroy slacks and a shirt with a blue vertical stripe on a white background. His socks were dark blue and he wasn't wearing shoes.

I said, "I want to talk with you about Paula Wittlauer."

His face fell apart and I forgot my three possibles forever because he was the man I wanted. He just stood there. I pushed the door open and stepped forward and he moved back automatically to make room for me. I drew the door shut after me and walked around him, crossing the room to the window. There wasn't a speck of dust or soot on the sill. It was immaculate, as well scrubbed as Lady Macbeth's hands.

I turned to him. His name was Lane Posmantur and I suppose he was around forty, thickening at the waist, his dark hair starting to go thin on top. His glasses were thick and it was hard to read his eyes through them but it didn't matter. I didn't need to see his eyes.

"She went out this window," I said. "Didn't she?"

"I don't know what you're talking about."

"Do you want to know what triggered it for me, Mr. Posmantur? I was thinking of all the things nobody noticed. No one saw her enter the building. Neither doorman remembered it because it wasn't something they'd be likely to remember. Nobody saw her go out the window. The cops had to look for an open window in order to know who the hell she was. They backtracked her from the window she fell out of.

"And nobody saw the killer leave the building. Now that's the one thing that would have been noticed, and that's the point that occurred to me. It wasn't that significant by itself but it made me dig a little deeper. The doorman was alert once her body hit the street. He'd remember who went in or out of the building from that point on. So it occurred to me that maybe the killer was still inside the building, and then I got the idea that she was killed by someone who *lived* in the building, and from that point on it was just a question of finding you because all of a sudden it all made sense."

I told him about the clothes on the chair. "She didn't take them off and pile them up like that. Her killer put her clothes like that, and he dumped them on the chair so that it would look as though she undressed in her apartment, and so that it would be assumed she'd gone out of her own window.

"But she went out of your window, didn't she?"

He looked at me. After a moment he said he thought he'd better sit down. He went to an armchair and sat in it. I stayed on my feet.

I said, "She came here. I guess she took off her clothes and you went to bed with her. Is that right?"

He hesitated, then nodded.

"What made you decide to kill her?"

"I didn't."

I looked at him. He looked away, then met my gaze, then avoided my eyes again. "Tell me about it," I suggested. He looked away again and a minute went by and then he started to talk.

It was about what I'd figured. She was living with Cary McCloud but she and Lane Posmantur would get together now and then for a quickie. He was a lab technician at Roosevelt and he brought home drugs from time to time and perhaps that was part of his attraction for her. She'd turned up that night a little after two and they went to bed.

She was really flying, he said, and he'd been taking pills himself, it was something he'd begun doing lately, maybe seeing her had something to do with it.

They went to bed and did the dirty deed, and then maybe they slept for an hour, something like that, and then she was awake and coming unglued, getting really hysterical, and he tried to settle her down and he gave her a couple of slaps to bring her around, except they didn't bring her around, and she was staggering and she tripped over the coffee table and fell funny, and by the time he sorted himself out and went to her she was lying with her head at a crazy angle and he knew her neck was broken and when he tried for a pulse there was no pulse to be found.

"All I could think of was she was dead in my apartment and full of drugs and I was in trouble."

"So you put her out the window."

"I was going to take her back to her own apartment. I started to dress her but it was impossible. And even with her clothes on I couldn't risk running into somebody in the hallway or on the elevator. It was crazy.

"I left her here and went to her apartment. I thought maybe Cary would help me. I rang the bell and nobody answered and I used her key and the chain bolt was on. Then I remembered she used to fasten it from outside. She'd showed me how she could do that. I tried with mine but it was installed properly and there's not enough play in the chain. I unhooked her bolt and went inside.

"Then I got the idea. I went back to my apartment and got her clothes and I rushed back and put them on her chair. I opened her window wide. On my way out the door I put her lights on and hooked the chain bolt again.

"I came back here to my own apartment. I took her pulse again and she was dead, she hadn't moved or anything, and I couldn't do anything for her, all I could do was stay out of it, and I, I turned off the lights here, and I opened my own window and dragged her body over to it, and, oh, God in heaven, God, I almost couldn't make myself do it but it was an accident that she was dead and I was so damned *afraid*—"

"And you dropped her out and closed the window." He nodded. "And if her neck was broken it was something that happened in the fall. And whatever drugs were in her system was just something she'd taken by herself, and they'd never do an autopsy anyway. And you were home free."

"I didn't hurt her," he said. "I was just protecting myself."

"Do you really believe that, Lane?"

"What do you mean?"

"You're not a doctor. Maybe she was dead when you threw her out the window. Maybe she wasn't."

"There was no pulse!"

"You couldn't find a pulse. That doesn't mean there wasn't any. Did you try artificial respiration? Do you know if there was any brain activity? No, of course not. All you know was that you looked for a pulse and you couldn't find one."

"Her neck was broken."

"Maybe. How many broken necks have you had occasion to diagnose? And people sometimes break their necks and live anyway. The point is that you couldn't have known she was dead and you were too worried about your own skin to do what you should have done. You should have phoned for an ambulance. You know that's what you should have done and you knew it at the time but you wanted to stay out of it. I've known junkies who left their buddies to die of overdoses because they didn't want to get involved. You went them one better. You put her out a window and let her fall twenty-one stories so that you wouldn't get involved, and for all you know she was alive when you let go of her."

"No," he said. "No. She was dead."

I'd told Ruth Wittlauer she could wind up believing whatever she wanted. People believe what they want to believe. It was just as true for Lane Posmantur.

"Maybe she was dead," I said. "Maybe that's your fault, too."

"What do you mean?"

"You said you slapped her to bring her around. What kind of a slap, Lane?"

"I just tapped her on the face."

"Just a brisk slap to straighten her out."

"That's right."

"Oh, hell, Lane. Who knows how hard you hit her? Who knows whether you may not have given her a shove? She wasn't the only one on pills. You said she was flying. Well, I think maybe you were doing a little flying yourself. And you'd been sleepy and you were groggy and she was buzzing around the room and being a general pain in the ass, and you gave her a slap and a shove and another slap and another shove and—"

"No!"

"And she fell down."

"It was an accident."

"It always is."

"I didn't hurt her. I liked her. She was a good kid, we got on fine, I didn't hurt her, I—"

"Put your shoes on, Lane."

"What for?"

"I'm taking you to the police station. It's a few blocks from here, not very far at all."

"Am I under arrest?"

"I'm not a policeman." I'd never gotten around to saying who I was and he'd never thought to ask. "My name's Scudder, I'm working for Paula's sister. I suppose you're under citizen's arrest. I want you to come to the precinct house with me. There's a cop named Guzik there and you can talk to him."

"I don't have to say anything," he said. He thought for a moment. "You're not a cop."

"No."

"What I said to you doesn't mean a thing." He took a breath, straightened up a little in his chair. "You can't prove a thing," he said. "Not a thing."

"Maybe I can and maybe I can't. You probably left prints in Paula's apartment. I had them seal the place a while ago and maybe they'll find traces of your presence. I don't know if Paula left any prints here or not. You probably scrubbed them up. But there may be neighbors who know you were sleeping with her, and someone may have noticed you scampering back and forth between the apartments that night, and it's even possible a neighbor heard the two of you struggling in here just before she went out the window. When the cops know what to look for, Lane, they usually find it sooner or later. It's knowing what you're after that's the hard part.

"But that's not even the point. Put your shoes on, Lane. That's right. Now we're going to go see Guzik, that's his name, and he's going to advise you of your rights. He'll tell you that you have a right to remain silent, and that's the truth, Lane, that's a right that you have. And if you remain silent and if you get a decent lawyer and do what he tells you I think you can beat this charge, Lane. I really do."

"Why are you telling me this?"

"Why?" I was starting to feel tired, drained, but I kept on with it. "Because the worst thing you could do is remain silent, Lane. Believe me, that's the worst thing you could do. If you're smart you'll tell Guzik everything you remember. You'll make a complete voluntary statement and you'll read it over when they type it up and you'll sign your name on the bottom.

"Because you're not really a killer, Lane. It doesn't come easily to you. If Cary McCloud had killed her he'd never lose a night's sleep over it. But you're not a psychopath. You were drugged and half-crazy and terrified and you did something wrong and it's eating you up tonight. Your face fell apart the minute I walked in here tonight. You could play it cute and beat this charge, Lane, but all you'd wind up doing is beating yourself.

"Because you live on a high floor, Lane, and the ground's only four seconds away. And if you squirm off the hook you'll never get it out of your head, you'll never be able to mark it Paid in Full, and one day or night you'll open the window and you'll go out of it, Lane. You'll remember the sound her body made when she hit the street—"

"No!"

I took his arm. "Come on," I said. "We'll go see Guzik."

WHERE IS HARRY BEAL?
John Lutz
FIRST APPEARANCE: *Buyer, Beware*, 1976

Alo Nudger first appeared in the novel *Buyer, Beware* (Putnam, 1976). It was written in the third person. When the character appeared in "Where Is Harry Beal?" in *Alfred Hitchcock's Mystery Magazine* in 1979 the point of view had changed to first person. The second novel, *Nightlines* (St. Martin's Press), was published in 1985, with the first-person point of view remaining. Through eight novels, the most recent being *Thicker than Blood* (St. Martin's Press, 1994), the Nudger series has remained one of the most popular and highly praised. The Nudger short story "What You Don't Know Can Hurt You" won the Shamus Award for best PI short story of 1982.

Mr. Lutz also writes about a PI named Carver, a somewhat different character in a no less popular series, but since Nudger was born first it is he who appears in this collection, at the author's choice.

"Mr. Nudger?" she said.

I said yes.

"It ain't every private detective that has a leaky trailer for an office." She closed her umbrella and stepped into my twelve-by-forty home and office.

"I like it," I told her. "I'm into moss and mushrooms."

She was a weary-looking blond, about forty, with brown eyes, a squarish homely face, and a nice shape except for thick ankles. "I want to hire you to find Harry Beal," she said.

"Who is?"

"My friend. More than a friend—my lover for the past year."

"How do you mean he's lost?"

"The police found his coat, shoes, and tie on the Jefferson Bridge last week."

"He sounds lost in the worst way," I said, motioning for the woman to sit down on the undersized sofa. "You haven't told me your name."

"Helen Farrow. I'm a cocktail waitress at the Blue Bull on Seventh Avenue."

I poured myself another cup of morning coffee, offering a cup to Helen Farrow, who refused. "So you've gone to the police?"

"They think Harry committed suicide."

"Why don't you think that?"

"The evening of his death, the police received a call from a public phone booth near the bridge. It was Harry, saying someone had threatened to kill him and was following him. When a patrol car got to the booth there was no one around but they found Harry's clothes on the bridge."

"If someone murdered him, it isn't likely they'd remove his coat, shoes, and tie. Is that what leads the police to believe it was suicide?"

"That's what they say."

But I knew that what had led to the easy conclusion of suicide was an undermanned and overworked police force. Lieutenant Catlin had told me about the department's troubles often enough.

"Have you got a photograph of Beal?"

She shook her head no.

"If it was murder, Beal's as dead as if it was suicide," I told her. "Either way, if a body hasn't washed up, the river's still got him—or maybe the ocean. People have jumped from that bridge and never been found."

"I don't think it was murder or suicide," she said stubbornly. "Neither one makes sense. I've drawn out all my savings. I want you to try to find Harry—alive."

"That sounds impossible."

"I know. But I'm paying your price and then some." A light came into her tired eyes that suggested a flinty toughness, an unexpected fineness of character to complement her desperation. She was one of those people who refuse to acknowledge hopelessness until they absolutely have to.

"Harry was sort of my last chance, Mr. Nudger. And you're my last chance to find him."

I sighed, slid open a shallow desk drawer, and got out one of my contracts for Helen Farrow to sign, reflecting that it was this type of case that invariably brought me pain and eventually would kill me. Still, I would take it. "Don't be optimistic," I told her.

But she was. I could tell. What's the matter with people?

Lieutenant Charles Catlin looked up from behind the desk in his sparse, efficient office at police headquarters. The office was the standard pale green that needed a fresh coat of paint and the drone of a dispatcher directing squad cars drifted in from a speaker in the booking area. From a portrait on the wall behind the desk, the commissioner seemed to be looking with stern disapproval over Catlin's shoulder.

"Hello, Nudger," Catlin said indifferently. He is a hulking man whose primal features belie a keen mind. "What brings you to this den of anticrime?"

"I'm on a job."

"The yellow pages strike again."

I sat down in the uncomfortable wooden chair alongside Catlin's desk. "Harry Beal," I said.

He nodded. "I talked to the girl he left behind him. She refuses to believe."

"She needs reassurance," I told him, "one way or the other. Fill me in on the case."

I knew Catlin would honor my request. We trade favors like Monopoly money. We both know neither of us is going to get rich in the real world.

Catlin repeated, in essence, Helen Farrow's short sad account of the night of Beal's disappearance.

"So why a finding of suicide?" I asked.

"Because there's more evidence suggesting suicide than there's evidence suggesting murder or accidental death—this year's budget being what it is."

"What about Beal himself?"

"Forty-eight years old, Caucasian, worked as an office-equipment salesman, no living relatives."

"Did his clothes tell you anything?"

"Check with Denning in the lab if you want. I'm busy

with more important things." He made a slight waving motion with the back of his hand and began filling out a form on his desk. Charm wasn't his strong suit.

I left and took the elevator down to the lab.

Denning recognized me and nodded a friendly hello. We discussed our mutual revulsion for Catlin, then I asked Denning to tell me whatever he could about Harry Beal.

"He wore a size ten shoe, a forty-four-regular coat, and favored loud neckties." He led me to where Beal's effects were stored, sliding open a metal file drawer long enough to contain a body.

The shoes were black wing tips, the suit coat a medium-priced material and blue, the tie a violent red, yellow, and gray. The soles of the shoes were about half worn, and there had been nothing in the suit-coat pockets.

"Anything off the record?" I asked.

"There were a few strands of red hair on the suit coat," Denning said. "Dyed, I think."

"Helen Farrow's hair is dyed blond."

"Who's Helen Farrow?"

"Beal's girlfriend. My client."

"Poor woman." He looked at me with his lab man's myopic gaze.

I left him without a kind word and drove my battered brown VW Rabbit to Helen Farrow's apartment. On the way I reviewed what I knew about the case, managed to start my nervous stomach churning, and popped an antacid tablet into my mouth. I have the knack but not the nerves for my profession.

Helen Farrow's apartment was in a declining part of town, on the third floor of a drab brick building with a chipped gargoyle on each side of the entrance. The apartment itself was small, cheaply furnished, and almost antiseptically clean and ordered. Helen Farrow was the kind who needed to know where things were and why. She let me in and I told her I'd come from headquarters.

"What did you find out?" she asked me.

"That Beal wore wing tip shoes. It's a start." I sat in a small vinyl chair and watched her pace. She stopped near a window overlooking the street and lighted a cigarette.

"Where did Beal work?" I asked.

"Gavner Enterprises, downtown. The police questioned Mr. Gavner, and I talked to him on the phone. He says Harry seemed depressed before his disappearance."

"I'll talk to Gavner," I told her, "but he'll most likely give me the same answers he gave the police."

She turned and stared at me, inhaling smoke from her cigarette as if it hurt her. I knew she wanted some words of encouragement. My opinion was that at that moment Harry Beal was somewhere under water, being nibbled by the fishes. But Helen wouldn't have been encouraged to hear that, so I left the apartment without saying anything.

Gavner Enterprises occupied an inconspicuous suite of offices in an inconspicuous building downtown. There was no receptionist in the small modern outer office, so I followed instructions on a sign telling visitors to press a button and wait.

Soon a voice boomed from the inner office, telling me to enter. I thought it was a bit unbusinesslike but I went in anyway.

The round-shouldered, gray-haired man behind the cluttered desk didn't stand as he acknowledged he was Gerald P. Gavner but he offered his hand. He appeared to be in his early fifties, but there was a keen and vital gleam in his eyes that suggested he might be an aging Romeo who chased the office girls around their desks.

I soon discovered I'd misinterpreted that gleam.

"I didn't approve of Beal living with that woman out of wedlock," Gavner said in a clipped, concise voice. "That might be an old-fashioned point of view, but I think that kind of behavior reflects on the company. Still, the man was my best salesman and I attribute his living with the woman to the depression he seemed to slide into the year before his suicide."

"Depression?"

"Oh, some people probably wouldn't have noticed. But Beal was usually such an enthusiastic person that for him normal behavior constituted depression. The woman probably never saw his real character and didn't realize he was in a depressed state."

"A year is a long time to stay depressed," I said.

"He might have pulled out of it if it hadn't been for the Farnworth murder."

My stomach jumped at the word "murder." "I don't know the case."

"Farnworth was the man who was tried and acquitted six years ago for the murder of Beal's wife and daughter in Texas. The feeling is that he was actually guilty but that he bought his way out of a conviction. Then, when Farnworth was killed last month, the police naturally suspected Beal. He had an ironclad alibi—wasn't within a thousand miles of the crime—but he was still questioned. Old wounds must have been opened, and I think that's what led him to do what he threatened."

"Beal had threatened suicide?"

"He'd made subtle references to it." Gavner folded his waxy hands, flashing a diamond pinky ring, and raised quizzical eyebrows. "Did the police tell you?"

"Our relationship is such that they seldom go into great detail."

I left Gavner and drove back to headquarters, where I was lucky enough to find Catlin still in.

"Tell me about the murder of Beal's wife and daughter," I said.

"It's irrelevant," he answered, "so I don't mind telling you." He leaned back in his squeaky swivel chair and clasped his hands behind his head. "Six years ago a wealthy womanizer named Farnworth was having an affair with Beal's wife. He turned out to be more than a little kinky. He strangled the wife and fourteen-year-old daughter—or at least he was arrested and tried for the murders. Money being all-important in this world, some key witnesses changed their testimony and Farnworth was acquitted."

"How did Beal react?"

"He took his insurance money and moved north to start over."

"What about Farnworth being murdered?" I asked.

"That happened two months ago, in Galveston. His body was discovered in a hotel. He'd been tortured before he was killed."

"So the law went to Beal as the logical suspect."

Catlin nodded. "Only Beal couldn't have killed Farn-worth. He was in New York at the time, at a company meeting. His boss, Gavner, and William Davis, Gavner Enterprises' New York office manager, swore to it. At the exact time of Farnworth's death in Galveston Beal was in conference in New York, discussing a new line of inter-locking file cabinets. I can show you Gavner's statement and the signed deposition the NYPD obtained from Davis." He smiled his ugly smile. "Like I told you—it's irrelevant."

I was prepared to admit that the Farnworth murder prob-ably had nothing to do with Beal's disappearance, but my stomach sensed otherwise. I unpeeled the foil from a roll of white discs, popped one into my mouth, and chewed reflectively.

"I bet you're developing an ulcer," Catlin said con-cernedly. "For your own sake, why don't you get into some other line of work and never come back here?"

"Tempting," I said, and meant it.

After leaving Catlin, I decided to pay another visit to Gavner and find out what, if anything, Beal had said to him about the Farnworth murder, and to discover Beal's reaction when he'd been informed of Farnworth's death. I phoned Gavner Enterprises from a booth on Twelfth Street, but a recorded voice informed me that Mr. Gavner was out and asked if I'd like to leave a message. After the tone, I informed the recorder that I had no message to leave and hung up. Apparently Gavner had departed for home after a hard day's work.

I stopped for a quick supper at a Culinary Cow steak house, took two antacid tablets, drove back to my trailer, and went to bed.

After sleeping late the next morning, I drove downtown to Gavner Enterprises and found the door locked. The build-ing manager told me that Gavner had moved out the day before. He'd rented the office on a month-to-month basis and had left no forwarding address. I talked the manager into letting me into the empty office in the hope of finding some clue as to where Gavner had gone, but the place was so bare it might as well have been hosed clean.

When I phoned Catlin to tell him about Gavner's sudden move, he seemed surprised but not particularly aroused.

"Moving isn't a crime," he said, "even if it is unusually fast."

"Maybe you ought to tell me what your investigation turned up on Gerald Gavner," I said.

"I'll indulge you," he said, and excused himself to get the file on Gavner. "Gavner was born in Plinton, Georgia," Catlin said, "on August twentieth, 1929. He lived in Georgia most of his life, then moved north to start Gavner Enterprises, which sells business equipment to various companies nationwide." Gavner had told the police he was single and listed his address as the Hawthorn Arms, a luxury apartment building on the west side of town.

"If you turn anything up," Catlin told me, "share it."

"You'd probably consider it irrelevant," I said, and hung up.

I was perspiring, and my stomach felt as if it were trying to digest metal filings. This wasn't my kind of case. When you get involved with murderers, things can get violent. The last time one of my cases turned violent, I was badly hurt. Though I didn't want that to happen again, I knew I was caught in currents I couldn't control. I drove to the plush Hawthorn Arms, asked for Gerald P. Gavner.

I was told the expected—that Gerald P. Gavner had moved out. He'd paid the last two months of the lease on his furnished apartment the day before, and the doorman had helped him with his two large suitcases and summoned a taxi.

I phoned Helen Farrow from the lobby and brought her up-to-date. She asked me to meet her at her apartment in an hour.

"I want you to find out about Gavner for me," she said as soon as I'd stepped in from the hall. "Whatever happened to Harry, Gavner knows about it."

"Not necessarily," I cautioned her. "There might be no connection. Gavner could have something to hide, and the police questioning him about Beal's death might have made him figure it was time to move on. Anyone investigating Beal's disappearance would be likely to tumble onto anything illegal Gavner Enterprises might have been involved in."

"I want you to investigate Gavner anyway," Helen persisted. She was smoking another cigarette in that seemingly painful manner. "Go to wherever he's from—find out everything."

"You're talking about money, Helen. More than I want to charge and more than you can pay."

She smiled and handed me something small, neatly folded, and faintly scented. It was a thousand-dollar bill.

"Ten of those came yesterday in the mail," she said. "There wasn't any note or anything in the envelope—just the ten bills." Her drab eyes brightened with the hope she was living on. "It means Harry's alive. I think you can find him through Gavner."

I asked her to show me the envelope the money had arrived in. It was a cheap manila envelope with her name and address typed on it. There was no return address.

"This could be Beal's way of telling you thanks and goodbye," I told her. She'd thought of that, judging by her guarded expression and the glint of tears in her eyes. "But what I think is happening," I continued, "is that we've scared somebody, and the money is that person's way of trying to buy you off so you'll stop searching for Beal."

"I want to use the money to find him," she said fervently.

"I don't know if that's smart, Helen. If it is someone trying to buy you off, he may try to stop you some other way."

Her answer was to hand me another thousand-dollar bill. "Use as much of it as you have to," she said. "Buy whatever information you need. I can't think of any way I'd rather spend the money." She glared challengingly at me. "I'm not afraid. Are you?"

"Yes. But I'll go to Gavner's hometown and start digging if you'll promise to put the rest of the money in the bank and keep your doors locked."

She smiled again. Soft light from the curtained window highlighted her features, and I decided that twenty years ago she must have been passable. "It's a deal," she said.

* * *

I was on the afternoon flight to Atlanta, and from the Atlanta airport I drove a rented car west to Plinton, Georgia. Plinton was a small town, and it didn't take me long to discover that the Gavner family, with their boy Gerald, had moved in 1930 to Carver, a hundred miles south.

In the small farming town of Carver I discovered some members of the Gavner family still living there. They told me that Gerald Gavner had died of internal injuries after being struck by a car. They gave me directions to his grave, and I stood in the neatly kept little cemetery and looked at the dates carved on the weather-smoothed tombstone: August 20, 1929–June 12, 1933.

I knew then what had happened. Someone had assumed Gerald Gavner's identity, obtaining a copy of his birth certificate from Plinton and using it to obtain various identification documents from library cards and gasoline credit cards to a driver's license, possibly even working up to a social security card. It's often done in the underworld, and the identification will stand up under a cursory investigation. The name on all the identification belongs to someone long dead, but someone who existed long enough to provide the foundation for the structure of phony identification. It's handy if the bearer of all that ID wants to engage in something illegal—like the operation of a dummy company to serve as a front for something profitable but risky.

I wanted to find out more about Gavner Enterprises, and I knew who could tell me. After booking into a motel on the outskirts of Carver, I phoned Helen and told her I was flying to New York the next day.

William Davis had vacated the New York office of Gavner Enterprises with the same abruptness with which Gavner himself had vacated the home office. So if Gavner had been involved in something crooked, Davis was too.

The New York office, in an undistinguished building on East Fifty-third Street, had been emptied as thoroughly as the home office, except for a skinny girl who was cleaning out the receptionist's desk and looking forlorn.

She said her name was Millie Ann and that Mr. Davis had given her notice the day before and left immediately.

"Left for where?" I asked.

She shook her frizzy blond head. "He didn't say. I didn't think it was my place to ask. I've only been working here a few months, part-time."

"Don't you have any idea? It's important, and I know he'd want to see me."

Millie Ann paused in her efforts to stuff several magazines and bottles of nail polish into a small paper bag. I could see she was debating with herself—and that she was miffed at losing her job on such short notice.

"You might try the Hangout—it's a bar on Fifty-second Street. Mr. Davis went there sometimes. Talk to Frank, the bartender."

"Were Frank and Mr. Davis friendly beyond a bartender-customer relationship?"

"I don't know." She rolled a romance magazine tightly. "But I was in there last night with my boyfriend and I saw Mr. Davis come in, talk to Frank, and hand him a big yellow envelope and some money. He acted real nervous. The skin under one of his eyes was jumping around, like."

"Did he see you?"

"No."

"What does Mr. Davis look like?" I asked.

She frowned. "Average size, I guess. About forty-five, maybe a little more. Not too bad-looking—red hair, a nice smile. He dressed pretty neat."

I thanked Millie Ann, told her I hoped she'd find work soon, and left.

The Hangout was a respectable-looking if dim lounge, with a long padded bar worked by a lanky man with a gleaming bald head and a down-turned mustache.

"Frank the bartender, I presume," I said, sitting near the end of the bar where he was stacking glasses.

He nodded and gave me a puzzled smile. I ordered a beer.

When he'd brought the beer I asked him if he knew where I could find Bill Davis.

He didn't pretend not to know Davis, but he shrugged and shook his head.

"It's important to both Davis and me that I find him," I said, placing a hundred-dollar bill on the bar.

Frank looked solemnly at the hundred. "I don't know where he is. If I did know, I'd tell you for sure."

"What about the envelope he gave you?"

Frank seemed surprised.

"That won't tell you where he's at."

"Did Davis say what was in the envelope?" My hand reached out as if to withdraw the crinkled bill on the bar.

"Sure," Frank said hastily, and my hand paused. He watched my hand. "All that's in it are some other smaller envelopes, addressed to somebody I never heard of. I'm supposed to mail one the first of every month for the next year."

"Let me look at one of those envelopes," I said. "Mr. Davis would want you to show it to me—believe me." I drew another hundred-dollar bill from my pocket and held it casually.

Frank shrugged as if the matter were really of no importance, went to a small safe in a cabinet behind the bar, and bent over it for a few minutes. Then he returned with a small white envelope. When I released my grip on the second bill and let it drop on top of the first, he set the envelope on the bar so I could read the address: "Mr. Norman Llewelyn, Hill Manor, Hillsboro, Missouri."

The next afternoon I turned my rented Chevy into a driveway beside a freshly painted metal sign lettered Hill Manor—Rest Home. Though only about fifty miles southwest of the St. Louis city limits, Hillsboro was very country, and Hill Manor, was secluded well off the main highway in low, densely wooded hills.

As I followed the curve of the narrow blacktop drive, the rest home came into view. It was a rambling three-story white frame structure that looked like a modernized and enlarged farmhouse. The grounds were neatly kept, the grass green and mowed beneath the two large elms that flanked the steps onto a wide gray-floored porch. A few people sat reading in the rocking chairs that lined the porch. They ignored me as I parked the car and went in through the double-doored entrance.

I was in a large, cool reception area. A television room off to the left emitted the sounds of soap opera. Beneath a large brass chandelier was a counter, and behind the counter stood a bespectacled elderly woman in a white uniform.

"I'm here to see Mr. Norman Llewelyn," I told her through one of my best smiles.

"He's in three twenty-six, at the end of the hall on the third floor," the woman said. "I'll ring upstairs and have someone tell him you're on your way up. What name should I give?"

"I'd rather surprise him," I said, and before she could answer I leaned over the counter and spoke confidentially. "I'm an old friend, and I came here primarily to make sure all of his bills are being paid."

"Oh, there's no problem there," she assured me. "Mr. Llewelyn has a wealthy aunt who sends cash every month to cover his expenses."

I nodded to her and walked toward the wide stairway.

When I entered room 326 without knocking, Llewelyn was sitting in a wicker chair by a tall window, gazing down at something. His back was to me; and I saw only a slumping, gray-haired form haloed by the fading afternoon light. One finger was rhythmically tapping the arm of the chair.

I said, "Hello, Harry Beal."

He turned and jumped halfway out of the chair, then sank back. His mobile face went through a series of expressions and settled on a pasty, resigned smile.

"I don't know what you're talking about or who you are," he said in a calm voice, but without real conviction. "My name is Norman Llewelyn. I'm here for a rest cure."

"You'd have succeeded but for Helen Farrow," I told him. "You had to murder Farnworth; you devoted your life to his death, planned it for six years. But with such a strong motive to kill him, you knew that even if he had seemed to die accidentally the police would suspect you of killing him. So you manufactured the perfect alibi for yourself. You used the names of dead people and their records of birth to build several identities—taking months, maybe years to establish them. You created synthetic lives—witnesses to provide you with a completely leakproof alibi for the time of Farnworth's murder."

"Whoever Farnworth is or was, I've never heard of him before." The wicker chair creaked softly.

"You were in New York, Gavner said—but *you* were Gavner. Davis corroborated your presence there—but *you* were Davis. You knew the Davis statement would be done by deposition, without the same people seeing either Gavner or Davis. But you effected mild disguises so your descriptions would differ. You wore a red wig as Davis, and you were careful not to stand up in your phony Gavner Enterprises office as Gavner so I wouldn't get an estimate of your height or build."

He began to squirm, a tic began under his right eye. "You're insane," he told me. Then his voice slipped into the concise efficient cadence of Gavner. "I demand that you leave—now!" Again his face and voice changed. He seemed to be slipping from personality to personality of the identities he'd created, as if the real Harry Beal had become lost among the long dead.

"I didn't figure on her loving me," he said finally, in a slow natural voice that probably was his own.

"You needed someone like Helen Farrow to substantiate your death," I said. "You phoned her to establish the possibility of murder, but left your clothes on the bridge to suggest suicide. That way, if the police suspected anything it would be your murder—and that would throw off the idea of you faking a suicide to go underground after killing Farnworth. Helen would keep the law moving in that direction if it was disposed to investigate your death."

"I didn't figure on her loving me," Beal repeated in a hoarse voice. "Not that much . . ."

I didn't know if he was actually mad or not. Llewelyn was just another of his carefully contrived false identities, the one he'd kept in reserve to slip into when his scheme was finished. He planned to stay at Hill Manor until he felt well enough to check out and return to New York, to reclaim what was left of the money he'd earmarked for his recuperation and left to be mailed regularly from the Hangout.

Leaving him slumped in the wicker chair, I walked from the suddenly stifling room and went downstairs to use the phone at the desk.

But I never completed the call.

I heard screams, then a commotion beyond the French windows at the far end of the reception area. I put down the receiver and went with the white-uniformed woman from behind the counter as she ran to open the French windows.

Beal was sprawled on the stones of the patio, where he had landed after plunging from his window.

This time he was definitely dead.

Standing there staring at his pathetically contorted corpse, I saw no real point in contacting the law. The easiest course for everyone was to keep Beal's death a suicide on the Jefferson Bridge—in another place, another time.

Amid hushed voices, sobbing, and confusion, I made my way around the side of the building to my rented car and drove away.

I would go home and explain to Helen Farrow that Beal was dead and better off that way, and that now she should pick up what was left of her life and forget him. I cringed at the thought of telling her—but hadn't I warned her when I accepted the case that she'd be disappointed?

As Beal had discovered, sometimes it's impossible to convince the Helen Farrows of the world of anything they refuse to believe.

I stopped for a red light and chewed an antacid tablet as I waited for it to change.

MERRILL-GO-ROUND
Marcia Muller
FIRST APPEARANCE: *Edwin of the Iron Shoes*, 1977

Marcia Muller's Sharon McCone first appeared in *Edwin of the Iron Shoes* (McKay, 1977), predating in novel form all of the contemporary female PIs. "Merrill-Go-Round" was her first short story appearance, published in *The Arbor House Treasury of Mystery and Suspense*. The next McCone novel was *Ask the Cards a Question* (St. Martin's Press, 1983), and the novels have been appearing regularly ever since. She has won a Shamus Award for best PI short story, and has been awarded the PWA Life Achievement Award, the first woman to receive it.

I clung to the metal pole as the man in the red coat and straw hat pushed the lever forward. The blue pig with the bedraggled whisk-broom tail on which I sat moved upward to the strains of "And the Band Played On." As the carousel picked up speed, the pig rose and fell with a rocking motion and the faces of the bystanders became a blur.

I smiled, feeling more like a child than a thirty-year-old woman, enjoying the stir of the breeze on my long black hair. When the red-coated attendant stepped onto the platform and began taking tickets I got down from the pig—reluctantly. I followed him as he weaved his way through lions and horses, ostriches and giraffes, continuing our earlier conversation.

"It was only yesterday," I shouted above the din of the music. "The little girl came in alone, at about three-thirty. Are you sure you don't remember her?"

The old man turned, clinging to a camel for support. His was the weathered face of one who has spent most of his

109

life outdoors. "I'm sure, Miss McCone. Look at them." He motioned around at the other riders. "This is Monday, and still the place is packed with kids. On a Sunday we get ten times as many. How do you expect me to remember one, out of all the rest?"

"Please, take another look at the picture." I rummaged in my shoulder bag. When I looked up the man was several yards away, taking a ticket from the rider of a purple toad.

I hurried after him and thrust the picture into the old man's hand. "Surely this child would stand out, with all that curly red hair."

His eyes, in their web of wrinkles, narrowed. He squinted thoughtfully at the photo, then handed it back to me. "No," he said. "She's a beautiful kid, and I'm sorry she's missing, but I didn't see her."

"Is there any way out of here except for the regular exit?"

He shook his head. "The other doors're locked. There's no way that kid could've left except through the exit. If her mother claims she got on the carousel and disappeared, she's crazy. Either the kid never came inside or the mother missed her when she left, that's all." Done collecting tickets, he leaned against a pony, his expression severe. "She's crazy to let the kid ride alone, too."

"Merrill is ten, over the age when they have to be accompanied."

"Maybe so, but when you've seen as many kids get hurt as I have, it makes you think twice about the regulations. They get excited, they forget to hang on. They roughhouse with each other. That mother was a fool to let her little girl ride alone."

Silently I agreed. The carousel was dangerous in many ways. Merrill Smith, according to her mother, Evelyn, had gotten on it the previous afternoon and never gotten off.

Outside the round blue building that housed the carousel I crossed to where my client sat on a bench next to the ticket booth. Although the sun was shining, Evelyn Smith had drawn her coat tightly around her thin frame. Her dull red hair fluffed in curls over her upturned collar, and her lashless blue eyes regarded me solemnly as I approached.

I marveled, for not the first time since Evelyn had given me Merrill's picture, that this homely woman could have produced such a beautiful child.

"Does the operator remember her?" Evelyn asked eagerly.

"There were so many kids here that he couldn't. I'll have to locate the woman who was in the ticket booth yesterday."

"But I bought Merrill's ticket for her."

"Just the same, she may remember seeing her." I sat down on the cold stone bench. "Look, Evelyn, don't you think it would be better if you went to the police? They have the resources for dealing with disappearances. I'm only one person, and—"

"No!" Her already pallid face whitened until it seemed nearly translucent. "No, Sharon, I want you to find her."

"But I'm not sure where to go next. You've already contacted Merrill's school and her friends. I can question the ticket-booth woman and the personnel at the children's playground, but I'm afraid their answers will be more of the same. And in the meantime your little girl has been missing—"

"No. Please."

I was silent for a moment. When I looked up, Evelyn's pale lashless eyes were focused intensely on my face. There was something coldly analytical about her gaze that didn't go with my image of a distressed mother. Quickly she looked away.

"All right," I said, "I'll give it a try. But I need your help. Try to think of someplace she might've gone on her own."

Evelyn closed her eyes in thought. "Well, there's the house where we used to live. Merrill was happy there; the woman in the first-floor flat was really nice to her. She might've gone back there; she doesn't like the new apartment."

I wrote down the address. "I'll try there, then, but if I haven't come up with anything by nightfall, promise me you'll go to the police."

She stood, a small smile curving her lips. "I promise, but I don't think that will be necessary."

Thrusting her hands deep in her pockets, she turned and walked away; I watched her weave through the brightly colored futuristic shapes of the new children's playground.

Why the sudden conviction that the case was all but solved? I wondered.

I remained on the bench for a few minutes. Traffic whizzed by on the other side of the eucalyptus grove that screened this southeast corner of Golden Gate Park, but I scarcely noticed it.

My client was a new subscriber to All Souls Legal Cooperative, the legal-services plan for which I was a private investigator. She'd come in this morning, paid her fee, and told her story to my boss, Hank Zahn. After she'd refused to allow him to call the police, he'd sent her to me.

It was Evelyn's unreasonable avoidance of the authorities that bothered me most about this case. Any normal middle-class mother—and she appeared to be just that—would have been on the phone to the Park Station minutes after Merrill's disappearance. But Evelyn had spent yesterday evening phoning her daughter's friends, then slept on the problem and contacted a lawyer. Why? What wasn't she telling me?

Well, I decided, when a client comes to you with a story that seems less than candid, the best place to start is with that client's own life. Perhaps the neighbor at the old address could shed some light on Evelyn's strange behavior.

By three that afternoon, almost twenty-four hours after Merrill's disappearance, I was still empty-handed. The old neighbor hadn't been home, and when I questioned the remaining park personnel, they couldn't tell me anything. Once again I drove to Evelyn's former address, on Fell Street across from the park's Panhandle—a decaying area that had gone further downhill after the hippies moved out and the hardcore addicts moved in. The house was a three-flat Victorian with a fire escape snaking up its facade. I rang the bell of the downstairs flat.

A young woman in running shorts answered. I identified myself and said Evelyn Smith had suggested I talk with her. "Her little girl has disappeared, and she thought she might've come back here."

"Evelyn? I haven't heard from her since she moved. You say Merrill's missing?"

I explained about her disappearance from the carousel. "So you haven't seen her?"

"No. I can't imagine why she'd come here."

"Her mother said Merrill had been happy here, and that you were nice to her."

"Well, I was, but as far as her being happy ... Her *un*-happiness was why I went out of my way with her."

"Why was she unhappy?"

"The usual. Evvie and Bob fought all the time. Then he moved out, and a few months later Evvie found a smaller place."

Evelyn hadn't mentioned a former husband. "What did they fight about?"

"Toward the end, everything, but mainly about the kid." The woman hesitated. "You know, that's an odd thing. I haven't thought of it in ages. How could two such homely people have such a beautiful child? Evvie—so awkward and skinny. And Bob, with that awful complexion. It was Merrill being so beautiful that caused their problems."

"How so?"

"Bob adored her. And Evvie was jealous. At first she accused Bob of spoiling Merrill, but later the accusations turned nasty—unnatural relationship, if you know what I mean. *Then* she started taking it out on the kid. I tried to help, but there wasn't much I could do. Evvie Smith acted like she hated her own child."

"Have you found out anything?" Evelyn asked.

I stepped into the small apartment in a bland modern building north of the park. "A little." But I wasn't ready to go into it yet, so I added, "I'd like to see Merrill's room."

She nodded and took me down the hallway. The room was decorated in yellow, with big felt cutouts of animals on the walls. The bed was neatly made up with ruffled quilts, and everything was in place except for a second-grade reader that lay open on the desk. Merrill, I thought, was an unnaturally orderly child.

Evelyn was staring at a grinning stuffed tiger on the bookcase under the window. "She's crazy about animals," she said softly. "That's why she likes the merry-go-round so much."

I ignored the remark, flipping through the reader and studying Merrill's name where she'd printed it in block letters on the flyleaf. Then I shut the book and said, "Why didn't you tell me about your former husband?"

"I didn't think it was important. We were divorced over two years ago."

"Where does he live?"

"Here in the city, on a houseboat at Mission Creek."

"And you didn't think that was important?"

She was silent.

"Is he the reason you didn't call the police?"

No reply.

"You think he's snatched Merrill, don't you?"

She made a weary gesture and turned away from me. "All right, yes. My ex-husband is a deputy district attorney. Very powerful, and he has a lot of friends on the police force. I don't stand a chance of getting Merrill back."

"So why didn't you tell me all this at the beginning?"

More silence.

"You knew that any lawyer would advise you to bring in the police and the courts. You knew an investigator would balk at snatching her back. So you couldn't come right out and ask me to do that. Instead, you wanted me to find out where she was on my own and bring her back to you."

"She's mine! She's supposed to be with me!"

"I don't like being used this way."

She turned, panic in her eyes. "Then you won't help me?"

"I didn't say that."

She needed help—more help, perhaps, than I could give her.

The late-afternoon fog was creeping through the redwood and eucalyptus groves of the park by the time I reached the carousel. It was shut for the night, but in the ticket booth a gray-haired woman was counting cash into a bank-deposit bag. The cashier I'd talked with earlier had told me her replacement came on in mid-afternoon.

"Yes," she said in answer to my initial question, "I worked yesterday."

I showed her Merrill's picture. "Do you remember this little girl?"

The woman smiled. "You don't forget such a beautiful child. She and her mother used to come here every Sunday afternoon and ride the carousel. The mother still comes. She sits on that bench over there and watches the children and looks sad as can be. Did her little girl die?"

It was more or less what I'd expected to hear.

"No," I said, "she didn't die."

It was dark by the time I parked at Mission Creek. All I could make out were the shapes of the boats moored along the ramshackle pier. Light from their windows reflected off the black water of the narrow channel, and waves sloshed against the pilings as I hurried along, my footsteps echoing loudly on the rough planking. Bob Smith's boat was near the end, between two hulking fishing craft. A dim bulb by its door highlighted its peeling blue paint, but little else. I knocked and waited.

The tie lines of the fishing craft creaked as the boats rose and fell on the tide. Behind me I heard a scurrying sound. Rats, maybe. I glanced over my shoulder, suddenly seized by the eerie sensation of being watched. No one—whom I could see.

Light footsteps sounded inside the houseboat. The little girl who answered the door had curly red-gold hair and widely spaced blue eyes. Her T-shirt was grimy and there was a rip in the knee of her jeans, but in spite of it she was beautiful. Beautiful and a few years older than in the picture I had tucked in my bag. That picture had been taken around the time she printed her name in block letters in the second-grade reader her mother kept in the neat-as-a-pin room Merrill no longer occupied.

I said, "Hello, Merrill. Is your dad home?"

"Uh, yeah. Can I tell him who's here?"

"I'm a friend of your mom."

Wrong answer; she stiffened. Then she whirled and ran inside. I waited.

Bob Smith had shaggy dark-red hair and a complexion pitted by acne scars. His body was stocky, and his calloused hands and work clothes told me Evelyn had lied about his job and friends on the police force. I introduced myself, showed him my license, and explained that his former wife had hired me. "She claims your daughter disappeared from the carousel in Golden Gate Park yesterday afternoon."

He blinked. "That's crazy. We were no place near the park yesterday."

Merrill reappeared, an orange cat draped over her shoulder. She peered anxiously around her father at me.

"Evelyn seems to think you took Merrill from the park," I said to Smith.

"Took? As in snatched?"

I nodded.

"Jesus Christ, what'll she come up with next?"

"You do have custody?"

"Since a little while after the divorce. Evvie was . . ." He glanced down at his daughter.

The cat chose that moment to wriggle free from her and dart outside. Merrill ran after it, calling, "Tigger! *Tigger!*"

"Evvie was slapping Merrill around," Smith went on. "I had to do something about it. Evvie isn't . . . too stable. She's got more problems than I could deal with, but she won't get help for them. Deep down, she loves Merrill, but . . . What did she do—ask you to kidnap her?"

"Not exactly. The way she went about it was complicated."

"Of course. With Evvie, it would be."

The orange cat brushed against my ankles—prodigal returned. Behind me Merrill said, "Dad, I'm hungry."

Smith opened his mouth to speak, but suddenly his features went rigid with shock.

I felt a rush of air and started to turn. Merrill cried out. I pivoted and saw Evelyn. She was clutching Merrill around the shoulders, pulling her back onto the pier.

"Daddy!"

Smith started forward. "Evvie, what the hell . . . ?"

Evelyn's pale face was a soapstone sculpture; her lips barely moved when she said, "Don't come any closer, Bob."

Smith pushed around me.

Evelyn drew back and her right hand came up, clutching a long knife.

I grabbed Smith's arm and stopped him.

Evelyn began edging toward the end of the pier, dragging Merrill with her. The little girl's feet scraped on the planking; her body was rigid, her small face blank with terror.

Smith said, "Christ, do something!"

I moved past him. Evelyn and Merrill were almost to the railing where the pier deadended above the black water.

"Evvie," I called, "please come back."

"No!"

"You've got no place to go."

"No place but the water."

Slowly I began moving toward them. "You don't want to go into it. It's cold and—"

"Stay back!" The knife glinted in the light from the boats. "I'll stay right where I am. We'll talk."

She pressed against the rail, tightening her grip on Merrill. The little girl hadn't made a sound, but her fingers clawed at her mother's arm.

"We'll talk," I said again.

"About what?"

"The animals."

"The *animals*?"

"Remember when you told me how much Merrill loved the animals on the carousel? How she loved to ride them?"

". . . Yes."

"If you go into the water and take her with you, she'll never ride them again."

Merrill's fingers stopped their frantic clawing. Even in the dim light I could see comprehension flood her features. She said, "Mom, what *about* the animals?"

Evelyn looked down at her daughter's head.

"What about the zebra, Mom? And the ostrich? What about the blue pig?"

I began edging closer.

"I *miss* the animals. I want to go see them again."

"Your father won't let you."

"Yes, he will. He will if I ask him. We could go on Sundays, just like we used to."

Closer.

"Would you really do that, honey? Ask him?"

"Uh-huh."

My foot slipped on the planking. Evelyn started and glanced up. She raised the knife and looked toward the water. Lowered it and looked back at me. "If he says yes, will you come with us? Just you, not Bob?"

"Of course."

She sighed and let the knife clatter to the planking. Then she let go of Merrill. I moved forward and kicked the knife into the water. Merrill began running toward her father, who stood frozen in front of his houseboat.

Then she stopped, looking back at her mother. Hesitated and reached out her hand. Evelyn stared at her for a moment before she went over and clasped it.

I took Evelyn's other hand and we began walking along the pier. "Are you okay, Merrill?" I asked.

"I'm all right. And I meant what I said about going to ride the carousel. If Mom's going to be okay. She is, isn't she?"

"Yes. Yes, she will be—soon."

THE STEINWAY COLLECTION
Robert J. Randisi

FIRST APPEARANCE: *This Story*, 1977

The Jacoby who appeared in "The Steinway Collection" (the story) in *Mystery Monthly* in 1977 is a somewhat different character from the one who later appeared in *Eye in the Ring* (Avon, 1982) and *The Steinway Collection* (the novel) (Avon, 1983). The basics are there, however. He's an ex-boxer turned New York PI, and his morals and sensibilities are about the same. He has appeared in six novels, the most recent being *Stand Up* (Walker & Co., 1994).

The man who answered the door was a painfully thin six foot four. He had gaunt hollows beneath his cheekbones, hooded gray eyes, a thin slit of a mouth, and gray hair that came to a widow's peak. He was dressed in an old sweatshirt, faded blue jeans, and sandals, so I knew he couldn't be the butler.

"Mr. Jacoby?" he asked, pronouncing it "Juh-*co*-bee," which is wrong.

"Miles *Jack*-uh-bee," I corrected, but he took no notice and stepped back.

"Come in, please," he said. I stepped past him and he closed the door and turned to me. "I am Aaron Steinway. I spoke to you on the phone this morning."

His voice was deep and his mouth barely moved when he spoke. The conversation he was referring to was an early morning phone call to my office that went something like this:

"Mr. Jacoby?" he had asked. I said I was and corrected his pronunciation, but he had taken no notice then either.

He went on to tell me about his missing pulp magazine

collection. He explained that he had one of the most extensive collections—including *Black Mask, Doc Savage, The Shadow*—in the world. He had gone on a business trip; when he got back the collection was gone.

He offered to pay me a generous fee to try and find it and suggested that I come out to his home in New Hyde Park to "look for clues." I stifled a trite remark about Sherlock Holmes magnifying glasses and told him I'd be there as soon as possible.

Now he led me down a long hallway to a room packed with comic books, magazines, and old hardcover and paperback books. You couldn't miss the spot where the pulps had been. Directly across from the door was almost a full wall of shelves. They were empty.

"That's where they were before I left," he told me. "Do you think you can find any clues? I've touched nothing." I looked at him and saw that he was serious. I humored him and walked to the empty shelves.

"Have you talked to the police?" I asked.

Behind me I heard him snort harshly. "They were here yesterday and didn't even bother to take fingerprints. Just looked around and told me they'd be in touch. If there isn't a clue they can trip over they close the case."

"Are you married, Mr. Steinway?" I asked.

"No," he answered. It didn't surprise me. He probably had little time to spare after his work and pulp collection. Certainly not enough time for a wife.

Looking down at my hands, which were black because I'd made the mistake of touching the shelves, I asked, "Could we go somewhere and talk about this? I'd like to ask some questions and perhaps . . . wash up."

He glanced at me for a moment as if he didn't see me, then shook his head. "Oh, yes, of course. This way."

We went to a smaller, cleaner room, his den. There were books here also, but they were newer and also cleaner. He showed me to a small bathroom where I washed my hands. When I came out he was seated behind his desk, staring into space.

"Mr. Steinway, how many people knew of your business trip?"

He thought for a moment, then answered, "My partner, Walter Brackett, of course. A few clients—"

"I'll want names, Mr. Steinway, and addresses. A list of people who knew you would be out of town. Another list of anyone who was interested in or made an offer for your collection recently." He nodded, took a pen and paper, and began the lists. Both were short. I made check marks next to the names that appeared on both: Walter Brackett, partner; James Denton, a client; Michael Walsh, another client. His partner's wife, Laura Brackett, appeared on both lists, but he had put a question mark next to her name on the list of people who knew about his trip. It probably depended on whether her husband told her. I checked her name, too.

I asked Steinway the nature of his business. He told me he was a stockbroker and an investment counselor. We discussed my fee and agreed on a retainer.

"I'll call the minute I find out anything, Mr. Steinway."

"Even if it's only one copy," he insisted anxiously.

"Yes, even if it's only one copy," I promised.

We shook hands and he got mine dirty again; he also mispronounced my name again, but this time I didn't correct him.

He'd paid for the privilege.

To tell the truth, I didn't really expect to find any trace of the books. Collections, no matter what kind, are usually broken up and fenced separately. However, as long as he was willing to pay me I was perfectly willing to go on looking.

I got out the yellow pages and looked up and visited every used and rare bookshop in the city. After four days of that I'd turned up nothing. I'd had Steinway look at a few copies of *Black Mask* and *Dime Detective,* but they weren't his. He was always able to tell, but they were all the same to me—dirty.

When I finished with the bookshops I was fairly certain that the collection had not been broken up and sold—at least not in the New York City area. I had put out some feelers with private investigators in New Jersey, Pennsylvania, upstate New York, and also with some other contacts

I had. I wanted to find out if anyone had been hired to do a number on Steinway's house while he was away.

With that done I began checking out the names my client had given me. I concentrated only on the ones that appeared on both lists Steinway had given me, the people who knew he would be away and who also had expressed interest in his collection.

I took his partner, Walter Brackett, first. I found him at home, a plush apartment house on Fifth Avenue and Sixty-first Street opposite Central Park.

Brackett explained that he himself had no desire to own his partner's collection; he had been trying to buy it for his wife, Laura.

"Aaron's collection is the reason Laura started one of her own, but over the past five years she hasn't been able to build it up anywhere near his." Then he leaned forward and said in a low voice, "I suppose that does make me a suspect, doesn't it? The fact that I've repeatedly tried to buy the collection?"

I nodded and said, "I'm afraid it does, Mr. Brackett."

He seemed amused by the idea. He was nudging his fifties in good shape and had dyed his hair and eyebrows black to help. He said, "Well then, before you ask: No, I did not steal Aaron's collection. I am a businessman. I deal in buying and selling, not stealing."

"What about your wife?" I asked.

His manner changed abruptly and he rose from behind his desk. "Good day, Mr. Jacoby."

"I apologize if I've offended you, Mr. Brackett, but I really would like to speak to your wife—"

"She is not at home. Good day."

Next I went to James Denton, who had made an offer the week before Steinway's trip. His address turned out to be a rundown hotel in the Village, on Jane Street. I thought that a man who lived in a dump like that would never have any reason to become a client of Aaron Steinway let alone make him a decent offer for his pulp collection.

He let me in to his third-floor room when I identified myself, but he was nervous. I asked him about his offer for Steinway's collection.

"It was an impulse," he told me, his brown eyes flicking

around the room, never looking at me. "I often buy things that way."

"You live here, and dress the way you do, and you expect me to believe that you buy anything on impulse?" I shook my head at him. "I don't buy it, Denton." I put my right hand on his chest. He was bigger than me, but I felt he would fold under a little pressure.

"Who were you acting for?" I asked, tapping his chest.

He looked down at my hand, then at my face. His nervous eyes went to the ceiling and he let out one word in a tone of disgust. "Brackett."

I patted his cheek and told him, "Thanks."

On the subway, on my way to interview Michael Walsh, Steinway's other client on the list, I went over what I'd just learned. Not only had Walter Brackett made repeated efforts to buy the collection from Steinway, he'd also hired someone else to front for him. Why? Did Brackett think that Steinway simply didn't want to sell to him?

Walsh didn't live in the city but did have a suite at the Statler Hilton while he was in town. He was a tall, handsome man approaching forty, with an open, friendly face.

I introduced myself and told him what I was working on.

"Damn it," he said, "now I'll never get that collection." He shook his head. "I didn't even want the whole thing, just a few issues, to round out my own collection."

"You mean you didn't make him an offer for all that he had?"

"Just the ones I needed. When he refused to break it up, I made him an offer for all of them, but he still refused. I'm sorry it was stolen. On second thought, I'm sorry it wasn't me who stole it."

"You didn't steal it?"

He smiled and shook his head. "No, I didn't steal it."

"Had you ever considered it?"

"I might have, if it were someone else," he admitted. "But Aaron has gotten me out of too many financial jams, including some alimony problems. That's why I say from someone else, but not from Aaron."

I thanked him and left.

Back at my office I called Steinway's house, but there was no answer, and the line at his New York apartment was busy. I decided to stop by after dinner and went downstairs to John's, right beneath my office on East Fiftieth Street. He was my landlord, and he also made the best roast beef in town.

It was eight o'clock when I got to Steinway's apartment house. There was no doorman on duty, so I stepped into the elevator and pressed the button marked Penthouse, where Steinway had his apartment.

When the doors opened and I stepped out, something struck me a blow on the back of my head. I went down, but not out. I struggled to my hands and knees, and turned my head. I saw the door to the stairway swing shut. Trying to shake the fuzziness from my head, I lurched toward the door. I could hear someone taking the steps fast and breathing raggedly. I started down, taking the steps two and three at a time. I finally spotted him four or five levels down. The lighting on the stairs was bad and I saw only his back, but at least I was gaining on him. From the sound of his breathing he was all run out.

I finally reached the top of one flight just as he was reaching its bottom. I took a chance and launched myself in a flat-out dive. I hit him high and we both went down. But I was slow in recovering because of the slug on my head. I grabbed for him: he hit me and the chase was over.

When I woke up I had to try a couple of times before I was able to get to my feet and support myself against the wall. I went through the stairway door and made my way to the elevator. When it arrived I leaned against the wall and pushed the Penthouse button again. When the elevator got there I went to Steinway's apartment. His door was wide open. Leaning against the doorjamb I felt for the wall switch and flicked the light on. I went slowly through the door.

I found Steinway in his study, seated at his desk. He was bloodier than I was and he was dead.

The phone on the desk was off the hook. It probably explained the busy signal I had heard earlier in the day. I called the police.

*   *   *

Someone was shaking me.

I woke up and stared at the person who was shaking me.

"Sergeant Dolan," he called, turning his head. He was young, fresh-faced, and in uniform. He was a cop.

He was joined by a red-haired man in his thirties who stared at me with intense blue eyes.

"Well, you're back with us," he said.

I frowned, trying to remember what had happened. After I phoned the police I must have passed out. I looked up from the chair I was sitting in and saw Steinway, still slumped over his desk. I tried to get up but the pain in my head forced me back down.

"Better sit tight, Jacoby," Dolan told me, "there's an ambulance on the way." He'd gotten my name from my wallet, which was in his hand. "The back of your head looks a little pulpy right now. How do you feel?"

"I've got a headache."

He nodded. "Think you can answer some questions?"

I waved a hand and found my wallet slapped into it. "I've got nothing better to do at the moment," I said.

"We found this on the dead man's desk," he said, and showed me one of my business cards. "Want to tell me about it?"

So I told him why Steinway had hired me, what I'd found out, and what had happened tonight. Including the fact that I hadn't seen the face of the guy who had hit me.

"Pulp magazines!" a hoarse voice said harshly from my left. I turned my head and saw a bulldog of a man in his late forties with gray hair. "What a bunch of crap!"

"My partner, Detective Connors," Dolan said. Then: "You say you phoned here about six-thirty and the line was busy?"

"I said I got a busy signal. When I got here it was off the hook. He could already have been dead."

"What about the guy who jacked you? Why would he hang around that long?"

"Maybe he searched the apartment after he killed him," I answered. It was a sound suggestion, assuming Steinway's murder and his collection were connected.

"One more thing," Dolan said. "Did you see the doorman?"

I told him I hadn't and had thought it odd at the time.

Just then the medical examiner and ambulance arrived. Dolan asked me to come downtown when I got a chance and do some paperwork. I told him I would and walked to the ambulance.

They stitched my head, told me I'd have a headache for a few days and to take aspirin for it. After that I went downtown and gave the cops my statement. I gave it to Sergeant Dolan. Connors was there, too. They told me they had found the doorman curled up with a bottle in the basement. He was an ex-alcoholic who had chosen tonight to become an *ex*ex-alcoholic.

I was about to leave when Dolan said, "Let us know if you find out anything."

"My client's dead," I told him. "I've no reason to look any further. Besides, murder is out of my league."

I opened the door to leave when Dolan did one of those Columbo takes.

"Oh, just one more thing. Steinway was killed at close range with a forty-five. Do you own a gun?"

"No."

"You don't?" Connors asked, surprised.

"I don't like them," I said. "They scare me."

In the morning I took a hot shower and some aspirin and then called my contacts and told them to send me a bill. When I got through paying them from my retainer I might have enough left for a few cups of coffee.

I thought about Steinway's murder and suddenly I realized that what I had told Dolan wasn't true. I did have reason to look further in this case. The reason was my curiosity.

I'd never been involved with murder before, so I didn't know exactly where to start. I decided to keep looking into the missing collection because if the two were connected, the connection might show up sooner or later. Besides, the cops were working on the murder and I didn't want to get in their way. Maybe we'd meet in midstream.

I found Brackett in his office.

"Terrible thing," he moaned. "The police were here this morning. When they told me what happened I couldn't believe it. Poor Aaron."

"What happens now?" I asked.

"I don't know, really. I'll have to confer with our—with my—with the firm's attorneys."

"Naturally you'll come into his half of the business," I remarked.

"I suppose."

"What about his personal property?"

"I don't know. There are no relatives." He shrugged and added, "Public auction, I imagine."

"I spoke to James Denton yesterday," I said. I threw it in that way to see what his reaction would be. I was disappointed.

"Who?" he asked politely.

"Denton, one of Steinway's clients. Aren't his clients your clients?"

He shook his head. "We are partners in name only, Mr. Jacoby. We never worked together for one client."

"Anyway, Denton told me that you hired him to make Steinway an offer for his collection."

"That's ridiculous." He looked confused. "Why, I don't even know the man. Really, Mr. Jacoby, Aaron is dead. Do you seriously intend to go on looking for his collection?"

I was puzzled because his reaction to Denton's name seemed real. I thought back to what Denton had told me when I had leaned on him. He had said one word: "Brackett." Of course.

"Would your wife have hired him?"

He sighed and seemed to sink into his chair. I thought he might get upset again, but he said, "I really couldn't tell you, Mr. Jacoby. You see, my wife and I are separated."

That surprised me. "Why didn't you tell me this yesterday?"

"I saw no reason to air my dirty laundry in front of you," he replied. Then he added, "However, now with this murder, I suppose it's better to hold nothing back. She moved out some three months ago and took an apartment uptown. I can give you the address if you like."

I had to ring the bell three times before she answered.

"I'm sorry," she apologized, "I was reading." She held up a worn copy of *Black Mask* with a half-dressed blond and the name Carroll John Daly on the cover.

"My name is Jacoby, Mrs. Brackett. I was working for Aaron Steinway at the time of his murder."

"Oh, yes," she murmured. "Come in, please." After she shut the door she asked me for identification. I showed her my license. She handed it back, saying, "I was just curled up with Race Williams. He's a private eye, too." She held up the book to show me where he did his private eyeing. I followed her into the living room.

"The police were already here, Mr. Jacoby, after they spoke to my husband." I didn't say anything. She continued, "Although I didn't like Aaron, I'm sorry he's dead, in much the same way I would be sorry if a dog or a cat was dead."

"You didn't like him because he wouldn't sell you his collection?"

"Among other things, yes."

"Did you hire James Denton to make him an offer?"

"Yes," she said, "I did. I knew Aaron would never sell to Walter knowing it was for me."

"Why?"

She settled herself on the couch and spread her arms out along the back, pushing her chest out. I figured her for her early thirties—about twenty years younger than her husband. She was tall, good-looking, with subtle curves, high cheekbones, and long legs. Her hair was black and hung down past her shoulders.

"He didn't like me because I wouldn't let him screw me," she said. She leaned forward, allowing me to peek down the front of her dress and said in a whisper, "I didn't like him. He was an old fart with fast hands, always grabbing for a piece of ass or tit."

I had trouble imagining that tall, cadaverous bookworm making a grab for anything but another book.

"How did you feel when Denton told you Steinway wouldn't sell?" I asked.

"Angry."

"Angry enough to kill him?"

She shook her pretty head. "No, Mr. Jacoby, not that

angry. That's hate. I didn't hate Aaron Steinway, I merely disliked him. Intensely."

"Mrs. Brackett, how badly did you want that collection?"

"Bad enough to make it part of my settlement with Walter. I told him if he could come up with the collection, I wouldn't take him for as much in court, and believe me we can take him for plenty."

Which probably meant she had something on him, but was willing to let him off the hook for the collection.

"Why do you want the collection so much?"

"Probably because it was so hard to get. From the beginning I knew how Aaron felt about that collection. Maybe it was my dislike for him that made me want it. I've been interested in comics and pulps since I was a kid. When I saw Aaron's collection, I started one of my own, but it never got to be as big as his. So I thought that the next best thing would be to acquire it. I've been trying for the past year." She looked at me and shook her head. "I really can't explain it any better than that."

"What do you have on your husband that would make it so easy for you to get a large settlement?"

"Ask him, Mr. Jacoby," she said.

I thanked her and left. Outside I went to a phone booth and called Brackett's office. His secretary told me he had gone home. I went there.

"Really, Jacoby," he said when he opened the door, "I think you're carrying this magazine business too far. How in the world do you expect to be paid—"

"It's a freebie, Brackett," I told him, pushing past him.

"Look here, man, who do you think—"

I turned to him. "I just had a nice chat with your wife, Brackett. She told me that if you couldn't get her Steinway's collection she had something on you—that she could squeeze a large settlement out of you."

"By blackmail, damn her!" He seemed to age in front of me and walked slowly to his desk. "She has photos . . ." he began, but couldn't continue. He tried again. "I've been indiscreet, Mr. Jacoby. My wife had me followed, had photos taken. I . . . I'm a man of peculiar sexual appetites—if my clients see those photos, it would ruin me."

"So when Steinway wouldn't sell his collection you stole it."

He shook his head. "I might have worked myself up to that, but before I could Aaron told me his house had been burglarized. I never believed that."

"You don't believe they've been stolen?" I asked.

He shook his head. "He hid it someplace. He just wanted to make it harder on me."

That sounded paranoid to me, but I didn't say so.

"Did he know about your wife's threat?"

"Not until I told him, last night."

"You were there last night? Was it you who hit me?"

"Yes, it was me. I went there to beg Aaron to sell me the collection. I told him about the photos, but he laughed and said I should have kept my indiscretions more of a secret."

"So you killed him!"

"No, no. I didn't. I wanted to. God knows I wanted to. I even brought a gun with me, to scare him. I put my hand in my pocket, to take it out and use it. . . . I got that far," Brackett continued, as if that alone should be worth something. "But in the end Laura was right. She always said I couldn't get the collection from him because I was afraid of him. She was right. He was always so overbearing, and I was always a coward. Even with a gun I was still afraid of him."

"So what did you do?"

He laughed. "I went out and got so drunk that I came back to Aaron's apartment to . . . to . . ."

"To kill him."

"To end his worthless life!" he cried.

"Did you?"

"He was already dead."

I hadn't expected that. I had come here hoping to get a confession.

"I panicked. I ran to the elevator and it opened. I didn't know it was you until I hit you. Then I ran. When you chased me and knocked me down I hit you again. I had never struck anyone before. I was pretty sure you hadn't seen my face, and the next morning, when you came over, I was sure."

Then he looked like he had just realized something and said, "You know, I really believed I would have done it if he hadn't already been dead."

"Did you see anything that might tell you who killed him?"

"Can you believe it?" he went on. "I really would have—"

"Come on, Brackett! Who killed your partner?" I was shouting now.

"How should I know, man? He was dead when I got there. I *would* have killed him myself, I know I would have, but he was already dead. Who killed him? Who robbed me of that pleasure? Who?" He was going a bit nuts. I started around the desk to shake him out of it when from the corner of my eye I saw someone standing in the doorway. I turned and found myself facing Michael Walsh.

He seemed to be in the act of leaving, but stopped, like a man caught where he shouldn't be.

"I'm sorry. I didn't mean to listen ..." he began. He seemed like a man in a daze, not at all the same easygoing, pleasant-faced man I'd spoken to the day before.

"How long have you been there?" I asked.

"Not long. The door was unlocked, so I came in. I wanted to talk to Brackett about ..." He stopped, as if he were going to say something he hadn't intended to say.

"About the collection?" I asked. He nodded and glanced at the door.

"Why talk to Brackett about it? Did you think he'd know where it was?"

"I thought maybe Steinway might have given it to Brackett to hold," he said slowly.

"Why would he do that and then say it was stolen?" I asked.

He shook his head and shut his eyes, as if trying to keep himself from answering. "Because he didn't want me to have it." He said it bitterly.

I was struck again by how much he'd changed since yesterday. Something was eating him up inside and I didn't have to be a genius to figure out what it was.

"Walsh, did you kill Steinway?" I gave him five slow

seconds to deny it, and when he didn't I knew what his answer would be.

He stood there staring at me, but not seeing me.

"Yes," he answered, looking totally surprised at the word that he had heard come from his mouth.

I suppose it is in all of us to kill, given the right circumstances. However, it is not in all of us to be able to handle what comes afterward. Walsh had been feeling the guilt from what he had done yesterday and he simply could not handle it because, although circumstances had made him kill, he was not a killer.

He sank into a chair and covered his face with his hands.

"Tell me what happened," I said.

He shrugged. "I killed him. I went there to ask him to lend me the copies I needed to complete my own collection. I only wanted to use them for one exhibition, so I could hear people talk about my collection, just once, the way they've been talking about his for years. But no, he had to taunt me, call my collection second rate, laugh at me. I became angry and I went for him. I was going to beat him. He grabbed a gun from his desk drawer. We struggled and it went off. I killed him."

"My God, Walsh, it was an accident," I told him. "You didn't kill him on purpose, it was an accident."

He looked at me and said, "But I killed him. I panicked. I took the gun and threw it in a garbage can in an alley somewhere. Then I ran. . . ." He stopped talking and stared at the floor.

I turned to Brackett. He had been staring at Walsh. Now he looked at me. "*I* wouldn't feel guilty if *I* killed him," Brackett said proudly. "I wish I had killed him."

I looked at Walsh, a man consumed by guilt for something that was accidental, and I had to agree with Brackett. He *should* have been the one to kill Steinway.

It would have made it easier for me to call the cops.

When Dolan had arranged for Walsh and Brackett to be taken downtown, one to be booked and one to sign a statement, he invited me to ride with him.

"You mean you're dropping the case?" he asked in the car.

I shrugged. "I have no client. Who'll pay me if I find it? If I find it, who do I turn it in to? And if Steinway did hide it, he's the only one who would know where it is and he's dead."

Dolan didn't reply.

ROBBERS' ROOST
Loren D. Estleman
FIRST APPEARANCE: *Motor City Blue*, 1980

Detroit PI Amos Walker first appeared in the novel *Motor City Blue* (Houghton Mifflin, 1980). He has gone on to appear in ten highly praised novels, with no end in sight. He is consistently hailed as the contemporary PI who comes the closest to Raymond Chandler's Philip Marlowe in ethics and personal moral code. Mr. Estleman has won three Shamus Awards with his popular character, one for best PI novel and two for best PI short story.

"Robbers' Roost" was published in a short-lived magazine called *Mystery* in 1982.

1

I was met at the door by a hatchet-faced woman in a nurse's uniform who took my card and asked me to accompany her to Dr. Tuskin's office. I hadn't come to see anyone by that name, but I said okay. I have another set of manners when my checks don't bounce. On the way we passed some old people in wheelchairs whose drugged eyes followed us the way the eyes of sunning lizards follow visitors to the zoo. The place was a nursing home for the aged.

"I can't let you see Mr. Chubb," announced Dr. Tuskin, after we had shaken hands and the nature of my visit was established. The nurse had withdrawn. "Perhaps I can help you, Mister"—he glanced down at my card—"Walker?"

He was tall and plump with very white hair and wore a three-piece suit the color of creamed anything. His office wore a lot of cedar and the desk he was standing behind was big and glossy and bare but for the card. I didn't think he'd scooped any paperwork into a drawer on my account.

"I doubt it," I said. "I got a telephone call from Mr. Chubb requesting my services. If he hasn't confided in you we've nothing to discuss."

"He is infirm. I can't imagine what reasons he'd have for engaging a private investigator at this time in his life." But his frost-blue eyes were uneasy. I played on that.

"I don't think they have anything to do with the operation of this home or he wouldn't have made the call from one of your telephones." I dropped the reassuring tone. "But I have a friend on the *News* who might be interested in finding out why a private investigator was denied access to one of your patients."

His face tightened. "That sounds like blackmail."

"I was hoping it would."

After a moment he pressed something under his desk. Reappearing, Hatchet Face was instructed to take me to Oscar Chubb's room on the second floor. Dr. Tuskin didn't say goodbye as we left.

Upstairs lay a very old man in bed, his pale, hollow-templed head almost lost amidst the pillow and heavy white quilt. The nurse awakened him gently, told him who I was, and moved to draw the blinds over the room's only window, which looked out over the choppy blue-green surface of Lake St. Clair.

"Leave it," he bleated. "It's taken me eighty years to get to Grosse Pointe. I like to be reminded."

She went out, muttering something about the glare and his cataract.

"As if it mattered." He mined a bony arm in a baggy pajama sleeve out from under the heavy spread, rested it a moment, then used the remote control atop the spread to raise himself to a sitting position. He waved me into the chair next to the bed.

"I hear you're good."

"Good's a pretty general term," I said. "I'm good in some areas. Missing persons, yeah. Divorce, no. I have a low gag threshold."

"Have you ever heard of Specs Kleinstein?"

"Racketeer. Retired, lives in Troy."

He nodded feebly. His eyes were swollen in the shriveled face and his head quaked. "I want him in jail."

"You, the Detroit Police, and the FBI." I stuck a cigarette in my mouth, then remembered where I was, and started to put it away. He told me to go ahead and smoke. I said, "Sure?"

"Don't worry about killing me. I'm hardier than I look."

"You'd almost have to be."

He smiled, or tried to. The corners of his lipless mouth tugged out a tenth of an inch. "You remind me of Eddie."

"Eddie?" I lit up.

"He's the reason I want Specs behind bars. The reason you're here. You know about Robbers' Roost?"

I blew smoke away from the bed. "If I answer this one right, do I get the range or the trip to Hawaii?"

"Indulge my senility. You won't find the Roost on any map, but if you ask any old-time Detroiter about it he'll grin and give you directions a blind man could follow. It covers ten blocks along the river in Ecorse where rumrunners from Canada used to dock during Prohibition. Eddie and I grew up there."

"Eddie was your brother?"

"Yes and no. His last name was Stoner. My folks adopted him in 1912 after his folks were killed in a streetcar accident on Woodward. You ever see an old Warner Brothers picture called *Angels with Dirty Faces*?"

"A time or twelve."

"Well, it was Eddie and me right on the button. We were the same age, but he grew up faster on account of a four-alarm temper and a pair of fists like pistons. When college time came and my parents could afford to send only one of us, it was Eddie who stepped aside. After graduation I joined the Ecorse Police Department. Eddie got a job delivering bootleg hooch for Specs Kleinstein.

"I asked him how far he thought I'd get in the force when it got out that I had Mob connections. He said, 'Probably chief,' and I knocked him down for the first and only time in my life. He moved out soon after."

Chubb closed his eyes. Whatever breathing he was doing wasn't enough to stir the quilt over his chest. But his nostrils were quivering and I relaxed.

"One day I pulled over a big gray Cadillac for running a stop sign on Jefferson," he went on. "Eddie was behind the wheel with a girl in the passenger's seat and ten cases of Old Log Cabin stacked in back. The girl was Clara Baxter, Kleinstein's mistress. Eddie laughed when I told him to watch his butt. Well, I took them in, car and all. They were back on the street an hour later with everything returned, including the liquor. That was how things worked back then."

"Back then." I flicked some ash into a pants cuff.

Chubb ignored the comment. "I never saw him again. That winter the river froze over, and the boats went into dry dock while old cars were used to ferry the stuff across. I still have the clipping."

A yellow knuckle twitched at the bed stand. In the drawer was a square of brown newsprint fifty years old. Bootlegger Dies as Ice Collapses, bellowed the headline. I read swiftly.

"It says it was an accident," I said. "The ice gave way under Stoner's car and he went to the bottom."

"Yeah. It was just coincidence that Specs found out about Eddie stealing his woman the day before the accident and threatened to kill him. I have that on good authority."

"You tried to nail him for it?"

"For thirty-two years, until retirement. No evidence."

"What made you decide to try again now?"

He opened his huge eyes and turned them on me. "In confidence?"

I nodded.

"This morning I had a little stroke. I still can't grip anything with my right hand. Nobody here even knows about it. But I won't survive another."

I smoked and thought. "I wouldn't know where to start after all this time."

"You do if your recommendation is any good. Try Walter Barnes in Ecorse. He was my partner for fourteen years and he knows as much about the case as I do. Then you might see what you can do about recovering Eddie's remains.

"He's still down there?"

"I never could get the city to pay out to raise a gangster's body. The car isn't a hazard to navigation."

I folded away the clipping inside my jacket and stood. "My fee's two-fifty a day plus expenses."

"See my son. His number's on the back of the clipping."

"Be seeing you."

"Don't count on it."

2

I found Walter Barnes watering the lawn of his brick split-level on Sunnyside, a tall man in his early seventies with pinkish hair thinning in front and a paunch that strained the buttons on his fuzzy green sweater. He wore a hearing aid, so naturally I started the interview at the top of my lungs.

"Stop shouting or I'll spray you," he snapped. "Who'd you say you were?"

I handed him my card. He moved his lips as he read.

"Amos Walker, huh? Never heard of you."

"You're in the majority. What can you tell me about Eddie Stoner?"

"Who'd you say you're working for?" His eyes were narrow openings in thickets of wrinkles.

"Oscar Chubb. You used to be partners."

His face softened. "Oscar. How is he?"

"Dying."

"I been hearing that for ten years. Who was it you asked me about?"

"Eddie Stoner." I made strangling motions with my hands in my pockets.

His lips drew back over his dentures. "Eddie was bad. He was the reason Oscar took so long getting his stripes. The brass didn't like having a hoodlum's brother on the force, blood kin or no."

"Tell me about Eddie's death."

His story was loaded with repetitions and back-telling, but I gathered that it was one of Barnes's snitches who had carried the tale of Kleinstein's death threat. Clara Baxter had blurted out the details of her fling during an argument. A scuffle with Eddie followed; Kleinstein's eyeglasses got broken along with his nose, and he sputtered through the blood that Stoner wouldn't see Thursday.

"Way I see it," the ex-cop wrapped up, "Specs wormed his way back into Eddie's confidence somehow, then let him have it in the car that night on the ice. Then he got out a spud and chopped a circle around the car so it broke through, and headed back on foot. But we never could prove they were together that night."

"What happened to Clara Baxter?"

"She left town right after the fight. Last I heard she was back and living in Detroit. Married some guy named Fix or Wicks, something like that. I heard he died. Hell, her too, probably, by now."

"Thanks, Mr. Barnes. Who do I see about fishing Eddie's remains out of the river?"

He turned off the nozzle and started rolling up the hose with slow, deliberate movements of his spotted hands. "In this town, no one. Money's too tight to waste solving a murder no one cares about anymore."

"I hope you're wrong, Mr. Barnes," I said. "About no one caring, I mean."

He made no reply. For all I knew, his hearing aid needed fresh batteries.

3

A Clara Wicks and two C. Fixes were listed in the Detroit directory. I tried them from my office. The first was a thirty-year-old divorcée who tried to rape me over the telephone and the others were men. Then I got tricky and dialed the number for C. Hicks. No answer. Next I rang Lieutenant John Alderdyce on Detroit Homicide, who owed me a favor. He collected on a poker debt from a cop on the Ecorse Police, whose wife's brother knew a member of the city council, who had something on the mayor. Half an hour later Alderdyce called back to say that dragging for the submerged car would start first thing in the morning. Democracy is a system of checks and balances.

There was still no answer at the Hicks number. The house was on Livernois. I thought I'd check it out, and had my hand on the door handle of my war-torn Cutlass when two guys crowded in on either side of me. Together they'd have filled Tiger Stadium.

"You got a previous engagement, chum," said the one on my left, a black with scar tissue over both eyes and a sagging lower lip that left his bottom teeth exposed. His partner wasn't as pretty.

I was hustled into the rear of a dark blue Lincoln in the next slot down, where Gorgeous sat next to me while the other drove. After that the conversation lagged.

Kleinstein was leaning on a cane in the living room of his Troy townhouse when we entered. His white hair was fine over shiny scalp and his neck and hands were spotted, but aside from that he was the Specs whose picture I'd seen in books about Prohibition, down to the thick eyeglasses that had earned him his nickname. He had on a pastel blue sport shirt and gray trousers with pleats.

"You're working for Oscar Chubb." His Yiddish accent was faint but there. "Why?"

"I'm supporting a habit. I have to eat every now and then."

His cane slashed upward. A black light burst inside my temple. I reeled, then lurched forward, but the gargoyles who had brought me stepped between us. Unarmed that day, I relaxed.

"Next time don't be flip," warned the old man. "What've you found out?"

"If you hit me with that cane again I'll make you eat it."

Gorgeous lumbered toward me, dropping one shoulder. I pivoted and kicked. The side of my sole met his kneecap with an audible snap. Howling, he grasped it and staggered backward until he fell into an overstuffed chair. He started to blubber. His partner roared and lunged, but Kleinstein smacked the cane across his chest, halting him.

"All right, you're a hard case. The cemetery's full of them. Some guys are just too dumb to scare. You're here because I want you to know I didn't kill Stoner."

"Who told you I cared?"

He smiled dryly. The spectacles magnified his eyes to three times their normal size. "Let's stick to the subject. Five witnesses swore I was nowhere near the river that night."

"My client says different."

"Your client is senile."

"Maybe. We'll know for sure tomorrow. The City of Ecorse is raising the car Stoner died in."

He didn't turn pale or try to walk on the ceiling. I hadn't really expected him to. "How much evidence do you think they'll find after fifty years?" He flushed. "Look at this house, Walker. I've lived like this a long time. Do you think I'd risk it on a cheap broad?"

"Maybe you wouldn't. The old Specs might have."

He spat on the carpet. The thug in him would always come through in moments like this. Turning to the uninjured flunky: "Take this punk back to his building and get a doctor for Richard on your way back." To me: "Step soft, Walker. Things have a way of blowing up around people I don't like."

I took him literally. When the gorilla dropped me off I checked under the hood before starting my car.

4

The Hicks home stood in a seedy neighborhood where old jalopies went to die, a once-white frame house with an attached garage and a swaybacked roof, surrounded by weeds. When no one answered my third knock I tried the door. It was unlocked.

The living room was cozy. Magazines and cheap paperbacks flung everywhere, assorted items of clothing slung over the shabby furniture and piled on the colorless rug. In the bedroom I found a single bed, unmade, and a woman's purse containing the usual junk and a driver's license in the name of Clara Hicks, aged sixty-eight. I was in the right place. A small, functional kitchen boasted an old refrigerator, a two-burner stove, and a sink and counter where a sack of groceries waited to be put away. The sack was wet. Two packages of hamburger were half thawed inside.

There was a throbbing noise behind a side door. My stomach dropped through a hole. I tore open the door and dashed into a wall of noxious smoke.

She was lying in the backseat of a six-year-old Duster with her hands folded demurely on her stomach. Her mousy gray hair was rumpled, but aside from that she was rigged for the street, in an inexpensive gray suit and floral print blouse. I recognized her sagging features from the picture on her driver's license. Coughing through my handkerchief, I reached over the seat to turn off the ignition and felt her throat for a pulse. After thirty seconds I gave up.

I climbed out and pulled up the garage door, gulped some air, then went back and steeled myself to run my fingers over her scalp. There was a sticky lump the size of a Ping-Pong ball above her left ear.

5

Two hours after I called him, I was still sitting in a chair in the kitchen talking to John Alderdyce. John's black, my age, and a spiffy dresser for a cop. In the garage they were still popping flashbulbs and picking up stray buttons.

"It could be suicide," I acknowledged. "She bought groceries today and left that hamburger thawing out in case you boys in Homicide got hungry."

The lieutenant made a disgusting noise. "That's what I can always count on from you, sincerity," he snarled. "The ME says she probably suffered cardiac arrest when the blow was struck, an hour or so before you found her. Who would you fit for it? Specs?"

"Maybe. I can't help wondering why, if he was going to do it, he didn't have her iced fifty years ago. The fact that I was with him about the time she took the blow means nothing. He could have had it catered. You'd better talk to Barnes."

"Not that I wasn't planning to anyway, but why?"

"Aside from Specs and Chubb, he was the only one who knew I was on the case. Someone had to tell Kleinstein."

"That opens up all sorts of unpleasant possibilities."

"Buying cops was invented in the twenties," I said. "Look up his record. Maybe he knows who dropped the contract on Eddie Stoner."

"That one's yours. I've got enough new murders on my hands. I don't have to tinker with old ones too."

I fumbled out a cigarette and stuck it between my lips without lighting it. My throat was raw from them as it was. "Someone doesn't agree with you. This particular old murder bothered him enough to make committing a new one seem worthwhile."

"Barnes is the one told you about the Baxter woman in the first place."

"He knew I'd suspect him if he didn't. He very conveniently forgot her married name, remember. Of course, I'm assuming she hasn't made enemies in the interim. That one's yours."

"Thanks. I wouldn't have known if you hadn't told me." He put away his notepad. "That'll do for now, Walker. Your help is appreciated."

I'd heard sweeter thanks from muggers. "Don't mention it. Finding little old ladies sapped and gassed is a favorite hobby of mine."

That night I dreamed I was out swimming on a warm evening when I came upon a vintage car sunk in the mud, moonlight shining on it through the water. Peering inside, I was snatched by flabby hands and found myself grappling with an old woman whose face was blotched gray with death. We rolled over and over, but her grip was like iron and I couldn't shake her. I awoke as drenched as if I had actually been in the water.

The telephone was ringing. It was John Alderdyce.

"Good news and bad news, shamus. Sheriff's men got Barnes at Metro Airport a few minutes ago, boarding a plane for L.A."

"What's the bad news?"

"We looked up his record. There's nothing to indicate he was anything but square. I wish to hell mine were as good."

That tore it as far as getting a good night's sleep was concerned. I sat up smoking cigarettes until dawn.

6

The day was well along when Alderdyce and I shared the Ecorse dock with a crowd of local cops and the curious, watching a rusty sedan rise from the river at the end of a cable attached to a derrick on the pier. Streaming water, the glistening hulk swung in a wide, slow arc and descended to a cleared section of dock. The crane's motor died. Water hissed down the archaic vehicle's boiler-shaped cowl and puddled around the rotted tires.

Uniforms held back the crowd while John and I inspected the interior. Decayed wooden crates had tumbled over everything. Something lay on the floor in front, swaddled in rags and what remained of the upholstery. White, turtle-gnawed bone showed through the tattered and blackened fabric.

"Not much hope of proving he was sapped or shot," said the lieutenant. "The denizens of the deep have seen to that."

"Even so," I said, "having a corpus delicti makes for a warm, cozy feeling. Is Barnes still in custody?"

"For the time being. We won't be able to hold him much longer without evidence. What is it?"

A longshoreman who had been pressed into service to unload the cargo had exclaimed as he lifted out the first of the crates. "Awful light for a box full of booze," he said, setting it down on the dock.

A crowbar was produced and the rotted boards gave way easily to reveal nothing inside. Alderdyce directed another crate to be opened, and another. They were equally unrewarding.

"I wonder why Eddie would risk his life for a carload of empty boxes," I mused, breaking the silence.

7

In the end, it was the boxes and not the body that broke him. After an hour of questioning, Alderdyce dropped the bombshell about the strange cargo, whereupon Barnes's face lost all color and he got so tongue-tied he couldn't keep his lies straight. When he started confessing, the stenographer had to ask him twice to slow down so she could keep up.

Outside Oscar Chubb's room that evening an orderly with shoulders you couldn't hike across grasped my upper arm as I started to push past and I asked him to let go. He squeezed harder, twisting the muscle and leering. I jabbed four stiffened fingers into the arch of his rib cage. When he doubled over I snatched hold of his collar and opened the door with his head. Inside, a gentle boot in the rump laid him out on his face.

Dr. Tuskin and the hatchet-faced nurse were standing on the other side of the bed. An oxygen tent covered Chubb's head and torso and he was wired to an oscilloscope whose feeble beep disconcertingly resembled a countdown. The noise echoed the beating of my client's heart.

"Call the police," Tuskin told the nurse.

"Uh-uh." I blocked her path. "What happened?"

Tuskin hesitated. "Stroke. It happened shortly after you left yesterday. What right have you to break in and batter my staff?"

I studied the gaunt face behind transparent plastic. "Is he conscious?"

Before the doctor could respond, Chubb's eyelids rolled open and the great eyes slewed my way. To Tuskin I said, "This will only take a minute. It'll be on tonight's news, so you can stay if you like."

He liked. I spoke for longer than a minute, but by then no one was watching the clock. The dying man lay with his eyes closed most of the time. I had only the peeping of the electronic whozis to tell me I still had an audience.

"I confirmed it in back issues of the *News* and *Free Press* at the library," I went on. "That wasn't the first load of hooch Specs paid for and never got. His rumrunning boats and cars had a habit of sinking and getting hijacked, more than those of his rivals. Eddie bought the stuff in Canada with the boss's money, stashed part of it to be picked up later, and saw to it that the empty crates he'd replaced it with got lost. He was making a respectable profit off each load. Kleinstein got wind of it and threatened him. Eddie and Clara never were an item. That was just Barnes's story."

Chubb's lips moved. I didn't need to hear him.

"Sure you saw them together," I said. "They were retrieving a load from one of their caches. If Barnes was Eddie's pipeline into the police department, as he's confessed, Clara was his spy in Specs's inner circle, ready to sound the alarm if he ever got suspicious. When he did, Barnes panicked and had Eddie taken out to keep him from talking."

I read his lips again and shook my head.

"No. I thought Barnes had killed him too until we checked out his alibi. The night Eddie went down, your partner was sitting vigil in a Harper Woods funeral parlor with a cousin's remains. Two people who were with him that night are still alive, and they've confirmed it. There was only one other person who had a stake in Eddie's death, who he would have trusted to go with him that last night."

His lips didn't move this time. I hurried on.

"It was the girl, Mr. Chubb. Clara Baxter. She shot him and spent all night chipping a hole under the car to cover the evidence. Barnes hasn't changed much in fifty years. When I started poking around he lost his head again and tipped Kleinstein anonymously to get me out of the way while he offed Clara. He knew she wouldn't confess to Eddie's murder, but if Specs got suspicious and wrung the truth about the swindle out of her, Barnes was cold meat. In court he stood a chance. The underworld doesn't offer one."

I waited, but he didn't respond. After a brief examination Dr. Tuskin announced that his patient had lapsed into coma.

I never found out if he was conscious long enough to appreciate the fact that he'd spent half a century hating a man for the wrong reason. He died early the next morning without telling his son about our arrangement, and I didn't have enough capital on hand to sue his estate. But I wasn't the biggest loser by far.

Three days after his arraignment on two counts of murder, while awaiting trial in the Wayne County Jail, Walter Barnes was found strangled to death in his cell with the cord from his hearing aid. The coroner called it suicide.

THE TAKAMOKU *JOSEKI*
Sara Paretsky

FIRST APPEARANCE: *Indemnity Only*, 1982

Chicago PI V. I. Warshawski burst onto the scene in the novel *Indemnity Only* (Dial Press, 1982). She and her creator were an immediate critical and popular hit, and their popularity has continued to grow through eight novels and one feature-length movie. The most recent novel was *Tunnel Vision* (Dell, 1994).

This story first appeared in *Alfred Hitchcock's Mystery Magazine* in 1983.

Written for S. Courtenay Wright
Christmas Day, 1982

I

Mr. and Mrs. Takamoku were a quiet, hardworking couple. Although they had lived in Chicago since the 1940s, when they were relocated from an Arizona detention camp, they spoke only halting English. Occasionally I ran into Mrs. Takamoku in the foyer of the old three-flat we both lived in on Belmont, or at the corner grocery store. We would exchange a few stilted sentences. She knew I lived alone in my third-floor apartment, and she worried about it, although her manners were too perfect for her to come right out and tell me to get myself a husband.

As time passed, I learned about her son, Akira, and her daughter, Yoshio, both professionals living on the West Coast. I always inquired after them, which pleased her.

With great difficulty I got her to understand that I was a private detective. This troubled her; she often wanted to know if I were doing something dangerous, and would shake her head and frown as she asked. I didn't see Mr.

147

Takamoku often. He worked for a printer and usually left long before me in the morning.

Unlike the De Paul students who formed an ever-changing collage on the second floor, the Takamokus did little entertaining, or at least little noisy entertaining. Every Sunday afternoon a procession of Asians came to their apartment, spent a quiet afternoon, and left. One or more Caucasians would join them, incongruous by their height and color. After a while, I recognized the regulars: a tall, bearded white man, and six or seven Japanese and Koreans.

One Sunday evening in late November I was eating sushi and drinking sake in a storefront restaurant on Halsted. The Takamokus came in as I was finishing my first little pot of sake. I smiled and waved at them, and watched with idle amusement as they conferred earnestly, darting glances at me. While they argued, a waitress brought them bowls of noodles and a plate of sushi; they were clearly regular customers with regular tastes.

At last, Mr. Takamoku came over to my table. I invited him and his wife to join me.

"Thank you, thank you," he said in an agony of embarrassment. "We only have question for you, not to disturb you."

"You're not disturbing me. What do you want to know?"

"You are familiar with American customs." That was a statement, not a question. I nodded, wondering what was coming.

"When a guest behaves badly in the house, what does an American do?"

I gave him my full attention. I had no idea what he was asking, but he would never have brought it up just to be frivolous.

"It depends," I said carefully. "Did they break up your sofa or spill tea?"

Mr. Takamoku looked at me steadily, fishing for a cigarette. Then he shook his head, slowly. "Not as much as breaking furniture. Not as little as tea on sofa. In between."

"I'd give him a second chance."

A slight crease erased itself from Mr. Takamoku's forehead. "A second chance. A very good idea. A second chance."

He went back to his wife and ate his noodles with the noisy appreciation that showed good Japanese manners. I had another pot of sake and finished about the same time as the Takamokus; we left the restaurant together. I topped them by a good five inches and perhaps twenty pounds, so I slowed my pace to a crawl to keep step with them.

Mrs. Takamoku smiled. "You are familiar with Go?" she asked, giggling nervously.

"I'm not sure," I said cautiously, wondering if they wanted me to conjugate an intransitive irregular verb.

"It's a game. You have time to stop and see?"

"Sure," I agreed, just as Mr. Takamoku broke in with vigorous objections.

I couldn't tell whether he didn't want to inconvenience me or didn't want me intruding. However, Mrs. Takamoku insisted, so I stopped at the first floor and went into the apartment with her.

The living room was almost bare. The lack of furniture drew the eye to a beautiful Japanese doll on a stand in one corner, with a bowl of dried flowers in front of her. The only other furnishings were six little tables in a row. They were quite thick and stood low on carved wooden legs. Their tops, about eighteen inches square, were crisscrossed with black lines which formed dozens of little squares. Two covered wooden bowls stood on each table.

"Go-ban," Mrs. Takamoku said, pointing to one of the tables.

I shook my head in incomprehension.

Mr. Takamoku picked up a covered bowl. It was filled with smooth white disks, the size of nickels but much thicker. I held one up and saw beautiful shades and shadows in it.

"Clamshell," Mr. Takamoku said. "They cut, then polish." He picked up a second bowl, filled with black disks. "Shale."

He knelt on a cushion in front of one of the tables and rapidly placed black and white disks on intersections of the lines. A pattern emerged.

"This is Go. Black plays, then white, then black, then white. Each tries to make territory, to make eyes." He showed me an "eye"—a clear space surrounded by black stones. "White cannot play here. Black is safe. Now white must play someplace else."

"I see." I didn't really, but I didn't think it mattered.

"This afternoon, someone knock stones from table, turn upside down, and scrape with knife."

"This table?" I asked, tapping the one he was playing on.

"Yes." He swept the stones off swiftly but carefully, and put them in their little pots. He turned the board over. In the middle was a hole, carved and sanded. The wood was very thick—I suppose the hole gave it resonance.

I knelt beside him and looked. I was probably thirty years younger, but I couldn't tuck my knees under me with his grace and ease: I sat cross-legged. A faint scratch marred the sanded bottom.

"Was he American?"

Mr. and Mrs. Takamoku exchanged a look. "Japanese, but born in America," she said. "Like Akira and Yoshio."

I shook my head. "I don't understand. It's not an American custom." I climbed awkwardly back to my feet. Mr. Takamoku stood with one easy movement. He and Mrs. Takamoku thanked me profusely. I assured them it was nothing and went to bed.

II

The next Sunday was a cold, gray day with a hint of snow. I sat in front of the television, in my living room, drinking coffee, dividing my attention between November's income and watching the Bears. Both were equally feeble. I was trying to decide on something friendlier to do when a knock sounded on my door. The outside buzzer hadn't rung. I got up, stacking loose papers on one arm of the chair and balancing the coffee cup on the other.

Through the peephole I could see Mrs. Takamoku. I opened the door. Her wrinkled ivory face was agitated, her eyes dilated. "Oh, good, good, you are here. You must come." She tugged at my hand.

I pulled her gently into the apartment. "What's wrong? Let me get you a drink."

"No, no." She wrung her hands in agitation, repeating that I must come, I must come.

I collected my keys and went down the worn, uncarpeted stairs with her. Her living room was filled with cigarette smoke and a crowd of anxious men. Mr. Takamoku detached himself from the group and hurried over to his wife and me. He clasped my hand and pumped it up and down.

"Good. Good you came. You are a detective, yes? You will see the police do not arrest Naoe and me."

"What's wrong, Mr. Takamoku?"

"He's dead. He's killed. Naoe and I were in camp during World War. They will arrest us."

"Who's dead?"

He shrugged helplessly. "I don't know name."

I pushed through the group. A white man lay sprawled on the floor. His face had contorted in dreadful pain as he died, so it was hard to guess his age. His fair hair was thick and unmarked with gray; he must have been relatively young.

A small dribble of vomit trailed from his clenched teeth. I sniffed at it cautiously. Probably hydrocyanic acid. Not far from his body lay a teacup, a Japanese cup without handles. The contents sprayed out from it like a Rorschach. Without touching it, I sniffed again. The fumes were still discernible.

I got up. "Has anyone left since this happened?"

The tall, bearded Caucasian I'd noticed on previous Sundays looked around and said "No" in an authoritative voice.

"And have you called the police?"

Mrs. Takamoku gave an agitated cry. "No police. No. You are detective. You find murderer yourself."

I shook my head and took her gently by the hand. "If we don't call the police, they will put us all in jail for concealing a murder. You must tell them."

The bearded man said, "I'll do that."

"Who are you?"

"I'm Charles Welland. I'm a physicist at the University of Chicago, but on Sundays I'm a Go player."

"I see ... I'm V. I. Warshawski. I live upstairs. I'm a private investigator. The police look very dimly on all citizens who don't report murders, but especially on PIs."

Welland went into the dining room, where the Takamokus kept their phone. I told the Takamokus and their guests that no one could leave before the police gave them permission, then followed Welland to make sure he didn't call anyone besides the police, or take the opportunity to get rid of a vial of poison.

The Go players seemed resigned, albeit very nervous. All of them smoked ferociously; the thick air grew bluer. They split into small groups, five Japanese together, four Koreans in another clump. A lone Chinese fiddled with the stones on one of the Go-bans.

None of them spoke English well enough to give a clear account of how the young man died. When Welland came back, I asked him for a detailed report.

The physicist claimed not to know his name. The dead man had only been coming to the Go club the last month or two.

"Did someone bring him? Or did he just show up one day?"

Welland shrugged. "He just showed up. Word gets around among Go players. I'm sure he told me his name—it just didn't stick. I think he worked for Hansen Electronic, the big computer firm."

I asked if everyone there was a regular player. Welland knew all of them by sight, if not by name. They didn't all come every Sunday, but none of the others was a newcomer.

"I see. Okay. What happened today?"

Welland scratched his beard. He had bushy, arched eyebrows which jumped up to punctuate his stronger statements. I thought that was pretty sexy. I pulled my mind back to what he was saying.

"I got here around one-thirty. I think three games were in progress. This guy"—he jerked his thumb toward the dead man—"arrived a bit later. He and I played a game. Then Mr. Hito arrived and the two of them had a game. Dr. Han showed up, and he and I were playing when the whole thing happened. Mrs. Takamoku sets out tea and snacks. We all wander around and help ourselves. About four, this guy took a swallow of tea, gave a terrible cry, and died."

"Is there anything important about the game they were playing?"

Welland looked at the board. A handful of black and white stones stood on the corner points. He shook his head. "They'd just started. It looks like our dead friend was trying one of the Takamoku *joseki*. That's a complicated one—I've never seen it used in actual play before."

"What's that? Anything to do with Mr. Takamoku?"

"The *joseki* are the beginning moves in the corners. Takamoku is this one"—he pointed at the far side—"where black plays on the five-four point—the point where the fourth and fifth lines intersect. It wasn't named for our host. That's just coincidence."

III

Sergeant McGonnigal didn't find out much more than I did. A thickset young detective, he had a lot of experience and treated his frightened audience gently. He was a little less kind to me, demanding roughly why I was there, what my connection with the dead man was, who my client was. It didn't cheer him up any to hear I was working for the Takamokus, but he let me stay with them while he questioned them. He sent for a young Korean officer to interrogate the Koreans in the group. Welland, who spoke fluent Japanese, translated the Japanese interviews. Dr. Han, the lone Chinese, struggled along on his own.

McGonnigal learned that the dead man's name was Peter Folger. He learned that people were milling around all the time watching each other play. He also learned that no one paid attention to anything but the game they were playing, or watching.

"The Japanese say the Go player forgets his father's funeral," Welland explained. "It's a game of tremendous concentration."

No one admitted knowing Folger outside the Go club. No one knew how he found out that the Takamokus hosted Go every Sunday.

My clients hovered tensely in the background, convinced that McGonnigal would arrest them at any minute. But they could add nothing to the story. Anyone who wanted to play was welcome at their apartment on Sunday afternoon. Why should he show a credential? If he knew how to play, that was the proof.

McGonnigal pounced on that. Was Folger a good player? Everyone looked around and nodded. Yes, not the best— that was clearly Dr. Han or Mr. Kim, one of the Koreans— but quite good enough. Perhaps first *kyu,* whatever that was.

After two hours of this, McGonnigal decided he was getting nowhere. Someone in the room must have had a connection with Folger, but we weren't going to find it by questioning the group. We'd have to dig into their backgrounds.

A uniformed man started collecting addresses while McGonnigal went to his car to radio for plainclothes reinforcements. He wanted everyone in the room tailed and wanted to call from a private phone. A useless precaution, I thought: the innocent wouldn't know they were being followed, and the guilty would expect it.

McGonnigal returned shortly, his face angry. He had a bland-faced, square-jawed man in tow, Derek Hatfield of the FBI. He did computer fraud for them. Our paths had crossed a few times on white-collar crime. I'd found him smart and knowledgeable, but also humorless and overbearing.

"Hello, Derek," I said, without getting up from the cushion I was sitting on. "What brings you here?"

"He had the place under surveillance," McGonnigal said, biting off the words. "He won't tell me who he was looking for."

Derek walked over to Folger's body, covered now with a sheet, which he pulled back. He looked at Folger's face and nodded. "I'm going to have to phone my office for instructions."

"Just a minute," McGonnigal said. "You know the guy, right? You tell me what you were watching him for."

Derek raised his eyebrows haughtily. "I'll have to make a call first."

"Don't be an ass, Hatfield," I said. "You think you're impressing us with how mysterious the FBI is, but you're not, really. You know your boss will tell you to cooperate with the city if it's murder. And we might be able to clear this thing up right now, glory for everyone. We know Folger worked for Hansen Electronic. He wasn't one of your guys working undercover, was he?"

Hatfield glared at me. "I can't answer that."

"Look," I said reasonably. "Either he worked for you and was investigating problems at Hansen, or he worked for them and you suspected he was involved in some kind of fraud. I know there's a lot of talk about Hansen's new Series J computer—was he passing secrets?"

Hatfield put his hands in his pockets and scowled in thought. At last he said, to McGonnigal, "Is there some place we can go and talk?"

I asked Mrs. Takamoku if we could use her kitchen for a few minutes. Her lips moved nervously, but she took Hatfield and me down the hall. Her apartment was laid out like mine and the kitchens were similar, at least in appliances. Hers was spotless; mine had that lived-in look.

McGonnigal told the uniformed man not to let anyone leave or make any phone calls, and followed us.

Hatfield leaned against the back door. I perched on a bar stool next to a high wooden table. McGonnigal stood in the doorway leading to the hall.

"You got someone here named Miyake?" Hatfield asked.

McGonnigal looked through the sheaf of notes in his hand and shook his head.

"Anyone here work for Kawamoto?"

Kawamoto is a big Japanese electronics firm, one of Mitsubishi's peers and a strong rival of Hansen in the mega-computer market.

"Hatfield, are you trying to tell us that Folger was passing Series J secrets to someone from Kawamoto over the Go boards here?"

Hatfield shifted uncomfortably. "We only got onto it three weeks ago. Folger was just a go-between. We offered him immunity if he would finger the guy from Kawamoto. He couldn't describe him well enough for us to make a pickup. He was going to shake hands with him or touch him in some way as they left the building."

"The Judas trick," I remarked.

"Huh?" Hatfield looked puzzled.

McGonnigal smiled for the first time that afternoon.

"The man I kiss is the one you want. You should've gone to Catholic school, Hatfield."

"Yeah. Anyway, Folger must've told this guy Miyake we were closing in." Hatfield shook his head disgustedly. "Miyake must be part of that group, just using an assumed name. We got a tail put on all of them." He straightened up and started back toward the hall.

"How was Folger passing the information?" I asked.

"It was on microdots."

"Stay where you are. I might be able to tell you which one is Miyake without leaving the building."

Of course, both Hatfield and McGonnigal started yelling at me at once. Why was I suppressing evidence, what did I know, they'd have me arrested.

"Calm down, boys," I said. "I don't have any evidence. But now that I know the crime, I think I know how it was done. I just need to talk to my clients."

Mr. and Mrs. Takamoku looked at me anxiously when I came back to the living room. I got them to follow me into the hall. "They're not going to arrest you," I assured them. "But I need to know who turned over the Go board last week. Is he here today?"

They talked briefly in Japanese, then Mr. Takamoku said, "We should not betray guest. But murder is much worse. Man in orange shirt, named Hamai."

Hamai, or Miyake, as Hatfield called him, resisted valiantly. When the police started to put handcuffs on him, he popped a gelatin capsule into his mouth. He was dead almost before they realized what he had done.

Hatfield, impersonal as always, searched his body for the microdot. Hamai had stuck it to his upper lip, where it looked like a mole against his dark skin.

IV

"How did you know?" McGonnigal grumbled, after the bodies had been carted off and the Takamokus' efforts to turn their life savings over to me successfully averted.

"He turned over a Go board here last week. That troubled my clients enough that they asked me about it. Once I knew we were looking for the transfer of information, it was obvious that Folger had stuck the dot in the hole under the board. Hamai couldn't get at it, so he had to turn the whole board over. Today, Folger must have put it in a more accessible spot."

Hatfield left to make his top-secret report. McGonnigal followed his uniformed men out of the apartment. Welland held the door for me.

"Was his name Hamai or Miyake?"

"Oh, I think his real name was Hamai—that's what all his identification said. He must have used a false name with Folger. After all, he knew you guys never pay attention to each other's names—you probably wouldn't even notice what Folger called him. If you could figure out who Folger was."

Welland smiled; his busy eyebrows danced. "How about a drink? I'd like to salute a lady clever enough to solve the Takamoku *joseki* unaided."

I looked at my watch. Three hours ago I'd been trying to think of something friendlier to do than watch the Bears get pummeled. This sounded like a good bet. I slipped my hand through his arm and went outside with him.

LONG GONE
Sue Grafton

FIRST APPEARANCE: *"A" Is for Alibi*, 1982

Sue Grafton appeared on the scene with her Kinsey Millhone novel *"A" Is for Alibi* (Holt, 1982). The most recent novel to appear was *"K" Is for Killer* (Holt, 1994). She is presently a staple on all of the national best-seller lists. She has won the Shamus Award for best PI novel twice.

This story first appeared in *Redbook* in 1986 under the title "She Didn't Come Home." "Long Gone" is Ms. Grafton's preferred title.

September in Santa Teresa. I've never known anyone yet who doesn't suffer a certain restlessness when autumn rolls around. It's the season of new school clothes, fresh notebooks, and finely sharpened pencils without any teeth marks in the wood. We're all eight years old again and anything is possible. The new year should never begin on January 1. It begins in the fall and continues as long as our saddle oxfords remain unscuffed and our lunch boxes have no dents.

My name is Kinsey Millhone. I'm female, thirty-two, twice divorced, "doing business as" Kinsey Millhone Investigations in a little town ninety-five miles north of Los Angeles. Mine isn't a walk-in trade like a beauty salon. Most of my clients find themselves in a bind and then seek my services, hoping I can offer a solution for a mere thirty bucks an hour, plus expenses. Robert Ackerman's message was waiting on my answering machine that Monday morning at nine when I got in.

"Hello. My name is Robert Ackerman and I wonder if you could give me a call. My wife is missing and I'm wor-

ried sick. I was hoping you could help me out." In the
background, I could hear whiney children, my favorite kind.
He repeated his name and gave me a telephone number. I
made a pot of coffee before I called him back.

A little person answered the phone. There was a murmured child-size hello and then I heard a lot of heavy
breathing close to the mouthpiece.

"Hi," I said. "Can I speak to your daddy?"

"Yes." Long silence.

"Today?" I added.

The receiver was clunked down on a tabletop and I could
hear the clatter of footsteps in a room that sounded as if it
didn't have any carpeting. In due course, Robert Ackerman
picked up the phone.

"Lucy?"

"It's Kinsey Millhone, Mr. Ackerman. I just got your
message on my answering machine. Can you tell me what's
going on?"

"Oh wow, yeah—"

He was interrupted by a piercing shriek that sounded
like one of those policeman's whistles you use to discourage
obscene phone callers. I didn't jerk back quite in time. Shit,
that hurt.

I listened patiently while he dealt with the errant child.

"Sorry," he said when he came back on the line. "Look,
is there any way you could come out to the house? I've
got my hands full and I just can't get away."

I took his address and brief directions, then headed out
to my car.

Robert and the missing Mrs. Ackerman lived in a housing
tract that looked like it was built in the forties before anyone ever dreamed up the notion of family rooms, country
kitchens, and his 'n' hers solar spas. What we had here was
a basic drywall box, cramped living room with a dining L,
a kitchen, and one bathroom sandwiched between two
nine-by-twelve-foot bedrooms. When Robert answered the
door I could just about see the whole place at a glance.
The only thing the builders had been lavish with was the
hardwood floors, which, in this case, was unfortunate. Little
children had banged and scraped these floors and had

brought in some kind of foot grit that I sensed before I was even asked to step inside.

Robert, though harried, had a boyish appeal; a man in his early thirties perhaps, lean and handsome, with dark eyes and dark hair that came to a pixie point in the middle of his forehead. He was wearing chinos and a plain white T-shirt. He had a baby, maybe eight months old, propped on his hip like a grocery bag. Another child clung to his right leg, while a third rode his tricycle at various walls and doorways, making quite loud sounds with his mouth.

"Hi, come on in," Robert said. "We can talk out in the backyard while the kids play." His smile was sweet.

I followed him through the tiny disorganized house and out to the backyard, where he set the baby down in a sand-pile framed with two-by-fours. The second child held on to Robert's belt loops and stuck a thumb in its mouth, staring at me while the tricycle child tried to ride off the edge of the porch. I'm not fond of children. I'm really not. Especially the kind who wear hard brown shoes. Like dogs, these infants sensed my distaste and kept their distance, eyeing me with a mixture of rancor and disdain.

The backyard was scruffy, fenced in, and littered with the fifty-pound sacks the sand had come in. Robert gave the children homemade-style cookies out of a cardboard box and shooed them away. In fifteen minutes the sugar would probably turn them into lunatics. I gave my watch a quick glance, hoping to be gone by then.

"You want a lawn chair?"

"No, this is fine," I said, and settled on the grass. There wasn't a lawn chair in sight, but the offer was nice anyway.

He perched on the edge of the sandbox and ran a distracted hand across his head. "God, I'm sorry everything is such a mess, but Lucy hasn't been here for two days. She didn't come home from work on Friday and I've been a wreck ever since."

"I take it you notified the police."

"Sure. Friday night. She never showed up at the baby-sitter's house to pick the kids up. I finally got a call here at seven asking where she was. I figured she'd just stopped off at the grocery store or something, so I went ahead and picked 'em up and brought 'em home. By ten o'clock when

I hadn't heard from her, I knew something was wrong. I called her boss at home and he said as far as he knew she'd left work at five as usual, so that's when I called the police."

"You filed a missing persons report?"

"I can do that today. With an adult, you have to wait seventy-two hours, and even then, there's not much they can do."

"What else did they suggest?"

"The usual stuff, I guess. I mean, I called everyone we know. I talked to her mom in Bakersfield and this friend of hers at work. Nobody has any idea where she is. I'm scared something's happened to her."

"You've checked with hospitals in the area, I take it."

"Sure. That's the first thing I did."

"Did she give you any indication that anything was wrong?"

"Not a word."

"Was she depressed or behaving oddly?"

"Well, she was kind of restless the past couple of months. She always seemed to get excited around this time of year. She said it reminded her of her old elementary school days." He shrugged. "I hated mine."

"But she's never disappeared like this before."

"Oh, heck no. I just mentioned her mood because you asked. I don't think it amounted to anything."

"Does she have any problems with alcohol or drugs?"

"Lucy isn't really like that," he said. "She's petite and kind of quiet. A homebody, I guess you'd say."

"What about your relationship? Do the two of you get along okay?"

"As far as I'm concerned, we do. I mean, once in a while we get into it, but never anything serious."

"What are your disagreements about?"

He smiled ruefully. "Money, mostly. With three kids, we never seem to have enough. I mean, I'm crazy about big families, but it's tough financially. I always wanted four or five, but she says three is plenty, especially with the oldest not in school yet. We fight about that some—having more kids."

"You both work?"

"We have to. Just to make ends meet. She has a job in an escrow company downtown, and I work for the phone company."

"Doing what?"

"Installer," he said.

"Has there been any hint of someone else in her life?"

He sighed, plucking at the grass between his feet. "In a way, I wish I could say yes. I'd like to think maybe she just got fed up or something and checked into a motel for the weekend. Something like that."

"But you don't think she did."

"Uh-uh, and I'm going crazy with anxiety. Somebody's got to find out where she is."

"Mr. Ackerman—"

"You can call me Rob," he said.

Clients always say that. I mean, unless their names are something else.

"Rob," I said, "the police are truly your best bet in a situation like this. I'm just one person. They've got a vast machinery they can put to work and it won't cost you a cent."

"You charge a lot, huh?"

"Thirty bucks an hour plus expenses."

He thought about that for a moment, then gave me a searching look. "Could you maybe put in ten hours? I got three hundred bucks we were saving for a trip to the San Diego Zoo."

I pretended to think about it, but the truth was, I knew I couldn't say no to that boyish face. Anyway, the kids were starting to whine and I wanted to get out of there. I waived the retainer and said I'd send him an itemized bill when the ten hours were up. I figured I could put a contract in the mail and reduce my contact with the short persons who were crowding around him now, begging for more sweets. I asked for a recent photograph of Lucy, but all he could come up with was a two-year-old snapshot of her with the two older kids. She looked beleaguered even then, and that was before the third baby came along. I thought about quiet little Lucy Ackerman whose three strapping sons had legs the size of my arms. If I were she, I know where I'd be. Long gone.

*   *   *

Lucy Ackerman was employed as an escrow officer for a small company on State Street not far from my office. It was a modest establishment of white walls, rust-and-brown plaid furniture, with burnt orange carpets. There were Gauguin reproductions all around, and a live plant on every desk. I introduced myself first to the office manager, a Mrs. Merriman, who was in her sixties, had tall hair, and wore lace-up boots with stiletto heels. She looked like a woman who'd trade all her pension monies for a head-to-toe body tuck.

I said, "Robert Ackerman has asked me to see if I can locate his wife."

"Well, the poor man. I heard about that," she said with her mouth. Her eyes said, "Fat chance!"

"Do you have any idea where she might be?"

"I think you'd better talk to Mr. Sotherland." She had turned all prim and officious, but my guess was she knew something and was just dying to be asked. I intended to accommodate her as soon as I'd talked to him. The protocol in small offices, I've found, is ironclad.

Gavin Sotherland got up from his swivel chair and stretched a big hand across the desk to shake mine. The other member of the office force, Barbara Hemdahl, the bookkeeper, got up from her chair simultaneously and excused herself. Mr. Sotherland watched her depart and then motioned me into the same seat. I sank into leather still hot from Barbara Hemdahl's backside, a curiously intimate effect. I made a mental note to find out what she knew, and then I looked, with interest, at the company vice-president. I picked up all these names and job titles because his was cast in stand-up bronze letters on his desk, and the two women both had white plastic name tags affixed to their breasts, like nurses. As nearly as I could tell, there were only four of them in the office, including Lucy Ackerman, and I couldn't understand how they could fail to identify each other on sight. Maybe all the badges were for customers who couldn't be trusted to tell one from the other without the proper IDs.

Gavin Sotherland was large, an ex-jock to all appearances, maybe forty-five years old, with a heavy head of blond hair thinning slightly at the crown. He had a slight paunch, a slight stoop to his shoulders, and a grip that was damp with sweat. He had his coat off, and his once-starched white shirt was limp and wrinkled, his beige gabardine pants heavily creased across the lap. Altogether, he looked like a man who'd just crossed a continent by rail. Still, I was forced to credit him with good looks, even if he had let himself go to seed.

"Nice to meet you, Miss Millhone. I'm so glad you're here." His voice was deep and rumbling, with confidence-inspiring undertones. On the other hand, I didn't like the look in his eyes. He could have been a con man, for all I knew. "I understand Mrs. Ackerman never got home Friday night," he said.

"That's what I'm told," I replied. "Can you tell me anything about her day here?"

He studied me briefly. "Well, now, I'm going to have to be honest with you. Our bookkeeper has come across some discrepancies in the accounts. It looks like Lucy Ackerman has just walked off with half a million dollars entrusted to us."

"How'd she manage that?"

I was picturing Lucy Ackerman, free of those truck-busting kids, lying on a beach in Rio, slurping some kind of rum drink out of a coconut.

Mr. Sotherland looked pained. "In the most straightforward manner imaginable," he said. "It looks like she opened a new bank account at a branch in Montebello and deposited ten checks that should have gone into other accounts. Last Friday, she withdrew over five hundred thousand dollars in cash, claiming we were closing out a big real estate deal. We found the passbook in her bottom drawer." He tossed the booklet across the desk to me and I picked it up. The word VOID had been punched into the pages in a series of holes. A quick glance showed ten deposits at intervals dating back over the past three months and a zero balance as of last Friday's date.

"Didn't anybody else double-check this stuff?"

"We'd just undergone our annual audit in June. Everything was fine. We trusted this woman implicitly and had every reason to."

"You discovered the loss this morning?"

"Yes, ma'am, but I'll admit I was suspicious Friday night when Robert Ackerman called me at home. It was completely unlike that woman to disappear without a word. She's worked here eight years and she's been punctual and conscientious since the day she walked in."

"Well, punctual at any rate," I said. "Have you notified the police?"

"I was just about to do that. I'll have to alert the Department of Corporations too. God, I can't believe she did this to us. I'll be fired. They'll probably shut this entire office down."

"Would you mind if I had a quick look around?"

"To what end?"

"There's always a chance we can figure out where she went. If we move fast enough, maybe we can catch her before she gets away with it."

"Well, I doubt that," he said. "The last anybody saw her was Friday afternoon. That's two full days. She could be anywhere by now."

"Mr. Sotherland, her husband has already authorized three hundred dollars' worth of my time. Why not take advantage of it?"

He stared at me. "Won't the police object?"

"Probably. But I don't intend to get in anybody's way, and whatever I find out, I'll turn over to them. They may not be able to get a fraud detective out here until late morning, anyway. If I get a line on her, it'll make you look good to the company *and* to the cops."

He gave a sigh of resignation and waved his hand. "Hell, I don't care. Do what you want."

When I left his office, he was putting the call through to the police department.

I sat briefly at Lucy's desk, which was neat and well organized. Her drawers contained the usual office supplies; no personal items at all. There was a calendar on her desktop, one of those loose-leaf affairs with a page for each day. I checked back through the past couple of months. The only personal notation was for an appointment at the Women's Health Center August 2 and a second visit last Friday afternoon. It must have been a busy day for Lucy, what with a doctor's appointment and ripping off her company for half a million bucks. I made a note of the address she'd penciled in at the time of her first visit. The other two women in the office were keeping an eye on me, I noticed, though both pretended to be occupied with paperwork.

When I finished my search, I got up and crossed the room to Mrs. Merriman's desk. "Is there any way I can make a copy of the passbook for that account Mrs. Ackerman opened?"

"Well, yes, if Mr. Sotherland approves," she said.

"I'm also wondering where she kept her coat and purse during the day."

"In the back. We each have a locker in the storage room."

"I'd like to take a look at that, too."

I waited patiently while she cleared both matters with her boss, and then I accompanied her to the rear. There was a door that opened onto the parking lot. To the left of it was a small rest room and, on the right, there was a storage room that housed four connecting upright metal lockers, the copy machine, and numerous shelves neatly stacked with office supplies. Each shoulder-high locker was marked with a name. Lucy Ackerman's was still securely padlocked. There was something about the blank look of that locker that seemed ominous somehow. I looked at the lock, fairly itching to have a crack at it with my little set of key picks, but I didn't want to push my luck with the cops on the way.

"I'd like for someone to let me know what's in that locker when it's finally opened," I remarked while Mrs. Merriman ran off the copy of the passbook pages for me.

"This, too," I said, handing her a carbon of the withdrawal slip Lucy'd been required to sign in receipt of the cash. It had been folded and tucked into the back of the booklet. "You have any theories about where she went?"

Mrs. Merriman's mouth pursed piously, as though she were debating with herself about how much she might say.

"I wouldn't want to be accused of talking out of school," she ventured.

"Mrs. Merriman, it does look like a crime's been committed," I suggested. "The police are going to ask you the same thing when they get here."

"Oh. Well, in that case, I suppose it's all right. I mean, I don't have the faintest idea where she is, but I do think she's been acting oddly the past few months."

"Like what?"

"She seemed secretive. Smug. Like she knew something the rest of us didn't know about."

"That certainly turned out to be the case," I said.

"Oh, I didn't mean it was related to that," she said hesitantly. "I think she was having an affair."

That got my attention. "An affair? With whom?"

She paused for a moment, touching at one of the hairpins that supported her ornate hairdo. She allowed her gaze to stray back toward Mr. Sotherland's office. I turned and looked in that direction too.

"Really?" I said. No wonder he was in a sweat, I thought.

"I couldn't swear to it," she murmured, "but his marriage has been rocky for years, and I gather she hasn't been that happy herself. She has those beastly little boys, you know, and a husband who seems determined to spawn more. She and Mr. Sotherland ... Gavie, she calls him ... have ... well, I'm sure they've been together. Whether it's connected to this matter of the missing money, I wouldn't presume to guess." Having said as much, she was suddenly uneasy. "You won't repeat what I've said to the police, I hope."

"Absolutely not," I said. "Unless they ask, of course."

"Oh. Of course."

"By the way, is there a company travel agent?"

"Right next door," she replied.

I had a brief chat with the bookkeeper, who added nothing to the general picture of Lucy Ackerman's last few days at work. I retrieved my VW from the parking lot and headed over to the health center eight blocks away, wondering what Lucy had been up to. I was guessing birth control and probably the permanent sort. If she were having an affair (and determined not to get pregnant again in any event), it would seem logical, but I hadn't any idea how to verify the fact. Medical personnel are notoriously stingy with information like that.

I parked in front of the clinic and grabbed my clipboard from the backseat. I have a supply of all-purpose forms for occasions like this. They look like a cross between a job application and an insurance claim. I filled one out now in Lucy's name and forged her signature at the bottom where it said Authorization to Release Information. As a model, I used the Xerox copy of the withdrawal slip she'd tucked in her passbook. I'll admit my methods would be considered unorthodox, nay illegal, in the eyes of law-enforcement officers everywhere, but I reasoned that the information I was seeking would never actually be used in court, and therefore it couldn't matter *that* much how it was obtained.

I went into the clinic, noting gratefully the near-empty waiting room. I approached the counter and took out my wallet with my California Fidelity ID. I do occasional insurance investigations for CF in exchange for office space. They once made the mistake of issuing me a company identification card with my picture right on it that I've been flashing around quite shamelessly ever since.

I had a choice of three female clerks and, after a brief assessment, I made eye contact with the oldest of them. In places like this, the younger employees usually have no authority at all and are, thus, impossible to con. People without authority will often simply stand there, reciting the rules like mynah birds. Having no power, they also seem to take a vicious satisfaction in forcing others to comply.

The woman approached the counter on her side, looking at me expectantly. I showed her my CF ID and made the form on the clipboard conspicuous, as though I had nothing to hide.

"Hi. My name is Kinsey Millhone," I said. "I wonder if you can give me some help. Your name is what?"

She seemed wary of the request, as though her name had magical powers that might be taken from her by force. "Lillian Vincent," she said reluctantly. "What sort of help did you need?"

"Lucy Ackerman has applied for some insurance benefits and we need verification of the claim. You'll want a copy of the release form for your files, of course."

I passed the forged paper to her and then busied myself with my clipboard as though it were all perfectly matter-of-fact.

She was instantly alert. "What is this?"

I gave her a look. "Oh, sorry. She's applying for maternity leave and we need her due date."

"Maternity leave?"

"Isn't she a patient here?"

Lillian Vincent looked at me. "Just a moment," she said, and moved away from the desk with the form in hand. She went to a file cabinet and extracted a chart, returning to the counter. She pushed it over to me. "The woman has had a tubal ligation," she said, her manner crisp.

I blinked, smiling slightly as though she were making a joke. "There must be some mistake."

"Lucy Ackerman must have made it then if she thinks she can pull this off." She opened the chart and tapped significantly at the August 2 date. "She was just in here Friday for a final checkup and a medical release. She's sterile."

I looked at the chart. Sure enough, that's what it said. I raised my eyebrows and then shook my head slightly. "God. Well. I guess I better have a copy of that."

"I should think so," the woman said, and ran one off for me on the desktop dry copier. She placed it on the counter and watched as I tucked it onto my clipboard.

She said, "I don't know how they think they can get away with it."

"People love to cheat," I replied.

It was nearly noon by the time I got back to the travel agency next door to the place where Lucy Ackerman had worked. It didn't take any time at all to unearth the reservations she'd made two weeks before. Buenos Aires, first class on Pan Am. For one. She'd picked up the ticket Friday afternoon just before the agency closed for the weekend.

The travel agent rested his elbows on the counter and looked at me with interest, hoping to hear all the gory details, I'm sure. "I heard about that business next door," he said. He was young, maybe twenty-four, with a pug nose, auburn hair, and a gap between his teeth. He'd make the perfect costar on a wholesome family TV show.

"How'd she pay for the tickets?"

"Cash," he said. "I mean, who'd have thunk?"

"Did she say anything in particular at the time?"

"Not really. She seemed jazzed and we joked some about Montezuma's revenge and stuff like that. I knew she was married and I was asking her all about who was keeping the kids and what her old man was going to do while she was gone. God, I never in a million *years* guessed she was pulling off a scam like that, you know?"

"Did you ask why she was going to Argentina by herself?"

"Well, yeah, and she said it was a surprise." He shrugged. "It didn't really make sense, but she was laughing like a kid, and I thought I just didn't get the joke."

I asked for a copy of the itinerary, such as it was. She had paid for a round-trip ticket, but there were no reservations coming back. Maybe she intended to cash in the return ticket once she got down there. I tucked the travel docs onto my clipboard along with the copy of her medical forms. Something about this whole deal had begun to chafe, but I couldn't figure out quite why.

"Thanks for your help," I said, heading toward the door.

"No problem. I guess the other guy didn't get it either," he remarked.

I paused, midstride, turning back. "Get what?"

"The joke. I heard 'em next door and they were fighting like cats and dogs. He was pissed."

"Really?" I said. I stared at him. "What time was this?"

"Five-fifteen. Something like that. They were closed and so were we, but Dad wanted me to stick around for a while until the cleaning crew got here. He owns this place, which is how I got in the business myself. These new guys were starting and he wanted me to make sure they understood what to do."

"Are you going to be here for a while?"

"Sure."

"Good. The police may want to hear about this."

I went back into the escrow office with mental alarm bells clanging away like crazy. Both Barbara Hemdahl and Mrs. Merriman had opted to eat lunch in. Or maybe the cops had ordered them to stay where they were. The book-keeper sat at her desk with a sandwich, an apple, and a carton of milk neatly arranged in front of her, while Mrs. Merriman picked at something in a plastic container she must have brought in from a fast-food place.

"How's it going?" I asked.

Barbara Hemdahl spoke up from her side of the room. "The detectives went off for a search warrant so they can get in all the lockers back there, collecting evidence."

"Only one of 'em is locked," I pointed out.

She shrugged. "I guess they can't even peek without the paperwork."

Mrs. Merriman spoke up then, her expression tinged with guilt. "Actually, they asked the rest of us if we'd open our lockers voluntarily, so of course we did."

Mrs. Merriman and Barbara Hemdahl exchanged a look. "And?"

Mrs. Merriman colored slightly. "There was an overnight case in Mr. Sotherland's locker and I guess the things in it were hers."

"Is it still back there?"

"Well, yes, but they left a uniformed officer on guard so nobody'd walk off with it. They've got everything spread out on the copy machine."

I went through the rear of the office, peering into the storage room. I knew the guy on duty and he didn't object to my doing a visual survey of the items, as long as I didn't touch anything. The overnight case had been packed with all the personal belongings women like to keep on hand in case the rest of the luggage gets sent to Mexicali by mistake. I spotted a toothbrush and toothpaste, slippers, a filmy nightie, prescription drugs, hairbrush, extra eyeglasses in a case. Tucked under a change of underwear, I spotted a round plastic container, slightly convex, about the size of a compact.

Gavin Sotherland was still sitting at his desk when I stopped by his office. His skin tone was gray and his shirt was hanging out, big rings of sweat under each arm. He was smoking a cigarette with the air of a man who's quit the habit and has taken it up again under duress. A second uniformed officer was standing just inside the door to my right.

I leaned against the frame, but Gavin scarcely looked up.

I said, "You knew what she was doing, but you thought she'd take you with her when she left."

His smile was bitter. "Life is full of surprises," he said.

I was going to have to tell Robert Ackerman what I'd discovered and I dreaded it. As a stalling maneuver, just to demonstrate what a good girl I was, I drove over to the police station first and dropped off the data I'd collected, filling them in on the theory I'd come up with. They didn't exactly pin a medal on me, but they weren't as pissed off as I thought they'd be, given the number of penal codes I'd violated in the process. They were even moderately courteous, which is unusual in their treatment of me. Unfortunately, none of it took that long and before I knew it, I was standing at the Ackermans' front door again.

I rang the bell and waited, bad jokes running through my head. Well, there's good news and bad news, Robert. The good news is we've wrapped it up with hours to spare so you won't have to pay me the full three hundred dollars we agreed to. The bad news is your wife's a thief, she's probably dead, and we're just getting out a warrant now, because we think we know where the body's stashed.

The door opened and Robert was standing there with a finger to his lips. "The kids are down for their naps," he whispered.

I nodded elaborately, pantomiming my understanding, as though the silence he'd imposed required this special behavior on my part.

He motioned me in and together we tiptoed through the house and out to the backyard, where we continued to talk in low tones. I wasn't sure which bedroom the little rug rats slept in, and I didn't want to be responsible for waking them.

Half a day of playing papa to the boys had left Robert looking disheveled and sorely in need of relief.

"I didn't expect you back this soon," he whispered.

I found myself whispering too, feeling anxious at the sense of secrecy. It reminded me of grade school somehow;

the smell of autumn hanging in the air, the two of us perched on the edge of the sandbox like little kids, conspiring. I didn't want to break his heart, but what was I to do?

"I think we've got it wrapped up," I said.

He looked at me for a moment, apparently guessing from my expression that the news wasn't good. "Is she okay?"

"We don't think so," I said. And then I told him what I'd learned, starting with the embezzlement and the relationship with Gavin, taking it right through to the quarrel the travel agent had heard. Robert was way ahead of me.

"She's dead, isn't she?"

"We don't know it for a fact, but we suspect as much."

He nodded, tears welling up. He wrapped his arms around his knees and propped his chin on his fists. He looked so young. I wanted to reach out and touch him. "She was really having an affair?" he asked plaintively.

"You must have suspected as much," I said. "You said she was restless and excited for months. Didn't that give you a clue?"

He shrugged one shoulder, using the sleeve of his T-shirt to dash at the tears trickling down his cheeks. "I don't know," he said. "I guess."

"And then you stopped by the office Friday afternoon and found her getting ready to leave the country. That's when you killed her, isn't it?"

He froze, staring at me. At first, I thought he'd deny it, but maybe he realized there wasn't any point. He nodded mutely.

"And then you hired me to make it look good, right?"

He made a kind of squeaking sound in the back of his throat, and sobbed once, his voice reduced to a whisper again. "She shouldn't have done it—betrayed us like that. We loved her so much."

"Have you got the money here?"

He nodded, looking miserable. "I wasn't going to pay your fee out of that," he said incongruously. "We really did have a little fund so we could go to San Diego one day."

"I'm sorry things didn't work out," I said.

"I didn't do so bad, though, did I? I mean, I could have gotten away with it, don't you think?"

I'd been talking about the trip to the zoo. He thought I

was referring to his murdering his wife. Talk about poor communication. God.

"Well, you nearly pulled it off," I said. Shit, I was sitting there trying to make the guy *feel* good.

He looked at me piteously, eyes red and flooded, his mouth trembling. "But where did I slip up? What did I do wrong?"

"You put her diaphragm in the overnight case you packed. You thought you'd shift suspicion onto Gavin Sotherland, but you didn't realize she'd had her tubes tied."

A momentary rage flashed through his eyes and then flickered out. I suspected that her voluntary sterilization was more insulting to him than the affair with her boss.

"Jesus, I don't know what she saw in him," he breathed. "He was such a pig."

"Well," I said, "if it's any comfort to you, she wasn't going to take *him* either. She just wanted freedom, you know?"

He pulled out a handkerchief and blew his nose, trying to compose himself. He mopped his eyes, shivering with tension. "How can you prove it, though, without a body? Do you know where she is?"

"I think we do," I said softly. "The sandbox, Robert. Right under us."

He seemed to shrink. "Oh, God," he whispered. "Oh, God, don't turn me in. I'll give you the money, I don't give a damn. Just let me stay here with my kids. The little guys need me. I did it for them. I swear I did. You don't have to tell the cops, do you?"

I shook my head and opened my shirt collar, showing him the mike. "I don't have to tell a soul," I said, and then I looked over toward the side yard.

For once, I was glad to see Lieutenant Dolan amble into view.

C IS FOR COOKIE
Rob Kantner

FIRST APPEARANCE: *This Story*, 1982

Rob Kantner is one of only two writers who has won four Shamus Awards. The other is Lawrence Block. Pretty good company, huh? His detective, Ben Perkins, first appeared in this story in *Alfred Hitchcock's Mystery Magazine* in 1982. He has gone on to appear in eight novels since *The Back Door Man* (Bantam, 1986).

"No" isn't a word I like to say to pretty women. But I'd said it to Charlotte Ambrose, in no uncertain terms, when she disappeared from the restaurant, leaving me stuck with her screaming two-year-old charge.

I hadn't wanted to meet her in the first place. Charlotte and I were an old deal, long dead and a bitter memory. But in that excited, rich-broad, enthusiastic way of hers, she'd persuaded me on the phone to meet her at Mr. Mike's in Westland to talk over an "assignment." There was money in it for me, she said. That tipped the scales in favor of going, if only barely.

It had been twelve years so she looked older, but she was still the white-blond, creamy Nordic, limber, and sensual Charlotte that I remembered. And the money she offered was my usual rate—two fifty per day plus expenses. But the job was crap, a locate job on a boyfriend of hers who'd disappeared. I turned her down without a second thought, partly because I didn't like the sound of the job and partly for the satisfaction of saying no to her just once and, in that small, petty way, getting back at her for what she'd done to me years before. And then, without the slightest warning, she excused herself to go to the rest room and just plain dropped out of sight.

I didn't realize it at first, of course. I finished my beer and smoked a cigar and stared absently around the restaurant at the handful of people there. Then the kid, a chubby little blue-eyed boy named Will, commenced to screaming. I fidgeted, offering him crackers to eat and utensils to play with, but he sent up a howl to the ceiling, his plump face red like a balloon. Charlotte's pit stop stretched abnormally long, and I finally sent a waitress to check up on her. Gone, she said. Not in the parking lot, either. Leaving me alone with the brat.

"I know she's a bitch," Kate said, "but why would she abandon her kid? With you?"

We were in my apartment in Belleville and the kid was clinging to my leg, staring at Kate. He'd stopped hollering about halfway back from Mr. Mike's and was doing the shy wide-eyed bit, occasionally issuing a hiccup. Kate was staying with me for a few days because her ex-husband, whose name is, apparently, That Jerk, was conducting his semiannual harassment campaign against her and she needed a place to hide out. I said, "The kid's not hers. She told me she was baby-sitting him for a friend who was away for a few days."

Kate was a short shaggy off-blond, painfully thin and gaunt, and she wore her usual expression of half skepticism and half harried patience. "You know, in the six years we've been involved, I've seen you get people shot in my house, and I've seen you rough up deputy sheriffs, and I've seen you take some of the sleaziest characters in the world out for dinner. But I never imagined you'd bring home an abandoned toddler."

"That's why you should stick around, kid. Officially I may be just an apartment maintenance guy, but there's always more to Perkins than that." I disengaged Will from my leg and headed into the kitchen to build a drink and figure out what to do. Kate went over to the kid. "Are you hungry, Will?"

"Ha," he said seriously, his face still flushed.

To Kate's arched eyebrow I interpreted, having picked up a little of the kid's jargon, "Yes."

"See cookie," Will added.

"I'll check," she answered. As she pawed through the cupboards, I poured myself some straight Jack Daniel's. Groping among the boxes, wrappers, and debris, she said, "I take it you turned her down."

"I did."

She found a bag of stale Oreos and handed one to the boy, who practically inhaled it, looking hopefully and much more happily at Kate. "What was the job?"

"Some boyfriend of hers disappeared. She wanted him found. I wasn't up for it."

"Sure, Ben. But now you're stuck with the kid. What do you plan to do about that?"

Will had found the bathroom and I heard the toilet flush. Thank God—a good, disciplined, toilet-trained little kid. He came out of the bathroom sans jeans and trailing a long stream of toilet paper. As Kate and I both dived to gather it up, I said, "She's just peevish. Sooner or later she'll call me and tell me who the kid's mother is. Or, even better, I'll call her." I left Kate to pull the kid's pants back on, shoved the bundle of toilet paper into the wastebasket, and went to the phone, where I found taped to it a slip with a telephone number.

"The Kroger's store in Belleville called," Kate said from behind me. "Apparently the check you passed there bounced."

"I didn't *pass* a check, I *gave* them one. And if it bounced, it's probably some screwup." At least I hoped so, since my checking account seemed to have a mind of its own. I reached for the phone and it rang as my hand touched the receiver.

"Enjoying the baby-sitting?" Charlotte asked sweetly.

I sighed. "Nice gag, Charlotte."

Kate leaned her blue-jeaned fanny against the edge of the counter, listening. The boy was studiously opening and closing cupboard doors but apparently was well brought up enough not to mess with anything inside. In my ear, Charlotte laughed and said, "I *do* rather fancy the idea of your taking care of a little baby boy, but I must confess that humor wasn't my only motive."

Charlotte never did anything that didn't redound to her advantage. "So fill me in," I said evenly.

"You do the job, Ben," she said. "Find Chuck Crane for me. And then I'll tell you where the kid belongs. Don't worry, nobody's looking for him right now. You've got enough time, if you're at all as talented at your work as I'm told you are. And I'll pay you as agreed."

The boy, having decided I was okay, I guess, was giving me a sunny, radiant look, which was about all I needed just then.

I said, "This is one sick, twisted game you're playing, Charlotte."

"But effective. And don't think about trying to track me down. I'm where you could never, ever find me. You'll never find the boy's mother, either. When you have the answer, call my home number and leave word on my message box. Within four hours I'll call you back and we'll meet someplace. Do it fast, Ben." She hung up.

I slammed the phone down and banged my fist against the wall, which got me nothing but sore knuckles. Kate looked more gaunt than usual. I told her the story and she said immediately, "So turn the kid over to the cops. Simple enough."

I sat down on a chair and lit a small cork-tipped cigar. After a long pause I said, "Nope. Not right now, anyway."

"Why, for God's sake?"

"Because," I said without looking at her, "I take care of things myself. I don't dump them off on someone else. You know that."

"So you're going to let that ruthless swine strong-arm you," she jibed.

The boy stood between us, eyes wide, not understanding the words but picking up on the tone, for sure. "I can't win every point, Kate."

"Yeah," she said grimly, pushing herself away from the counter and going to the sink. She made herself speciously busy with some dishes. "You just want to do it. This is just a convenient excuse to get involved with her again. You just don't learn, do you."

It was a dumb argument and one I'd run out of patience with. Getting to my feet, I said, "You got a choice. Come with me while I try to get a line on this Crane fella, or sit here and sulk."

"I'll stay here, thanks," she said. "The boy's had enough moving around for one day. You go and help your girlfriend."

Kate could sure turn on a person, I reflected as I headed out I-94 in my seventy-one Mustang. It had been getting worse lately, worse than ever. After six years, it was finally going sour. I knew it and she knew it; what we hadn't got around to yet was what Bob Seger calls "the famous final scene."

She came close to starting one with that girlfriend crack, though—as if I wanted to do the job, as if Charlotte meant anything to me anymore. Fact was, I was feeling nothing but cold burning fury at what she'd done, exploiting a helpless two-year-old and the boy's unknowing family. But it was like her.

We'd met in the mid-sixties under the most clichéd of circumstances: her mother and my mom fixed us up. The two women couldn't have been more different. Charlotte's mother was your typical Franklin Village matron, and my mom was a nursing home supervisor who boarded kids for rich folks to make a few extra bucks. (Sidelines, you see, are an old Perkins family tradition, though my mom's moonlighting was far more respectable than mine.)

One of my mom's boarders—and a real brat as I recall—was Charlotte's younger brother. My mom thought it would be good for me to find a "nice girl" from a "good family" and settle down. And forget the questionable job I had as aide to a union boss with a smudged reputation. What Charlotte's mother thought isn't on the record, although I suspect she welcomed the suit of a no-frills straight arrow like me after seeing a steady parade of giggle-headed rich kids march through Charlotte's life. Shy Charlotte wasn't.

It started for laughs and got heavy quick, quicker than either of us expected. Unlike most of the women I'd known until then, Charlotte was dynamic. Her considerable physical attributes aside, she was bright, enthusiastic, challenging, tough-minded, and exciting. Her bright light burned white hot, attracting people to her; and sometimes I'd sit and wonder what she saw in me, a straight, sober, hard-edged Detroit boy on the make.

We got ourselves a house in the Jefferson-Chalmers neighborhood. It was one of the older ones, a rambling yellow brick place on the Detroit River with its own boat-house. My job was increasingly intense and dangerous, and Charlotte was meteoric and unpredictable and not the easiest person in the world to live with, and yet, all these years later, I remember those days as being tranquil. I remember barbecue dinners out on the big airy porch; long walks along the river; card games and beer of an evening with one or two of the young couples who lived around us; evenings spent in debate; sunrise strolls around the Belle Isle fountain; afternoons making love in the enormous second-story riverfront bedroom while the curtains floated in the air and freighters glided by outside in ghostly silence.

The riot in 1967 changed things for keeps. My mom's nursing home got torched and she died on the second day, trying to get an inmate out. The feds came after my boss and some others on tax and racketeering charges and they zeroed in on me, trying to make me Public Snitch Number One. I refused to talk, even though they gave me immunity; my name got in the papers; and one day, when it looked as if I was going to jail on contempt charges, I came home to find Charlotte gone. Not a word. Just empty closets and her car gone from the garage.

Things bottomed out then, thank God. The feds made their case via the net worth method, the defendants went off to Lewisburg, and I went off the hook. A lot of years passed and I never heard of Charlotte again—and thought of her as little as possible, which is to say once a day.

But I didn't rehash ancient history on my way to South-field. Instead, I tried to piece together what I'd half heard from Charlotte as she told me about her mysterious Chuck Crane. A thin, wiry, athletic man, she said, in his mid-thirties. She'd met him on St. Patrick's Day at one of the Irish bars on the west side. He lived in the Franklin Park Towers and drove a Corvette. He had lots of clothes, man-ners, style, money, and smarts, and he never seemed to work. He called himself an "investor." He and Charlotte made several long trips together, one to Switzerland, one to the Bahamas, and she introduced him to her daddy, whom I once sarcastically referred to as the "oil seal king." By Charlotte's standards the affair was serious.

Until he disappeared a month ago.

The Franklin Park Towers sprawl at the intersection where the Lodge Freeway dumps out onto I-696 heading west and Telegraph Road shoots north toward Pontiac. There's a lot of government land there, including a couple of military reserve outfits and an old Nike missile base; there are also shopping centers, synagogues, and endless miles of well-heeled subdivisions with names like Bingham Farms, Mayfair, and Beverly Hills. I've often thought of it as the place where Detroit busted open and gushed people north.

The apartments are huge and glum looking, the style known as Twentieth-Century Insane Asylum. Pretty they aren't, but they happen to be one of the prestige addresses of the Detroit area. I found Crane's apartment and, with the timely help of a skeleton key I'd acquired at great cost some years before (its previous owner is now a guest of the state at Marquette), gained entry.

It was a single-bedroom place, conspicuously neat and sterile; rented furniture, nothing personal on the walls, none of the little debris of personality in the place at all. I had the bizarre feeling that I'd broken by accident into the complex's model apartment—a place everyone looked at but no one lived in—not a place where a wealthy young man had lived for several years. Judging from the dry sink, the painstaking orderliness of the silverware and plates, the clean dry tub, and the absence of dirty linen, it looked to me as if no one had lived there for a month or more, maybe. There was also a feeling of emptiness. Like a personality had been there once but had left for good.

The resident rental agent wasn't much help. He had, after all, a huge number of tenants to keep track of, and he didn't know any of them personally, let alone Chuck Crane. I also don't think he was overly impressed with my cover story that I was an investigator for Mass Mutual Insurance. He glumly went through his records anyway, giving me beady little hostile looks. Yes, Crane had rented the apartment. He'd paid his rent a year in advance (and the thought occurred to me: who in his right mind does *that*?). No, there were never any complaints about him. Where Crane worked was not the agent's business. The only concrete thing I could get out of him was Crane's license plate number. A thin, very frail thread, but the best I could do.

I headed south on Telegraph to the huge, cylindrical Holiday Inn, went inside to a bank of phones, and called a friend in Lansing. She's a financial analyst for the state of Michigan, and a damned good one, and she has that invaluable resource for a fellow in my line of work, direct and unlimited access to the state's computer records. She even carries a portable terminal home, which was where I found her. I think helping me is a kick for her, even though she fusses a lot about my occasional requests. I help her out with things from time to time, and buy her lunch in Detroit once a month, so it evens out. Sort of.

She put me on hold and was gone quite a while firing up her terminal and going into the computer on her second telephone line. She came back to tell me that Crane's car was registered to a firm called Pan Peninsular Products— such a Michigan kind of name I was surprised they didn't throw a "Wolverine" in—based in the Penobscot Building in Detroit. I asked, in passing, for a rundown on the company and she said it would take some time and she'd get back to me on it later that night.

It was pushing late afternoon by then, but I headed straight down to the Penobscot. It was tired looking and half empty, like many downtown office buildings since the Renaissance Center went up a few years back. Pan Peninsular occupied a suite on the tenth floor. I stood in the echoing hallway and did my magic act with a skeleton key again. I found the suite stripped clean—nothing left but the stink of cigarettes, a couple of rickety, ready-for-junkyard desks, and severed coils of telephone cables. Pan Peninsular no longer existed, as far as I could tell, except for the name neatly stenciled on the rippled glass door.

The TV flickered color into the otherwise dark living room of my apartment as I entered. In the strange strobelike light, Kate's gaunt face looked stark and stony. She turned to me as I closed the door and said without greeting, "Garden City Medical Center called while you were gone. That check you sent them on your Uncle Dan's account bounced."

I went purposefully into the kitchen, poured myself a big shot of Jack Daniel's black, and rescued a bottle of Stroh's from the refrigerator. Back in the living room I saw that Kate wasn't drinking—a bad sign. I said, "Where's the boy?"

"Sleeping in your bed. He fell asleep about eight, after wiping out your Oreo supply, two hot dogs, and an entire can of pork and beans. God, if my kids had eaten like that. . . . What's with your checking account lately, anyway? You underfinanced, or something?"

"Nah, that's not it," I said absently. I sat down at the other end of the couch from her and noted that she made no move to slide down and join me. In a feeble attempt to get past our awkwardness, I told her what I'd found out—which amounted to a big fat zero. I finished, "So Crane's a big phony. The only question is, what was his game and where did he go? Hopefully Lansing will get me some information tonight. Maybe I'll get it ironed out and get the kid back home tomorrow."

"And if not you can call the cops," she said flatly.

I got the telephone off the hi-fi cabinet, sat on the couch, shucked my shoes, and dialed Lansing. My friend picked the phone up before the second ring.

"Pan Peninsular's a shell, Ben," she told me.

"What do you mean?"

"It's hollow. Business license and incorporation papers only. No assets, no taxes, the officers are professional front guys. The outfit, as far as the state of Michigan is concerned, is a company in name only."

"Okay, kid, do me some blue-sky. In your experience, what does this mean?"

There was a brief hissing of long-distance silence and then she said, "All right, but this is off the record."

"Always. Always."

"It's one of two things," she said slowly. "Either it's an organization front, for laundering money or something, or . . . just maybe . . . it's a government front, one of those 'sting' operations. I've seen it happen both ways. You get enough official paper to stand a cursory inspection, and go from there."

I got my last cigar out of my shirt pocket and lit it from a wood match struck against my thumbnail. The smoke showed translucent gray, like a navy ship, in the light of the TV set. "Anything more you can tell me? Who do I talk to now?"

She laughed. "Either the organization or someone in Justice. You know the players better than I do, Ben."

"I hear you. Thanks, kid."

"Listen, for this you owe me London Chop House."

"And here I had a nice A and W root beer all picked out for you."

I heard her laugh as I hung up. Kate was watching "The Dukes of Hazzard" and I pondered for a moment. Sure, I knew the players all right, but it had to be approached with great precision. Finally I picked up the phone, searched my memory, and dialed tentatively. My contact wasn't available, which was the routine; I hung up and a few minutes later the phone rang. I snatched it up. My contact was upset, highly upset. He spoke in that business-speak dialect that indicated he was worried about my phone's being tapped, despite the number of years he's known me.

I gave him a few pieces of information, but didn't muscle him, partly because I've never needed to, and partly because it wouldn't have worked. My strongest selling point was that Pan Peninsular had closed up shop and Crane had disappeared, so it was old business and there was no reason not to give me the story. My contact hemmed and hawed and then certified to me that Chuck Crane was not known among his colleagues, in either the Detroit or Pontiac operations, and that there had been no business involving such a person. I hung up, knowing that the next call would tell the tale.

The "Dukes" were on commercial. Kate stirred and said, "You know, it's a pity."

"What's that, kid?"

"We're alone in the room and you're not even here."

Hell of a time for heavy mysteries. "Look, it's late and I've got a few more calls to make, okay?"

She shrugged. I picked up the phone again and called

the highest police authority I knew, Detective Captain Elvin Dance of the Detroit Police Department.

I first got to know Elvin when he was a strikebreaker with one of the car companies in the early sixties. Fortunately, he went legit after that and joined the police department and did very well for himself. To no one's surprise. Elvin is a good, solid, practical cop, half politician and half lawman, a remarkable combination for a man who grew up in a slum and earned his Ph.D. at night at Wayne State. He was on duty, which wasn't unusual, and at his desk, which was.

"Run that by one more time, Ben."

"What I said was," I said distinctly, "you find whoever you have to and tell them I know about Crane and the sting operation he was running. I don't know what his game was and I don't care. All I want to know is where the man is." I felt my heart pounding. "Or I'll go to every media organ in town and turn them loose on it. Confidentiality guaranteed. This is information for a client of mine not involved in the business."

"You know, Ben," he said, his voice a coarse growl, "there's been some heavy federal action round here lately. Mucho sensitive. How much of that big nose of yours you want whacked off? I'm just asking, as a friend of yours."

I said, "You get the word out now. I want a call back from a top player tonight. That happens, and nothing further gets said to anybody."

He sighed, "I'll look into it, man."

The Duke boys were headed toward their showdown with the Boss, and I didn't feel welcome to interrupt. Instead I morosely smoked my cigar, thinking about the downside: red lights in the parking lot, handcuffs on the wrists, the fast hustle to the waiting car, the grim professional faces firing tough professional questions. I'd come close to it before, but usually for better reasons than helping a selfish, strong-willed adrenaline junkie.

And the phone rang. I picked it up with a slippery hand. It was Bill Scozzafava, the bartender at my local watering hole, Under New Management.

"You ever heard of uttering and publishing, stupid?"

It was his polite and legal way of informing me that one

of my Detroit Bank drafts had gone rubber on him. I smoothed him over, promising him cash money the next day. I cut off the conversation as quickly as I could and hung up. I was getting tired and my mind was wandering and it seemed like only moments later when the phone rang again.

The voice was, as might be expected, unknown to me. Anonymous, masculine, bland, purposeful. It said, "You have made inquiries about a man named Crane. You have made certain guarantees. We accept the guarantees because we have the means to enforce them, as you probably recall from your encounter with us in the late sixties. What you need to know about the story is as follows . . ."

When I hung up, Kate was gone. I found her sleeping with Will in my bed. It was a pretty picture. I went back to the living room and with thick fingers punched out Charlotte's number. Her answering machine gave a perky spiel and when the tone sounded I told her to meet me at the Belle Isle fountain at seven. Good a place as any.

I found a thin summer blanket in my linen closet and wrapped it around me like a shroud and fell into an awkward and restless sleep on the couch.

She wore a white blouse open to the breasts and white deck pants over white sandals, and she sat on the rim of the defunct Belle Isle fountain. A short distance away on the curving drive was a knee-high, stainless steel DeLorean that I assumed was hers. I parked behind it and walked over to her. The sun was rising over Windsor to the south, bathing her white-blond hair and casting ambivalent shadows of darkness and light over the pathetic grandeur of the dry fountain. I sat down a piece away from her and lit a cigar, filling my rusted mouth and lungs with good coarse smoke.

"You owe me a name."

With an amused and triumphant look, she retorted, "*You* owe *me* the story."

"Know anybody in cocaine, Charlotte?"

She squinted into the sun and smiled at me, her impossibly white and even teeth glinting in the new sun. "Of course. Doesn't everybody?"

"I'm talking traffic, not the trendy geeks into an occasional party snort."

"You know me," she said smugly. "I only deal with the top people in any field."

"Seen any of them around lately?" I asked wearily.

In the silence she slowly straightened and began, by God, to look a little uncertain. "No, it's gotten pretty quiet. What are you getting at, Ben?"

"Your friend Crane was DEA. That's Drug Enforcement Administration, the Justice arm that handles drugs since the FBI has never had jurisdiction in that particular area. Crane's part of a real small, elite group. They're called the Flying Squad. They're moles, Charlotte. They move into an area and live three, four, five years undercover. They work their way into the drug traffic, build the book on the top people in it, turn the case, and disappear. They never even stay around to testify, their work is that thorough. They don't have names. They don't have real identities or lives. The case is their whole life."

I hadn't noticed it before, but the sharp uncaring sunlight was showing a pattern of lines and creases in her face that weren't there twelve years ago. Apparently the years hadn't been any kinder to her than I was. It occurred to me how vital her flip, arrogant attitude was to her good looks. She said flatly, "So he busted them."

"He's in St. Louis now, burrowing his way in. You'll never see him again. It wasn't real to him, Charlotte, it was just a case and you were part of it."

She stood up angrily. "It was more than that to him. Believe me, I know." She thought of something. "After all, he protected me. He didn't turn me in with the rest."

She was asking for it and I didn't hesitate to give it to her. "You're a dilettante, Charlotte. A thrill-seeking groupie. He's a pro and he sized you up right away. He knew, with your social connections, he could ride you right into the mainstream. But once he had the case nailed down, you were nothing to him anymore. He got the principals but didn't bother with you because you were nothing but small fry. And guys like him have no use for small fry."

She smiled, but it was forced, the bright light extinguished. "You know," she said, cocking her head to one side as she narrowed her eyes, "I had other reasons for wanting to see you. The assignment wasn't the only thing. I did care for you—"

"You didn't care for me. You loved my game. The union, the scandal, the investigation, the notoriety. I finally worked that out for myself, when I was trying to deal with the fact that you ran like a rat when my back was to the wall. You wanted the game but you couldn't take the heat."

"No," she shouted, her face lean and ugly, "I left because you were just what you are now: nothing! Look at you! A maintenance man and ... and a detective! All you've gotten is older. You haven't gotten anywhere, after all these years, haven't achieved a thing, just another flunky."

"As opposed to you, presumably."

After a long silence, she nodded abruptly and hooked her thumbs in the waistband of her pants. "Well, I got what I wanted." She took a step to go, then hesitated. "I wish I hadn't had to use the kid to muscle you, but the results speak for themselves. His mother will be out at your place this morning to pick Will up. She'll never speak to me again, of course, but that's not a big price to pay."

She turned. "Good-bye, Ben."

"Just a minute," I said roughly, taking her arm. She turned, her blue eyes directed indifferently at me. "You're into this flunky for a day and some gas money. Call it two seventy-five and we're quits."

She smiled contemptuously, went into her purse, and counted out two C-notes and four twenties. I curled them into a stiff tube and stuck them into my shirt pocket, then fished out a crumpled five and gave it to her. Without another word or look, I headed back to my car. She called something that the rising wind muffled. It might have been thanks but, knowing Charlotte, it probably wasn't.

The tension was electric in my kitchen. The boy was hunkered on his knees on one of my chairs at the small dinette, spooning Cheerios sloppily into his mouth. Kate was at the other end of the table, cupping a mug of coffee in her hands. And another woman sat between her and Will, a tall medium blond with a long voluptuous figure and a Lady Diana haircut. She rose, a worried, uncertain smile on her face, and Kate said to me, "This is Will's mother, Ben. Carole Somers."

Mrs. Somers wore a one-piece denim dress that ended just below her knees, revealing elegant long legs beneath. Her eyes warmed up as she held out her hand and I shook it. "From what Kate's been telling me, Mr. Perkins, I owe you a ton of thanks—and a certain ex-friend a punch in the jaw." Despite the words, her dark brown eyes were merry, her smile as golden as her hair.

"Name's Ben, Carole. No thanks needed. Charlotte mentioned you were an old friend of hers?" I let her hand go, still feeling its warmth in my palm.

The boy was giving me that radiant, adoring look again, and this wasn't lost on Carole, who smiled. "Past tense, for sure. You too?"

"With seniority." I grinned. Kate sat straight-faced, watching me as I poured myself a cup of coffee and leaned back against the counter. "You leave the boy with her often?"

Carole shrugged. "Once in a while, when I have to travel. When I got in at Metro this morning there was a message from her telling me where to pick Will up. I was curious but not alarmed. Not until Kate told me the story." She gave the boy a smile. "You sure took good care of him."

"It was Kate," I admitted.

"No trouble," Kate shrugged.

"See cookie," Will announced.

"We're all out," Kate said. "This kid and cookies—"

"Oh, that's not what he means," Carole laughed. "He watches 'Sesame Street' and that's a song the Cookie Monster sings. " 'C is for Cookie, that's good enough for me.' "

Kate wasn't exactly mirthful that morning, but she laughed with us at that. Carole got up then, gathered up Will, and headed for the door. I followed her and found out as she thanked me effusively that she lived in Berkley and wanted to keep in touch with me. Well, that made two of us.

Back in the kitchen, Kate handed me the phone, which I hadn't heard ring. "Detroit Bank."

The lady was very upset with me. I bank by mail, mainly, and I'd sent in a couple of payroll checks and forgotten to endorse them. They promptly mailed them back for endorsement, but since I'm pretty lazy and don't open my mail more than once a week, I didn't know what had gone wrong until the bank, nervous, began bouncing my checks all over the place. I endured the lecture, promised to stop in and correct the problem, and hung up.

Kate was at the door, lugging her overnight bag. "What do you say?" she asked lightly.

Theoretically, after six years, plenty. But I inquired, "What about That Jerk?"

"He's probably given up by now. If not I'll run him off. God knows I've done it before." She opened the door and turned to me, at the very edge of her composure. "Isn't it the damndest thing. C is for Cookie. Sometimes we forget." Then she hefted her bag and left quickly.

I shut the door and thought that, if she'd stayed, I'd probably have replied that C also stands for cocaine, checks, conspiracies. But I've found that you usually don't get to say everything you want to during the famous final scene.

I suppose you could say I netted out on the deal. Kate was gone, but there was Carole, whom I saw lot of in the time that followed. And I made friends with a damned nice little kid, my first brush with domesticity.

Ironic, I guess.

Charlotte wanted something badly but didn't get it. I came into the situation not wanting or expecting anything, but got plenty. And got paid besides.

THE STRAWBERRY TEARDROP
Max Allan Collins
FIRST APPEARANCE: *True Detective*, 1983

With *True Detective* (St. Martin's Press, 1983), his first Nathan Heller novel, Max Collins virtually created a new genre for himself, the historical private eye novel. Over the course of six novels he has won the Shamus for best PI novel twice. Only he, Lawrence Block, and Sue Grafton have achieved that feat.

The most recent Heller novel is *Blood and Thunder.*

This story first appeared in *The Eyes Have It* (Mysterious Press, 1984).

In a garbage dump on East Ninth Street near Shore Drive, in Cleveland, Ohio, on August 17, 1938, a woman's body was discovered by a cop walking his morning beat.

I got there before anything much had been moved. Not that I was a plainclothes dick—I used to be, but not in Cleveland; I was just along for the ride. I'd been sitting in the office of Cleveland's public safety director, having coffee, when the call came through. The safety director was in charge of both the police and fire department, and one would think that a routine murder wouldn't rate a call to such a high muckety-muck.

One would be wrong.

Because this was the latest in a series of anything-but-routine, brutal murders—the unlucky thirteenth, to be exact, not that the thirteenth victim would seem any more unlucky than the preceding twelve. The so-called Mad Butcher of Kingsbury Run had been exercising his ghastly art sporadically since the fall of '35, in Cleveland—or so I understood. I was an out-of-towner, myself.

So was the woman.

Or she used to be, before she became so many dismembered parts flung across this rock-and-garbage-strewn dump. Her nude torso was slashed and the blood, splashed here, streaked there, was turning dark, almost black, though the sun caught scarlet glints and tossed them at us. Her head was gone, but maybe it would turn up. The Butcher wasn't known for that, though. The twelve preceding victims had been found headless, and had stayed that way. Somewhere in Cleveland, perhaps, a guy had a collection in his attic. In this weather it wouldn't smell too nice.

It's not a good sign when the medical examiner gets sick; and the half dozen cops, and the police photographer, were looking green around the gills themselves. Only my friend, the safety director, seemed in no danger of losing his breakfast. He was a ruddy-cheeked six-footer in a coat and tie and vest, despite the heat; hatless, his hair brushed back and pomaded, he still seemed—years after I'd met him— boyish. And he was only in his mid-thirties, just a few years older than me.

I'd met him in Chicago, seven or eight years ago, when I wasn't yet president (and everything else) of the A-1 Detective Agency, but still a cop; and he was still a Prohibition agent. Hell, *the* Prohibition agent. He'd considered me one of the more or less honest cops in Chicago—emphasis on the less, I guess—and I made a good contact for him, as a lot of the cops didn't like him much. Honesty doesn't go over real big in Chicago, you know.

Eliot Ness said, "Despite the slashing, there's a certain skill displayed here."

"Yeah, right," I said. "A regular ballet dancer did this."

"No, really," he said, and bent over the headless torso, pointing. He seemed to be pointing at the gathering flies, but he wasn't. "There's an unmistakable precision about this. Maybe even indicating surgical training."

"Maybe," I said. "But I think the doctor lost this patient."

He stood and glanced at me and smiled, just a little; he understood me: he knew my wise-guy remarks were just my way of holding on to my own breakfast.

"You ought to come to Cleveland more often," he said.

"You know how to show a guy a good time, I'll give you that, Eliot."

He walked over and glanced at a forearm, which seemed to reach for an empty soapbox, fingers stretched toward the Gold Dust twins. He knelt and studied it.

I wasn't here on a vacation, by any means. Cleveland didn't strike me as a vacation city, even before I heard about the Butcher of Kingsbury Run (so called because a number of the bodies, including the first several, were found on that Cleveland street). This was strictly business. I was here trying to trace the missing daughter of a guy in Evanston who owned a dozen diners around Chicago. He was one of those self-made men who started out in the greasy kitchen of his own first diner, fifteen or so years ago; and now he had a fancy brick house in Evanston and plenty of money, considering the times. But not much else. His wife had died four or five years ago, of consumption; and his daughter—who he claimed to be a good girl and by all other accounts was pretty wild—had wandered off a few months ago, with a taxi dancer from the Northside named Tony.

Well, I'd found Tony in Toledo—he was doing a floor show in a roadhouse with a dark-haired girl named FiFi; he'd grown a little pencil mustache and they did an apache routine—he was calling himself Antoine now. And Tony/Antoine said Ginger (which was the Evanston restaurateur's daughter's nickname) had taken up with somebody named Ray, who owned (get this) a diner in Cleveland.

I'd gotten here yesterday, and had talked to Ray, and without tipping I was looking for her, asked where was the pretty waitress, the one called Ginger, I think her name is. Ray, a skinny balding guy of about thirty with a silver front tooth, leered and winked and made it obvious that not only was Ginger working as a waitress here, she was also a side dish, where Ray was concerned. Further casual conversation revealed that it was Ginger's night off—she was at the movies with some girlfriends—and she'd be in tomorrow, around five.

I didn't push it further, figuring to catch up with her at the diner the next evening, after wasting a day seeing Cleveland and bothering my old friend Eliot. And now I was in a city dump with him, watching him study the severed forearm of a woman.

"Look at this," Eliot said, pointing at the outstretched fingers of the hand.

I went over to him and it. Not quickly, but I went over.

"What, Eliot? Do you want to challenge my powers of deduction, or just make me sick?"

"Just a lucky break," he said. "Most of the victims have gone unidentified; too mutilated. And a lot of 'em have been prostitutes or vagrants. But we've got a break, here. Two breaks actually."

He pointed to the hand's little finger. To the small gold filigree band with a green stone.

"A nice specific piece of jewelry to try to trace," he said, with a dry smile. "And even better ..."

He pointed to a strawberry birthmark, the shape of a teardrop, just below the wrist.

I took a close look; then stood. Put a hand on my stomach.

Walked away and dropped to my knees and lost my breakfast.

I felt Eliot's hand patting my back.

"Nate," he said. "What's the matter? You've seen homicides before ... even grisly ones like this ... brace up, boy."

He eased me to my feet.

My tongue felt thick in my mouth, thick and restless.

"What is it?" he said.

"I think I just found my client's daughter," I said.

Both the strawberry birthmark and the filigree ring with the green stone had been part of my basic description of the girl; the photographs I had showed her to be a pretty but average-looking young woman—slim, brunet—who resembled every third girl you saw on the street. So I was counting on those two specifics to help me identify her. I hadn't counted on those specifics helping me in just this fashion.

I sat in Eliot's inner office in the Cleveland city hall; the mayor's office was next door. We were having coffee with some rum in it—Eliot kept a bottle in a bottom drawer of his rolltop desk. I promised him not to tell Capone.

"I think we should call the father," Eliot said. "Ask him to come and make the identification."

I thought about it. "I'd like to argue with you, but I don't see how I can. Maybe if we waited till . . . Christ. Till the head turns up . . ."

Eliot shrugged. "It isn't likely to. The ring and the birth-mark are enough to warrant notifying the father."

"I can make the call."

"No. I'll let you talk to him when I'm done, but that's something I should do."

And he did. With quiet tact. After a few minutes he handed me the phone; if I'd thought him cold at the scene of the crime, I erased that thought when I saw the damp-ness in his gray eyes.

"Is it my little girl?" the deep voice said, sounding tinny out of the phone.

"I think so, Mr. Jensen. I'm afraid so."

I could hear him weeping.

Then he said: "Mr. Ness said her body was . . . dismem-bered. How can you say it's her? How . . . how can you know it's her?"

And I told him of the ring and the strawberry teardrop.

"I should come there," he said.

"Maybe that won't be necessary." I covered the phone. "Eliot, will my identification be enough?"

He nodded. "We'll stretch it."

I had to argue with Jensen, but finally he agreed for his daughter's remains to be shipped back via train; I said I'd contact a funeral home this afternoon, and accompany her home.

I handed the phone to Eliot to hang up.

We looked at each other and Eliot, not given to swear-ing, said, "I'd give ten years of my life to nail that butch-ering bastard."

"How long will your people need the body?"

"I'll speak to the coroner's office. I'm sure we can send her home with you in a day or two. Where are you staying?"

"The Stadium Hotel."

"Not anymore. I've got an extra room for you. I'm a bachelor again, you know."

We hadn't gotten into that yet; I'd always considered Eliot's marriage an ideal one, and was shocked a few months back to hear it had broken up.

"I'm sorry, Eliot."

"Me too. But I am seeing somebody. Someone you may remember; another Chicagoan."

"Who?"

"Evie MacMillan."

"The fashion illustrator? Nice-looking woman."

Eliot smiled slyly. "You'll see her tonight, at the country club ... but I'll arrange some female companionship for you. I don't want you cutting my time."

"How can you say such a thing? Don't you trust me?"

"I learned a long time ago," he said, turning to his desk full of paperwork, "not to trust Chicago cops—even ex-ones."

Out on the country club terrace, the ten-piece band was playing Cole Porter and a balmy breeze from Lake Erie was playing with the women's hair. There were plenty of good-looking women here—low-cut dresses, bare shoulders—and lots of men in evening clothes for them to dance with. But this was no party, and since some of the golfers were still here from late afternoon rounds, there were sports clothes and a few business suits (like mine) in the mix. Even some of the women were dressed casually, like the tall, slender blond in pink shirt and pale green pleated skirt who sat down next to me at the little white metal table and asked me if I'd have a Bacardi with her. The air smelled like a flower garden, and some of it was flowers, and some of it was her.

"I'd be glad to buy you a Bacardi," I said, clumsily.

"No," she said, touching my arm. She had eyes the color of jade. "You're a guest. I'll buy."

Eliot was dancing with his girl Evie, an attractive brunet in her mid-thirties; she'd always struck me as intelligent but sad, somehow. They smiled over at me.

The blond in pink and pale green brought two Bacardis over, set one of them in front of me, and smiled. "Yes," she said wickedly. "You've been set up. I'm the girl Eliot promised you. But if you were hoping for somebody in an evening gown, I'm not it. I just *had* to get an extra nine holes in."

"If you were looking for a guy in a tux," I said, "I'm not it. And I've never been on a golf course in my life. What else do we have in common?"

She had a nicely wry smile, which continued as she sipped the Bacardi. "Eliot, I suppose. If I have a few more of these, I may tell you a secret."

And after a few more, she did.

And it was a whopper.

"*You're* an undercover agent?" I said. A few sheets to the wind myself.

"Shhhh," she said, finger poised uncertainly before pretty lips. "It's a secret. But I haven't been doing it much lately."

"Haven't been doing what?"

"Well, undercover work. And there's a double entendre there that I'd rather you didn't go looking for."

"I wouldn't think of looking under the covers for it."

The band began playing a tango.

I asked her how she got involved, working for Eliot. Which I didn't believe for a second, even in my cups.

But it turned out to be true (as Eliot admitted to me when he came over to see how Vivian and I were getting along, when Vivian—which was her name, incidentally—went to the powder room with Evie).

Vivian Chalmers was the daughter of a banker (a solvent one), a divorcée of thirty with no children and a lot of social pull. An expert trapshooter, golfer, tennis player, and "all 'round sportswoman," with a sense of adventure. When Eliot called on her to case various of the gambling joints he planned to raid—as a socialite she could take a fling in any joint she chose, without raising any suspicion—she immediately said yes. And she'd been an active agent in the first few years of Eliot's ongoing battle against the so-called Mayfield Road Mob which controlled prostitution, gambling, and the policy racket in the Cleveland environs.

"But things have slowed down," she said, nostalgically. "Eliot has pretty much cleaned up the place, and, besides, he doesn't want to use me anymore."

"An undercover agent can only be effective so long," I said. "Pretty soon the other side gets suspicious."

She shrugged, with resigned frustration, and let me buy the next round.

We took a walk in the dark, around the golf course, and ended up sitting on a green. The breeze felt nice. The flag on the pin—thirteen—flapped.

"Thirteen," I said.

"Huh?"

"Victim thirteen."

"Oh. Eliot told me about that. Your 'luck' today, finding your client's missing daughter. Damn shame."

"Damn shame."

"A shame, too, they haven't found the son of a bitch."

She was a little drunk, and so was I, but I was still shocked—well, amused—to hear a woman, particularly a "society" woman, speak that way.

"It must grate on Eliot, too," I said.

"Sure as hell does. It's the only mote in his eye. He's a hero around these parts, and he's kicked the Mayfield Mob in the seat of the pants, and done everything else from clean up a corrupt police department to throw labor racketeers in jail, to cut traffic deaths in half, to founding Boy's Town, to . . ."

"You're not in love with the guy, are you?"

She seemed taken aback for a minute, then her face wrinkled into a got-caught-with-my-pants-down grin. "Maybe a little. But he's got a girl."

"I don't."

"You might."

She leaned forward.

We kissed for a while, and she felt good in my arms; she was firm, almost muscular. But she smelled like flowers. And the sky was blue and scattered with stars above us, as we lay back on the golf green to look up. It seemed like a nice world, at the moment.

Hard to imagine it had a Butcher in it.

I sat up talking with Eliot that night; he lived in a little converted boathouse on the lake. The furnishings were sparse, spartan; it was obvious his wife had taken most of the furniture with her and he'd had to all but start over.

I told him I thought Vivian was a terrific girl.

Leaning back in a comfy chair, feet on an ottoman, Eliot, tie loose around his neck, smiled in a melancholy way. "I thought you'd hit it off."

"Did you have an affair with her?"

He looked at me sharply; that was about as personal as I'd ever got with him.

He shook his head no, but I didn't quite buy it.

"You knew Evie MacMillan in Chicago," I said.

"Meaning what?"

"Meaning nothing."

"Meaning I knew her when I was still married."

"Meaning nothing."

"Nate, I'm sorry I'm not the Boy Scout you think I am."

"Hey, so you've slept with girls before. I'll learn to live with it."

There was a stone fireplace, in which some logs were trying to decide whether to burn anymore or not; we watched them trying.

"I love Evie, Nate. I'm going to marry her."

"Congratulations."

We could hear the lake out there; could smell it some, too.

"I'd like that bastard's neck in my hands," Eliot said.

"What?"

"That Butcher. That goddamn Butcher."

"What made you think of him?"

"I don't know."

"Eliot, it's been over three years since he first struck, and you *still* don't have anything?"

"Nothing. A few months ago, last time he hit, we found some of the ... body parts, bones and such ... in a cardboard box in the Central Market area. There's a Hooverville over there or what used to be a Hooverville ... it's a shantytown, is more like it, genuine hoboes as opposed to just good folks down on their luck. Most of the victims—before today—were either prostitutes or bums ... and the bums from that shantytown were the Butcher's meat. So to speak."

The fire crackled.

Eliot continued: "I decided to make a clean sweep. I took twenty-five cops through there at one in the morning, and rousted out all the 'bo's and took 'em down and fingerprinted and questioned all of 'em."

"And it amounted to . . . ?"

"It amounted to nothing. Except ridding Cleveland of that shantytown. I burned the place down that afternoon."

"Comes in handy, having all those firemen working for you. But what about those poor bastards whose 'city' you burned down?"

Sensing my disapproval, he glanced at me and gave me what tried to be a warm smile, but was just a weary one. "Nate, I turned them over to the relief department, for relocation and, I hope, rehabilitation. But most of them were bums who just hopped a freight out. And I did 'em a favor by taking them off the potential victims list."

"And made room for Ginger Jensen."

Eliot looked away.

"That wasn't fair," I said. "I'm sorry I said that, Eliot."

"I know, Nate. I know."

But I could tell he'd been thinking the same thing.

I had lunch the next day with Vivian in a little outdoor restaurant in the shadow of Terminal Tower. We were served lemonade and little ham and cheese and lettuce and tomato sandwiches with the crusts trimmed off the toasted bread. The detective in me wondered what became of the crusts.

"Thanks for having lunch with me," Vivian said. She had on a pale orange dress; she sat crossing her brown pretty legs.

"My pleasure," I said.

"Speaking of which . . . about last night . . ."

"We were both a little drunk. Forget it. Just don't ask *me* to."

She smiled as she nibbled her sandwich.

"I called and told Eliot something this morning," she said, "and he just ignored me."

"What was that?"

"That I have a possible lead on the Butcher murders."

"I can't imagine Eliot ignoring that . . . and it's not like it's just *anybody* approaching him—you *did* work for him. . . ."

"Not lately. And he thinks I'm just . . ."

"Looking for an excuse to be around him?"

She nibbled at a little sandwich. Nodded.

"Did you resent him asking you to be with me as a blind date last night?"

"No," she said.

"Did . . . last night have anything to do with wanting to 'show' Eliot?"

If she weren't so sophisticated—or trying to be—she would've looked hurt; but her expression managed to get something else across: disappointment in me.

"Last night had to do with showing *you*," she said. "And . . . it had a little to do with Bacardi rum. . . ."

"That it did. Tell me about your lead."

"Eliot has been harping on the 'professional' way the bodies have been dismembered. He's said again and again he sees a 'surgical' look to it."

I nodded.

"So it occurred to me that a doctor—anyway, somebody who'd at least been in medical school for a time—would be a likely candidate for the Butcher."

"Yes."

"And medical school's expensive, so, it stands to reason, the Butcher just might run in the same social circles as yours truly."

"Say, you *did* work for Eliot."

She liked that.

She went on: "I checked around with my friends, and heard about a guy whose family has money, plenty of it. Name of Watterson."

"Last name or first?"

"That's the family name. Big in these parts."

"Means nothing to me."

"Well, Lloyd Watterson used to be a medical student. He's a big man, very strong—the kind of strength it might take to do some of the things the Butcher has done. And he has a history of mental disturbances."

"What kind of mental disturbances?"

"He's been going to a psychiatrist since he was a schoolboy."

"Do you know this guy?"

"Just barely. But I've heard things about him."

"Such as?"

"I hear he likes boys."

Lloyd Watterson lived in a two-story white house at the end of a dead-end street, a Victorian-looking miniature mansion among other such houses, where expansive lawns and towering hedges separated the world from the wealthy who lived within.

This wasn't the parental home, Vivian explained; Watterson lived here alone, apparently without servants. The grounds seemed well tended, though, and there was nothing about this house that said anyone capable of mass murder might live here. No blood spattered on the white porch; no body parts scattered about the lawn.

It was midafternoon, and I was having second thoughts.

"I don't even have a goddamn gun," I said.

"I do," she said, and showed me a little .25 automatic from her purse.

"Great. If he has a dog, maybe we can use that to scare it."

"This'll do the trick. Besides, a gun won't even be necessary. You're just here to talk."

The game plan was for me to approach Watterson as a cop, flashing my private detective's badge quickly enough to fool him (and that almost always worked), and question him, simply get a feel for whether or not he was a legitimate suspect, worthy of lobbying Eliot for action against. My say-so, Vivian felt, would be enough to get Eliot off the dime.

And helping Eliot bring the Butcher in would be a nice wedding present for my old friend; with his unstated but obvious political ambitions, the capture of the Kingsbury Run maniac would offset the damage his divorce had done him in conservative, mostly Catholic Cleveland. He'd been the subject of near hero worship in the press here (Eliot was always good at getting press—Frank Nitti used to refer to him as "Eliot Press"); but the ongoing if sporadic slaughter of the Butcher was a major embarrassment for Cleveland's fabled safety director.

So, leaving Vivian behind in the roadster (Watterson might recognize her), I walked up the curved sidewalk and went up on the porch and rang the bell. In the dark hardwood door there was opaque glass through which I could barely make out movement, coming toward me.

The door opened, and a blond man about six-three with a baby face and ice blue eyes and shoulders that nearly filled the doorway looked out at me and grinned. A kid's grin, on one side of his face. He wore a polo shirt and short white pants; he seemed about to say, "Tennis, anyone?"

But he said nothing, as a matter of fact; he just appraised me with those ice blue, somewhat vacant eyes. I now knew how it felt for a woman to be ogled—which is to say, not necessarily good.

I said, "I'm an officer of the court," which in Illinois wasn't exactly a lie, and I flashed him my badge, but before I could say anything else, his hand reached out and grabbed the front of my shirt, yanked me inside, and slammed the door.

He tossed me like a horseshoe, and I smacked into something—the stairway to the second floor, I guess; I don't know exactly, because I blacked out. The only thing I remember is the musty smell of the place.

I woke up minutes later, and found myself tied in a chair in a dank, dark room. Support beams loomed out of a packed dirt floor. The basement.

I strained at the ropes, but they were snug; not so snug as to cut off my circulation, but snug enough. I glanced around the room. I was alone. I couldn't see much—just a shovel against one cement wall. The only light came from a window off to my right, and there were hedges in front of the window, so the light was filtered.

Feet came tromping down the open wooden stairs. I saw his legs first, white as pastry dough.

He was grinning. In his right hand was a cleaver. It shone, caught a glint of what little light there was.

"I'm no butcher," he said. His voice was soft, almost gentle. "Don't believe what you've heard. . . ."

"Do you want to die?" I said.

"Of course not."

"Well then cut me loose. There's cops all over the place, and if you kill me, they'll shoot you down. You know what happens to cop killers, don't you?"

He thought that over, nodded.

Standing just to one side of me, displaying the cold polished steel of the cleaver, in which my face's frantic reflection looked back at me, he said, "I'm no butcher. This is a surgical tool. This is used for amputation, not butchery."

"Yeah. I can see that."

"I wondered when you people would come around."

"Do you want to be caught, Lloyd?"

"Of course not. I'm no different than you. I'm a public servant."

"How ... how do you figure that, Lloyd?" My feet weren't tied to the chair; if he'd just step around in front of me ...

"I only dispose of the flotsam. Not to mention jetsam."

"Not to mention that."

"Tramps. Whores. Weeding out the stock. Survival of the fittest. You know."

"That makes a lot of sense, Lloyd. But I'm not flotsam *or* jetsam. I'm a cop. You don't want to kill a cop. You don't want to kill a fellow public servant."

He thought about that.

"I think I have to, this time," he said.

He moved around the chair, stood in front of me, stroking his chin, the cleaver gripped tight in his right hand, held about breastbone high.

"I *do* like you," Lloyd said, thoughtfully.

"And I like you, Lloyd," I said, and kicked him in the balls.

Harder than any man tied to a chair should be able to kick; but you'd be surprised what you can do, under extreme circumstances. And things rarely get more extreme than being tied to a chair with a guy with a cleaver coming at you.

Only he wasn't coming at me, now: now, he was doubled over, and I stood, the chair strapped to my back; managed, even so, to kick him in the face.

He tumbled back, gripping his groin, his head leaning

back, stretching, tears streaming down his cheeks, cords in his neck taut; my shoe had caught him on the side of the face and broken the skin. Flecks of blood, like little red tears, spattered his cheeks, mingling with the real tears.

That's when the window shattered, and Vivian squeezed down and through, pretty legs first.

And she gave me the little gun to hold on him while she untied me.

He was still on the dirt floor, moaning, when we went up the stairs and out into the sunny day, into a world that wasn't dank, onto earth that was grass-covered and didn't have God knows what buried under it.

We asked Eliot to meet us at his boathouse; we told him what had happened. He was livid; I never saw him angrier. But he held Vivian for a moment, and looked at her and said, "If anything had happened to you, I'd've killed you."

He poured all of us a drink; rum as usual. He handed me mine and said, "How could you get involved in something so harebrained?"

"I wanted to give my client something for his money," I said.

"You mean his daughter's killer."

"Why not?"

"I've been looking for the bastard three years, and you come to town and expect to find him in three days."

"Well, I did."

He smirked, shook his head. "I believe you did. But Watterson's family will bring in the highest-paid lawyers in the country and we'd be thrown out of court on our cans."

"What? The son of a bitch tried to cut me up with a cleaver!"

"Did he? Did he swing on you? Or did you enter his house under a false pretense, misrepresenting yourself as a law officer? And as far as that goes, *you* assaulted *him*. We have very little."

Vivian said, "You have the name of the Butcher."

Eliot nodded. "Probably. I'm going to make a phone call."

Eliot went into his den and came out fifteen minutes later.

"I spoke with Franklin Watterson, the father. He's agreed to submit his son for a lie detector test."

"To what end?"

"One step at a time," Eliot said.

Lloyd Watterson took the lie detector test twice—and on both instances denied committing the various Butcher slayings; his denials were, according to the machine, lies. The Watterson family attorney reminded Eliot that lie detector tests were not admissible as evidence. Eliot had a private discussion with Franklin Watterson.

Lloyd Watterson was committed, by his family, to an asylum for the insane. The Mad Butcher of Kingsbury Run—which to this day is marked "unsolved" in the Cleveland police records—did not strike again.

At least not directly.

Eliot married Evie MacMillan a few months after my Cleveland visit, and from the start their marriage was disrupted by crank letters, postmarked from the same town as the asylum where Watterson had been committed. "Retribution will catch up with you one day," said one postcard, on the front of which was a drawing of an effeminate man grinning from behind prison bars. Mrs. Ness was especially unnerved by these continuing letters and cards.

Eliot's political fortunes waned, in the wake of the "unsolved" Butcher slayings. Known for his tough stance on traffic violators, he got mired in a scandal when one pre-dawn morning in March of 1942, his car skidded into an oncoming car on the West Shoreway. Eliot and his wife, and two friends, had been drinking. The police report didn't identify Eliot by name, but his license number—EN-1, well known to Cleveland citizens—was listed. And Eliot had left the scene of the accident.

Hit-and-run, the headlines said. Eliot's version was that his wife had been injured, and he'd raced her to a hospital—but not before stopping to check on the other driver, who confirmed this. The storm blew over, but the damage was done. Eliot's image in the Cleveland press was finally tarnished.

Two months later he resigned as safety director.

About that time, asylum inmate Lloyd Watterson managed to hang himself with a bedsheet, and the threatening mail stopped.

How much pressure those cards and letters put on the marriage I couldn't say; but in 1945 Eliot and Evie divorced, and Eliot married a third time a few months later. At the time he was serving as federal director of the program against venereal disease in the military. His attempt to run for Cleveland mayor in 1947 was a near disaster: Cleveland's one-time fairhaired boy was a has-been with a hit-run scandal and two divorces and three marriages going against him.

He would not have another public success until the publication of his autobiographical book, *The Untouchables*, but that success was posthumous; he died shortly before it was published, never knowing that television and Robert Stack would give him lasting fame.

I saw Eliot, now and then, over the years; but I never saw Vivian again.

I asked him about her, once, when I was visiting him in Pennsylvania, in the early '50s. He told me she'd been killed in a boating accident in 1943.

"She's been dead for years, then," I said, the shock of it hitting me like a blow.

"That's right. But shed a tear for her, now, if you like. Tears and prayers can never come too late, Nate."

Amen, Eliot.

AUTHOR'S NOTE: I wish to express my indebtedness to two nonfiction works, Four Against the Mob *by Oscar Fraley (Popular Library, 1961) and* Cleveland—The Best Kept Secret *by George E. Condon (Doubleday, 1967). Fact, speculation, and fiction are freely mixed in the preceding story; with the exception of Eliot Ness, all characters—while in many cases having real-life counterparts—are fictional.*

TILL TUESDAY
Jeremiah Healy

FIRST APPEARANCE: *Blunt Darts*, 1984

Blunt Darts (Walker, 1984) was the first John Francis Cuddy novel. Since then there have been ten novels, the most recent being *Rescue* (Pocket Books, 1995). Mr. Healy's *The Staked Goat* (Pocket Books) won the Shamus Award for best PI novel of 1986.

"'Till Tuesday" was first published in *Alfred Hitchcock's Mystery Magazine* in 1988.

Cambridge, Massachusetts, is home to Harvard University, boutique restaurants, and people who believe that Anthony Lewis editorials really make a difference. The two men sitting across from me lived there, but I pictured them more as *Wall Street Journal* than *New York Times*.

The one on the right was an architect, Michael Atlee. Atlee was lanky and angular; his brown hair showed licks of white at the temples. He fit poorly into an expensive blue tweed sports jacket and red rooster tie over slacks a little too pale to contrast correctly with his coat. Atlee held a pipe by its bowl in his hand, but made no effort to light it.

The man next to him spelled and smelled lawyer through and through. Thayer Lane, Esq., was on his business card, followed by his firm's four named partners and an upscale address. Slim, with black hair, Lane wore a charcoal pin-striped uniform of power and a muted paisley tie.

I guessed both men to be perched on the far side of forty-five. Neither seemed especially comfortable having a conference on the Wednesday after Labor Day in a one-room office with John Francis Cuddy, Confidential Investigations on the door.

After the introductions, Lane said, "Mr. Cuddy, we are here on a matter which cannot be discussed with the police. You come highly recommended, especially in the categories of loyalty and discretion."

"Thank you."

"I should say that while Mr. Atlee will be your client in this regard, he is uncomfortable with speaking at length. Hence, he asked me to accompany him here today."

I looked at Atlee. "What seems to be the problem?"

Atlee said, "Thayer?"

Lane took his cue. "Mr. Atlee—Michael—is a designer of buildings. Perhaps you're familiar with some of his works?"

Lane ticked off five recent commercial towers. I recognized two of them. I thought they looked like I-beams wearing Tina Turner dresses, but I kept it to myself. "Is the difficulty related to one of the buildings?"

"No, Mr. Cuddy," said Lane. "Let me try to outline the situation for you."

"Go ahead. And please call me John."

"John." Lane spoke as if he might otherwise forget the name. "John, are you married?"

"Widower."

"Ah, sorry. Well . . ." Lane took a deep breath. "Michael is married. However, he has been engaged in an affair for three years with a woman, Gina Fiore. Michael believes that Ms.—Gina, has disappeared, and he would like you to find her."

I looked over to Atlee, who sucked on his unlit pipe and blew imaginary smoke at me. His facial movements masked any emotion.

"How long has she been missing?"

"That's uncertain. Michael last saw her this past Thursday but couldn't reach her yesterday."

Atlee said, "Tell him all of it."

Lane glanced at Atlee and sighed. "Every Labor Day Michael hosts a family retreat at his summer home on Parker Pond in Maine. We all go up on Thursday night, scour and spruce the place up with paint and so forth against the elements, then relax and shoot skeet Sunday and Monday."

"You shoot skeet on a lake on Labor Day weekend?"

Atlee said, "I've got ten acres. It's private enough."

I said to Atlee, "So she could be gone for as long as six days."

"Right."

"Or as little as twenty hours."

Lane stuck in, "My point precisely."

Atlee said, "Doesn't matter. She's gone."

"Where does Gina live?"

Atlee nodded to Lane, who took over again. "Gina lives in a condominium on Revere Beach that Michael purchased as an investment. Part of their, ah, arrangement is that she is to be available at all times. By telephone and in person."

Lovely. I said to Lane, "A few minutes ago you said 'we'?"

"I'm sorry?"

"You were talking about the lake thing being a family event but you said 'we all went up to the summer place.'"

"Oh, quite. Michael is a client of my firm, but we're also best friends. Roomed together at Harvard and prepped at Choate before that. My wife and I are like family to Michael and Winnie, and Seth's my godson."

I said to Atlee, "Winnie's your wife and Seth's your son?"

He nodded and bit down on the pipe stem.

"Any reason for Gina to take off?"

"None." Decisively.

"Who else knows about your relationship with Gina?"

Lane said, "A woman named Marla—I'm afraid we don't have her last name—lives in the next unit in Gina's building and is aware of, ah . . ."

"Anybody else?"

Atlee fidgeted in his chair, I thought at first from impatience. Then he said, "Seth knows, or suspects. Same damned thing, I guess. Saw us once together a couple of years ago in a bar over there. Slumming with one of his swim-team chums. Damned bad luck, but there it is."

I had the impression I'd been treated to Atlee's longest speech of the decade. "Any point in my talking with him?"

"No." Case closed.

Lane said, "That would be rather difficult anyway, John."

"Why is that?"

"You see, Seth is a junior at Stanford this year, and he always leaves the morning after Labor Day to head out there."

Atlee said, "Damned fool has to drive his Jeep three thousand miles. Can't take the plane like a normal person."

"In any case," said Lane, "I had a call from him last night. He was near Pittsburgh and wasn't sure of his next destination."

I said, "He called you?"

Lane seemed affronted. "I am his godfather."

"All right. I'll need a photo of Gina and her address over in Revere."

Atlee said, "Don't have a photo."

"I'm sure you understand," said Lane.

Before I could reply, Atlee leaned forward, tapping his pipe on my desk for emphasis. "Just understand this. I really care for that girl. I may not show it, but I do. And I want you to find her."

TWO

Revere Beach is an incongruous strip of old clam shacks and new high-rise towers along a slightly polluted stretch of sand and ocean about ten miles north of Boston. I flashed the key Atlee had given me at the security guard, who smiled deferentially and used his magazine to wave me into the lobby. I took an elevator to the ninth floor.

Unit 9A was at the end of the hall. I had a little trouble with the lock, rattled it and the knob twice before the tumbler would turn. Inside, the apartment was airy, with a striking view of the Atlantic through sliding glass doors to a narrow balcony. Versatile sectional furniture for couch and chairs. Track lighting overhead, a wall unit with stereo, color TV, and even a few books.

I entered the bedroom and had been drawn toward some framed photos on the bureau when I thought I heard the snap and creak of a quick entry at the front door. I managed two steps before a perfectly tanned woman in a European string bikini appeared in the doorway to the living room. She leveled a tiny automatic at me and said, "My boyfriend told me to just keep firing until the guy falls."

I got the hint.

"Gina and me watch each other's places, you know?"

"Good system."

"Look, at least I can make you a drink or something, huh?"

She was trying hard, a little too hard, to make up for the gun scene. My investigator's ID had convinced her I wasn't a "real" burglar, and she was pleased to introduce herself as Marla, the girl next door. I'd seen everything except the bedroom closet with nothing to show for it. Now she was watching me rummage through Gina's dresses, slacks, and shoes.

"So Mikey figures Gina's flown on him, huh?"

I liked her using "Mikey." I said over my shoulder, "That the way you see it?"

"Without telling me? And leaving all her stuff like this?" She paused. "Hard to say for sure, though. Gina's been a little restless lately."

I stopped searching and turned around. "Restless?"

"Yeah, well, it's not so easy being somebody's sweet harbor, you know? Waiting for a phone call, planning your life around a lunch here or there and some afternoon delight."

Somehow the phrase sounded sweeter in the song. "Would she have left on her own?"

"Not likely. Gina enjoyed being took care of, even by a creep like Mikey."

"How do you mean?"

"Aw, we double-dated a coupla months ago. Her and Mikey and this guy called himself 'Jim.' We drove up to Swampscott to go sailing, like they was afraid to do the class thing and go all the way to Marblehead, maybe one of their big shot friends sees them there with two bimbettes from Revere."

"You ever see this Jim again?"

"No, but like I said, that wasn't his real name. Stupid guy, he drives us all up there in this big green Mercedes, like we're too dumb to know how to run a plate at the registry."

"You ran his license plate?"

"Yeah. Turns out he's another Cambridge high roller with, get this, the name Thayer Lane."

Ah, Mr. Lane. "This Lane seem interested in Gina?"

"Coulda been. I kept him pretty interested that day, I'll tell you. Never did hear back from him, though. Good old 'Jim.' "

"Gina ever mention Atlee's son?"

"Not really. Just that the father and him didn't get along too well."

"Some families are like that."

"Boy, you got that right." Her tone changed. "You got any pressing commitments after this here?"

I stuck my head back into the closet. There were three matching pieces of luggage; the size just up from the smallest seemed to be missing.

"Well, do you?"

"Marla," I said, pointing, "does Gina have a full set of these bags?"

She came over, pressing and rubbing more than my request required. "Uh-huh. Gina uses the other one for day hops." She was wearing some kind of coconut-scented lotion.

"Meaning not overnight?"

Marla stepped back without answering. She kept going until her calves touched the bed, then sat back and onto her elbows, in one languid motion. She hooded her eyes. "Doesn't have to take all night, sugar."

Walking to the bureau, I picked up one of the photos. A girl about Marla's age, long frosted curls, winking at the lens.

"This Gina?"

She licked her lips. "Uh-huh."

"Recent?"

"Hair's a little shorter now. Let's talk about you. And me."

I think she was laughing as I went through the front door.

I stood up, put my hands in my pockets. "Mrs. Feeney told me what they were, but it was some Latin name, and I forget it."

"What happened to that elaborate altar boy training?"

I looked at the purplish flowers with yellowish petals, then at her stone. Elizabeth Mary Devlin Cuddy. "Won't help me much with this one, Beth."

What's the problem?

I told her.

An architect's mistress. Sordid.

"It's about to get worse."

How?

"Tomorrow I intend to see his wife about their son."

THREE

The next morning I stopped at the office to hoke up a manila file folder and some documents, then took Memorial Drive to Cambridge. The Atlees' home was on one of those short streets off Brattle. An aggressively traditional mini-manse, it was surrounded by an outside fence nearly as tall as the trees behind it. I tapped a button on the intercom at the wrought-iron entrance and a minute later received a metallic, female "Yes?"

"Mrs. Atlee?"

"Yes?"

"My name is John Cuddy. I'm a private investigator and I'm here about your son."

"My son? Is there some kind of problem?"

"No, no, ma'am. It's just that, well, it would be easier if I could show you the file."

Hesitation, then the grating buzz and click that tell you to push on the gate.

"And you say my son witnessed an accident?"

"Yes, ma'am." I slid the folder over to her, holding my index finger on the document in the middle of the Acco-clipped bunch till she held the place for herself and began reading it.

She was about Atlee's age, with strawberry blond hair pulled severely behind her head. A peasant dress heightened the sense of bony strength about her. Striking, not beautiful, she probably sat an English saddle well, given some of the bronzed trophies on shelves in the den. The other statuettes looked like awards for swimming and shooting.

"But this isn't even my son's handwriting."

"No, ma'am. That's the handwriting of our Mr. Green, who's no longer our Mr. Green because he fouled up so much, like here when he took down your son's statement then forgot to have him date or sign it over ... there."

She shook her head and handed me back the file. "Well, I'm sure if Seth were here he'd be glad to help you, but he left for California on Tuesday."

I let my face fall. "Gee, Mrs. Atlee, this case is coming up for trial and all. Do you have a number where I can reach him?"

"Yes. Well, no. Not for a few more days. You see, he drives there, to return to Stanford, and he rather dawdles really, taking roads that interest him and stopping wherever."

"Does he call you?"

"Sometimes. Other times no. If we hear from him, we could ask him to call you, but it would probably be late at night and perhaps not at all."

"Is there anyone else he might call?"

She considered it. "Yes. His friend Doug Cather. Seth and Doug were on the swim team together at prep school. Doug's at Harvard now."

I looked past her to a photo on the mantel. A family portrait of a younger Atlee and wife behind a seated teenager.

"Is that Seth?"

She twisted around and looked back at me. "Yes." She darkened. "Is there something else?"

"No, no. He looks like a fine boy."

Doug Cather lived in Kirkland House, part of the not-quite-quadrangle of more-than-dorms nestled near the Charles River. He was tall, broad-shouldered, and completely hairless.

"We shave our heads."

"Why?"

"For swimming. Cuts down on the drag effect in the water."

Anything for dear old Harvard, I guess. Cather accepted my bogus accident story.

"No, I haven't heard from Seth, which is kind of funny."

"You two stay in touch that closely?"

"Not really. It's just that he always calls me when he leaves for school, and I kind of waited around for it yesterday morning. Cut classes and all."

"Wait a minute. I thought Seth left for California on Tuesday. Yesterday was Wednesday."

Cather's face clouded over.

I said, "There's something you're not telling me."

"There's something I don't think is any of your business."

"Something about Seth?"

"Yeah."

"Look, I'm not going to give you a long song and dance about confidentiality. You don't know me at all, so you don't know if you can trust me."

"That's right."

"Okay. Here's my problem. I've got to find your friend. You can help me, or I can do it the hard way. Go see other people, his dad, whoever. That might mean I find out worse things than I need to know. All I can say is if you tell me what's going on, I'll try to keep it to myself."

Cather didn't speak.

"We want Seth as a witness for us on this collision. I'm not about to spread rumors that would make him look bad."

"It's not ..." He seemed to search inside for a moment. "I want your promise anyway. You won't tell anybody?"

"Promise."

He blew out a breath. "Okay, it's like this. After we graduated from Choate, Seth and I bounced around for the summer. One day we decide to go to Revere Beach, kind of scope out the other half, you know? Well, we dare each other to go into this bar. I mean, we're way underage and nobody's ever gonna serve us without ID, but we try it anyway. Right off, I spot Seth's father in one of the booths, with a real tough ... a really sharp-looking chick just a couple of years older than us. So I start to say something, and Seth sees them and gets all uptight. He's kind of impulsive anyhow, and he bolts out of there and like won't even talk with me all the way home."

"What's that got to do with his driving to California?"

"Well, it didn't take a genius to see what his dad was doing there, and I guess Seth and him had a real blowup over it. Anyway, Seth decides not to go out for swimming at Stanford, like to punish his dad, I guess. But every year his family has this Labor Day thing to please his mom. So, okay, after Seth gets home from the weekend each year, he goes back up there."

"Seth goes back?"

"Right. He tells his parents he's leaving for school, and he does, sort of, but first he drives up to Parker Pond and does the swim."

"The swim."

"Yeah. He swims out from their property to this little island and back. It's like a ritual, I guess, to prove he can still go the distance. And maybe to think about when he was younger and he didn't, well, know about his dad."

"Would Seth sleep over in Maine on that Tuesday night?"

"Definitely. It's almost four hours to get there, and he probably wouldn't leave his parents in Cambridge much before lunchtime."

"You ever been to this Parker Pond house?"

"Sure. Lots of times."

"Can you draw me a map?"

FOUR

Even with Doug Cather's sketch, I had to stop at an inn on the main road for supplemental directions. A turnoff went from paved to gravel to hard-packed dirt. Then I saw rutted tracks curve off the road, a primitive driveway running under a white tollgate. Leaving the car, I walked up to the gate. A single horizontal bar, very freshly painted, was hinged on one of two posts and swung inward freely.

The day was warm, the only sounds the wind in the trees and a woodpecker pocking away nearby. I decided to approach more quietly than my old Fiat would allow. I tossed my sport coat into the front seat and switched on the hazard lights. Ducking under the gate bar, I started walking.

The driveway doglegged right to insure privacy and squiggled here and there to avoid particularly substantial pines. Passing the last big tree, I spotted the back of the house.

A black Jeep Wrangler was parked at the mouth of an adjoining shed.

I moved through the underbrush and approached the shed, keeping it between me and the large chalet-style house behind it. I stopped at the side of the shed to listen. No noise from inside.

Edging toward the front, I looked through the webby pane at the shed's door. Paint buckets, rake and lawn mower, gasoline can, etc. The Jeep was stuffed to the roof with the odd-lot cartons and containers students use to return to college.

I circled around the house. Every door and window seemed sealed tight. The wind was really howling lakeside, kicking whitecaps against the shoreline.

At the back door, I knocked, waited, and knocked again louder. Inside I could see the kitchen area. Using a rock to break the glass, I was hit with the stench as I opened the door itself. I gagged and tried to close off my nasal passages with the back of my tongue. Grabbing a dish rag off the rack over the sink, I took it to the shed and doused it with gasoline. I held the rag to my face and went back inside.

He was lying on the floor of the great room, cathedral ceiling above him. A dry pair of swim trunks and a beach towel lay on a chair next to him. At his side, a carefully carved and scrolled double-barreled shotgun, one hand around the trigger mechanism. His face was bloated, the head connected only by the few tendons the blast had left of his neck. Seth Atlee, a marionette past all mending.

Gina was on the open, slatted staircase leading to the upper level. Naked, she'd taken the other barrel between the shoulder blades and would have been dead before her nose struck the tenth step.

The house was twenty degrees hotter than the ambient

temperature outside. I didn't think my gasoline filter would support a telephone call indoors.

I pulled the door closed and walked slowly down the driveway. At the gate, I noticed what seemed to be a grass stain on the house side of the swing bar, stark against the gleaming white. Like someone had scraped the inner edge of the bar against a car.

I started the Fiat and drove to the inn to learn about law enforcement in Maine.

FIVE

The funeral was scheduled for Saturday afternoon, beginning from a mortuary on Massachusetts Avenue in Cambridge. I got there early and parked a block away. Even announced murder-suicides draw large numbers of sincere mourners these days. I watched the arrivals of Michael and Winnie Atlee, Doug Cather, and Thayer Lane with a woman I took to be his wife.

Forty minutes later, the crowd came back out, repairing to private cars to form the procession. I left the Fiat. Pausing at Lane's Mercedes, I could see the lawyer on the porch of the funeral home, bending slightly at the waist and using both hands to shake hands gently with a short, elderly woman. I caught his eye. He glared at me. I smiled and beckoned. He excused himself, moving stiff-legged over to me.

"Counselor."

"Mr. Cuddy, don't you think it a bit tasteless for you to appear here?"

"What I think is that Seth didn't kill Gina or himself."

Lane stopped fussing.

I said, "How long did you figure it'd take before they were found?"

"I beg your pardon?"

"The bodies. Buttoned up in the house and all. Seth would be reported missing by his college after a while, but who would think to check the lake place?"

"What in the world kind of question is that?"

"You see, the longer the wait, the tougher to peg time

of death. After a couple of weeks, no one would swear to anything shorter than a few, bracketed, days."

"Mr. Cuddy, I really must get back."

"You didn't want me searching for Gina so quickly after Atlee couldn't raise her. You double-dated with him, Gina, and Marla once. Gina was restless, maybe you caught each other's fancy."

"Preposterous."

"But Atlee's a big client and an old friend. So you needed a safe place to try your luck. None safer than the summer home you helped close up the day before."

"I'm not going to—"

"Listen any more? You've listened too much as it is, Lane. An innocent man would have walked already."

He clenched his teeth. "Finish it then."

"You didn't know about Seth's ritual swim. I'm guessing you were in the sack with Gina when Seth burst in downstairs. He would have seen your car. Did he call out to you? 'Hey, Uncle Thayer, you upstairs?' "

Lane looked clammy, unsteady.

"You jump out of bed, try to pull some clothes on. Seth's in good shape, though, takes the steps two at a time. Sees you in the nearly altogether with the woman he recognizes as his dad's mistress. He goes nuts, runs back downstairs, gets a skeet gun. He loads it and comes back, back to purge the stain from the one place he still thought was family inviolate."

"No, no."

"You try to reason with him in the great room, Gina following you down the stairs. A struggle, the gun wavers toward Seth as somebody hits the trigger. Seth goes down, Gina yells, "You murdered him!" Or maybe she just starts screaming, screaming till you lock onto her as a target and she—"

"You can't prove a word of this!"

"No?" I gestured toward the hood of his Mercedes. "Those gouge marks. You put them there when you swung the gate in to leave the place on Tuesday."

He blinked, trying to make the scratches go away. "They . . . they . . ."

"Freshly painted gate, two days before. If you'd taken a

piece out of the car driving back Monday, the missus would remember it. The kind of thing that would spoil the whole weekend."

"Seth, he called me . . ."

I shook my head. "Nobody called you Tuesday night, because Seth didn't call his friend Wednesday morning. I'm betting the medical examiner saw the bodies soon enough to place both deaths on Tuesday afternoon. The phone alibi would have been perfect in a few more weeks. Now it's going to hang you."

"Thayer? Thayer!"

We both turned.

Michael Atlee was chopping his hand toward the lead limousine. For the godfather.

Lane whispered. "What are you . . ."

"Going to do? I'm going to give you a chance here, Thayer. Mikey there is your best friend, right?"

"I . . . yes he is, but—"

"Then sometime in the next two days you're going to tell him all about it."

"Money. You want money."

"I don't want money, Thayer. I was hired to find Gina Fiore. I found her and was paid. Now you're going to do your job. You're going to be the first to tell your best friend how his mistress and son really died."

"Thayer!" called Atlee, striding determinedly toward us.

Lane said, "But for God's sake, Cuddy, that's not how it happened! The way you said, it wasn't like that."

"Maybe not. You've got till Tuesday to come up with a better version."

I walked back to my car.

LUCKY PENNY
Linda Barnes

FIRST APPEARANCE: *This Story*, 1986

After four novels featuring ex-private eye turned actor Michael Sraggue, Ms. Barnes states she "auditioned" Carlotta Carlyle in this story, which appeared for the first time in *New Black Mask* in 1986. Since then she has concentrated on Carlotta, who has appeared in six novels, the last of which was *Hardware* (Dell, 1995).

Lieutenant Mooney made me dish it all out for the record. He's a good cop, if such an animal exists. We used to work the same shift before I decided—wrongly—that there was room for a lady PI in this town. Who knows? With this case under my belt, maybe business'll take a 180-degree spin, and I can quit driving a hack.

See, I've already written the official report for Mooney and the cops, but the kind of stuff they wanted: date, place, and time, cold as ice and submitted in triplicate, doesn't even start to tell the tale. So I'm doing it over again, my way.

Don't worry, Mooney. I'm not gonna file this one.

The Thayler case was still splattered across the front page of the *Boston Globe*. I'd soaked it up with my midnight coffee and was puzzling it out—my cab on automatic pilot, my mind on crime—when the mad tea party began.

"Take your next right, sister. Then pull over, and douse the lights. Quick!"

I heard the bastard all right, but it must have taken me thirty seconds or so to react. Something hard rapped on the cab's dividing shield. I didn't bother turning around. I hate staring down gun barrels.

I said, "Jimmy Cagney, right? No, your voice is too high. Let me guess, don't tell me—"

"Shut up!"

"*Kill* the lights, *turn off* the lights, okay. But *douse* the lights? You've been tuning in too many old gangster flicks."

"I hate a mouthy broad," the guy snarled. I kid you not.

"Broad," I said. "Christ! *Broad*? You trying to grow hair on your balls?"

"Look, I mean it, lady!"

"Lady's better. Now you wanna vacate my cab and go rob a phone booth?" My heart was beating like a tin drum, but I didn't let my voice shake, and all the time I was gabbing at him, I kept trying to catch his face in the mirror. He must have been crouching way back on the passenger side. I couldn't see a damn thing.

"I want all your dough," he said.

Who can you trust? This guy was a spiffy dresser: charcoal gray three-piece suit and rep tie, no less. And picked up in front of the swank Copley Plaza. *I* looked like I needed the bucks more than he did, and I'm no charity case. A woman can make good tips driving a hack in Boston. Oh, she's gotta take precautions, all right. When you can't smell a disaster fare from thirty feet, it's time to quit. I pride myself on my judgment. I'm careful. I always know where the police checkpoints are, so I can roll my cab past and flash the old lights if a guy starts acting up. This dude fooled me cold.

I was ripped. Not only had I been conned, I had a considerable wad to give away. It was near the end of my shift, and like I said, I do all right. I've got a lot of regulars. Once you see me, you don't forget me—or my cab.

It's gorgeous. Part of my inheritance. A '59 Chevy, shiny as new, kept on blocks in a heated garage by the proverbial dotty old lady. It's the pits of the design world. Glossy blue with those giant chromium fins. Restrained decor: just the phone number and a few gilt curlicues on the door. I was afraid all my old pals at the police department would pull me over for minor traffic violations if I went whole hog and painted Carlotta's Cab in ornate script on the hood. Some do it anyway.

So where the hell were all the cops now? Where are they when you need 'em?

He told me to shove the cash through that little hole they leave for the passenger to pass the fare forward. I told him he had it backward. He didn't laugh. I shoved bills.

"Now the change," the guy said. Can you imagine the nerve?

I must have cast my eyes up to heaven. I do that a lot these days.

"I mean it." He rapped the plastic shield with the shiny barrel of his gun. I checked it out this time. Funny how big a little .22 looks when it's pointed just right.

I fished in my pockets for change, emptied them.

"Is that all?"

"You want the gold cap on my left front molar?" I said.

"Turn around," the guy barked. "Keep both hands on the steering wheel. High."

I heard jingling, then a quick intake of breath.

"Okay," the crook said, sounding happy as a clam, "I'm gonna take my leave—"

"Good. Don't call this cab again."

"Listen!" The gun tapped. "You cool it here for ten minutes. And I mean frozen. Don't twitch. Don't blow your nose. Then take off."

"Gee, thanks."

"Thank *you*," he said politely. The door slammed.

At times like that, you just feel ridiculous. You *know* the guy isn't going to hang around waiting to see whether you're big on insubordination. *But,* he might. And who wants to tangle with a .22 slug? I rate pretty high on insubordination. That's why I messed up as a cop. I figured I'd give him two minutes to get lost. Meantime I listened.

Not much traffic goes by those little streets on Beacon Hill at one o'clock on a Wednesday morn. Too residential. So I could hear the guy's footsteps tap along the pavement. About ten steps back, he stopped. Was he the one in a million who'd wait to see if I turned around? I heard a funny kind of whooshing noise. Not loud enough to make me jump, and anything much louder than the ticking of my

watch would have put me through the roof. Then the footsteps patted on, straight back and out of hearing.

One minute more. The only saving grace of the situation
was the location: District One. That's Mooney's district.
Nice guy to talk to.

I took a deep breath, hoping it would have an encore,
and pivoted quickly, keeping my head low. Makes you feel
stupid when you do that and there's no one around.

I got out and strolled to the corner, stuck my head
around a building kind of cautiously. Nothing, of course.

I backtracked. Ten steps, then whoosh. Along the sidewalk stood one of those new Keep Beacon Hill Beautiful
trash cans, the kind with the swinging lid. I gave it a shove
as I passed. I could just as easily have kicked it; I was in
that kind of funk.

Whoosh, it said, just as pretty as could be.

Breaking into one of those trash cans is probably tougher
than busting into your local bank vault. Since I didn't even
have a dime left to fiddle the screws on the lid, I was forced
to deface city property. I got the damn thing open and
dumped the contents on somebody's front lawn, smack in
the middle of a circle of light from one of those ritzy Beacon Hill gas streetlamps.

Halfway through the whiskey bottles, wadded napkins,
and beer cans, I made my discovery. I was being thorough.
If you're going to stink like garbage anyway, why leave
anything untouched, right? So I was opening all the brown
bags—you know, the good old brown lunch-and-bottle
bags—looking for a clue. My most valuable find so far
had been the moldy rind of a bologna sandwich. Then I hit
it big: one neatly creased brown bag stuffed full of cash.

To say I was stunned is to entirely underestimate how I
felt as I crouched there, knee-deep in garbage, my jaw
hanging wide. I don't know what I'd expected to find.
Maybe the guy's gloves. Or his hat, if he'd wanted to get
rid of it fast in order to melt back into anonymity. I pawed
through the rest of the debris fast. My change was gone.

I was so befuddled I left the trash right on the front
lawn. There's probably still a warrant out for my arrest.

District One headquarters is off the beaten path, over on

New Sudbury Street. I would have called first, if I'd had a dime.

One of the few things I'd enjoyed about being a cop was gabbing with Mooney. I like driving a cab better, but face it, most of my fares aren't scintillating conversationalists. The Red Sox and the weather usually covers it. Talking to Mooney was so much fun, I wouldn't even consider dating him. Lots of guys are good at sex, but conversation—now there's an art form.

Mooney, all six-foot-four, 240 linebacker pounds of him, gave me the glad eye when I waltzed in. He hasn't given up trying. Keeps telling me he talks even better in bed.

"Nice hat," was all he said, his big fingers pecking at the typewriter keys.

I took it off and shook out my hair. I wear an old slouch cap when I drive to keep people from saying the inevitable. One jerk even misquoted Yeats at me: "Only God, my dear, could love you for yourself alone and not your long red hair." Since I'm seated when I drive, he missed the chance to ask me how the weather is up here. I'm six-one in my stocking feet and skinny enough to make every inch count twice. I've got a wide forehead, green eyes, and a pointy chin. If you want to be nice about my nose, you say it's got character.

Thirty's still hovering in my future. It's part of Mooney's past.

I told him I had a robbery to report and his dark eyes steered me to a chair. He leaned back and took a puff of one of his low-tar cigarettes. He can't quite give 'em up, but he feels guilty as hell about 'em.

When I got to the part about the bag in the trash, Mooney lost his sense of humor. He crushed a half-smoked butt in a crowded ashtray.

"Know why you never made it as a cop?" he said.

"Didn't brownnose enough."

"You got no sense of proportion! Always going after crackpot stuff!"

"Christ, Mooney, aren't you interested? Some guy heists a cab, at gunpoint, then tosses the money. Aren't you the least bit *intrigued*?"

"I'm a cop, Ms. Carlyle. I've got to be more than in-trigued. I've got murders, bank robberies, assaults—"

"Well, excuse me. I'm just a poor citizen reporting a crime. Trying to help—"

"Want to help, Carlotta? Go away." He stared at the sheet of paper in the typewriter and lit another cigarette. "Or dig me up something on the Thayler case."

"You working that sucker?"

"Wish to hell I wasn't."

I could see his point. It's tough enough trying to solve any murder, but when your victim is *the* Jennifer (Mrs. Justin) Thayler, wife of the famed Harvard Law prof, and the society reporters are breathing down your neck along with the usual crime-beat scribblers, you got a special kind of problem.

"So who did it?" I asked.

Mooney put his size twelves up on his desk. "Colonel Mustard in the library with the candlestick! How the hell do I know? Some scumbag housebreaker. The lady of the house interrupted his haul. Probably didn't mean to hit her that hard. He must have freaked when he saw all the blood, 'cause he left some of the ritziest stereo equipment this side of heaven, plus enough silverware to blind your average hophead. He snatched most of old man Thayler's god-damn idiot art works, collections, collectibles—whatever the hell you call 'em—which ought to set him up for the next few hundred years, if he's smart enough to get rid of them."

"Alarm system?"

"Yeah, they had one. Looks like Mrs. Thayler forgot to turn it on. According to the maid, she had a habit of forget-ting just about anything after a martini or three."

"Think the maid's in on it?"

"Christ, Carlotta. There you go again. No witnesses. No fingerprints. Servants asleep. Husband asleep. We've got word out to all the fences here and in New York that we want this guy. The pawnbrokers know the stuff's hot. We're checking out known art thieves and shady museums—"

"Well, don't let me keep you from your serious busi-ness," I said, getting up to go. "I'll give you the collar when I find out who robbed my cab."

"Sure," he said. His fingers started playing with the typewriter again.

"Wanna bet on it?" Betting's an old custom with Mooney and me.

"I'm not gonna take the few piddling bucks you earn with that ridiculous car."

"Right you are, boy. I'm gonna take the money the city pays you to be unimaginative! Fifty bucks I nail him within the week."

Mooney hates to be called "boy." He hates to be called "unimaginative." I hate to hear my car called ridiculous. We shook hands on the deal. Hard.

Chinatown's about the only chunk of Boston that's alive after midnight. I headed over to Yee Hong's for a bowl of wonton soup.

The service was the usual low-key, slow-motion routine. I used a newspaper as a shield; if you're really involved in the *Wall Street Journal*, the casual male may think twice before deciding he's the answer to your prayers. But I didn't read a single stock quote. I tugged at strands of my hair, a bad habit of mine. Why would somebody rob me and then toss the money away?

Solution Number One: he didn't. The trash bin was some Mob drop, and the money I'd found in the trash had absolutely nothing to do with the money filched from my cab. Except that it was the same amount—and that was too big a coincidence for me to swallow.

Two: the cash I'd found was counterfeit and this was a clever way of getting it into circulation. Nah. Too baroque, entirely. How the hell would the guy know I was the pawing-through-the-trash type? And if this stuff was counterfeit, the rest of the bills in my wallet were too.

Three: it was a training session. Some fool had used me to perfect his robbery technique. Couldn't he learn from TV like the rest of the crooks?

Four: it was a frat hazing. Robbing a hack at gunpoint isn't exactly in the same league as swallowing goldfish.

I closed my eyes.

My face came to a fortunate halt about an inch above a bowl of steaming broth. That's when I decided to pack it in and head for home. Wonton soup is lousy for the complexion.

I checked out the log I keep in the Chevy, totaled my fares: $4.82 missing, all in change. A very reasonable robbery.

By the time I got home, the sleepiness had passed. You know how it is: one moment you're yawning, the next your eyes won't close. Usually happens when my head hits the pillow; this time I didn't even make it that far. What woke me up was the idea that my robber hadn't meant to steal a thing. Maybe he'd left me something instead. You know, something hot, cleverly concealed. Something he could pick up in a few weeks, after things cooled off.

I went over that backseat with a vengeance, but I didn't find anything besides old Kleenex and bent paper clips. My brainstorm wasn't too clever after all. I mean, if the guy wanted to use my cab as a hiding place, why advertise by pulling a five-and-dime robbery?

I sat in the driver's seat, tugged my hair, and stewed. What did I have to go on? The memory of a nervous thief who talked like a B movie and stole only change. Maybe a mad tollbooth collector.

I live in a Cambridge dump. In any other city, I couldn't sell the damned thing if I wanted to. Here, I turn real-estate agents away daily. The key to my home's value is the fact that I can hoof it to Harvard Square in five min-utes. It's a seller's market for tarpaper shacks within walk-ing distance of the Square. Under a hundred thou only if the plumbing's outside.

It took me a while to get in the door. I've got about five locks on it. Neighborhood's popular with thieves as well as gentry. I'm neither. I inherited the house from my weird Aunt Bea, all paid for. I consider the property taxes my rent, and the rent's getting steeper all the time.

I slammed my log down on the dining room table. I've got rooms galore in that old house, rent a couple of them to Harvard students. I've got my own office on the second floor. But I do most of my work at the dining room table. I like the view of the refrigerator.

I started over from square one. I called Gloria. She's the late-night dispatcher for the Independent Taxi Owners

Association. I've never seen her, but her voice is as smooth as mink oil and I'll bet we get a lot of calls from guys who just want to hear her say she'll pick 'em up in five minutes.

"Gloria, it's Carlotta."

"Hi, babe. You been pretty popular today."

"Was I popular at one thirty-five this morning?"

"Huh?"

"I picked up a fare in front of the Copley Plaza at one thirty-five. Did you hand that one out to all comers or did you give it to me solo?"

"Just a sec." I could hear her charming the pants off some caller in the background. Then she got back to me.

"I just gave him to you, babe. He asked for the lady in the '59 Chevy. Not a lot of those on the road."

"Thanks, Gloria."

"Trouble?" she asked.

"Is mah middle name," I twanged. We both laughed and I hung up before she got a chance to cross-examine me.

So. The robber wanted my cab. I wished I'd concentrated on his face instead of his snazzy clothes. Maybe it was somebody I knew, some jokester in midprank. I killed that idea; I don't know anybody who'd pull a stunt like that, at gunpoint and all. I don't want to know anybody like that.

Why rob my cab, then toss the dough?

I pondered sudden religious conversion. Discarded it. Maybe my robber was some perpetual screwup who'd ditched the cash by mistake.

Or . . . Maybe he got exactly what he wanted. Maybe he desperately desired my change.

Why?

Because my change was special, valuable beyond its $4.82 replacement cost.

So how would somebody know my change was valuable?

Because he'd given it to me himself, earlier in the day.

"Not bad," I said out loud. "Not bad." It was the kind of reasoning they'd bounced me off the police force for, what my so-called superiors termed the "fevered product of an over-imaginative mind." I leaped at it because it was the only explanation I could think of. I do like life to make some sort of sense.

I pored over my log. I keep pretty good notes: where I

pick up a fare, where I drop him, whether he's a hailer or
a radio call.

First, I ruled out all the women. That made the task
slightly less impossible: sixteen suspects down from thirty-
five. Then I yanked my hair and stared at the blank white
porcelain of the refrigerator door. Got up and made myself
a sandwich: ham, swiss cheese, salami, lettuce, and tomato,
on rye. Ate it. Stared at the porcelain some more until the
suspects started coming into focus.

Five of the guys were just plain fat and one was decidedly
on the hefty side; I'd felt like telling them all to walk. Might
do them some good, might bring on a heart attack. I
crossed them all out. Making a thin person look plump is
hard enough; it's damn near impossible to make a fatty
look thin.

Then I considered my regulars: Jonah Ashley, a tiny
blond southern gent; muscle-bound "just-call-me-Harold"
at Longfellow Place; Dr. Homewood getting his daily ferry
from Beth Israel to MGH; Marvin of the gay bars; and
Professor Dickerman, Harvard's answer to Berkeley's sixties radicals.

I crossed them all off. I could see Dickerman holding
up the First Filthy Capitalist Bank, or disobeying civilly at
Seabrook, even blowing up an oil company or two. But my
mind boggled at the thought of the great liberal Dickerman
robbing some poor cabbie. It would be like Robin Hood
joining the Sheriff of Nottingham on some particularly rotten peasant swindle. Then they'd both rape Maid Marian
and go off pals together.

Dickerman *was* a lousy tipper. That ought to be a crime.

So what did I have? Eleven out of sixteen guys cleared
without leaving my chair. Me and Sherlock Holmes, the
famous armchair detectives.

I'm stubborn; that was one of my good cop traits. I stared
at that log till my eyes bugged out. I remembered two of
the five pretty easily; they were handsome and I'm far from
blind. The first had one of those elegant bony faces and
far-apart eyes. He was taller than my bandit. I'd ceased
eyeballing him when I'd noticed the ring on his left hand;
I never fuss with the married kind. The other one was built,
a weight lifter. Not an Arnold Schwarzenegger extremist,

but built. I think I'd have noticed that bod on my bandit. Like I said, I'm not blind.

That left three.

Okay. I closed my eyes. Who had I picked up at the Hyatt on Memorial Drive? Yeah, that was the salesman guy, the one who looked so uncomfortable that I'd figured he'd been hoping to ask his cabbie for a few pointers concerning the best skirt-chasing areas in our fair city. Too low a voice. Too broad in the beam.

The log said I'd picked up a hailer in Kenmore Square when I'd let out the salesman. Ah yes, a talker. The weather, mostly. Don't you think it's dangerous for you to be driving a cab? Yeah, I remembered him, all right: a fatherly type, clasping a briefcase, heading to the financial district. Too old.

Down to one. I was exhausted but not the least bit sleepy. All I had to do was remember who I'd picked up on Beacon near Charles. A hailer. Before five o'clock which was fine by me because I wanted to be long gone before rush hour grid-locked the city. I'd gotten onto Storrow and taken him along the river into Newton Center. Dropped him off at the BayBank Middlesex, right before closing time. It was coming back. Little nervous guy. Pegged him as an accountant when I'd let him out at the bank. Measly, undernourished soul. Skinny as a rail, stooped, with pits left from teenage acne.

Shit. I let my head sink down onto the dining room table when I realized what I'd done. I'd ruled them all out, every one. So much for my brilliant deductive powers.

I retired to my bedroom, disgusted. Not only had I lost $4.82 in assorted alloy metals, I was going to lose fifty to Mooney. I stared at myself in the mirror, but what I was really seeing was the round hole at the end of a .22, held in a neat gloved hand.

Somehow, the gloves made me feel better. I'd remembered another detail about my piggy bank robber. I consulted the mirror and kept the recall going. A hat. The guy wore a hat. Not like my cap, but like a hat out of a forties gangster flick. I had one of those: I'm a sucker for hats. I plunked it on my head, jamming my hair up underneath— and I drew in my breath sharply.

A shoulder-padded jacket, a slim build, a low slouched hat. Gloves. Boots with enough heel to click as he walked away. Voice? High. Breathy, almost whispered. Not unpleasant. Accentless. No Boston "R."

I had a man's jacket and a couple of ties in my closet. Don't ask. They may have dated from as far back as my ex-husband, but not necessarily so. I slipped into the jacket, knotted the tie, tilted the hat down over one eye.

I'd have trouble pulling it off. I'm skinny, but my build is decidedly female. Still, I wondered—enough to traipse back downstairs, pull a chicken leg out of the fridge, go back to the log, and review the feminine possibilities. Good thing I did.

Everything clicked. One lady fit the bill exactly: mannish walk and clothes, tall for a woman. And I was in luck. While I'd picked her up in Harvard Square, I'd dropped her at a real address, a house in Brookline: 782 Mason Terrace, at the top of Corey Hill.

Jojo's garage opens at seven. That gave me a big two hours to sleep.

I took my beloved car in for some repair work it really didn't need yet and sweet-talked JoJo into giving me a loaner. I needed a hack, but not mine. Only trouble with that Chevy is it's too damn conspicuous.

I figured I'd lose way more than fifty bucks staking out Mason Terrace. I also figured it would be worth it to see old Mooney's face.

She was regular as clockwork, a dream to tail. Eight-thirty-seven every morning, she got a ride to the Square with a next-door neighbor. Took a cab home at five-fifteen. A working woman. Well, she couldn't make much of a living from robbing hacks and dumping the loot in the garbage.

I was damn curious by now. I knew as soon as I looked her over that she was the one, but she seemed so blah, so *normal*. She must have been five-seven or -eight, but the way she stooped, she didn't look tall. Her hair was long and brown with a lot of blond in it, the kind of hair that would have been terrific loose and wild, like a horse's mane. She tied it back with a scarf. A brown scarf. She wore suits. Brown suits. She had a tiny nose, brown eyes

under pale eyebrows, a sharp chin. I never saw her smile.
Maybe what she needed was a shrink, not a session with
Mooney. Maybe she'd done it for the excitement. God
knows if I had her routine, her job, I'd probably be dressing
up like King Kong and assaulting skyscrapers.

See, I followed her to work. It wasn't even tricky. She
trudged the same path, went in the same entrance to Harvard Yard, probably walked the same number of steps
every morning. Her name was Marcia Heidegger and she
was a secretary in the admissions office of the College of
Fine Arts.

I got friendly with one of her co-workers.

There was this guy typing away like mad at the desk in
her office. I could just see him from the side window. He
had grad student written all over his face. Longish wispy
hair. Gold-rimmed glasses. Serious. Given to deep sighs and
bright velour V necks. Probably writing his thesis on
"Courtly Love and the Theories of Chrétien de Troyes."

I latched onto him at Bailey's the day after I'd tracked
Lady Heidegger to her Harvard lair.

Too bad Roger was so short. Most short guys find it hard
to believe that I'm really trying to pick them up. They look
for ulterior motives. Not the Napoleon type of short guy;
he assumes I've been waiting years for a chance to dance
with a guy who doesn't have to bend to stare down my
cleavage. But Roger was no Napoleon. So I had to engineer
things a little.

I got into line ahead of him and ordered, after long delib-
eration, a BLT on toast. While the guy made it up and
shoved it on a plate with three measly potato chips and a
sliver of pickle you could barely see, I searched through
my wallet, opened my change purse, counted out silver, got
to $1.60 on the last five pennies. The counterman sang out:
"That'll be a buck eighty-five." I pawed through my pockets, found a nickel, two pennies. The line was growing res-
tive. I concentrated on looking like a damsel in need of a
knight, a tough task for a woman over six feet.

Roger (I didn't know he was Roger then) smiled ruefully
and passed over a quarter. I was effusive in my thanks. I
sat at a table for two, and when he'd gotten his tray (ham-

and-cheese and a strawberry ice cream soda), I motioned him into my extra chair.

He was a sweetie. Sitting down, he forgot the difference in our height, and decided I might be someone he could talk to. I encouraged him. I hung shamelessly on his every word. A Harvard man, imagine that. We got around slowly, ever so slowly, to his work at the admissions office. He wanted to duck it and talk about more important issues, but I persisted. I'd been thinking about getting a job at Harvard, possibly in admissions. What kind of people did he work with? Where they congenial? What was the atmosphere like? Was it a big office? How many people? Men? Women? Any soul mates? Readers? Or just, you know, office people?

According to him, every soul he worked with was brain-dead.

I had to be more obvious. I interrupted a stream of complaint with, "Gee, I know somebody who works for Harvard. I wonder if you know her."

"It's a big place," he said, hoping to avoid the whole endless business.

"I met her at a party. Always meant to look her up." I searched through my bag, found a scrap of paper, and pretended to read Marcia Heidegger's name off it.

"Marcia? Geez, I work with Marcia. Same office."

"Do you think she likes her work? I mean I got some strange vibes from her," I said. I actually said "strange vibes" and he didn't laugh his head off. People in the Square say things like that and other people take them seriously.

His face got conspiratorial, of all things, and he leaned closer to me.

"You want it, I bet you could get Marcia's job."

"You mean it?" What a compliment—a place for me among the brain-dead.

"She's gonna get fired if she doesn't snap out of it."

"Snap out of what?"

"It was bad enough working with her when she first came over. She's one of those crazy neat people, can't stand to see papers lying on a desktop, you know? She almost threw out the first chapter of my thesis!"

I made a suitably horrified noise and he went on.

"Well, you know, about Marcia, it's kind of tragic. She doesn't talk about it."

But he was dying to.

"Yes?" I said, as if he needed egging on.

He lowered his voice. "She used to work for Justin Thayler over at the law school, that guy in the news, whose wife got killed. You know, her work hasn't been worth shit since it happened. She's always on the phone, talking real soft, hanging up if anybody comes in the room. I mean, you'd think she was in love with the guy or something, the way she—"

I don't remember what I said. For all I know, I may have volunteered to type his thesis. But I got rid of him somehow and then I scooted around the corner of Church Street and found a pay phone and dialed Mooney.

"Don't tell me," he said. "Somebody mugged you, but they only took your trading stamps."

"I have just one question for you, Moon."

"I accept. A June wedding, but I'll have to break it to Mother gently."

"Tell me what kind of junk Justin Thayler collected."

I could hear him breathing into the phone.

"Just tell me," I said, "for curiosity's sake."

"You onto something, Carlotta?"

"I'm curious, Mooney. And you're not the only source of information in the world."

"Thayler collected Roman stuff. Antiques. And I mean old. Artifacts, statues—"

"Coins?"

"Whole mess of them."

"Thanks."

"Carlotta—"

I never did find out what he was about to say because I hung up. Rude, I know. But I had things to do. And it was better Mooney shouldn't know what they were, because they came under the heading of illegal activities.

When I knocked at the front door of the Mason Terrace house at ten A.M. the next day, I was dressed in dark slacks, a white blouse, and my old police department hat. I looked very much like the guy who reads your gas meter. I've never heard of anyone being arrested for impersonating the gas man. I've never heard of anyone really giving the gas man a second look. He fades into the background and that's exactly what I wanted to do.

I knew Marcia Heidegger wouldn't be home for hours. Old Reliable had left for the Square at her usual time, precise to the minute. But I wasn't 100 percent sure Marcia lived alone. Hence the gas man. I could knock on the door and check it out.

Those Brookline neighborhoods kill me. Act sneaky and the neighbors call the cops in twenty seconds, but walk right up to the front door, knock, talk to yourself while you're sticking a shin in the crack of the door, let yourself in, and nobody does a thing. Boldness is all.

The place wasn't bad. Three rooms, kitchen and bath, light and airy. Marcia was incredibly organized, obsessively neat, which meant I had to keep track of where everything was and put it back just so. There was no clutter in the woman's life. The smell of coffee and toast lingered, but if she'd eaten breakfast she'd already washed, dried, and put away the dishes. The morning paper had been read and tossed in the trash. The mail was sorted in one of those plastic accordion files. I mean she folded her underwear like origami.

Now coins are hard to look for. They're small; you can hide 'em anywhere. So this search took me one hell of a long time. Nine out of ten women hide things that are dear to them in the bedroom. They keep their finest jewelry closest to the bed, sometimes in the nightstand, sometimes right under the mattress. That's where I started.

Marcia had a jewelry box on top of her dresser. I felt like hiding it for her. She had some nice stuff and a burglar could have made quite a haul with no effort.

The next favorite place for women to stash valuables is the kitchen. I sifted through her flour. I removed every Kellogg's Rice Krispie from the giant economy-sized box— and returned it. I went through her place like no burglar ever will. When I say thorough, I mean thorough.

I found four odd things. A neatly squared pile of clippings from the *Globe* and the *Herald,* all the articles about the Thayler killing. A manila envelope containing five dif-

ferent safe-deposit box keys. A Tupperware container full
of superstitious junk, good luck charms mostly, the kind of
stuff I'd never have associated with a straight arrow like
Marcia: rabbits' feet galore, a little leather bag on a string
that looked like some kind of voodoo charm, a pendant in
the shape of a cross surmounted by a hook, and, I swear
to God, a pack of worn tarot cards. Oh yes, and a .22
automatic, looking a lot less threatening stuck in an ice
cube tray. I took the bullets; the loaded gun threatened a
defenseless box of Breyers mint chocolate chip ice cream.

I left everything else just the way I'd found it and went
home. And tugged my hair. And stewed. And brooded.
And ate half the stuff in the refrigerator, I kid you not.

At about one in the morning, it all made blinding,
crystal-clear sense.

The next afternoon, at five-fifteen, I made sure I was the
cabbie who picked up Marcia Heidegger in Harvard
Square. Now cabstands have the most rigid protocol since
Queen Victoria; you do not grab a fare out of turn or your
fellow cabbies are definitely not amused. There was nothing
for it but bribing the ranks. This bet with Mooney was
costing me plenty.

I got her. She swung open the door and gave the Mason
Terrace number. I grunted, kept my face turned front, and
took off.

Some people really watch where you're going in a cab,
scared to death you'll take them a block out of their way
and squeeze them for an extra nickel. Others just lean back
and dream. She was a dreamer, thank God. I was almost
at District One headquarters before she woke up.

"Excuse me," she said, polite as ever. "That's Mason
Terrace in *Brookline*."

"Take the next right, pull over, and douse your lights,"
I said in a low Bogart voice. My imitation was not that
good, but it got the point across. Her eyes widened and
she made an instinctive grab for the door handle.

"Don't try it, lady," I Bogied on. "You think I'm dumb
enough to take you in alone? There's a cop car behind us,
just waiting for you to make a move."

Her hand froze. She was a sap for movie dialogue.

"Where's the cop?" was all she said on the way up to Mooney's office.

"What cop?"

"The one following us."

"You have touching faith in our law enforcement system," I said.

She tried a bolt, I kid you not. I've had experience with runners a lot trickier than Marcia. I grabbed her in approved cop hold number three and marched her into Mooney's office.

He actually stopped typing and raised an eyebrow, an expression of great shock for Mooney.

"Citizen's arrest," I said.

"Charges?"

"Petty theft. Commission of a felony using a firearm." I rattled off a few more charges, using the numbers I remembered from cop school.

"This woman is crazy," Marcia Heidegger said with all the dignity she could muster.

"Search her," I said. "Get a matron in here. I want my four dollars and eighty-two cents back."

Mooney looked like he agreed with Marcia's opinion of my mental state. He said, "Wait up, Carlotta. You'd have to be able to identify that four eighty-two as yours. Can you do that? Quarters are quarters. Dimes are dimes."

"One of the coins she took was quite unusual," I said. "I'm sure I'd be able to identify it."

"Do you have any objection to displaying the change in your purse?" Mooney said to Marcia. He got me mad the way he said it, like he was humoring an idiot.

"Of course not," old Marcia said, cool as a frozen daiquiri.

"That's because she's stashed it somewhere else, Mooney," I said patiently. "She used to keep it in her purse, see. But then she goofed. She handed it over to a cabbie in her change. She should have just let it go, but she panicked because it was worth a pile and she was just babysitting it for someone else. So when she got it back, she hid it somewhere. Like in her shoe. Didn't you ever carry your lucky penny in your shoe?"

"No," Mooney said. "Now, Miss—"

"Heidegger," I said clearly. "Marcia Heidegger. She used to work at Harvard Law School." I wanted to see if Mooney picked up on it, but he didn't. He went on: "This can be taken care of with a minimum of fuss. If you'll agree to be searched by—"

"I want to see my lawyer," she said.

"For four dollars and eighty-two cents?" he said. "It'll cost you more than that to get your lawyer up here."

"Do I get my phone call or not?"

Mooney shrugged wearily and wrote up the charge sheet. Called a cop to take her to the phone.

He got JoAnn, which was good. Under cover of our old-friend-long-time-no-see greetings, I whispered in her ear.

"You'll find it fifty well spent," I said to Mooney when we were alone.

"I don't think you can make it stick."

"We'll see, won't we?"

JoAnn came back, shoving Marcia slightly ahead of her. She plunked her prisoner down in one of Mooney's hard wooden chairs and turned to me, grinning from ear to ear.

"Got it?" I said. "Good for you."

"What's going on?" Mooney said.

"She got real clumsy on the way to the pay phone," JoAnn said. "Practically fell on the floor. Got up with her right hand clenched tight. When we got to the phone, I offered to drop her dime for her. She wanted to do it herself. I insisted and she got clumsy again. Somehow this coin got kicked clear across the floor."

She held it up. The coin could have been a dime, except the color was off: warm, rosy gold instead of dead silver. How I missed it the first time around I'll never know.

"What the hell is that?" Mooney said.

"What kind of coins were in Justin Thayler's collection?" I asked. "Roman?"

Marcia jumped out of the chair, snapped her bag open, and drew out her little .22. I kid you not. She was closest to Mooney and she just stepped up to him and rested it above his left ear. He swallowed, didn't say a word. I never realized how prominent his Adam's apple was. JoAnn froze, hand on her holster.

Good old reliable, methodical Marcia. Why, I said to

myself, *why* pick today of all days to trot your gun out of
the freezer? Did you read bad luck in your tarot cards?
Then I had a truly rotten thought. What if she had two
guns? What if the disarmed .22 was still staring down the
mint chip ice cream?

"Give it back," Marcia said. She held out one hand,
made an impatient waving motion.

"Hey, you don't need it, Marcia," I said. "You've got
plenty more. In all those safe-deposit boxes."

"I'm going to count to five—" she began.

"Were you in on the murder from day one? You know,
from the planning stages?" I asked. I kept my voice low,
but it echoed off the walls of Mooney's tiny office. The
hum of everyday activity kept going in the main room. Nobody noticed the little gun in the well-dressed lady's hand.
"Or did you just do your beau a favor and hide the loot
after he iced his wife? In order to back up his burglary
tale? I mean, if Justin Thayler really wanted to marry you,
there is such a thing as divorce. Or was old Jennifer the
one with the bucks?"

"I want that coin," she said softly. "Then I want the two
of you"—she motioned to JoAnn and me—"to sit down
facing that wall. If you yell, or do anything before I'm out
of the building, I'll shoot this gentleman. He's coming
with me."

"Come on, Marcia," I said, "put it down. I mean, look
at you. A week ago you just wanted Thayler's coin back.
You didn't want to rob my cab, right? You just didn't know
how else to get your good luck charm back with no questions asked. You didn't do it for money, right? You did it
for love. You were so straight you threw away the cash.
Now here you are with a gun pointed at a cop—"

"Shut up!"

I took a deep breath and said, "You haven't got the
style, Marcia. Your gun's not even loaded."

Mooney didn't relax a hair. Sometimes I think the guy
hasn't ever believed a word I've said to him. But Marcia
got shook. She pulled the barrel away from Mooney's skull
and peered at it with a puzzled frown. JoAnn and I both
tackled her before she got a chance to pull the trigger. I
twisted the gun out of her hand. I was almost afraid to

look inside. Mooney stared at me and I felt my mouth go dry and a trickle of sweat worm its way down my back.

I looked.

No bullets. My heart stopped fibrillating, and Mooney actually cracked a smile in my direction

So that's all. I sure hope Mooney will spread the word around that I helped him nail Thayler. And I think he will; he's a fair kind of guy. Maybe it'll get me a case or two. Driving a cab is hard on the backside, you know?

MARY, MARY, SHUT THE DOOR
Benjamin M. Schutz
FIRST APPEARANCE: Embrace the Wolf, 1985

Ben Schutz had already won a Shamus Award for best PI novel with *A Tax in Blood* (Tor, 1987) when along came this story. "Mary, Mary, Shut the Door" was published in *Deadly Allies* (Doubleday, 1992) and swept both the Shamus and the Edgar awards for best short story. His sixth Haggerty novel, *Mexico Is Forever* (St. Martin's Press), was published in 1994.

Enzo Scolari motored into my office and motioned me to sit. What the hell, I sat. He pulled around to the side of my desk, laced his fingers in his lap, and sized me up.

"I want to hire you, Mr. Haggerty," he announced.

"To do what, Mr. Scolari?"

"I want you to stop my niece's wedding."

"I see. And why is that?"

"She is making a terrible mistake, and I will not sit by and let her do it."

"Exactly what kind of mistake is she making?"

"She knows nothing about him. They just met. She is infatuated, nothing more. She knows nothing about men. Nothing. The first one to pay any attention to her and she wants to get married."

"You said they just met. How long ago, exactly?" Just a little reality check.

"Two weeks. Can you believe it? Two weeks. And I just found out about it yesterday. She brought him to the house last night. There was a party and she introduced him to everyone and told us she was going to marry him. How can you marry someone you've known for two weeks? That's ridiculous. It's a guarantee of failure and it'll break her heart. I can't let that happen."

"Mr. Scolari, I'm not sure we can help you with this. Your niece may be doing something foolish, but she has a right to do it. I understand your concern for her well-being, but I don't think you need a detective, maybe a priest or a therapist. We don't do premarital background checks. Our investigations are primarily criminal."

"The crime just hasn't happened yet, Mr. Haggerty. My niece may be a foolish girl, but he isn't. He knows exactly what he's doing."

"And what is that?"

"He's taking advantage of her naïveté, her innocence, her fears, her loneliness, so he can get her money. That's a crime, Mr. Haggerty."

And a damn hard one to prove. "What are you afraid of, Mr. Scolari? That he'll kill her for her money? That's quite a leap from an impulsive decision to marry. Do you have any reason to think that this guy is a killer?"

He straightened up and gave that one some thought. Enzo Scolari was wide and thick with shoulders so square and a head so flat he could have been a candelabra. His snow white eyebrows and mustache hung like awnings for his eyes and lips.

"No. Not for that. But I can tell he doesn't love Gina. Last night I watched him. Every time Gina left his side his eyes went somewhere else. A man in love, his eyes follow his woman everywhere. No, he's following the maid or Gina's best friend. Gina comes back and he smiles like she's the sunrise. And she believes it.

"He spent more time touching the tapestries than he did holding her hand. He went through the house like a creditor, not a guest. No, he doesn't want Gina, he wants her money. You're right, murder is quite a step from that, but there are easier ways to steal. Gina is a shy, quiet woman who has never had to make any decisions for herself. I don't blame her for that. My sister, God rest her soul, was terrified that something awful would happen to Gina and she tried to protect her from everything. It didn't work. My sister was the one who died and it devastated the girl. Now Gina has to live in the world and she doesn't know how.

If this guy can talk her into marrying him so quickly, he'll have no trouble talking her into letting him handle her money."

"How much money are we talking about here?"

"Ten million dollars, Mr. Haggerty." Scolari smiled, having made his point. People have murdered or married for lots less.

"How did she get all this money?"

"It's in a trust for her. A trust set up by my father. My sister and I each inherited half of Scolari Enterprises. When she died, her share went to Gina as her only child."

"This trust, who manages it?"

"I do, of course."

Of course. Motive number two just came up for air. "So, where's the problem? If you control the money, this guy can't do anything."

"I control the money as trustee for my sister. I began that when Gina was still a little girl. Now she is of age and can control the money herself if she wants to."

"So you stand to lose the use of ten million dollars. Have I got that right?"

Scolari didn't even bother to debate that one with me. I liked that. I'll take naked self-interest over the delusions of altruism any day.

"If they've just met, how do you know that this guy even knows that your niece has all this money?"

Scolari stared at me, then spat out his bitter reply. "Why else would he have pursued her? She is a mousy little woman, dull and plain. She's afraid of men. She spent her life in those fancy girls' schools where they taught her how to set the table. She huddled with her mother in that house, afraid of everything. Well, now she is alone and I think she's latched onto the first person who will rescue her from that."

"Does she know how you feel?"

He nodded. "Yes, she does. I made it very clear to her last night."

"How did she take it?"

"She told me to mind my own business." Scolari snorted. "She doesn't even know that that's what I'm doing. She said she loved him and she was going to marry him, no matter what."

"Doesn't sound so mousy to me. She ever stand up to you before?"

"No, never. On anything else, I'd applaud it. But getting married shouldn't be the first decision you ever make."

"Anyone else that might talk to her that she'd listen to?"

"No. She's an only child. Her father died when she was two in the same explosion that killed my father and took my legs. Her mother died in an automobile accident a little over a year ago. I am a widower myself and Gina was never close to my sons. They frightened her as a little girl. They were loud and rough. They teased her and made her cry." Scolari shrugged as if boys would be boys. "I did not like that and would stop it whenever I caught them, but she was such a timid child, their cruelty sprouted whenever she was around. There is no other family."

I picked up the pipe from my desk, stuck it in my mouth, and chewed on it. A glorified pacifier. Kept me from chewing up the inside of my mouth, though. Wouldn't be much of a stretch to take this one on. What the hell, work is work.

"Okay, Mr. Scolari, we'll take the case. I want you to understand that we can't and we won't stop her wedding. There are guys who will do that, and I know who they are, but I wouldn't give you their names. We'll do a background check on this guy and see if we can find something that'll change her mind or your mind. Maybe they really love each other. That happens, you know. This may be a crazy start, but I'm not sure that's a handicap. What's the best way to run a race when you don't know where the finish is?" I sure didn't have an answer and Scolari offered none.

"Mr. Haggerty, I am not averse to taking a risk, but not a blind one. If there's information out there that will help me calculate the odds, then I want it. That's what I want you to get for me. I appreciate your open mind, Mr. Haggerty. Perhaps you will change my mind, but I doubt it."

"Okay, Mr. Scolari. I need a description of this guy, his name and anything else you know about him. First thing Monday morning, I'll assign an investigator and we'll get on this."

"That won't do, Mr. Haggerty. You need to start on this immediately, this minute."

"Why is that?"

"Because they flew to St. Mary's this morning to get married."

"Aren't we a little late, then?"

"No. You can't apply for a marriage license on St. Mary's until you've been on the island for two days."

"How long to get the application approved?"

"I called the embassy. They say it takes three days to process the application. I'm looking into delaying that, if possible. Once it's issued they say most people get married that day or the next."

"So we've got what, five or six days? Mr. Scolari, we can't run a complete background check in that period of time. Hell, no one can. There just isn't enough time."

"What if you put everyone you've got on this, round the clock?"

"That gets you a maybe and just barely that. He'd have to have a pimple on his backside the size of Mount Rushmore for us to find it that fast. If this guy's the sneaky, cunning opportunist that you think he is, then he's hidden that, maybe not perfectly, but deep enough that six days won't turn it up. Besides, I can't put everyone on this, we've got lots of other cases that need attention."

"So hire more staff, give them the other cases, and put everyone else on this. Money is no object, Mr. Haggerty. I want you to use all your resources on this."

My jaw hurt from clamping on the dead pipe. Scolari was old enough to make a foolish mistake. I told him it was a long shot at best. What more could I tell him? When did I become clairvoyant, and know how things would turn out? Suppose we did find something, like three dead ex-wives? Right! Let's not kid ourselves—all the staff for six days— round the clock—that's serious money. What was it Rocky said? When you run a business, money's always necessary but it's never sufficient. Don't confuse the two and what you do at the office won't keep you up at night.

I sorted everything into piles and then decided. "All right, Mr. Scolari, we'll do it. I can't even tell you what it'll cost. We'll bill you at our hourly rates plus all the expenses.

I think a reasonable retainer would be thirty thousand dollars."

He didn't even blink. It probably wasn't a week's interest on ten million dollars.

"There's no guarantee that we'll find anything, Mr. Scolari, not under these circumstances. You'll know that you did everything you could, but that's all you'll know for sure."

"That's all you ever know for sure, Mr. Haggerty."

I pulled out a pad to make some notes. "Do you know where they went on St. Mary's?"

"Yes. A resort called the Banana Bay Beach Hotel. I have taken the liberty of registering you there."

"Excuse me." I felt like something under his front wheel.

"The resort is quite remote and perched on the side of a cliff. I have been assured that I would not be able to make my way around. I need you to be my legs, my eyes. If your agents learn anything back here, someone has to be able to get that information to my niece. Someone has to be there. I want that someone to be you, Mr. Haggerty. That's what I'm paying for. Your brains, your eyes, your legs, to be there because I can't."

I stared at Scolari's withered legs and the motorized wheelchair he got around in. More than that he had money, lots of money. And money's the ultimate prosthesis.

"Let's start at the top. What's his name?"

The island of St. Mary's is one of lush green mountains that drop straight into the sea. What little flat land there is, is on the west coast, and that's where almost all the people live. The central highlands and peaks are still wild and pristine.

My plane banked around the southern tip of the island and headed toward one of those flat spots, the international airport. I flipped through the file accumulated in those few hours between Enzo Scolari's visit and my plane's departure. While Kelly, my secretary, made travel arrangements I called everyone into the conference room and handed out jobs. Clancy Hopper was to rearrange caseloads and hire temporary staff to keep the other cases moving. Del Winslow was to start investigating our man Derek Marshall. We had a name, real or otherwise, an address, and a phone number. Del would do the house-to-house with the drawing we made from Scolari's description. Larry Burdette would be smilin' and dialin'. Calling every computerized data base we could access to get more information. Every time Marshall's name appeared he'd take the information and hand it to another investigator to verify every fact and then backtrack each one by phone or in person until we could recreate the life of Derek Marshall. Our best chance was with the St. Mary's Department of Licenses. To apply for a marriage license Marshall had to file a copy of his passport, birth certificate, decrees of divorce if previously married, death certificate if widowed, and proof of legal name change, if any. If the records were open to the public, we'd get faxed copies or I'd go to the offices myself and look at them personally. I took one last look at the picture of Gina Dalesandro and then the sketch of Derek Marshall, closed the file, and slipped it into my bag as the runway appeared outside my window.

I climbed out of the plane and into the heat. A dry wind moved the heat around me as I walked into the airport. I showed my passport and had nothing to declare. They were delighted to have me on their island. I stepped out of the airport and the cab master introduced me to my driver. I followed him to a battered Toyota, climbed into the front seat, and stowed my bag between my feet. He slammed the door and asked where to.

"Banana Bay Beach Hotel," I said as he turned the engine on and pulled out.

"No problem."

"How much?" We bounced over a sleeping policeman.

"Eighty ecee."

Thirty-five dollars American. "How far is it?"

"Miles or time?"

"Both."

"Fifteen miles. An hour and a half."

I should have gotten out then. If the road to hell is paved at all, then it doesn't pass through St. Mary's. The coast road was a lattice of potholes winding around the sides of the mountains. There were no lanes, no lights, no signs, and no guardrails. The sea was a thousand feet below and we were never more than a few inches from visiting it.

Up and down the hills, there were blue bags on the trees.

"What are those bags?" I asked.

"Bananas. The bags keep the insects away while they ripen."

I scanned the slopes and tried to imagine going out there to put those bags on. Whoever did it, they couldn't possibly be paying him enough. Ninety minutes of bobbing and weaving on those roads like a fighter on the ropes and I was exhausted from defying gravity. I half expected to hear a bell to end the trip as we pulled up to the resort.

I checked in, put my valuables in a safe-deposit box, took my key and information packet, and headed up the hill to my room. Dinner was served in about an hour. Enough time to get oriented, unpack, and shower.

My room overlooked the upstairs bar and dining area and below that the beach, the bay, and the surrounding cliffs. I had a thatched-roof veranda with a hammock and clusters of flamboyant and chenille red-hot cattails close enough to pluck. The bathroom was clean and functional. The bedroom large and sparely furnished. Clearly, this was a place where the attractions were outdoors and rooms were for sleeping in. The mosquito netting over the bed and the coils on the dresser were not good signs. It was the rainy season and Caribbean mosquitoes can get pretty cheeky. In Antigua one caught me in the bathroom and pulled back the shower curtain like he was Norman Bates.

I unpacked quickly and read my information packet. It had a map of the resort, a list of services, operating hours, and tips on how to avoid common problems in the Caribbean such as sunburn, being swept out to sea, and a variety of bites, stings, and inedible fruits. I familiarized myself with the layout and took out the pictures of Gina and Derek. Job one was to find them and then tag along unobtrusively until the home office gave me something to work with.

I showered, changed, and lay down on the bed to wait for dinner. The best time to make an appearance was midway through the meal. Catch the early birds leaving and the stragglers on their way in.

Around eight-thirty, I sprayed myself with insect repellent, slipped my keys into my pocket, and headed down to dinner. The schedule said that it would be a barbecue on the beach.

At the reception area I stopped and looked over the low wall to the beach below. Scolari was right, he wouldn't be able to get around here. The rooms jutted out from the bluff and were connected by a steep roadway. However, from this point on, the hillside was a precipice. A staircase wound its way down to the beach. One hundred and twenty-six steps, the maid said.

I started down, stopping periodically to check the railing. There were no lights on the trail. Late at night, a little drunk on champagne, a new bride could have a terrible accident. I peered over the side at the concrete roadway below. She wouldn't bounce and she wouldn't survive.

I finished the zigzagging descent and noted that the return trip would be worse.

Kerosene lamps led the way to the beach restaurant and bar. I sat on a stool, ordered a yellowbird, and turned to look at the dining area. Almost everyone was in couples, the rest were families. All white, mostly Americans, Canadians, British, and German. At least that's what the brochure said.

I sipped my drink and scanned the room. No sign of them. No problem, the night was young even if I wasn't. I had downed a second drink when they came in out of the darkness. Our drawing of Marshall was pretty good. He was slight, pale, with brown hair parted down the middle, round-rimmed tortoiseshell glasses, and a deep dimpled smile he aimed at the woman he gripped by the elbow. He steered her between the tables as if she had a tiller.

They took a table and I looked about to position myself. I wanted to be able to watch Marshall's face and be close enough to overhear them without looking like it. One row over and two up a table was coming free. I took my drink from the bar and ambled over. The busboy cleared the table and I took a long sip from my drink and set it down.

Gina Dalesandro wore a long flower-print dress. Strapless, she had tan lines where her bathing suit had been. She ran a finger over her ear and flipped back her hair. In profile she was thin-lipped, hook-nosed, and high-browed. Her hand held Marshall's, and then, eyes on his, she pulled one to her and kissed it. She moved from one knuckle to the next, and when she was done she took a finger and slowly slid it into her mouth.

"Gina, please, people will look," he whispered.

"Let them," she said, smiling around his finger.

Marshall pulled back and flicked his eyes around. My waitress had arrived and I was ordering when he passed over me. I had the fish chowder, the grilled dolphin with stuffed christophine, and another drink.

Gina picked up Marshall's hand and held it to her cheek and said something soothing because he smiled and blew her a kiss. They ordered and talked in hushed tones punctuated with laughter and smiles. I sat nearby, watching, waiting, her uncle's gargoyle in residence.

When dessert arrived, Gina excused herself and went toward the ladies' room. Marshall watched her go. I read nothing in his face or eyes. When she disappeared into the bathroom, his eyes wandered around the room, but settled on no one. He locked in on her when she reappeared and led her back to the table with his eyes. All in all it proved nothing.

We all enjoyed the banana cake and coffee and after a discreet pause I followed them back toward the rooms. We trudged silently up the stairs, past the bar and the reception desk, and back into darkness. I kept them in view as I went toward my room and saw that they were in room 7, two levels up and one over from me. When their door clicked closed, I turned around and went back to the activities board outside the bar. I scanned the list of trips for tomorrow to see if they had signed up for any of them. They were down for the morning trip to the local volcano. I signed aboard and went to arrange a wake-up call for the morning.

After a quick shower, I lit the mosquito coils, dialed the lights way down, and crawled under the netting. I pulled the phone and my book inside, propped up the pillows, and called the office. For his money, Scolari should get an answer. He did.

"Franklin Investigations."

"Evening, Del. What do we have on Derek Marshall?"

"Precious little, boss, that's what."

"Well, give it to me."

"Okay, I canvassed his neighborhood. He's the invisible man. Rented apartment. Manager says he's always on time with the rent. Nothing else. I missed the mailman, but I'll catch him tomorrow. See if he can tell me anything. Neighbors know him by sight. That's about it. No wild parties. Haven't seen him with lots of girls. One thought he was seeing this one particular woman but hasn't seen her around in quite a while."

"How long has he been in the apartment?"

"Three years."

"Manager let you look at the rent application?"

"Leo, you know that's confidential. I couldn't even ask for that information."

"We prosper on the carelessness of others, Del. Did you ask?"

"Yes, and he was offended and indignant."

"Tough shit."

"Monday morning we'll go through court records and permits and licenses for the last three years, see if anything shakes out."

"Neighbors tell you anything else?"

"No, like I said, they knew him by sight, period."

"You find his car?"

"Yeah. Now that was a gold mine. Thing had stickers all over it."

"Such as?"

"Bush-Quayle. We'll check him out with Young Republican organizations. Also, Georgetown Law School."

"You run him through our directories?"

"Yeah, nothing. He's either a drone or modest."

"Call Walter O'Neil, tonight. Give him the name, see if he can get a law firm for the guy, maybe even someone who'll talk about him."

"Okay. I'm also going over to the school tomorrow, use the library, look up yearbooks, et cetera. See if we can locate a classmate. Alumni affairs will have to wait until Monday."

"How about NCIC?"

"Clean. No warrants or arrests. He's good or he's tidy."

"Anything else on the car?"

"Yeah, a sticker for something called Ultimate Frisbee. Nobody here knows anything about it. We're trying to track down an association for it, find out where it's played, then we'll interview people."

"Okay. We've still got three, maybe four days. How's the office doing? Are the other cases being covered?"

"Yeah, we spread them around. Clancy hired a couple of freelancers to start next week. Right now, me, Clancy, and Larry are pulling double shifts on this. Monday when the offices are open and the databases are up, we'll probably put the two new guys on it."

"Good. Any word from the St. Mary's registrar's office?"

"No. Same problem there. Closed for the weekend. Won't know anything until Monday."

"All right. Good work, Del." I gave him my number. "Call here day or night with anything. If you can't get me directly, have me paged. I'll be out tomorrow morning on a field trip with Marshall and Gina, but I should be around the rest of the day."

"All right. Talk to you tomorrow."

I slipped the phone under the netting. Plumped the pillows and opened my book. Living alone had made me a voracious reader, as if all my other appetites had mutated into a hunger for the words that would make me someone else, put me somewhere else, or at least help me to sleep. The more I read, the harder it was to keep my interest. Boredom crept over me like the slow death it was. I was an old jaded john needing ever kinkier tricks just to get it up, or over with. Pretty soon nothing would move me at all. Until then, I was grateful for Michael Malone and the jolts and length of *Time's Witness.*

I woke up to the telephone's insistent ring, crawled out of bed, and thanked the front desk for the call. A chameleon darted out from under the bed and headed out the door. "Nice seeing you," I called out, and hoped he'd had a bountiful evening keeping my room an insect-free zone. I dressed and hurried down to breakfast.

After a glass of soursop, I ordered salt fish and onions with bakes and lots of coffee. Derek and Gina were not in the dining room. Maybe they'd ordered room service, maybe they were sleeping in and wouldn't make it. I ate quickly and kept checking my watch while I had my second cup of coffee. Our driver had arrived and was looking at the activities board. Another couple came up to him and introduced themselves. I wiped my mouth and left to join the group. Derek and Gina came down the hill as I checked in.

Our driver told us that his name was Wellington Bramble and that he was also a registered tour guide with the Department of the Interior. The other couple climbed into the back of the van, then Derek and Gina in the middle row. I hopped in up front, next to Wellington, turned, and introduced myself.

"Hi, my name is Leo Haggerty."

"Hello, I'm Derek Marshall and this is my fiancée, Gina Dalesandro."

"Pleasure to meet you."

Derek and Gina turned and we were all introduced to Tom and Dorothy Needham of Chicago, Illinois.

Wellington stuck his head out the window and spoke to one of the maids. They spoke rapidly in the local patois until the woman slapped him across the forearm and waved a scolding finger at him.

He engaged the gears, pulled away from the reception area, and told us that we would be visiting the tropical rain forests that surround the island's active volcano. All this in perfect English, the language of strangers and for strangers.

Dorothy Needham asked the question on all of our minds. "How long will we be on this road to the volcano?"

Wellington laughed. "Twenty minutes, ma'am, then we go inland to the volcano."

We left the coast road and passed through a gate marked St. Mary's Island Conservancy—Devil's Cauldron Volcano and Tropical Rain Forest. I was first out and helped the women step down into the muddy path. Wellington lined us up and began to lead us through the jungle, calling out the names of plants and flowers and answering questions.

There were soursop trees, lime trees, nutmeg, guava, ba-nanas, coconuts, cocoa trees, ginger lilies, lobster-claw plants, flamboyant and hibiscus, impression fern, and che-nille red-hot cattails. We stopped on the path at a large fern. Wellington turned and pointed to it.

"Here, you touch the plant, right here," he said, pointing at Derek, who eyed him suspiciously. "It won't hurt you."

Derek reached out a finger and touched the fern. In-stantly the leaves retracted and curled in on themselves.

"That's Mary, Mary, Shut the Door. As you can see, a delicate and shy plant indeed."

He waved us on and we followed. Gina slipped an arm through Derek's and put her head on his shoulder. She squeezed him once.

"Derek, you know I used to be like that plant. Before you came along. All closed up and frightened if anybody got too close. But not anymore. I am so happy," she said, and squeezed him again.

Other than a mild self-loathing, I was having a good time, too. We came out of the forest and were on the volcano. Wellington turned to face us.

"Ladies and gentlemen, please listen very carefully. We are on top of an active volcano. There is no danger of an eruption, because there is no crust, so there is no pressure buildup. The last eruption was over two hundred years ago. That does not mean that there is no danger here. You must stay on the marked path at all times and be very careful on the sections that have no guardrail. The water in the volcano is well over three hundred degrees Fahrenheit; should you stumble and fall in, you would be burned alive. I do not wish to alarm you unreasonably, but a couple of years ago we did lose a visitor, so please be very careful. Now follow me."

We moved along, single file and well spaced through a setting unlike any other I'd ever encountered. The circular top of the volcano looked like a wound on the earth. The ground steamed and smoked and nothing grew anywhere. Here and there black water leaked out of crusty patches like blood seeping from under a scab. The smell of sulfur was everywhere.

I followed Derek and Gina and watched him stop a couple of times and test the railings before he let her proceed. Caution, Derek? Or a trial run?

We circled the volcano and retraced our path back to the van. As promised, we were back at the hotel twenty minutes later. Gina was flushed with excitement and asked Derek if they could go back again. He thought that was possible, but there weren't any other guided tours this week, so they'd have to rent a car and go themselves. I closed my eyes and imagined her by the side of the road, taking a picture perhaps, and him ushering her through the foliage and on her way to eternity.

We all went in for lunch and ate separately. I followed them back to their room and then down to the beach. They moved to the far end of the beach and sat facing away from everyone else. I went into the bar and worked my way through a pair of long necks.

A couple in the dining room was having a spat, or maybe it was a tiff. Whatever, she called him a *schwein* and really tagged him with an open forehand to the chops. His face lit up redder than a baboon's ass.

She pushed back her chair, swung her long blond hair in an about-face, and stormed off. I watched her go, taking each step like she was grinding out a cigarette under her foot. Made her hips and butt do terrible things.

I pulled my eyes away when I realized I had company. He was leering at me enthusiastically.

I swung around slowly. "Yes?"

It was one of the local hustlers who patrolled the beach, as ubiquitous and resourceful as the coconuts that littered the sand.

"I seen you around, man. Y'all alone. That's not a good thin', man. I was thinkin' maybe you could use some company. Someone to share paradise wit'. Watcha say, man?"

I shook my head. "I don't think so."

He frowned. "I know you ain't that way, man. I seen you watch that blond with the big ones. What'sa matter? What you afraid of?" He stopped and tried to answer that one for me. "She be clean, man. No problem."

When I didn't say anything, he got pissed. "What is it then? You don't fuck strange, man?"

"Watch my lips, bucko. I'm not interested. Don't make more of it than there is."

He sized me up and decided I wasn't worth the aggravation. Spinning off his stool, he called me something in patois. I was sure it wasn't "sir."

I found a free lounge under a bohio and kept an eye on Derek and Gina. No sooner had I settled in than Gina got up and headed across the cocoa-colored volcanic sands to the beach bar. She was a little pink around the edges. Probably wouldn't be out too long today. Derek had his back to me, so I swiveled my head to keep her in sight. She sat down and one of the female staff came over and began to run a comb through her hair. Cornrowing. She'd be there for at least an hour. I ordered a drink from a wandering waiter, closed my eyes, and relaxed.

Gina strolled back, her hair in tight little braids, each one tipped with a series of colored beads. She was smiling and kicking up little sprays of water. I watched her take Derek by the hands and pull him up out of his chair. She twirled around and shook her head back and forth, just to watch the braids fly by. They picked up their snorkels and fins and headed for the water. I watched to see which way they'd go. The left side of the bay had numerous warning signs about the strong current including one on the point that said Turn Back—Next Stop Panama.

They went right and so did I. Maybe it was a little fear, maybe it was love, but she held on to his hand while they hovered over the reef. I went farther out and then turned back so I could keep them in sight. The reef was one of the richest I'd ever been on and worthy of its reputation as one of the best in the Caribbean.

I kept my position near the couple, moving when they did, just like the school of squid I was above. They were in formation, tentacles tucked in, holding their position by undulating the fins on each lateral axis. When the school moved, they all went at once and kept the same distance from each other. I drifted off the coral to a bed of sea grass. Two creatures were walking through the grass. Gray-green, with knobs and lumps everywhere, they had legs and wings! They weren't toxic-waste mutants, just the flying gurnards. I dived down on them and they spread their violet wings and took off.

When I surfaced, Derek and Gina were heading in. I swam downstream from them and came ashore as they did. Gina was holding her side and peeking behind her palm. Derek steadied her and helped get her flippers off.

"I don't know what it was, Derek. It just brushed me and then it felt like a bee sting. It really burns," Gina said.

I wandered by and said, "Looks like a jellyfish sting. When did it happen?"

"Just a second ago." They answered in unison.

"Best thing for that is papaya skins. Has an enzyme that neutralizes the toxin. The beach restaurant has plenty of them. They keep it just for things like this. You better get right over, though. It only works if you apply it right away."

"Thanks. Thanks a lot," Derek said, then turned to help Gina down the beach. "Yes, thank you," she said over his shoulder.

"You're welcome," I said to myself, and went to dry off.

I sat at the bar, waiting for dinner and playing backgammon with myself. Derek and Gina came in and went to the bar to order. Her dress was a swirl of purple, black, and white and matched the color of the beads in her hair. Derek wore lime green shorts and a white short-sleeved shirt. Drinks in hand, they walked over to me. I stood up, shook hands, and invited them to join me.

"That tip of yours was a lifesaver. We went over to the bar and got some papaya on it right away. I think the pain was gone in maybe five minutes. How did you know about it?" Gina asked.

"I've been stung myself before. Somebody told me about it. Now I tell you. Word of mouth."

"Well, we're very grateful. We're getting married here on the island and I didn't want anything to mess this time up for us," Derek said.

I raised my glass in a toast. "Congratulations to you. This is a lovely place to get married. When is the ceremony?" I asked, sipping my drink.

"Tomorrow," Gina said, running her arm through Derek's. "I'm so excited."

I nearly drowned her in rerouted rum punch but managed to turn away and choke myself instead. I pounded my chest and waved off any assistance.

"Are you okay?" Derek asked.

"Yes, yes, I'm fine," I said as I got myself under control. Tomorrow? How the hell could it be tomorrow? "Sorry. I was trying to talk when I was drinking. Just doesn't work that way."

Derek asked if he could buy me another drink and I let him take my glass to the bar.

"I read the tourist brochure about getting married on the island. How long does it take for them to approve an application? They only said that you have to be on the island for two days before you can submit an application."

Gina leaned forward and touched my knee. "It usually takes two or three days, but Derek found a way to hurry things up. He sent the papers down early to the manager here and he agreed to file them for us as if we were on the island. It'll be ready tomorrow morning and we'll get married right after noon."

"That's wonderful. Where will the ceremony be?" My head was spinning.

"Here at the hotel. Down on the beach. They provide a cake, champagne, photographs, flowers. Would you join us afterward to celebrate?"

"Thank you, that's very kind. I'm not sure that I'll still be here, though. My plane leaves in the afternoon, and you know with that ride back to the airport, I might be gone. If I'm still here, I'd be delighted."

Derek returned with drinks and sat close to Gina and looped an arm around her.

"Honey, I hope you don't mind, but I invited Mr. Haggerty to join us after the ceremony." She smiled anxiously.

"No, that sounds great, love to have you. By the way, it sounded like you've been to the islands before. This is our first time. Have you ever gone scuba diving?" Derek was all graciousness.

"Yeah, are you thinking of trying it?"

"Maybe, they have a course for beginners tomorrow. We were talking about taking the course and seeing if we liked it," he said.

"I'm a little scared. Is it really dangerous?" Gina asked.

Absolutely lethal. Russian roulette with one empty chamber. Don't do it. Wouldn't recommend it to my worst enemy.

"No, not really. There are dangers if you're careless, and they're pretty serious ones. The sea is not very forgiving of our mistakes. But if you're well trained and maintain some respect for what you're doing, it's not all that dangerous."

"I don't know. Maybe I'll just watch you do it, Derek."

"Come on, honey. You really liked snorkeling. Can you imagine how much fun it would be if you didn't have to worry about coming up for air all the time?" Derek gave Gina a squeeze. "And besides, I love the way you look in that new suit."

I saw others heading to the dining room and began to clean up the tiles from the board.

"Mr. Haggerty, would you—" Gina began.

"I'm sure we'll see Mr. Haggerty again, Gina. Thanks for your help this afternoon," Derek said, and led her to the dining room.

I finished my drink and took myself to dinner. After that, I sat and watched them dance to the *shak-shak* band. She put her head on his shoulder and molded her body to his. They swayed together in the perfect harmony only lovers and mothers and babies have.

They left that way, her head on his shoulder, a peaceful smile on her lips. I could not drink enough to cut the ache I felt and went to bed when I gave up trying.

Del was in when I called and gave me the brief bad news.

"The mailman was a dead end. I went over to the school library and talked to teachers and students. So far, nobody's had anything useful to tell us. I've got a class list and we're working our way through it. Walt did get a lead on him, though. He's a junior partner in a small law firm, a 'boutique' he called it."

"What kind of law?" Come on, say tax and estate.

"Immigration and naturalization."

"Shit. Anything else?"

"Yeah, he's new there. Still don't know where he came from. We'll try to get some information from the partners first thing in the morning."

"It better be first thing. Our timetable just went out the window. They're getting married tomorrow at noon."

"Jesus Christ, that puts the screws to us. We'll only have a couple of hours to work with."

"Don't remind me. Is that it?"

"For right now. Clancy is hitting bars looking for people that play this 'Ultimate Frisbee' thing. He's got a sketch with him. Hasn't called in yet."

"Well, if he finds anything, call me no matter what time it is. I'll be around all morning tomorrow. If you don't get me direct, have me paged, as an emergency. Right now we don't have shit."

"Hey, boss, we just ran out of time. I'm sure in a couple of days we'd have turned something up."

"Maybe so, Del, but tomorrow around noon somebody's gonna look out over their heads and ask if anybody has anything to say or forever hold your peace. I don't see myself raising my hand and asking for a couple of more days, 'cause we're bound to turn something up."

"We did our best. We just weren't holding very good cards is all."

"Del, we were holding shit." I should have folded when Scolari dealt them.

I hung up and readied my bedroom to repel all boarders. Under the netting, I sat and mulled over my options. I had no reason to stick my nose into Gina's life. No reason at all to think that Derek was anything but the man she'd waited her whole life for. Her happiness was real, though. She was blossoming under his touch. I had seen it. And happiness is a fragile thing. Who was I to cast a shadow on hers? And without any reason. Tomorrow was a special day for her. How would she remember it? How would I?

I woke early from a restless night and called the office. Nothing new. I tried Scolari's number and spoke briefly to him. I told him we were out of time and had nothing of substance. I asked him a couple of questions and he gave me some good news and some bad. There was nothing else to do, so I went down to see the betrothed.

They were in the dining room holding hands and finishing their coffee. I approached and asked if I could join them.

"Good morning, Mr. Haggerty. Lovely day, isn't it?" Gina said, her face aglow.

I settled into the chair and decided to smack them in the face with it. "Before you proceed with your wedding, I have some news for you."

They sat upright and took their hands, still joined, off the table.

"Gina's uncle, Enzo Scolari, wishes me to inform you that he has had his attorneys activate the trustee's discretionary powers over Miss Dalesandro's portion of the estate so that she cannot take possession of the money or use it in any fashion without his consent. He regrets having to take this action, but your insistence on this marriage leaves him no choice."

"You son of a bitch. You've been spying on us for that bastard," Derek shouted, and threw his glass of water at me. I sat there dripping while I counted to ten. Gina had gone pale and was on the verge of tears. Marshall stood up. "Come on, Gina, let's go. I don't want this man anywhere near me." He leaned forward and stabbed a finger at me. "I intend to call your employer, Mr. Scolari, and let him know what a despicable piece of shit I think he is, and that goes double for you." He turned away. "Gina, are you coming?"

"Just a second, honey," she whispered. "I'll be along in just a second." Marshall crashed out of the room, assaulting chairs and tables that got in his way.

"Why did you do this to me? I've waited my whole life for this day. To find someone who loves me and wants to live with me and to celebrate that. We came here to get away from my uncle and his obsessions. You know what hurts the most? You reminded me that my uncle doesn't believe that anyone could love me for myself. It has to be my money. What's so wrong with *me*? Can you tell me that?" She was starting to cry and wiped at her tears with her palms. "Hell of a question to be asking on your wedding day, huh? You do good work, Mr. Haggerty. I hope you're proud of yourself."

I'd rather Marshall had thrown acid in my face than the

words she hurled at me. "Think about one thing, Miss Dalesandro. This way you can't lose. If he doesn't marry you now, you've avoided a lot of heartache and maybe worse. If he does, knowing this, then you can relax knowing it's you and not your money. The way I see it, either way you can't lose. But I'm sorry. If there had been any other way, I'd have done it."

"Yes, well, I have to go, Mr. Haggerty." She rose, dropped her napkin on the table, and walked slowly through the room, using every bit of dignity she could muster.

I spent the rest of the morning in the bar waiting for the last act to unfold.

At noon, Gina appeared in a long white dress. She had a bouquet of flowers in her hands and was trying hard to smile. I sipped some anesthetic and looked away. No need to make it any harder now. I wasn't sure whether I wanted Marshall to show up or not.

Derek appeared at her side in khaki slacks and an embroidered white shirt. What will be, will be. They moved slowly down the stairs. I went to my room, packed, and checked out. By three o'clock I was off the island and on my way home.

It was almost a year later when Kelly buzzed me on the intercom to say that a Mr. Derek Marshall was here to see me.

"Show him in."

He hadn't changed a bit. Neither one of us moved to shake hands. When I didn't invite him to sit down, he did anyway.

"What do you want, Marshall?"

"You know, I'll never forget that moment when you told me that Scolari had altered the trust. Right there in public. I was so angry that you'd try to make me look bad like that in front of Gina and everyone else. It really has stayed with me. And here I am, leaving the area. I thought I'd come by and return the favor before I left."

"How's Gina?" I asked with a veneer of nonchalance over trepidation.

"Funny you should ask. I'm a widower, you know. She

had a terrible accident about six months ago. We were scuba diving. It was her first time. I'd already had some courses. I guess she misunderstood what I'd told her and she held her breath coming up. Ruptured a lung. She was dead before I could get her to shore."

I almost bit through my pipe stem. "You're a real piece of work, aren't you? Pretty slick, death by misinformation. Got away with it, didn't you?"

"The official verdict was accidental death. Scolari was beside himself, as you can imagine. There I was, sole inheritor of Gina's estate, and according to the terms of the trust her half of the grandfather's money was mine. It was all in Scolari stock, so I made a deal with the old man. He got rid of me and I got paid fifty percent more than the shares were worth."

"You should be careful, Derek, that old man hasn't got long to live. He might decide to take you with him."

"That thought has crossed my mind. So I'm going to take my money and put some space between him and me."

Marshall stood up to leave. "By the way, your bluff wasn't half-bad. It actually threw me there for a second. That's why I tossed the water on you. I had to get away and do some thinking, make sure I hadn't overlooked anything. But I hadn't."

"How did you know it was a bluff?" You cocky little shit.

Marshall pondered that a moment. "It doesn't matter. You'll never be able to prove this. It's not on paper anywhere. While I was in law school I worked one year as an unpaid intern at the law firm handling the estate of old man Scolari, the grandfather. This was when Gina's mother died. I did a turn in lots of different departments. I read the documents when I was xeroxing them. That's how I knew the setup. Her mother's share went to Gina. Anything happens to her and the estate is transferred according to the terms of Gina's will. An orphan, with no siblings. That made me sole inheritor, even if she died intestate. Scolari couldn't change the trust or its terms. Your little stunt actually convinced Gina of my sincerity. I wasn't in any hurry to get her to write a will and she absolutely refused to do it when Scolari pushed her on it.

"Like I said, for a bluff it wasn't half-bad. Gina believed

you, but I think she was the only one who didn't know anything about her money. Well, I've got to be going, got a plane to catch." He smiled at me like he was a dog and I was his favorite tree.

It was hard to resist the impulse to threaten him, but a threat is also a warning and I had no intention of playing fair. I consoled myself with the fact that last time I only had two days to work with. Now I had a lifetime. When I heard the outer door close, I buzzed Kelly on the intercom.

"Yes, Mr. Haggerty?"

"Reopen the file on Derek Marshall."

ACKNOWLEDGMENTS

I'd like to thank the following people for their contributions to this story: Joyce Huxley of Scuba St. Lucia for her information on hyperbaric accidents; Michael and Alison Weber of Charlottesville for the title and good company; and John Cort and Rebecca Barbetti for including us in their wedding celebration and tales of "the spork" among other things.

MYSTERY ANTHOLOGIES

TANTALIZING MYSTERY ANTHOLOGIES

☐ **MORE MYSTERY CATS by Lilian Jackson Braun, Ellis Peters, Dorothy L. Sayers, P. G. Wodehouse, and ten others.** Cats and crime make an irresistible combination in this collection that even the most finicky mystery lover will devour with gusto! (176898—$5.99)

☐ **MYSTERY CATS III More Feline Felonies by Lilian Jackson Braun, Patricia Highsmith, Edward D. Hoch, and fourteen other modern masters of mystery.** Cats just seem to have a nose for crime. So *Mystery Cats* returns with a third volume featuring more "pick of the litter" tales of murder, mayhem, and meows. (182936—$4.99)

☐ **MORE MURDER MOST COZY More Mysteries in the Classic Tradition by Agatha Christie, P.D. James, and others.** Battling, intriguing, and wonderfully engaging murder returns to vicarages and villages, boarding houses and quaint seaside resorts. These eight superb stories are the perfect treat for the mystery connoisseur. (176499—$5.99)

*Prices slightly higher in Canada